C000088925

The Greenmen

BOOK TWO IN
The Hero's Arc

Linden Forster

CORDATE

Also by Linden Forster

For Rowan, the first eyes to find my words.

To Michelle

Thank you for joining
me in my story

LR Foster

Amber keeps yesterday, watches today and envisions tomorrow.

Prologue

Somewhere out there, beyond our stars, a planet drifts through the cosmos. Not merely a planet, but a world, with life. Most of the life in the universe is akin to the food in takeaways which people stumble into at three o'clock in the morning. The only real difference is pouring hot sauce over outer-space lifeforms does not usually offer any improvement. What separates this world apart is the calibre of its life, which has the capacity to operate on a few realms of complexity above amoebae.

Animal arrival to the world was elicited by the usual suspects: massive god like beings and a sizeable amount of chance. Soon after their introduction they set about establishing feuds among themselves, many of which have remained resolute through the ages. Will time and space and authors ever let dwarves and goblins get along?

At its birth the universe began as most of us do; with lots of kicking and screaming, demanding of attention and generally being very vocal about its new-found existence and making sure everyone noticed. In short, with a big bang.

Out of nothing burst light and darkness and matter. Everything spreading from the epicentre of creation. Raw

9

unsolicited matter found itself coming together to form shapes and objects. Colour was formed.

Before long, a singularity of matter thought it should do something with the light scattered around the place. The organism started to gather it up. It tried and tried, but no matter how much it absorbed there always seemed to be more light cluttering up the place. In fact, the poor little photosynthesiser wasn't convinced that it was making any difference at all. So it decided that the best thing would be to have some assistance. It squeezed itself very hard and there was an unsticking sound, followed by a pop and then there were two green blobby things bobbing along in space.

This did not provoke a radical reduction in the quantity of lumens firing around the universe. So *Quercus* thought, I will get bigger. I will be able to absorb more. That will help.

Bryo felt they should multiply and send their *spores*, as he called them, across the galaxy to harvest as much light as they could. Whereas *Quercus* was wary of what would happen to their children if they did this. He wished to find a safe place for his offspring to grow and develop. To do this, he said they should spread themselves out on these amazing things called *roots* until they found a place suitable to raise young.

In the early days, it was *Bryo* who proved more successful. A portion of his energy went towards increasing his own mass, but most of it was put into catapulting his seed in all directions.

Millions of miles away, two hooligans had decided to have a snowball fight.

Normally life does not need to be concerned with the rumblings from a few galaxies over, but in this case the hooligans in question were star giants.

When Ukta started to think about their snowball fight he realised that the whole thing was redundant. The whole point in a snowball fight is to hit your opponent, and there is no point in hitting them if you can't see them. Which was a real issue for Ukta, whose friend, Kraktor, was standing lightyears away.

So Ukta had an idea. He would conceal a stone at the centre of his snowball. That way, when he next saw Kraktor he would be able to see the bruise it left. He snatched an asteroid from a nearby belt and padded a thin layer of snow over top.

The rock was on a safe trajectory to miss *Quercus* and *Bryo* by a few billion miles until Kraktor's head got in the way and rerouted the projectile. Much to Kraktor's annoyance.

Quercus was in the middle of de-sporing himself from a particularly aggressive botanical explosion from *Bryo* when:

Wham!

The space rock crashed into them both.

Bryo's blobby body burst, sending every cell it had once contained in a different direction. Some were scattered into the atmosphere and rained back down to the rock. Others drifted into space, possibly to find their own, less confrontational, rock. In a way *Bryo* lived on, a little part of himself finding many corners of the universe.

The impact shattered a number of *Quercus*'s roots, but it was thanks to them that he survived. His disc of limbs had grown to such a size that it spread the blow over a wide area. Only crippling, rather than destroying.

The meteor hurtled through the universe and *Quercus* dug in and held on.

The rock tumbled and rolled through the cold black expanse, but eventually found a star.

It was sucked into an orbit and as quickly as possible changed its Social Meteor status to "in a solar system". Not long after that it had two moons and everyone commented how happy they were for it. Next the planet announced that it had life growing on its surface. This panicked many of the world's Friends as they wondered why they didn't have a botanic yet and when things were going to work out for them. Others simply laughed at the world and questioned how it possibly expected to raise life when it couldn't tell its pole from its equator.

Much of the life was thanks to *Bryo*. Although he was destroyed, his legacy lived on. His body and seed colonised the globe and quickly adapted to a host of climates and environments. The plants diversified into grasses to cover the plains, weeds to fill the seas and flowers so men had something to help them apologise.

While all that was going on *Quercus* was not resting on his laurels. His roots were well established and now with the sun's influence, he developed green solar panels to harness as much light as he could during the day. He decided a broad shape would be best, and lots of them. Soon he found that he didn't have enough space to put all his valuable *leaves*, so he reimagined his root idea to create *branches* with enough space for all the leaves he desired. With the leaves proving effective, *Quercus* did not feel it was necessary for the rest of his body to be able to make use of light anymore, and the collision had made him paranoid and fearful, so he built himself armour and named it *bark*.

One of the drawbacks to leaves, *Quercus* found, was that they had a tendency to dry out in the heat of the sun. He had the solution. His roots were wet; he could feel it. All he needed to do was get it to his leaves. He built tubes up inside himself from his roots all the way up his trunk, through his branches and to the leaves. When he was ready, he turned the tips of his roots into sponges.

Quercus found he was lonely.

From a different core branch that spread far and wide, *Quercus* crafted a seed. Each of its own size and shape. He let them drop from his branches, but ensured each was cradled by his root system. He watched for years as the seeds germinated and rose from the soil. He enjoyed the sensation as their roots developed and intertwined with his.

He watched over them as the Primes rose from the earth and grew from seedlings into saplings.

That is when the wind came.

Something great fell from the sky and plunged into the sea, causing a splash so vast it sent a pulse of air coursing around the globe.

When the wind wave reached *Quercus,* it ripped many of his branches from him. What was once an immense arching mushroom canopy covering the Primes was stripped to little more than a forking on his trunk.

Quercus mourned the loss of his limbs, but it did not distract from the deaths of his children. Over half of the Primes had perished. Some of those that survived did so through flexibility or from being so small the wind did not trouble them. Though most of those who remained owed their survival to *Quercus*'s sheltering branches.

As the remaining Primes grew into trees, *Quercus* sought to recreate those that had been lost, but all he could manage were primitive recreations of his own image. He grew angry and threw these substandard seeds from the Garden.

However, through his rage, he always ensured they did not fall far from one of his roots.

When the Primes were old enough he requested that they develop their own disciples. The Primes were excited and did their best to mimic their own image in their offspring. *Quercus* issued only two rules to them: no disciple may ever grow within the Garden and the Primes must always ensure that every one of their children have contact with one of their roots.

The story goes that *Quercus*'s desire to protect all that he had created was so strong that he even cast his roots to the disciples of the Primes, as well as his own.

If this is true, *Quercus* truly never rested on his laurels; the laurels rested on him.

Where Were We?

Aereon, a spotty, scrawny teenager whose body had recently decided to add gangly to that alluring list, was chopping wood. There have been better heroes: stronger, more handsome, more charismatic, heroic heroes, but he's still young and where there is youth there is hope. Young people can always change, that's what being young is all about. The old get to dig their heels in and damn the approaching tide with an appropriate salute.

To his left were a couple more tree stumps and two men with axes working their way through their own wood piles.

Behind the three of them was a growing mound of chopped material.

Like a wolverine with a dead caribou, a growling dwarf dragging a huge branch backed out of the forest. He grunted and switched his grip as he attempted to wrap his arms around the limb and manoeuvre it over the root matted ground. Eventually, he wrestled it into the clearing. 'Another branch for you fine gents,' he said, wiping his brow.

'Bring it over here. I'm almost done with this one,' said Koel, the burliest of the three choppers.

The dwarf's eyes, which were concealed by thick frowning

eyebrows, flared at the speaker. His lips pursed, and his tongue stuck into his cheek, neither of which were visible beneath his bushy brown beard. A drawback of dwarves' glorious facial hair is it does put a bit of a dampener on their expressions.

He stuck his hands on his hips and glared at the man. Koel continued to swing his axe.

'Yes! Fine! No problem at all,' said the dwarf.

Silvor slung his arm over the branch and hauled it to what just so happened to be the furthest away chopping block.

'Just pop it down there,' said Koel.

Silvor did pop it down, unceremoniously, and waited for a "thank you". None came. The dwarf brandished a chubby finger threateningly and opened his mouth.

'How is everyone getting on?' said Lars.

Silvor shut his gob and turned as Lars strode out of the trees. Over his shoulder was a branch even wider than the one Silvor had been struggling with.

As Lars walked towards them the tips of the branch emerged from the trees, complete with a second dwarf dangling off the end.

Lars rolled the load off his shoulder and it crashed to the ground. Volris, the dwarf, had to tuck and roll to avoid becoming even dwarfer.

Oblivious to any mild-peril, Lars rubbed his hands and approached his workers.

Aereon chucked some more chopped wood onto the pile and hefted the axe into his stump. 'We're getting along fine,' he declared.

Lars folded his arms and his gaze fell on the wood pile. 'So I see.'

'Are we nearly finished?' asked Edin, who had also seized the opportunity to cease manual labour. Edin was a slender man and no matter how he slept, what he did or what happened to him his hair always seemed to bounce back into a perfect quiff and his face a smug smirk.

Lars smiled through his blonde goatee. 'Not yet. Two more days, at the least. How about some lunch, for now?'

The distinct sound of enthusiastic people trying hard not to sound too enthusiastic murmured though the group.

Lars gave them a knowing smile and led them from the clearing. They passed through a thin layer of trees before they reached Lars's lodge, at the edge of the wood.

The windowless log cabin had one room, a stone floor, and a beamed ceiling. In the centre of the room, a blocky fireplace rose into a chimney. Scattered around the lodge were a number of quilts and animal pelts, showing where Lars's guests were sleeping. In one corner was a long wooden bed where Lars found rest when he desired it.

The chunky wooden table was surrounded by an eclectic assortment of chairs. Everyone chose one to meet their needs. Except Lars, who had a sniff of the pot suspended in the fireplace and reached for his fire-starters.

Once the kindling had taken, he grabbed a log and gently placed it into the hearth.

Lunch was stew and had been for dinner, breakfast, lunch, dinner and breakfast already, but Lars's stews were something of an event and no one complained. Aereon did raise a hand. He was not one to cause a fuss, but he was vegetarian after all. He had told Lars previously, but it was the sort of detail the Woodsman was prone to forget. As his memory jogged, he gave Aereon a smile and was happy to cater to his needs.

Lars also baked. He specialised in broad dense bread and they always got through two loafs at meals, with the dwarves usually polishing off one all to themselves. Lars stared down at them when they did this, but whenever they sheepishly caught his gaze he would burst into a hearty chuckle and offer them more.

If Lars wasn't such a skilled carpenter, the chairs might have groaned after the meal. Instead the dwarves, who were first to finish, rested their hands on their engorged bellies, clapped their lips in satisfaction and then started to snore with their feet dangling pleasantly under the table. Lars smiled at them as he cleared away their bowls. The other three desperately clung to theirs, fearful that they might be sucked across the table and snorted into the dwarves' formidable nostrils.

Once everyone else was finished and with some regret, Lars knocked on the dwarves' drooped heads.

Somewhat bleary, the dwarves bumbled down off their seats and sauntered through the door.

Lars selected his favoured axe from the umbrella stand next to the door and closed the door behind him.

They left the others to their chopping and returned to the forest. While Lars scoured the trees the two brothers shuffled in his wake. Every now and then, Lars approached a tree. He'd prop his axe against the trunk and place his hands gently on the bark, then press his ear to it. Most times he would simply pick up his axe and walk away. Or he might give the tree an experimental tap with his knuckles. But, on the odd occasion, he would turn and say, 'Who wants to give me a lift up?'

Dwarves are proud creatures.

Pride can take a number of forms. For instance, if the

average man asked them such a question they would proudly give them the finger. For dwarves this is the index finger; they've never had much tolerance for bows, crossbows are their ranged weapon of choice. So, when the situation calls for it they proudly brandish their trigger finger.

Dwarves respect strength. And good, wholesome cooking. And anything with facial hair.

So when Lars asked them for a hand up the tree, it was with great pride that both dwarves threw themselves on all fours in helpful service.

'I can do it,' grovelled Volris.

'I can do it better,' snivelled Silvor.

Lars's brow wrinkled. 'What have I told you two about that sort of thing?'

'Sorry, mister Lars.'

'Sorry, sir.'

'That's bet–' began Lars '–hang on. Now that's enough of that. You hear? No more of this *sir* and *mister* stuff. I haven't been treated to such a fuss in all my life. Now one of you get over here so I've got something to stand on.'

After a bit of a scuffle between the brothers, both dwarves tensed as they each received a big boot on the back.

Lars lined up to the chosen branch and swung his axe.

Not much later the limb crashed to ground, only a few inches from Volris and Silvor's heads.

Lars stepped down and inspected the severed limb.

The wood within looked healthy enough. They would be able to extract some good material from it. Further up, where the branch started to fork, there was a scar in the bark.

Lars could see black infection had started to seep into the grain beneath. What little foliage remained beyond it was sparse and sickly discoloured.

'You two can get up now.'

The dwarves sprang to their feet like eager pups.

'Silvor, take this to the clearing. Make sure to remind them that anything infected is to be burned.'

Silvor saluted and dragged the branch away.

On the first day of working with Lars, Silvor had questioned that wasn't *all* the wood to be burned? Lars had told him no. He said the logs were for fire wood. Fires have purpose. Some wood though, some wood just needed to be burned.

'Shall I fetch the balm?' asked Volris.

'Do you remember where we left it?' Volris nodded dutifully. 'Off you go then,' said Lars, frowning slightly. Feeling his point about not doting on him had not been taken in by the dwarves.

When Volris returned, he was rolling a huge wooden barrel in front of him. To Lars it looked as though the cask had taken to racing across the mossy forest floor entirely of its own volition.

It stopped just in front of him and he peered over the top at the grinning dwarf on the other side.

Lars righted it and cracked open the lid with his powerful fingers. He dipped his hands into the cloudy whitish green mixture and looked down to find Volris already in position.

After Lars was happy with the coating, he stepped off Volris and brushed his hands on the trunk.

'What is this stuff anyway?' Volris asked, trying to peer over the rim of the barrel.

'In simple terms, it works with the trees sap to protect the open wound against infection. It is a very old recipe.' Lars pinned the lid back over the mixture. 'Come on. Leave that here for now.'

'What about Silvor? Should we wait for him?'

'I'm sure he'll find us,' replied Lars, without turning around.

Volris scuttled after him and before long Lars was knocking on trees again.

'Why do you do that?' the dwarf asked. 'I've noticed you only do it to trees with damaged branches. But, sometimes we take the branch and sometimes we take the whole tree and sometimes we leave it entirely. How do you know what to do? What are you looking for?'

Lars slowly turned away from the tree he was examining and looked down at the dwarf from his greatly superior height. Volris shifted in his shadow.

'You have a lot of questions today.'

It wasn't a question, but Volris felt as though something was expected of him. 'My Thane always taught me not to ask questions.'

'Yes. Today you have many.'

Volris considered this. 'Well, it's like if someone had an arrow sticking out of their head it would be rude to ask about it on preface, but after a while, you might sort of say "hey, what's with the arrow?" kind of thing.'

'I see. So your argument is: a suitable amount of time has passed for you to feel it's acceptable to ask me about my work?'

'That's what I'm saying,' said Volris, cheerfully.

'Very well,' said Lars. 'I knock on the trees, master dwarf, to see if their souls are still intact.'

*

As Silvor set off after Lars and Volris, Edin dragged the offered branch over to his station. He took his axe and removed the dead parts and threw them onto the discard pile. He positioned what remained for the chop when a knot in the wood made him stop. Back home, in his Shack, next to his bed, there was one just like it. He lowered the axe and his fingers found the mark.

'What do you think is happening on Krank right now?'

Koel rose from his work. 'Panic, I would imagine. Ask Aereon. Aereon,' began Koel, raising his voice, 'do you think Krank is still in a panic after Edin and I left?'

Aereon gawked, then he choked and started to cough uncontrollably.

It took several thumps in the back until he stopped. When he did, he straightened himself out and composed himself as best he could.

'Panic?' he asked, innocently.

'Yes. Panic,' said Koel, who had done the thumping. 'What were people like when we left?'

'...Panic?' asked Aereon again.

'Yes! Panic! You know. People running around screaming and shouting, smashing things. General hysteria.'

'There were some hysterics, when you left, certainly,' said Aereon, truthfully.

'Well, what about the King?' asked Edin. 'Did Codrich miss us?'

'Yes actually,' nodded Aereon, pleased at the opportunity to answer a question without much bowdlerize. 'He was rather distraught when you two failed your debut launch and he lost his beloved fabricators.'

Edin and Koel shared a look. 'We did not fail!'

'No?' said Aereon. 'You were supposed to simply cross the estuary, find out what was beyond our borders and come back. How is this –' Aereon raised his arms to their surroundings '– not a failure? You forgot your paddles and got swept out to sea. Then I had to go out of my way to build a second floyancy. Then I literally had to go out of my way and come rescue you.'

'Look here, you. We're just –' Edin waved his hands around, searching for the right words '– broadening the scope of our task. Why stop at the land just beyond our borders, when we could come out here and learn so much more.'

'That's right,' said Koel. 'Come on Aereon, where's your sense of adventure?'

Aereon did not offer comment.

'And who asked you to come after us anyway?'

'The King,' mumbled Aereon.

'Because we, certainly didn't,' continued Edin. 'We were getting along just fine without you.'

'What about the ogres?' Aereon demanded.

'What about them?'

'They captured you!' protested Aereon. 'They were making you fight to the death.'

'A minor hiccough,' shrugged Koel.

Aereon dropped his jaw. 'A minor–'

'And we did fight to the death. And look at us.' Edin patted himself down. 'Still alive. We even managed to break out all by ourselves, at which point you showed up and tried to take all the credit.'

'You wouldn't have been able to escape if I hadn't been there to distract the ogres.'

'I thought it was the yetis, by way of Lars, that distracted the ogres?' Edin said, smugly. 'And I'm sure I remember hearing that the whole thing was his plan.'

'Yes,' said Aereon, who had picked up his jaw and found it was made of granite. 'It was Lars that lured the yetis into the ogre camp. And yes, it was his plan.'

'Ah ha!'

'While he was doing that it was my job to find your cage and release you,' explained Aereon.

'Which we had already escaped from. Thanks to Lars's diversion.'

'But Lars never would have been there if it wasn't for me! It was me who found you and me who convinced him to come!'

'Yes, yes. That's fine, Aereon,' said Edin. 'I'll be sure to show Lars my sincere gratitude when he comes back.'

'And by soul you mean…?'

Lars's stare was penetrative. 'Do you believe that you have a soul, master Volris?'

'Yes, sir,' said Volris. 'All dwarves have souls. They play a key role in our physiology. When we turn to golems and begin to settle it is our souls that shape what gems and metals grow within us. Of course, Thanes have more. That is to be expected. They are needed to support the Oth. But, all mountains develop riches within them and a soul determines the abundance of each. For example, a dwarf who was known for his fierce temper and strong resolve will nurture a cavern of rubies. Only the most honourable dwarves will become mountains with diamonds in any real quantity or quality. A ranger, who felt most at home in the wilderness will raise great mines of emeralds. And those dwarves who were happiest on the mountain slopes often harbour sapphires in their midst.

'If a dwarf was a renowned warrior the metal within his mountain will be almost all iron. Whereas, if he was disposed towards culture and finer things then he will develop more silver and Gold.'

It is a very rare dwarf indeed that can say gold without capitalising it.

Lars looked at Volris for a long time. 'If a dwarven soul can do all that, why is it inconceivable that a tree might have a soul?'

'Because it's a tree,' shrugged Volris.

Lars began searching through the forest again. Ignorance was not something he was known to tolerate.

'Wait!' Volris chased after Lars's broad steps. 'Why wouldn't a tree's soul be intact?'

'When a tree is threatened this can cause the spirit to rip from the body and flee. In this forest there is power though, spirits drawn from the wood are given a physical presence and they stay to fight for their tree's safety. Forests further from here have spirits with decreasing physicality to the point where they can no longer defend themselves and their only choice is to run from the attacker and desert their home.'

'That's quite sad,' said Volris, eventually.

Lars nodded in agreement.

'What are you guys talking about?'

Lars turned half a head to Silvor. 'Life.'

'That old chestnut, eh?'

'No, it's a beech.'

It was a little after lunch when the day started to darken.

The clouds closed in and brought with them a thick downpour. They covered the piles to keep them dry and headed indoors.

The Creators found cushions and placed themselves next to the fire. The dwarves pulled out an old wooden box from the cabinet and carried it over to the table. Aereon found himself a corner and rested his forearms on his knees and his chin on this forearms – a sure sign of someone who is troubled and wants people to know it.

In no time at all, everyone was cosy and beginning to steam.

Lars busied himself making them all his rich, honeyed tea. So thick you had to suck it out the mug.

He passed Edin and Koel with little word, as with Aereon.

When he reached the dwarves they had opened the box and were busy setting up its contents. He smiled as he rested a tankard next to each of them. 'You two going at it again?'

'Yes, mmmii... Yes, Lars,' said Silvor, after a warning stare from his host. 'Would you like to play?'

'No, that's alright. I think you two should practise a little more before you play me again,' teased Lars.

Silvor looked offended. 'We are good players! Volris has even beaten Fenrik.'

Lars rubbed his chin and his fingers disappeared into his coarse beard. 'Well then I can only assume that he is also a poor player. Either that or he let you win.'

Silvor's entire face tightened, but it is very hard to take anyone who has syrup running down their beard seriously. 'Right! You'll see. We're good players. You'll see.'

Karplaw is an ancient game of dwarf conception. Each player takes control of an army with its own set of objectives.

For the dwarves they have to ensure that none of the enemy crosses their side of the table. For the goblin player, they have to get one of their pieces to cross their opponent's side of the table. When the game was first invented these were the only two armies, but it was quickly discovered that dwarves did not like playing as goblins. Now every craftsman includes two sets of dwarf armies. Later editions saw the introduction new races, such as of trolls who simply have to obliterate the enemy force and men who must kill the adversary's leader without losing their own.

The game is won by achieving your army's objective or by preventing your opponents.

As it was, Volris and Silvor always opted to play as the dwarves. They each set a stoic battle line across their board edge and sent tiny brigades across the board to find the holes in the enemy line and nine times out of ten these were massacred.

It was a game of patience and Lars had aptly wound up Silvor so Volris won the first two games easily.

The third was closer, but Silvor still lost in the end and went off to sulk.

'Fancy a game?' asked Volris.

Lars nodded in Silvor's direction. 'You're not going to act like that when you lose, are you?'

Volris shook his head.

'Alright then. One game.'

Lars was an expert at commanding all of the armies, but his favourite were the trolls. He liked the simplicity of their approach. Just wipe out the enemy or, alternatively, when fighting dwarves, make it off the opponent's table edge. Not that there wasn't strategy to it. The board was covered in various types of terrain to provide cover and hazards.

Volris lined up his troops all the way along the mountain peaks, taking up a commanding position.

Lars placed his trolls in a circle in the middle of his table edge, with the exception of a small force that he positioned in the bog on the right of the board.

Lars went first. On his first turn his main army moved as far forward as they were allowed, but his trolls in the swamp were hindered by the sticky terrain.

The trolls were still out of range from Volris's trebuchets and ballistas and he did not wish to move his army forward so he did nothing.

In Lars's second turn his trolls in the swamp reached the river which flowed from the mountains. Trolls are not natural swimmers and thus they began to sink, and drown. For any other race this would be a real issue, but trolls have a handy survival trait that they can never die. They simply adapt to become something that would survive whatever was killing them. This had been incorporated into the game and the trolls changed physiology into river trolls.

By Volris's second turn, Silvor was back at the table and watching keenly as his brother opened up a volley from his war machines. The trolls were still half a board away and there were only a couple hits. Those struck morphed into stone trolls and shook off the blows.

For Lars's third turn the Creators were at the table and even Aereon had taken an interest from his corner. Lars's main force reached the forest in the centre of the board while the river trolls sped through the waters.

Everyone watched as Volris sent more bolts, arrows and rocks flying after the main body of trolls, but there was only one hit.

The river trolls emerged and started to climb the lower slopes of the mountains, while the trolls and stone trolls continued through the forest.

Volris shot quarrels, bolts and boulders at the rising river trolls and by the end of his turn, four had been knocked from the mountains and all had been turned to stone.

Three trolls landed on their back and one got up. By the end of Lars's turn almost all the trolls were on the mountain.

The game ended with Volris frantically trying to knock the trolls from his mountains, but ultimately there were too many and they broke through the ranks and reached the board edge.

'It's not fair!' Volris moaned. 'The trolls are too good.'

'Ep! Ep! What did I say about throwing a wobbly?'

'Sorry,' said Volris.

'Better. That's enough Karplaw for one night. Clear it away. I'll get dinner started'

Before he could even get to his feet, there was a knock at the door.

'Who's that now?'

Lars pushed open the door and found an armed force on this doorstep.

As it turned out, only one out of three parts of that statement was correct. Firstly, it probably took more than a baker's dozen for something to be classified as a force. Secondly, the demi-force was very aware of who lived on the premises and therefore took several respectful steps back from the doorstep. They were armed though, and armoured. The rain bounced and sung off their shiny helmets and breastplates.

The closest one removed his helmet and neatly tucked it

under his arm.

Lars observed. 'What can I do for you, Sergeant?'

The Captain wisely chose not to correct. 'Good evening to you, Woodsman. We are looking for the individual known as Aereon Cusith of Krank. We have reason to believe you might be harbouring him.'

Lars's arms folded. '*Harbouring* is a very strong word.'

Captain Morj, whose hair was starting to plaster to his face, knew he should be in the pub at this hour and was in no mood for a tactful conversation. 'Is he here or not?'

When people aren't in the mood for being tactful they tend to act very stupidly indeed.

Lars stared.

'I... er... the King. That is, King Victarian,' began Morj, desperately trying to regain some composure, 'I have an order from King Victarian for Aereon Cusith... I um... I was told he had been seen here... that he was staying here.' Captain Morj pointed a finger. 'That's him there, isn't it?'

Lars looked down past his elbow at Aereon, who was peering around the door frame as were the dwarves and Creators. Lars's gaze returned to the Captain. 'Might be.'

'Look, I'm just trying to do my job sir–'

'I'm not a sir.'

'I hear the King just wants to have a chat with him, if that helps?'

'It doesn't. If this were Aereon, then he wouldn't have to go anywhere.'

'Fine!' said Captain Morj. His accusing finger extended further out in front of him. 'You just continue to hide behind your protector Aereon, see where it... where it... what are you doing?'

Lars had stepped out into the rain and was closing the gap between himself and the Captain. He stopped half a step in front of Morj, blocking his view of the door.

'There,' said Lars. 'Now he's not hiding behind me. Now you're standing in front of me. What do you make of that?'

'Uh…'

'"Uh…"?' questioned Lars.

'Uh… I have to go?'

Lars smiled. The Captain tried to smile back, but he didn't have much control over what his face was doing. It seemed to be trying to peel itself as far away from the Woodsman as possible. Lars clapped him on the shoulder and his whole body flinched. 'That's the spirit. Off you pop now.'

The Captain's men turned at his order and he herded them away from the lodge. Morj felt that a lack of impending comeuppance may cause rumblings when he recounted events to King Victarian, but waited until they were at a safe distance before turning back to Lars and shouting, 'This isn't over!' He shook his fist for good measure.

He watched and waited until he was sure the Woodsman wasn't going to start running at him, then turned back to his troop and smiled. That hadn't gone too badly, all things considered. In fact, a well-deserved celebratory drink was probably in order.

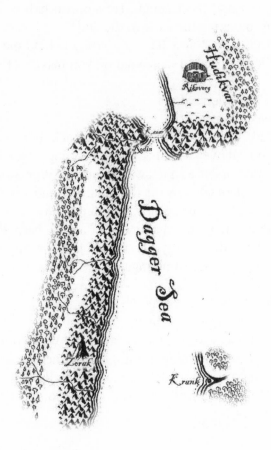

Moonrise

Sunrise

Sunset

Moonset

Hudkvar

Rikeverg

Aedin

Dagger Sea

Zorak

K.runk

Wanted Adolescent

Two more days thought Lars.

Just two more days, then they'd have enough wood for the Kingdom to use while he was gone. All they had to do was make it two more days.

Contrary to standard procedure when someone utters a phrase to the effect of "all we have to do is X and we'll be fine" the group did not spontaneously combust.

In fact, they made it through the entire day without episode. The weather even held so it was long and productive too.

Once the work was done and everyone was inside, the dwarves took it upon themselves to teach the Krankians the rules to Karplaw. Like excited children, they thought the best way to do this was to play amongst themselves several times and wait for the humans to pick up just enough to stumble their way through a game.

Aereon never played. He preferred to watch. Silvor shrugged and told him it was his loss. The Creators meanwhile experienced actual losses, as both were systematically thrashed.

Lars was in his apron again and bustling around, snatching

up ingredients. The stew had finally run out and it was on to cottage pie with salted boar. The dwarves and Koel had offered to go out and rustle up something a bit fresher, but Lars had refused them. He was determined to get through his larder before they left. He hated the idea of food going to waste.

As he chopped the potatoes, his eyes flickered over the flames in the fireplace.

'Would someone mind fetching some more firewood?'

Aereon got his feet, 'I'll go.'

Lars nodded vaguely and got back to chopping things and dropping them into the pot of warming water.

The door closed behind Aereon with a solid clunk. To the rear of the lodge was Lars's personal supply of logs, protected by the overhang of the roof. Aereon scooped up two armfuls worth.

He made his way back around the lodge, but was stopped in his tracks by the beauty of the sunset.

The horizon was awash with orange and purple haze that faded up into an azure sky wisped with pink kissed clouds.

In the centre of it all, there was a black figure. The silhouette moved closer.

A couple more steps and he could see it was Kajsha. She seemed like quite a mousy girl at first glance, but Aereon now knew she had a strong personality underneath.

It had been Kajsha who had introduced Aereon to Lars. After Aereon's initial appeal to the King of Hudikvar to help rescue Edin and Koel had been refused by Victarian, Kajsha had found him and suggested Lars could help.

Aereon was not the only one who had emotional investment in the quest to free the Creators from the clutches of the ogres. In fact, Kajsha probably had a great deal more to lose. If Aereon didn't retrieve Edin and Koel and they died at the hands of the ogres, he would be brandished a failure. He had failed before, he could deal with that, and his emotional connection to the Creators was not the deepest. Whereas Kajsha risked losing her great idol. Asta, the Night Bandit, had also been captured and forced to fight for the ogres' amusement.

Aereon did not arrive in time to rescue her and ended up breaking the news to not only Kajsha, but her friends as well. All of which lived in one decrepit tent and had nothing for themselves but what Asta stole for them.

On his return Aereon confronted the King of Hudikvar and went on to give him a degrading verbal bollocking. It had gone quite well. Usually an action like that resulted in a King taking the bollocker down a notch or two, or however many a head amassed to.

Chiefly though, Aereon neglected to mention that Asta had died.

Built on the emotions of the moment and his despise for King Victarian, Aereon had given a passionate speech to the lost boys and girls of Hudikvar. He may have encouraged the rudderless kids to rise against the ruling powers and continue Asta's work in feeding the needy. Which presumably had something to do with why Victarian was after him and why Kajsha was standing before him now.

'Hello,' he said.

'Hi,' she said.

It was riveting stuff.

Kajsha looked at her feet. Aereon tried to do the same, but the logs were in the way. So he looked at them instead.

'It's good to see you,' one of them managed.

'You too,' said the other.

In the silence, Aereon felt like a machete would have been useful.

'What have you been up to?' he blurted.

'Surviving,' replied Kajsha. She smiled, then as an afterthought added, 'And you?'

'Just been chopping wood for Lars,' Aereon lifted the bundle in his arms slightly. 'He says he wants to leave enough for everyone in Hudikvar to use while he is away.'

'How long does he think that will be?' asked Kajsha.

'Hasn't said. We haven't asked. We just work on getting the pile big enough before we leave.'

'When will that be?'

'Two days, I think.'

'…Oh.'

It would be unfair on Aereon to say that he did not notice any signs of dismay. He certainly did. He just had absolutely no idea what they meant. He decided the best thing was to continue talking. 'Yes, Lars thinks we can get the remaining work done tomorrow. Then we'll rest up and leave at first light the following morning.'

'… I see.'

This was totally beyond Aereon.

There must have been something he'd said to upset her. They'd said hello to each other. They had told each other what they were up to. She had said she was "surviving". Maybe he was supposed to have asked her to elaborate on that, it was always hard to tell. Then he'd told her he was leaving in two days...

… Nope, couldn't be that. People tended not to offer a

great emotional response when he was about to leave. In fact, as Aereon understood it, that usually happened immediately afterwards.

He was at a loss.

Mercifully she started talking again.

'You'll come and see me before you leave won't you, Reon?'

When Kajsha had first learned Aereon's name there had been a slight miscommunication, but Aereon liked the way the abbreviation purred off her lips and he'd never bothered to correct her.

'Uh... Yes?' said Aereon, a little taken aback. 'I can do that, I guess. Tomorrow night?'

'Won't you need to rest up for your journey through the forest?'

'Nah, I never get any sleep with Volris and Silvor around anyway. They snore something dreadful.'

She looked pleased. 'Well, tomorrow night works for me.'

'I'll see you then. That is, if Victarian doesn't get his hands on me first.'

'What?' asked Kajsha with wide eyes.

Aereon shifted uneasily under their focus. 'There was a group of soldiers here last night. Apparently Victarian wants to see me. Lars scared them off.'

'I think that might have been my fault.'

'Did you tell them this is where I was?' suggested Aereon. 'That's ok. They would have found out anyway.'

'No. No they don't know who I am. They don't know that I know you,' said Kajsha. She started to whisper nervously. 'A couple nights ago, we raided one of the farms.'

Aereon stared at her and lowered his voice, 'How did it go?

Did any of you get caught?'

'No. I guess you wouldn't have heard,' she began. 'There was an ogre attack that night. People were distracted. We were able to sneak in and take as much as we could carry.'

'You used ogres as a diversion, while vaguely innocent people were being attacked and their land ravaged, so you could skulk about and ravage their land for yourself?' Kajsha looked at her feet again. Aereon smiled, 'Asta would have been proud.'

'Do you really think so?' her voice was barely audible now.

The Night Bandit had been many things, hypocritical was one of them. Her philosophy of stealing from the poor and giving to the poorer so the rich didn't end up with everything had some questionable economics. Mainly, that it involved bringing the poor farmers down to the same level as the growing jobless and landless citizens of Hudikvar. Whatever she lacked in a divine principle she more than made up for in her clear and decisive execution of her ideology. Asta was a brave woman and she believed in her beliefs with absolute believity.

That is why Aereon was able to say with surety, 'Yes. She would have done the same.'

'I miss her so much.'

Tears beaded.

'I know. She was a good woman. Strong and brave.'

'Kind...' added Kajsha. She took a step closer, '...Selfless. You remind me of her a bit, you know? In some respects. You have a way about you.'

She embraced him. Her arms wrapped around his neck and her head rested on his collar.

'Uh…'

She lifted her head.

'Op. Watch out there, precious cargo.' Aereon gestured with the logs.

Kajsha retracted her arms and looked down at the firewood she had craned over to get to Aereon.

'Sorry,' she said. 'I'll see you tomorrow?'

She took a step back.

'Oh yeah. You. Yeah. Me. Yes. Tomorrow. I'll see you tomorrow. We'll see each other tomorrow. Definitely.'

Another step back and blushes on pale cheeks.

'Ok, I'll see you then. Good night.'

She turned and started towards the glowing lights of Hudikvar's capital, Rjkovorg.

Aereon wanted to watch her until she was out of sight. He was only given a chance to see her out of earshot though.

'What didn't you do that for?'

Aereon's neck snapped at Edin, who was leaning against the lodge with a broad grin on his impossibly smug face.

'Why didn't I do what?' asked Aereon.

'Kiss her!' Edin pushed off the wall and approached Aereon. 'She seemed like a sweet girl.'

'She's… Were you spying on me?'

'A little. When you didn't come back Lars sent me out to check you were ok. The King is looking for you after all.'

'Shove off,' said Aereon, oozing machoism. 'Besides, I already have a girlfriend.'

He tried to push past Edin, but a hand shot out and grabbed his arm. 'Whoa, whoa, whoa. What do you mean you've already got a girlfriend? Who is this girlfriend? Just tell me it's not that god-awful spawn of the Hartilbys.'

The logs fells to the ground and a finger found itself inches from Edin's chin. 'Now you listen here. Lirna is… if I was a religious man I'd say she was an angel. If I was a dwarf I'd say she was a gem.'

'You are neither of those things. So what is she?'

'She's… she's…'

'Yes?'

'She's perfect, alright!'

Edin's palm acquainted itself with his forehead, 'Give me a break. She is not perfect. She's a schemer. You must have seen the way she acts, smiling and waving. She always has time for everyone. Come on, nobody is that nice. She does it so she can get what she wants from them when she needs it.'

'No,' protested Aereon. 'She's not like that. She's not that nice… What I mean is she did all that stuff because she felt she had to. She started when she was young and then ever since she's felt like she has to be friendly to everyone, because that's what they expect.'

'She said that, did she?' enquired Edin. 'She's got you wrapped around her little finger, doesn't she? Listen to my words, Aereon. *Watch out for that girl*. She's a snake in the grass. A thorn on a rose bush. She looks all nice and idyllic, but she is actually concealing something dreadful.'

'Have you ever seen a snake or a rose bush?'

'Irrelevant.'

'I don't care what you say!' shouted Aereon. 'Nothing will make me change the way I feel about her. She is waiting for me and I won't treat her the same way you treat Frilla. Or is it Carylron? Or Maggie?'

'You can only name th–' began Edin '– I assure you, I have no idea what you're talking about.'

Aereon shook himself free from Edin's grip and scrambled to get the fire wood back in his arms. He stormed to the front of the lodge and glared at the entrance for a moment before he put his temper on simmer and turned back to Edin sheepishly, 'Could you open the door, please?'

Tensions were high during dinner.

Aereon informed the table that he planned to go see Kajsha the following evening. Lars said he thought it was a fine idea. Koel responded by saying he thought it was a terrible idea.

Lars went as far to say that Aereon should take the whole day off to spend with Kajsha, which caused a little disgruntlement from the dwarves, a snide remark from Edin and further deliberations from Koel, who argued that Aereon should not be off gallivanting when the King of Hudikvar was looking for him. It was safer for them all to stick together.

Regardless, the next day Aereon set off to seek out Kajsha and the rest went to work on finishing the wood pile for the residents of Hudikvar. Lars was not someone who believed in having a lie in. He did not believe in anyone else having a lie in either. He probably had little grasp about what a lie in was. So when Aereon was turfed out he had a bit of time on his hands. What with Kajsha and her gang being mostly in their teens and therefore having no idea what a sunrise was.

Aereon took it slow. The forest gradually fell behind him as he headed into the roaming moraines that surrounded the capital of Hudikvar. He strolled peacefully in between them and wound his way towards Kajsha's tent.

Its faded maroon canvas appeared around a ridge and Aereon approached. The day was still young and unsurprisingly he did not hear anything from inside, except a faint wheezing from one of the corners.

Aereon left them and climbed the mound next to the tent.

The sun had pulled itself over the horizon but an orange glow still stuck to the landscape and the sky.

Aereon sat himself down on a not uncomfortable patch of moss and hugged his knees.

The shadow of Rjkovorg's great wooden wall loomed ahead. The fortification had been constructed from thick tree trunks, reinforced with structural supports within, designed to help keep things out. Aereon had initially given the King the benefit of the doubt and assumed it was meant for the ogres, but now he wondered, maybe the King lived in fear of his own people. If there ever was a rebellion it would surely stem from beyond Rjkovorg. It would be the rest of Hudikvar that would rise up. If that happened the King would need a place to defend against the insurgence.

Rjkovorg and its wall were far more ancient than Victarian. Maybe the Kings of old had been no different. Or maybe peasants had been coaxed into building the wall with the promise that it would be used to shelter them in the event of an ogre attack. Maybe the first Kings truly had meant it for the people of Hudikvar, but now the wall only protected the residents of Rjkovorg.

Beyond the city, the land flattened as it sloped to the shimmering water. The sea had a golden quality in the young day. Aereon knew that across the other side there were mountains. It stuck him as odd that he couldn't see them.

It wasn't for the first time someone had considered this phenomenon.

At that very moment, somewhere in the world, a man armed with a compass, a map and a telescope was seeing to the issue, and the word *epiphany* was certainly going to get its monies worth by the time he'd finished his studies. At that moment, he had just made the discovery that the unequivocally flat world was slightly domed.

Due to a lack of any nautical transportation until very recently, the people of the world were yet to learn about anything like poles or the idea of the world having more than two dimensions. That would be ridiculous; people would fall off. Of course people could also fall off a two-dimensional planet, but only if they got too close to the edge and that was just natural selection at its finest.

As it was, the people of the world who required things like maps marked the four points as Sunrise, Moonset, Sunset and Moonrise. While the sun worked on making a nice warm equator, the world's twin moons decided that they were too good for it and set their orbit over the world's poles. Cicar achieved full orbit in a day, while Endos took thirty.

The sun continued to rise and slowly the Kingdom of Hudikvar came alive.

Aereon was roused from his thoughtless tranquillity by the heavy clunking sound caused by large pieces of wood shifting. The gate of Rjkovorg opened and out spilled the guard to check all was well. It never was, but they rarely did anything about it. Their orders were to protect the capital. Rjkovorg was positioned as far to Moonrise as the realm went, the ogres had plenty of people to occupy themselves with before they got anywhere near it, so they never did.

The ogres were not the only things terrorising the people of Hudikvar. Victarian's troops had been commanded to redouble their efforts and bring him the body (he wasn't specific on what condition) of the Night Bandit.

This was going to prove difficult. The ogres could have

done anything with it after Asta fell in the fighting pits. Most likely they burnt it to appease their god who they believed was responsible for the monthly lunar eclipse. Every cycle they host a great games where many people from a host of races perish. On the final day, when the day turns black, they light a great pyre in the hope that the god of life will smile kindly on them and bring back the light and the warmth.

Victarian was convinced the key to finding the Night Bandit was finding Aereon. He'd found Aereon. He was living with the Woodsman. A difficult man to manoeuvre. A spy had been deployed to scout it out and find a point of weakness, and a weakness he'd found. The spy had lurked in a tree and listened in on Aereon and Kajsha's conversation. He'd learned of a bond between the two and their plan to meet.

'Excellent,' the King had said at the news. 'Let that be a lesson to you all: never get involved with women, they'll bring you nothing but trouble.'

A guard had raised a hand.

'Yes?' snapped Victarian.

'Didn't you get involved with a woman? It's just with you having a son and all, I thought that maybe at one time there might have been a lady in your life?'

'Shut up.'

'Shutting up, sire.' A metal gauntlet twanged off a helmet.

'You,' said Victarian, turning to the spy. 'Before you go, tell me what in the world happened to your face?'

The spy's face was badly bloodied and his shirt stained. One of his eyes seemed determined to puff itself out its socket in dark purple bruise. 'After I retrieved the information, the girl left and Aereon and the man headed inside. I planned to follow the girl when I felt something. A sense I was being watched. Are you familiar with the sensation?' The King rested his hand on his cheek, but did not respond. 'I turned around and above me was this pair of glowing orange eyes. Just staring at me. I started to edge away, you know, to get down the tree when it launched itself at me. This huge bird, the biggest I've ever seen, flew right at me and knocked me out the tree. I figured it was because it had a nest there or something, but it landed next to me and started pecking away until I managed to get to my feet. Then it damn-well nearly chased me all the way to Rjkovorg.'

'Curious.'

'I suppose it worked out ok, I was able to catch up with the girl and find out where she lives. Although, this does sting a bit.'

'Yes. And a burgundy yurt I believe you said?'

'I think I said maroon tent.'

'A burgundy yurt?' encouraged the King.

'Uh… yes,' said the spy, feeling it would be tricky to explain to his wife why he'd lost his head over such a remedial argument. 'A burgundy yurt, you can't miss it.'

Victarian had gone on to give instructions to Captain Morj and politely informed him that failure a third time was not an option. The Captain had pointed out that he had only failed once so far. The King told him he was well aware of that, but he was offering him a second opportunity, and if he failed, there would not be a third chance to fail. Morj suggested in future he say "there will not be a third opportunity" to eliminate the confusion. Several members of his squad nodded in agreement. After a little more thought, Morj also felt that this was not a decapitation worthy issue so he dropped it and King Victarian dismissed him and ordered him to return with the girl.

The Captain took his men and left Rjkovorg. Equipped with the spy's information, they wound through the moraines that led to Kajsha's tent.

Fortunately, the Captain liked to keep an informal company and the men sang as they went, which gave Aereon just enough time to duck down into the grass before they rounded a bend and came into view of the burgundy yurt.

After a final flourishing chorus the Captain silenced his men and they encircled the tent. Aereon was asked later exactly what the song was about and all he could recall was there had been a lot of questionable language and something about dropping a crab into a pint to get it so drunk it started walking forwards.

Aereon watched the Captain remove his helmet and pat down his hair. Then he marched straight through the tent door with his arm stretched out in front of him in a "halt" sort of fashion.

'By order of the King I am under instruction to – by buggery there's a lot of you,' the Captain's voice was clearly audible through the thin canvas. 'I am looking for a young woman of the description – ah yes, I think that is you in corner. If you would be so good as to come with me, the King requires your presence presently. There's a good lass. At ease the rest of you.

'I see you've got a lot of our wanted Night Bandit posters. That's very good, awareness is half the battle. I'm pleased to see you kids taking the initiative. You know, it was actually one of my buddies who did the artwork. Quite a likeness. Well, so I hear anyway, never actually seen her myself. I suppose that's why the price is so high. Would be much simpler if everybody knew her. That's it dear, come along.' Aereon could see Kajsha through the fold of the door flaps. 'What's this you've all drawn on it?'

'Oh no,' muttered Aereon.

Being the fans they were of Asta, all the occupants in the tent had a poster over their beds and every one of them had defaced it to read "THE KNIGHT BANDIT" (It is mandatory that all wanted posters, regardless of universe or time, are written in capitals).

'Knight Bandit,' Aereon heard the Captain say thoughtfully. 'Knight Bandit,' he repeated uneasily.

Several things happened at once. The Captain screamed 'Treason!' and lunged for Kajsha who burst out the door only to be snatched by one of the guards. The rest ran to their Captain and all crashed into the side of the tent, which collapsed under the strain as youths squeezed out underneath the tarp and made a break for it past the struggling guards.

When the squabble was over, all the children had been caught and each guard stood with one in a vice like grip. Each guard accept Captain Morj who was trying to find his way out of the vast cloth draped over him.

All eyes were on the peak as it shifted this way and that, searching for the door.

The Captain conceded. 'Alright, do one of you chaps want to come over here and show me the way out?'

'No can do Cap,' replied one of his men. 'The number of hostages—'

'Captives,' whispered another.

'Right, right. The number of *captives* directly corresponds to the number of Constables. Twelve for twelve. So, you see, we don't have a man to assist you there, Cap.'

'Typical! That is just bloody typical. Right. Fine. I'll do it myself.'

The bell-shaped sunken tent started to wriggle about again, with the Captain reaching several dead ends and uttering several unprintable words.

'You know what you remind me of, Cap? When I wake up in the morning and look down. Hur hur hur.'

The point stopped shuffling as it considered this. 'Wilkinson, there are earth worms with more decorum than you.'

'Why don't you just use your sword, Cap?' Suggested another guard, once everyone had settled down.

'This happens to be someone's home, Grunson. Now don't get me wrong, I'll dismantle a home. That's just good policing that is. But, if you damage a home you'll be looking at a swift bill for the costs to repair it.'

'That's very smart, Cap,' said Constable Grunson.

'That's why I earn the big bucks. Where is the bloody – here we are.'

The Captain emerged looking quietly chuffed with himself.

'Olle,' he began, signalling one of the guards, 'hand me my helmet would you?'

'Um… you took it in with you, Cap,' replied Olle.

The Captain's fists clenched and he bounced on the balls of his feet as his body trembled with rage. 'Well,' he said quietly 'it's a good thing I don't have my helmet now, otherwise' his voice rose, 'I'd bloody well kick it over that sodding hill.'

He stormed back to the tent, lifted the door over his head

48

and crawled through it.

'That's a paradox,' said one of the captives, 'because if he had his helmet then he wouldn't be angry so he would have no reason to kick it away.'

'Ah huh,' said the guard vaguely.

Several minutes later, Captain Morj crawled like a dog out a kennel through the flat tent door. 'Found it,' he called triumphantly. He got to his feet and rammed his helmet on his head. 'Right, shall we go then?'

The troop set off and as they rounded a mossy mound, Aereon could just make out the Captain say, 'So kids, how would you like to learn a dirty song?'

The Final Meeting

The Long House was a simple construction, with little in the way of ornate flourishes. Its stone base was strong. Its wooden walls were thick. And its thatched roof was – in desperate need of repair, actually.

Inside the King was burrowed in like a tick.

The light was dim and concealed the decrepit state of the ancient shields, old pelts and used weapons which decorated the walls. Underneath the ornaments, twenty Royal Guard lined the inside of the building at all times.

At the far end of the hall there was a small step. Only two people ever set foot on the risen floor. King Victarian and Dagny, the Captain of the Royal Guard. The landing was carpeted with pelts, contrasting to the harsh flagstone in the rest of the hall. The throne stood at the head of the platform, where the King would sit in front of citizens wishing for his audience and they would be commanded to kneel.

He sat behind the throne now, at his desk, tending to kingly business. Beyond him was a door that led to his quarters.

Victarian had all his meals brought to him and it was heavily rumoured among the people that he never left the Long House's foundations anymore.

The King was roused from his notes by a ruckus from outside. Initially his eyes bulged in concern, but then he recognised the tune and grimaced instead. He dropped his quill and struggled to his feet. He was seated on his throne as the noise grew and the words became audible.

'*Oh! I thought you said:*
That little ducking duck ducked my knife!
I DIDN'T SAY THAT!
Oh no! I told you.
There was no ducking involved at all.
He was no duck, though I would like to pluck him.
And it was not a knife, but my wife!'

The door thrust open and a tide of giggles flushed through the room. Guards and children alike were wiping their eyes as they stumbled down the hall.

'Are Captain Morj and the Greased Elbows quite finished?' asked Victarian, sourly. The King named all the units within the guard, and had taken particularly joy in coming up with a name for Captain Morj's troop. When it had proved that they excelled at carrying out jobs in the scummy areas of Hudikvar he had named them the Greased Elbows. The King had been furious to find the Captain and his men had taken it as a term of endearment.

'Oh yes, sire. Final verse that,' informed the Captain.

'Good. That is good,' said Victarian, with feeling. 'And who are all these people you have brought with you?'

'Traitors, your highness.'

'Traitors?' the King raised an eyebrow at the Captain. 'You sing and have merriment with traitors?'

'Well sire, it's always been my belief that if you enjoy your job you'll never have to work a day in your life.'

'I do not pay you to enjoy yourself,' Victarian spat.

'Right you are, sire. Today you paid me to find the girl and bring her to you. I've done that and to-boot rounded up a band of miscreants. I call that a successful day. What difference does it make if I did all that with a song in my heart and a spring in my step?'

'*All* the difference,' wavered the King. 'It's about image. People need to see that the guard are respectable. A force capable of protection as well as aggression should you cross them.'

'Oh, I couldn't agree more sire, image is very important. You can't put a price on it. You there,' said the Captain, and pointed to one of his detainees who happened to still be sniggering away. 'Do you feel you were captured in a prompt and professional manner today?'

'Ah hee ah heehee ah heeheehee – yes, sir.'

The Captain pulled a face and raised his arms to suggest he felt this was solid evidence. The King did not seem to share his view, so Morj continued. 'And if you saw something happening on the streets that you didn't feel should be happening, would you be happy to approach me or one of my men and draw the situation to our attention?'

'Oh yes, sir.'

'See,' said the Captain, turning back to Victarian. 'What'd I tell you? I pride myself in being a respectable, professional and above all approachable protector of the people, your honour.'

'*Sire.*'

'Right, yes, sire.'

Victarian could see he was getting nowhere. He had the superior argument, he knew that, but debating with Captain Morj was like arming yourself with a sword and then waging war on a pond. 'Who said that any of these vile outlaws would live through the day to be given an opportunity to report crimes to you? Like they would do such a thing anyway, it would probably be them committing the crimes.'

'Oh, I think that's a little strong, sire. What we're looking at here is just a little bit of mild treason. Slap on the back of the wrist stuff.'

'Mild treason! *Mild treason*! There is no such thing as *mild* treason!'

'Sure there is,' retorted Morj. 'It's very treasonous to plot to kill a King. A big no-no in my book. About as treasonous as you can get that.' There was a murmur of agreement from the Greased Elbows. 'But scribbling on a poster, that's more what I would put under mild treason. Maybe even trivial. In fact, possibly charges of wasting police time are more appropriate. I tell you, I've got have a mind to–'

'Captain.'

'–yes, sire?'

'Enough.'

'Yes, sire.'

'You mentioned a poster?'

Captain Morj reached into the pouch on his belt and extracted a poster and handed it to the King.

The King looked at it. 'Did you fold this yourself?'

'Yes, sire.'

'It's dreadful.'

'Thank you, sire.'

The King unfolded the paper and his lips spelled out

"Knight Bandit" as his head did the math. '*Mild?*'

'Well it's just ink, isn't it? Not like it's blood.'

'Not yet,' said the King with some malice. 'Alright, which one's the girl?'

Morj signalled one of his men who brought Kajsha forward.

'Kneel,' commanded Dagny, which was generally all she ever added to conversation.

Kajsha did kneel and when she rose the King spoke in what he thought was his most pleasant voice.

'Now, what's your name dear?'

'Nunvior Biznus.'

'Well, Nunvior –' sniggers '– do you know why I had you brought here?'

'No idea.'

'Eh, sire?' said Morj.

'Not now!' snapped Victarian. 'It is because of our mutual friend, Aereon of Krank. I believe you met with him last night.'

Kajsha had assumed they had all been taken because the King had discovered that it was them who had pillaged the farm during the ogre attack. Kajsha relaxed a little. Despite the King's hatred of him, being an acquaintance of Aereon's was less incriminating than stealing from farmers. 'Um, yes I was.'

'Excellent. Honesty, that's what I appreciate, Nunvior. It really speeds things along. Now–'

'Uh, sire?'

'Not now, Captain!' The King shook his head at Morj. '*As I was saying*. I am curious as to what that relationship entails. The boy seems like a... brave, shall we say, individual. While you, my dear, are a delicate flower. I was young once. I know what it is to be consumed by desire. What strikes me as curious, is how you two kids were able to meet each other in such a short period of time.' Victarian lowered himself into his throne and made his old bones as comfortable as possible on the oak chair. 'In your own time.'

The morning had been successful for the lumberjacks. They had all worked hard and Lars reassured them that if they kept up this pace they would be finished before sunset.

For now, the sun was high in the sky and Lars was ushering everyone inside for some well-deserved lunch.

Sandwiches were on the menu. Lars's pantry was slowly depleting and what he didn't manage to get through they would take with them for the journey. He still had several loafs so he cut the bread thick. He loaded the bread with what he called *slices* of meat, although chunks may have been a more accurate description. He returned outside for the veggies.

Lars didn't have what one might call a vegetable patch. He had a fundamental disagreement with the principle of farming. He felt that everything should come from the land and everyone should hunt and gather their own food.

He had a nosey through the trees near his house. Occasionally he would swipe some foliage or dig out the root of something or even pick one of a number of edible fungi that grew in the woodland. He always took care never to pick too much from one spot. He spread his search and, when he had everything that he needed, returned to the lodge.

Before he went in he looked up at a nearby tree. He squinted at it for a while but eventually he did see the bark flutter in the wind. He smiled and opened the door.

Kajsha finished the tale of how she and Aereon met. And it was a tall tale.

She couldn't exactly have told the truth.

She didn't feel like it was wise to tell the King that she had befriended Aereon because she was a fan of the Night Bandit.

Victarian considered all that she had said. Along the way, he asked many questions in an attempt to expose any lies that Kajsha may have told, but her story held and when she was done the King was satisfied he had extracted the truth from her.

'Thank you for your honesty, Nunvior.' The children stifled their sniggers as did some of the Greased Elbows. 'Tie them up for now. I'll decide what to do with them later.'

Captain Morj stood aside as his men carried out the King's wish.

'Now Captain,' began Victarian, 'I believe there was something you were desperate to tell me?'

Morj looked over to Kajsha. Her hands were being tied behind her back, as were her friends'. They were all backed against the wall and forced to sit on the cold stone floor.

'It was nothing.'

The King threw up his arms. 'Sometimes I wonder, I really do, what goes on in that head of yours. I mean, my goodness, here I am trying to have a conversation and –'

'Oh yes! I remember now,' said Morj, thinking on his feet. He was good at that whenever he sensed a lecture on the horizon. 'I was just going to ask if you thought I should take my men back to the youths' yurt for when the boy shows up. We did… uh… disassemble it, to some extent, but we could reassemble it and wait inside for when he shows up.'

'I appreciate your thought process, Captain, but that won't be necessary,' the King smiled. 'You haven't been properly introduced to Aereon. Let me assure you, this is an individual who had no qualms in charging into an ogre camp to rescue his countrymen and the Night Bandit. I have no doubt that he will do the same again. Only this time he will be expected and this time he will not escape. When he sees her collapsed yurt, he will figure out what has happened and he will come running into our jaws. Some people see a mousetrap, Aereon sees free cheese and a challenge.

'Besides, the girl said they were not supposed to meet until close to dusk. I hardly think you standing around in a yurt all day is hardly an appropriate use of police time.'

'Yes, sire.'

'All we have to do is wait.'

The sun was falling into the woods and Lars had felled the final limb, the dwarves took it to Edin and Koel while he touched up the knot of the branch with his balm.

Lars returned the barrel to the lodge and joined the others in the clearing. The last of the wood was being chopped when he arrived. He smiled as Volris stood on his tip toes to place a piece on top of the pile.

'Shall I leave you to finish up out here and I'll get dinner started?'

There was much rejoicing.

Then the coo came from above.

'Somebody's up early,' said Lars, as he turned to the noise.

A great bird stretched its wings on one of the high branches and gave a groggy hoot.

Lars held out his hand and the bird dropped from its perch and glided down to a few inches off the ground before swooping up at the last moment to land with grace on Lars's closed hand.

'Hello there,' Lars rubbed his finger under her beak.

She tilted her head back and seemed to enjoy the sensation, but then her eyes flipped back open and she gave several vigorous hoots.

'Do you mean Kajsha?'

Lars had a passionate affinity for all animals, but he had a special relationship with the eagle owl known as Gwen. Little is known about how they met. Even less is known about how Lars could communicate with her. It's a flimsy plot point that will never be fully explained.

She hooted again.

'Just one?'

'What's she saying?' asked Volris.

'She said there was a man in her tree last night. She says he was listening to Aereon talking with Kajsha,' Lars turned back to the eagle owl. 'Where did he go? Why didn't you tell us this last night?'

Gwen pecked Lars's forearm and hooted angrily.

'Oy, this again,' mumbled Lars. 'I told you before, if I put windows in it will seriously compromise the insulation qualities.' She pecked him again. 'Why didn't you follow him all the way? We could have found out where he went.'

Gwen looked bashful.

She hooted quietly.

Lars sighed, 'Do you have to chase every one you see?'

More aggressive hooting followed.

'Alright. Alright. It's done now anyway. We need to get

down there and find out what has happened.'

'What's going on?'

'Gwen says she harassed the man back towards Rjkovorg. She thinks he was following Kajsha, but when she was distracted by a – ow! – was *justifiably* distracted by a rabbit. Presumably this was the work of an agent of the King and he will be operating under the assumption that Aereon is due at dusk. If we can get there before then, we may be able to warn everyone.'

'Who saw something like this coming?' asked a tempered Koel. 'Anyone? No one can think of anybody who thought letting Aereon go was a bad idea? Anybody?'

'I agree. I think we should do something,' said Volris, 'but you shouldn't Lars. This is your home. You provide a service that is important to the people as well as this forest. If the King learns of your involvement, if anyone sees you there, he will not allow you to continue to do this. Giving Aereon a roof is one thing. Helping him escape the King is another. We will go, and we will bring Aereon back. While we are away, you could get everything ready as we may need to leave in a hurry.'

Lars considered this for a long time. Eventually he said, 'Very well, but Gwen will go with you. They do not know of her and she knows where the girl lives. If you're too late and Aereon has already been taken, they will be expecting you in Rjkovorg. There is no way you will be able to enter through the gate.'

'You don't know what accomplished warriors we are,' said Silvor, smugly.

'There will be no bloodshed over this,' said Lars, forcefully. 'This is not an assault on the allies of the crown.

This is a rescue mission and no more. If you need to enter the city, there is another way. You will need to get to a stone's throw of the gate undetected. The two-hundred and seventy-fourth post from the right-hand side of the gate has a hole, two thirds of the way up. You must climb and you won't notice it from the ground as it is concealed by bark. It is imperative you make sure your counting is accurate.'

'How do you know all this?'

'That is not important right now. If Aereon is already inside those walls, that is the only way in.'

The dwarves and Edin nodded solemnly.

'Seriously, no names spring to mind?' protested Koel.

Day had merged into night and yet there was no sign of Aereon. For the first time, Victarian was beginning to feel he had made a mistake. Maybe Aereon wouldn't come. Maybe he would flee. Maybe that's all he was, a coward. No. He wouldn't do that. He would come. He had to come.

Morj watched the King's hand twitch restlessly. It had been a boring way to spend the day. Little humour was tolerated in the long house. Only Victarian's dry jokes.

Idle conversation was prohibited and on several occasions Morj was forced to shush his men to avoid further trouble from Victarian.

'You there, girl, tell me again when you two were supposed to meet?' barked the King.

'Before dusk,' answered Kajsha.

The King looked through the narrow windows below the roof and started to pace. 'He should be here by now.'

Morj was torn. He wasn't sure if offering a response or not offering one was more likely to draw the King's attention. In the end, he opted to say nothing, but a poorly timed cough from someone behind him spun the King's head.

'Say something, Captain?'

Morj mentally jumped up and down on the cougher's throat. 'I was just wondering if you would like me to perform a search for him?'

Victarian ran his hand over his stubble. 'Very well, but do it quietly.'

'Yes, sire. Thank you, sire,' said Morj.

He turned to the door and his men did the same. They followed him away from the throne and in the space they left, a lone figure stood staring down the King.

'Captain, you seem to be forgetting someone,' said the King.

Morj's head dropped. His hand had been inches from the door. *Inches!* He turned and made his way back down the hall. He recognised the armour. 'Bruts, what are you playing at?'

He drew level and Aereon lifted the guard's helmet and tossed it aside.

Gasps echoed around the room.

One of the youngest children pointed and shouted, 'Look it's the speech guy.'

The King merely smiled and gave a slow clap. 'Most impressive.' As Victarian spoke, Aereon continued to unbuckle straps resulting in various pieces of armour and equipment clanging on the floor. 'You had me worrying for a while there Aereon. I needn't have. My instinct was correct.'

'What did you do with Corporal Bruts?' breathed Morj.

Aereon turned to face him, ignoring the King for a moment. 'I had to hit him pretty hard, I'm afraid. I left him in his under armour. I'm sorry for any injury I caused him, but it was necessary to get myself in the building.'

The Captain's expression softened. 'Waking up with a woozy head in the middle of nowhere. He's used to the experience, I'm sure he'll pull through.'

'Certainly will, Cap. Usually he doesn't have his under armour on.'

The Greased Elbows burst into fits of giggles.

'Remember three pay days ago?'

'How could I forget? His missus hasn't let him out since.'

Morj turned to the King, 'I wonder if we might be excused, seeing as Aereon is here and all?' Reminiscing always got him in the mood for a drink.

'Yes, yes, very well,' the King waved them away dismissively.

'And remind me what time is our shift tomorrow?'

'You are on the late shift, Captain.'

There was a "Huzzah" from Morj's men. The Captain shushed them and turned to leave.

'Have a good evening, Sergeant,' said Aereon.

Morj snapped back at Aereon, 'That's *Captain* to you!'

'But, not to Lars?'

'Good god, no. Have you seen the size of that man? He can call me Nancy if he likes.'

Morj led his men from the building.

Outside everyone heard him shout, 'A one, a two, a one, two, three, four!'

'There once was a boring little sod of a crab.
Moving to his right he could go as fast as you like.
Wandering to his left he was absolutely fab.
But he would not go forward, that he disliked.

Here is the tale of this here boring little sod of a crab.

Oh! I was on the beach.
I WAS ON THE BEACH!
A rocky rocky beach.
A ROCKY ROCKY BEACH!
He was on the beach.
THE ROCKY ROCKY BEACH!
Walking sidie ways.
ALL OVER THE ROCKS!
He looked like a pisshead.
HE WAS A LITTLE PISSHEAD!
And I thought, we could be friends.
WE WILL BE FRIENDS!'

Nobody said a thing until the singing was out of hearing and when it was, it was Aereon who spoke first.

'He doesn't seem like your sort of servant.'

'He's not,' said Victarian with feeling, still tremoring from the after-effects of the song. 'But he has his uses. Now Aereon, you and I need to have a little chat.'

'Very well, but let them go.'

Victarian shot Aereon a quizzical eyebrow. 'What is your bargaining chip?'

'I don't have one,' Aereon shrugged. 'I am appealing to your sense of decency. I am the one you're after. So let them go. If you don't, everyone will know that you didn't.'

'What am I to make of this?' the King brandished the incriminating poster. 'I assume you know something about it?'

'Kids today,' said Aereon vaguely. 'No respect, if you ask me. But, that's not a punishable offence. They're just kids. They don't know any better. It's up to you to teach them. Not through pain,' he added hastily. 'You have a responsibility as their King to set an example. To create an environment for them to prosper in, but where there is also structure. A place where your people do not live in fear.'

'I see. You are going to play that card again.' The King took little time to consider. 'If it is all the same to you, I think I will hold onto them for now. They may be of use to help you cooperate. Now you are going to tell me everything you know about the Night Bandit. And that definitely did not have a *K* at the start of it.'

The red canvas sprawled across the grass and billowed gently in the breeze.

'I'm going to go out on a limb here,' Volris began, 'this does not bode well.'

'If only someone had foreseen something like this happening,' said Koel.

Everyone continued to ignore him. They pressed on towards Rjkovorg and it wasn't long before they stumbled across poor old Constable Bruts.

Silvor kicked his foot until his eyes flicked open. They blinked a few times and then focused on the faces above. 'Oh bugger, not you lot.'

'Yes. Us lot. Where is Aereon?'

'No idea.'

Silvor stomped on his ankle.

'Argh! Really, I don't know. That really hurt, how much do you weigh? No. No. No! Alright. We were here to get the girl. The one he met with. The King wanted her. He felt that if he had her then Aereon would come running to try and rescue her. We ended up taking them all. All the youths that lived in that tent. But, Aereon wasn't there I swear.'

'Really? Then who hit you on the back of the head and stole your armour?'

'Someone hit me on the – hey where are my – that little twerp. Where is he?'

Bruts tried to push himself up, but Edin and Koel shoved him back to the ground.

'Steady on, steady on,' said Silvor. 'You've had a nasty whack on the head. Best to keep your thoughts and actions at a glacial pace. Here.' Silvor offered the near naked guard a hand, which he grasped. He started to pull himself up, using the dwarf for support. Silvor's other had moved like lightning and he struck Bruts' forehead with the flat of his axe. The guard's eyes crossed and he slumped back down. 'Aereon's already in Rjkovorg. We need to move quickly.' He turned to Gwen who was perched on Volris's head, having found that the most stable place to be, 'You go back to Lars, tell him what we're doing. Tell him that everything needs to be ready to leave.'

Gwen hooted and took flight.

After some determined jogging from the dwarves and an accomplished power walk from the humans the gates of Rjkovorg came into view. The party slowed and ducked behind a small grassy mound.

'There it is,' said Volris. 'Can anyone make out the individual trunks?'

'I think we need to get closer still,' said Edin.

Silvor scuttled to the next piece of cover and everyone

followed. Light was rising from within the walls and spilling out the open gate. Battlements were stationed around the walls and the group only moved when the guards' backs were turned. Eventually they were close enough to see the structure of the wall clearly and they could count the beams as Lars had taught them.

Volris got to eight before Koel said, 'What in the name of Krank is that?'

'What?' asked Edin.

'Listen.'

'*HE WAS A LITTLE PISSHEAD!*
And I thought, we could be friends.
WE WILL BE FRIENDS!

There once was a boring little sod of a crab.
I took him to the pub and bought him a drink.
I asked him "how's life", he replied "it's bleeding drab".
I said "cheers", our glasses go clink.

This is the story of that boring little sod of a crab.

Oh! I was in the pub.
I WAS IN THE PUB!
A dodgy grimy pub.
A DODGY GRIMY PUB!
I was on my ninth drink.
IN THE DODGY GRIMY PUB!
Walking sidie ways.
ALL OVER THE WAITRESS!
I looked like pisshead.

The Greenmen

I AM A LITTLE PISSHEAD!

And I thought, is this sodding crab wantin' a scrap?

LET'S HAVE A SCRAP!'

Captain Morj's Greased Elbows disappeared into the darkest depths of Hudikvar to have themselves a good time.

In all the universes, parallel or otherwise, the gods of Fate and Chance dictate the course of events. It was Aereon's fate that he would survive that night, but the God of Chance must win sometimes. In another place, at another time the dwarves broke every characteristic in their body and ran from a confrontation, but not in a single universe did it occur to any of the gods that the Greased Elbows would not have a good time that night. Watching Morj and his men have a good time was just too much fun.

Volris started to count again.

When he reached twenty he mentally marked the embedded tree trunk and they scuttled further around the wall. He counted again and they moved again. The process was slow and the wind chilling, but eventually he was confident he had located post two-hundred and seventy-four.

Under Silvor's supervision they ran separately to the wall when no guards were watching.

With their backs to it they were safe from being seen from above.

'It's that one behind you,' rasped Volris to Koel.

'Right, I'll give someone a leg up.'

Silvor nominated himself and Koel cupped his hands for him to step on. A few quick movements and Silvor had sprung off Koel's shoulder and dug his axe as high up as he could reach. His free hand grasped the bark and his feet found something to rest on. He pulled himself up and released his axe, stretched up and embedded it again. The bark wobbled. With one slow push, Silvor's torso fell into the hollow. He pulled himself up and crawled deeper inside.

Silvor took out his rope and dropped one end to the ground. His brother grabbed it and gave him a thumb's up.

Silvor shuffled through the wall and delicately pulled at the bark at the other side. It came away just as easily and he placed it within the tunnel.

He dropped his rope through the other side and parasailed to the bottom. After a swift look to make sure the coast was clear he tugged at the rope and waited. Silvor leaned back and took the weight as the second person started to climb.

Victarian's subject was proving less than cooperative and he was not getting the answers he desired.

He had asked many questions about the Night Bandit. Where she lived? Where she came from? Did she have accomplices?

In Aereon's defence, he did not have the answers to these questions. He did have some answers, but it wasn't his fault that Victarian was asking the wrong questions.

'I don't know where you get your insolence from, boy. Where you come from the rulers must be very lenient indeed,' ranted Victarian, after another unsatisfactory answer.

'Quite the opposite, actually,' said Aereon.

And he was right. Aereon was used to dealing with the deadly sharpness of Queen Arburella, and the almost equally deadly bluntness of King Codrich. By comparison, Victarian was like a whimpering pup.

'Your bravery will soon wither.'

'Bring the girl?' Aereon guessed

'Bring the – yes. Very astute of you, Aereon,' complemented the King.

'Oh, I think we've both gotten to know each other quite well through these little meetings. For example, you knew I would come running to aid these people. You knew I was headstrong and would come without a plan. When I knocked out that guard and stole his armour I didn't have a plan,' Aereon started to pace. 'By the time we arrived here I had a vague plan, but it still took me all day to convince myself that it would work. You see, I've been wondering about you, like you've been wondering about me. What could I do to you? What does a man like Victarian care about enough for me to use against him?

'You're a proud man. Resolute. Unwavering. Traditional. These are not compliments by the way,' Aereon pointed out. 'You respect, above all, order and you believe the old ways are the best. New generations and ideas probably don't sit right with you. They probably keep you up at night. It's your ancestors you look to for strength. That's why you fill your home with their old hunting trophies, weapons and *shields*.'

All twelve captives leapt to their feet and each snatched an item off the wall.

The King was flustered. All his guards froze and allowed the youths to take up arms. All except Captain Dagny. In one swift movement, she drew her sword and held it across Aereon's neck.

She barked an order at her men and, with swords in hand, they advanced on the youngsters.

'*No!*' shrieked the King.

Aereon smiled.

'Those belonged to my forefathers. They are irreplaceable. Give them back at once!'

No one moved.

'Retrieve the possessions of the King,' commanded Dagny.

The Royal Guard edged forward.

'One more step and the buck gets it.'

Kajsha was wielding an ancient mace menacingly. She lifted it over her shoulder and prepared to swing at the companion next to her, who was hiding behind the head of a stag Victarian's great, great, great, great, great, great, great, great, great grandfather had bludgeoned with a spatula.

Victarian whimpered.

'Drop everything,' Dagny commanded. 'Or I shall kill your little boyfriend right now.'

The mace seemed to lower slightly as Kajsha looked at the blade inches from Aereon's throat.

'Just go,' said Aereon. 'She's not going to kill me.'

'Yes, I will.'

'She won't. I'm fine. You just get out of here.'

'You will not be fine,' assured Dagny who was getting quite agitated that she was not being taken seriously.

'I'm not worried. 'I'm in control of the situation.'.

If that was true or not, he didn't look worried and Kajsha believed him. It was possibly the "ok" sign he made with his hand and the un-surreptitious wink that convinced her.

She nudged the antlered thing next to her and slowly the group edged to the door. Without orders, the guards wilted and let them pass.

'Follow them,' barked Dagny, her blade now touching skin. 'Do not let them escape.'

The door flapped shut behind the last guard.

'Your friends will be caught,' spat Dagny. 'They do not have a hope of reaching the city gates. They will be surrounded, their loot will be taken from them and they will have no further value. I am sure that, when the time comes, the King will have an appropriate order to have you all executed.'

'It was a mistake for you to return,' said Victarian. His eyes had a glazed look, part of his brain still on his antiques. 'I have told you twice that your return to this city would be dealt with on pain of death –'

'True, but then you set a trap to lure me here. I'd say that was mixed signals.'

'– I will not provide such an offer a third time. You will not leave this city in one piece.' A remarkable improvement and far more clear than his threat to Captain Morj.

'My mother always taught me to quit while you have a head,' said Aereon. She of course had never said anything so crass, but it sounded like a cool thing to say. 'Too bad I've always been a terrible listener.'

Victarian opened his mouth to rebuttal but was interrupted by the commotion outside the door.

The ring of metal striking metal sounded though the hall. Victarian winced and contorted in his chair. The sound of strained gasps and searing pain echoed off the walls. Occasionally there was a worrying crack.

And then silence.

There was a scuffling of boots outside the double doors.

They both opened and two figures strolled inside.

It was Dagny who responded first, 'One more step and I kill him.'

Edin and Koel took a few more steps before they came to a halt.

'Who the hell are you?' asked the King.

'Ah, Victarian, I don't believe you've had the pleasure,' Aereon began. 'These are my fellow countrymen who I rescued from the ogres –'

'Well technically –' Edin began.

'Not now!' snapped Aereon. 'This here is Edin and that's Koel.'

'How do you do?' said Koel, offhandedly with a wave.

The King was overwhelmed, 'What happened out there?'

The Creators looked at one another, 'Us.'

'Just you?' asked Aereon, eyebrows raised.

Edin's hands found his hips, 'Is that so hard to believe?'

'Volris and Silvor aren't with you? That's what you're saying?'

'Who?' asked Victarian, totally lost.

'I'm not *not* saying that.'

'What?' demanded the King.

'And Lars? He didn't come either?'

'Don't get me started on that traitor,' Edin raised his voice and spoke slowly, so there was no misunderstanding made by the King. 'He betrayed us. He said he had been working for the King all along. He–'

'*How dare you say that about Lars? After all he's done for us. He –*'

Thump.

'*– What did you do that for? He –*'

Thump.

Dagny was swivelling on the spot, desperately trying to locate the muffled voice.

'You hit me one more time and I'm gonna –'

Crack!

The rotten roof gave way and a figure plummeted to the stone floor. When the dust cleared Silvor was covered in debris and dust with Dagny's sword pointed at his chest.

'Don't move a –'

Crack!

The decaying wood collapsed under Volris too and he landed squarely on Dagny's opportunely placed head. She crumpled under the impact and Volris found himself on top of the resulting heap. He looked over his shoulder at Dagny's masked face.

'Oh dear. She wasn't with us, was she?'

Aereon climbed to the King's platform and approached the throne.

The King sunk into the seat and pressed his spine to the back. Aereon grabbed the arms of the throne with his hands and lowered his face until it was level with Victarian's.

'It's funny how things work out. How quickly a scenario can turn on you. I want you to know something,' Aereon whispered. 'All evening you've been asking me questions about the Night Bandit. You were so desperate to know where she is and I'm going to tell you. Now that it's on my terms, I'm going to tell you.' Aereon stared into the King's pale eyes. 'The Night Bandit was in here tonight. The Night Bandits, I should say. Asta never left the ogre camp. They killed her, and that was your doing,' Aereon's voice started to rise as his anger grew. 'The Night Bandit lives on, though. She – he – it – they will always live on. They will always be here as long as someone like you is in charge. There will always be individuals who stand up to protect others. And soon it won't just be the group you caught today who are saying Knight Bandit – that did have a *K* at the start by the way.

'I just want you to know how close you were. You had them all in your grasp and you let them slip through your wrinkly old fingers.'

A blade flashed into those wrinkly old fingers and went for Aereon's throat.

Aereon instinctively moved to grab the King's hands.

The pair wrestled for control of the knife. Aereon's companions watched.

'Should we do something?' asked Koel.

'Shouldn't think so,' said Silvor. 'If this happens again and the only previous experience he has is asking his friends for help he'll kick himself.'

Slowly Aereon's young blood was winning and he started to push the blade towards Victarian. In a quick jerk, Aereon buckled the King's wrists on themselves and the dagger pierced a bony shoulder. Aereon let go and stepped back.

The King's hands slipped off the handle and a heavy breath escaped him.

'You're finished.' Aereon turned his back on the throne and his companions followed him into the night.

Into the Woods

A heavy deluge pummelled the muddy streets of Rjkovorg, hammering the thatched roofs of the city. The hustle and bustle of the capital was overrun and people darted through the torrent in search of cover.

It wasn't the sort of downpour that was totally concerned with *down* either. The wind was strong and lashed the rain at people's faces. The gale used the walls and streets of Rjkovorg to play tricks. The wind ploughed people from one side and then as quick as a switch came from the opposite direction.

Aereon stood atop the steps of the Long House, flanked by the dwarves and the Creators.

Scattered across the sodden ground, pinned to walls and in one instance even draped across a roof, were the Royal Guard. Aereon knew that Edin and Koel were no slouches in a fight. They had each survived two rounds in the ogre pits, but this was the Royal Guard. Each man and woman selected purely on their fighting ability to protect the King against any and all threats. The Creators would have done their part, but this was primarily the handiwork of Silvor and Volris. Aereon looked down at the former, who was smiling pleasantly at the groaning bodies.

Across the street, under an overhanging roof, Aereon could just make out Kajsha and her friends through the spitting rain.

He descended the steps and his clothes started to speckle.

Aereon gestured with his head. Everyone filled in behind him and they trudged towards the open gate.

Despite the haze, the guards at the gate saw them coming and could see that the group looked problematic. A pouty teenager and two men leading a ragtag gang of youths holding what appeared to be an assortment of rotten shields, rusty weapons and the odd moulting animal pelt. All flanked by two iron clad dwarves.

'Close the gates!' bellowed the Captain.

The troop sprang with obedience, all too eager to close the gates on the approaching rabble.

The Captain and his men were one of two units that operated the gates and had been aptly named by the King as the Gate Closers.

Every night, not long after sunset, they would close the gates and when they took over the shift at noon they would be open again. There was the occasional incident of having to turn away a group of peasants whose clothes and pronunciation did not meet standards, the riffraff as they called them, but other than that it was fairly straightforward. Of course, it was expected of both the Gate Openers and Gate Closers that if an enemy attacked the city they would be on duty to shut the gates to the approaching horde.

Such a scenario seemed to be upon them now. Aereon's party had broken into a run, and the Captain barked more orders at his men.

Say what you will about the Gate Closers. They may not

have been the brightest. They may not have been the fastest. They may not even have been the strongest. But, by golly, they could shut a gate.

Six men on each side of the gate pulled levers and turned wheels attached to cogs, connected to iron chains and the gate started to shut with dramatic pace.

'Come on, faster!' called the Captain and Aereon.

Bright-Spark Wendoson looked at the splashing outlaws quizzically. In a trance, his hands dropped off the wheel he had been turning and he sloshed over to the Captain.

'Wendoson! What the blazes are you doing? Get back to your post and shut this gate!'

'I've had a thought, Captain. You know how to get into either of the Gate teams you have to take the Defensive Vigilance Assessment?' said Wendoson.

'The DVA One-Oh-One. Yes.'

'And do you know the bit about responding to an assault on the gate?' continued Wendoson.

'The DVA One-Oh-One. Section Four – Appropriate Analysis and Response to Individuals and/or Companies Approaching the Gates of Rjkovorg. Yes, I'm aware of it.'

'Well, do you remember the question about when a party is approaching the gates how should you responds?'

'The DVA One-Oh-One. Section Four – Appropriate Analysis and Response to Individuals and/or Companies Approaching the Gates of Rjkovorg. Question Thirty-Seven – When an Individual and/or Companies are approaching the Gates of Rjkovorg at an Accelerated Velocity, How Might You Respond? Answer: "Close the gate, and right quick too." Yes, yes. Out with it man, they're almost on top of us.'

Behind him one door of the gate grinded to a halt and shut.

The other was still half open and struggling without its sixth man.

'Well, it just occurs to me, that question might have only been in reference to Individuals and/or Companies coming from outside Rjkovorg.'

The Captain stared as the rain *tinged* off his helmet, trying to beat some sense into him, and the wind rustled through his ear, but failed to stir up any thought by the time it came out the other.

Aereon ploughed between the two and slipped through the gap of the closing door.

The Captain still looked blank.

Edin and Koel both knocked into him as they passed, but the Captain seemed not to notice.

Next Kajsha and her band of miscreants bumbled their way to the ajar door and darted through.

Finally, the dwarves elbowed their way past the Captain and the gate shut.

The thud of it locking into place seemed to raise him from the depths of whatever field of consciousness he had been operating on.

'Right you are, Bright-Spark,' he said with a smile. He turned to the gate and his face fell.

Volris stood looking up at the thick wooden beams. His face; a perfect picture of the word *drat*. It was far too high to climb without an axe. He'd been a fraction too slow and a fraction too broad. He cursed all those heavy meals Lars had made over the last fortnight. Then instantly took it back.

He turned around slowly to face the guards.

They were all gazing at him with a combination of terror, accomplishment and curiosity. Like a cat who's dragged a squabbling pheasant through its flap and then realised that it actually looks quite threatening now it's trapped inside.

Volris's fingers twitched over the hammer tucked in his belt.

'Volris!' Silvor pounded the gate. 'Volris!'

'It's no use,' said Edin. 'The wood is too think.' Silvor brandished his axe. 'The wood is still too thick,' said Edin.

'We'll have to go around,' said Koel.

And Silvor was off.

'Go around?' asked Aereon. 'Go around where? What are you talking about? Where are we going?'

Edin had already gone after Silvor so Koel answered Aereon, 'We can get him out. I'll explain later. You go do whatever it is you are going to do and we'll meet you at the Lodge. Be sharpish though. It won't be long before the King has these gates open again and an army out looking for us,' Koel turned and ran.

Aereon turned to the youths. 'Come on.'

The Gate Closers had not put up much of a fight. Volris had fun with the Royal Guard, they were seasoned fighters, the best in the Kingdom, one or two of them even had some moves he was not familiar with, but the Gate Closers had been trained to shut the gates at the sight of a viral hedgehog. A good thing too, because if a virulent hedgehog ever made it inside Rjkovorg, they would be completely at a loss with what to do about it.

It had been no fun at all. It wasn't fighting. Not proper fighting. It was more like blindfolding a rabbit so it wouldn't see what happened next.

Volris tested the levers on the gates, but it was no use.

He scuttled into the shadow of a building and peered around the wall. The rain had cleared the streets of people and nobody saw him splash across the street to the adjacent building.

Volris looked left. He looked right. He took a confident step out into the street and a door opened.

Light spilled out and Volris flung himself back behind the wall as a figure stepped out.

The person was hooded and cloaked, and bowed their head to the wind.

The door closed and the figure turned towards him. Volris pulled away from the corner and pressed himself against the wall.

The figure continued to splash towards him and Volris's hand hovered over his hammer again. The shadow appeared around the corner, but ignored Volris and continued across the square to the house at the other side. It knocked on the door.

The door opened to a man's silhouette, which gazed down over the figure.

They seemed to recognise each other and a conversation began.

Volris was ready to turn and leave when the cloaked figure produced a knife. The blade flourished in the light.

The man in the house nodded and disappeared behind the door and when he returned he was hooded too. As he shut the door behind him, Volris could see a sword hilt sticking out his cloak.

Volris followed them. Curiosity may kill cats and trod on toads, but it tends to leave dwarves well enough alone.

The pair made their way to another door and looked over their shoulders before they knocked.

Volris stuck his head out from behind the barrel to see a woman answer. The hooded pair spoke to her and she too donned a cloak and concealed a weapon.

Three more houses and three of the same response. At the fourth, a tall man answered the door. He looked at them but said nothing. He stepped away from the door and they all followed him inside.

The last to enter scanned the streets for any watchers before shutting and locking the door.

Volris broke his cover and sprinted to the building.

He pressed an ear to the wall, but could hear nothing. No talking. No struggle. No screaming. Just the wind and the rain.

'Do you see anything?'

There was a shuffling sound and Silvor's face appeared out of the hole in the wall. 'No.'

'I'm sure everything is fine.'

Silvor grumbled. 'Something's wrong. He should have made been here by now. I'm going after him.'

'No. No! Then we'll have two missing dwarves. It's best for us all just to wait here for him.' Silvor had disappeared back into the tunnel of the wall. Koel turned to Edin and whispered, 'I knew we shouldn't have let him go up there. He's such a hot head.'

'What did you say?' asked Silvor as his head popped out again.

'Nothing,' smiled Koel.

Silvor glared, 'I'm going to look for him.' He disappeared again.

'No don't. It's –'

'He's here! Hold the rope.'

A little flustered, Edin and Koel grabbed the rope and tensed.

On Volris's first climb they lifted off the ground and smacked into the wall. On the other side Volris fell on his back. In the middle Silvor shouted, 'Confounded! Just hold the rope, would you.'

The Creators repositioned and planted into a broader stance.

'Ready,' called Edin. 'I think.'

They shifted slightly under Volris's weight, but held.

'Don't forget to replace the bark, Silvor,' Volris's voice echoed through the tunnel.

Aereon stopped at the treeline and turned to the lost boys and girls. They gathered around him with that expectant look he had come to expect. At the rear, some of the older teens were lending a hand to the smaller children. This is how it should be, felt Aereon. People in a position to take up responsibility should do so. They should guide those around them, not push and pull.

The last of the stragglers arrived and a little boy piped up, 'Why are we here?'

'You are here because of me. You are here because I put you in danger. Because of me you can never go home. I said some things that Victarian did not like. So he came looking for me. I should have known that he would send someone to track my movements. I should have warned you all to stay away. When Kajsha came to see me, someone must have followed her back to your tent. Now, because of my blindness, you can never go back there. I am sorry.'

'But you came to get us. You came to rescue us,' said the boy. 'So it's ok.'

Aereon smiled at him. 'As you all know, when I returned from the ogres I told Victarian that Asta had survived. I told him that I had rescued her and that she would continue her work,' the crowd murmured, the thought of Asta still touched on fragile feelings. 'Tonight I told him that was a lie. I told him that it is *you* he needs to fear. I told him that he does not have one Knight Bandit to fear anymore, but a team of them. And I know that you were not Asta's only supporters. There will be dozens, perhaps hundreds, of people she watched out for in Hudikvar. I encourage you to seek these people out. To build a resistance against the King and expose him for what he is. He is no man to rule this country. He is no man to rule you.'

Aereon raised his hands to quiet the jeering audience. 'I am not your leader,' he spoke slowly and clearly. 'You all need decide what is best for you. If you chose to continue the work of the Knight Bandit or track down Asta's supporters, you will have to operate carefully. The Guard will be looking for you now. You will have to move with great care and find a place to live where they cannot not find you. The forest will offer you shelter for tonight and may prove to be a good place for you to stay beyond that, I do not know. That is something for you to figure out for yourselves.'

'Aren't you going to stay?' asked the boy, with fiendish cuteness.

'I can't. I have my own Kingdom to get back to. I made a promise that I would return Edin and Koel safely. So that is what I must do. I wish you all the best, but I must go. My friends will be waiting.'

Everyone approached him individually and said their goodbyes. Last was Kajsha.

They both smiled weakly.

Aereon went first, 'Don't forget to make the most of all that stuff.' He gestured to the mace in her hand, 'I'm sure it will come in handy for something.'

'Oh right, yeah.'

'I've been thinking about Asta and the Knight Bandit,' said Aereon.

'Yes?'

'I'm not saying she wasn't a pioneer, a hero even, but I wonder if it might be a good time to pull away from her methods. The Knight Bandit needs to stand for more. Now that the King knows she is dead, he will surely tell the people. So I wonder if it's possible to try something new and achieve something that can get more people on to your side. Many of the people in Hudikvar are farmers, it seems foolish to alienate them to your cause. Sometime you may need them on your side, just a thought.'

'What will we do?' asked Kajsha.

'That's for you to work out, but I don't think you should steal from them.'

'I'm really going to miss you,' the mace fell to the ground and Kajsha launched herself at Aereon.

Instinctively he put his arms around her and she went stiff.

'Kajsha?'

She did not respond. He pushed her away and looked into her eyes. Her face was frozen.

Her gaze fixed on something over his shoulder.

*

The Creators and dwarves had worked themselves up to a run. They were soggy but the storm seemed to be passing. They squelched through the moraines as they made their way back to the forest.

The area between the hills was like a swamp, but the slopes were too sodden to climb.

'What took you so long anyway?' asked Edin, who was keen for a distraction.

'Oh, well,' began Volris, 'you know how it is. I had to deal with the guards at the gate. Then, as I made my way across Rjkovorg someone in a hood entered the streets. They knocked on a door and brandished a knife. The man inside donned a cloak and sworded his belt. Naturally I was curious.'

'Naturally,' agreed Silvor.

'So, I followed them and they knocked on four more doors, until there were six of them. Then, all armed, they knocked on another door. A man opened it and let them all inside. I tried to listen but I –'

'Hey!' Up ahead a nearly naked man lay in the mud. 'Hey you!' He pointed at them lazily.

'I got it,' said Koel.

Koel swung out a boot and caught Constable Bruts in the chin, who really was having the most dreadful day.

The group jogged on until they emerged from the moraines onto the open plain.

Koel and Edin stopped and the dwarves bumped into the back of them.

Volris rounded them and looked at their faces.

'What is it?' asked Silvor.

Kajsha didn't answer. She just raised a shaking hand.

Aereon slowly turned and peered over his shoulder.

Flames rose above the trees in the distance, piercing into the night. Sparks broke off and twinkled towards the stars.

'Lars...' Aereon squeezed Kajsha's shoulders. 'I have to go. Take care of yourself and your friends.'

He turned and ran.

He kept his head down until the trees streamed past. The backs of their trunks were given a glowing yellow tinge. He pushed himself to sprint the last part.

He could feel the heat of the fire. Only a few rows of trees were between him and it now. He looked around for a sign of Lars, or guards. Only the flames moved.

The fire was in a clearing of trees. Next to it he could see the tarp covered pile of firewood he had painstakingly cut. The fire was strong and its light spread far into the darkness. Aereon spotted Lars's lodge, still perfectly intact.

The lodge door opened.

Edin emerged.

'Ah, Aereon. Nice of you to join us.'

Koel followed him out.

'Where is Lars?' asked Aereon.

Next was Volris.

Koel pointed a thumb over his shoulder, 'He's just coming.'

Silvor emerged.

Then Lars. 'Come along Aereon. Don't dilly-dally. I've got your pack for you here.'

Lars placed it into his unresisting hands.

'But... the fire?'

'I told you all,' Lars continued, 'some wood just needs to be burned. I wasn't going to leave until I'd taken care of that rotten stack. Now, let's go.'

'What about Gwen?'

'Oh she's somewhere. She'll catch up. Now, come on. We need to put some distance between us and Rjkovorg.'

Getting Stabbed Makes People Angry

They knew better than to make themselves comfortable in his presence.

He found his chair and sat down.

'Why are you here?' dripping all over my floor.

'The time has come.' He turned his head to the speaker. 'We should move. Tonight there –'

'I am well versed in the events of this evening. Thank you, Erling. What is it that you have deduced from them, hmm?'

'That now is the time to strike.'

'I assume you all feel this way? That is why you have chosen to bear arms?'

He observed the quiet murmur and further inspection of shoes.

'Devoted underlings, these things take time. Yes, progress was made tonight, but there is still a long way to go.'

'He has taken an enormous fall. He cannot fall any further. You must see that, Victarian. You must.'

'He could take a more public fall. Many are fiercely loyal. He is their leader after all,' Victarian paused. His mind dwelled on the happenings of the evening. It had been an almighty embarrassment, that was true, but it had not been

88

witnessed by enough people. 'The time will come when he slips up and there are people there to see it, but this is not it. Return to your homes. Let the others know that the day is coming and those loyal to me will not go unrewarded.'

Victarian watched them all leave with their tails between their legs. He turned to his butler. 'Why is it that everyone is always so head strong, Herm?' Victarian asked, rhetorically. 'They realise that if they run at someone with their head it will cause some damage. They just never seem to grasp that most of it will be to themselves. They never consider what else a head can do. Why is it nobody ever thinks?'

'I do not know, Master,' said Herm.

Captain Morj did not feel good.

He'd woken up in a puddle of – in what he hoped was just a puddle.

His armour cocooned his wet clothes. His head hurt. His nose was running. He dabbed his finger against it and inspected: not blood at least. That was good. He wouldn't have to arrest anybody.

He seemed to be in a gutter of some kind, best not to read too much into that. Wouldn't want to stumble across a metaphor now, would we?

He stumbled to the end of the alley and spilled out into the street. He knew this place. The Curious Toad was just across the mud slicked road and was as good a place as any to start.

As he walked in, one hand was clutched to his head and the other was groping at the air, searching for some structural support.

Inside was a tavern. A proper tavern. Everything within had a purpose, usually to get sloshed upon or just reach a state of sloshed. There was no object there with aesthetics in mind, which made the whole place quite aesthetically pleasing. Everything was made of wood and nothing was straight. The roof curved in odd places. The walls bent at funny angles. Drinks slid off tables. But, the uneven surface that was current cause for concern for Morj was the floor.

The landlord was in the process of sweeping. At the sight of Morj, the landlord put his broom down and made his way to the bar.

Morj was doing the same. The stickiness, only years of spilt drinks can achieve, was providing some grip at least.

Morj edged onto a stool while the landlord picked up a cloth and started wiping surfaces. Which was peculiar because the cloth had sustained its entire existence without ever encountering soap.

'Morning, Ralf.'

'Morn, yourself,' said Ralf, picking up a cup and spitting in it.

'I made it this far last night, then?' asked Morj.

The Greased Elbows were the world's first and only contestants in a game they aptly titled *pub crawl*. The task was simple enough to understand: eighteen taverns, all with their own lethal brand of house ale. Morj, himself, had only ever reached the end pub and swallowed the last gulp of the final drink a handful of times, and all had been years ago. The premise was that any man who fell behind, was left behind. No hard feelings.

'You did.' The Curious Toad was stop number fifteen on the crawl, a respectable finish Morj felt. 'You were singing that song about what curiosity did to the toad again.'

'It trod on him,' said Morj, allowing himself a small smile.

'Yes, and I've told you, I don't like you singing that in here. I don't want my tavern associated with it. I swear, we're one incident away from it becoming our anthem!'

'Is that a challenge?'

'No!' said Ralf. 'Last night you had everyone up in arms. Singing away.'

'It's a good song. People like it and it brings you business. I don't see what the problem is.'

'It's *vulgar*.'

'That's why people like it,' Morj explained.

Ralf mumbled something and went back to cleaning his mug. Then his inner bartender took over and he offered Morj a drink.

'Go on then. Just one, to get the blood flowing.'

Are you sure it's still blood? thought Ralf. He tapped a keg while Morj fumbled with the pouch on his belt.

'This one's on the house.'

'Why?' asked Morj suspiciously.

'You may have tipped me two silvers last night,' said Ralf, bashfully looking the other way.

'I did what?'

'You said it was for being a top-notch bartender and that I was a really nice chap and that my hair smells like lilacs.'

'Uh, yes, sorry. I get like that sometimes.' Morj was at a crossroads, he could press the case and probably retrieve his grotesquely large tip, or he could drop the matter and hope it was never spoken of again. 'Give me the beer.'

He sipped at it experimentally then, once it stayed down, enjoyed mouthfuls.

'So, who else made it here?'

'Oh, the usual suspects,' began Ralf, 'Olle, Marius and

Noak. Although Noak looked as though he was on his last legs. Olle though, Olle was barely wobbling.'

'I've no idea how he does it,' said Morj, shaking his head. 'He's this big,' he held his hand out a few inches above the bar.

'Maybe he's got some dwarvish blood in him,' Ralf joked. 'Speaking of which what's the news on those two last night?'

'Olle and Marius? Who knows, probably made it to the Burrow. Probably still there now laughing at us lightweights.'

'No, the dwarves. You know the two that came with that boy. What's his face? You know, the one they're all talking about. Crayon the Rank, or something.'

'Aereon of Krank,' corrected Morj, solemnly.

'Yeah, that's the one. What happened to him and all his chums last night?'

'Oh, that. Nothing good I'd imagine. When we left, the King had him and a group of lost boys and girls.'

'You haven't heard?'

'Heard what?'

'They escaped. All of them. Apparently, the dwarves and Aereon's countrymen broke them all out.'

Morj's head smacked against the bar, 'Oh god.'

'Another drink?'

'And a nip please,' replied Morj without lifting his lips from the wood. 'He's going to be so mad.'

The sound of beverages hitting the bar raised Morj's head. He grasped the shot and took it in one. Then shut his eyes and waved his tongue out his mouth. 'Urgh.'

He grabbed the handle of the tankard and got to his feet.

'Aint you going to drink that here?'

'This one's for the road. I'm sure my grossly excessive tip

will stretch to cover the cost of the glass as well.'

'I want them found!' Victarian demanded.

A new unit within the Royal Guard was on duty, although they were feeling the loss of Dagny who was still reeling from having two-hundred pounds of armoured dwarf land on her head. The rest of the guards shifted uneasily. They liked having her as a buffer. Everything seemed more real now. Amiable threats seemed less amiable.

The current stream of abuse, however, was being aimed at the Search and Seekers. A wiry bunch, but good at what they do. The one who'd been mauled by Gwen was there. They hadn't actually done anything wrong, not yet. This was more of a pre-emptive bollocking, so the cost of failure was vivid in their minds.

'Do I make myself clear?' nobody said anything. 'Do I make myself *clear*?'

'Yes, sire.'

'Certainly, sire.'

'Yes.'

'Good. So, what are you all to do?'

'… Kill the dwarves?'

'Kill the dwarves!' shouted Victarian. 'Next.'

'… Kill the other two?'

'Kill the other two. Edin and Koel are their names and I would like to see their bodies as proof of your work. Anything else?'

'Bring Aereon back alive?'

'Bring Aereon back alive!' the King shrieked. 'I would like to see him before he dies. And during his death. And afterwards. Yes, bring that one back alive. He does not need to be in one piece, but definitely alive. And if you find the Woodsman with them, kill him too. You say he was not at his home?'

'No, sire. I mentioned the fire as well, right?'

'Yes, it was curious. Very well, examine the remains before you leave. They may have burned him. But be quick about it, you have much catching up to do.'

The Search and Seekers slinked out, just as Captain Morj came bumbling through the door.

'Captain!' cried Victarian. 'Where the hell have you been?'

'Sorry sire. I came as soon as I heard.'

Victarian studied the Captain with bulging eyes, 'Big night, was it?'

'No bigger than any other. Although I suppose the days are getting shorter, so in a sense–'

'Shut up.'

'Yes, sire.'

Victarian shifted uncomfortably.

'Goodness, what happened to your shoulder?'

'I was stabbed, Captain.'

Morj sucked in through his teeth 'Looks painful, sire.'

Victarian stared at him. He was looking for any hint of malice or humour in Morj's features. He found none. It was just good natured pleasantness. He hated that. 'It is very painful, thank you Captain.'

'Anytime sire. And where is Captain Dagny? We had plans.'

'She –' began the King, then he realised what had been said '– don't be absurd! She would never stoop so low. She was wounded in the line of duty.'

'Phewwwy,' Morj whistled. 'Sounds like quite the catastrophe. Glad I wasn't here for it. What happened to her?'

The King scowled. 'A dwarf was dropped on her.'

'A dwarf what?'

'Just a dwarf. One dwarf fell through the roof and landed on her. Well, a brace of dwarves fell through the roof in fact, which is why you will note, there are two holes in my ceiling.'

'Noted,' said Morj. 'Also sounds painful.'

'Can we diverge from the topic of things which are painful? Otherwise I shall have to add this conversation to the list.'

'As you wish, sire.'

'Where are your men, Captain?'

Morj didn't like to lie to the King if he could avoid it, 'On the streets, sire.'

'Whatever it is they are doing, I have something more important for them. My sources tell me that band of rough necks you caught yesterday did not join Aereon's party into the woods. They remained in Hudikvar somewhere. I want you to find them.'

'Them again,' said Morj. 'I thought we went through this.'

'We did. I'm glad you brought that up,' the King waged his finger at Morj, triumphantly. 'You see Aereon has informed me that Asta, the Night Bandit, was killed by the ogres and these youths have taken up her mantle. How does that sound for *mild* treason?'

'I suppose that is slightly stronger cheddar. What will you do to them if I find them?'

'When,' assured the King. 'I will do nothing. You will kill them on sight. As I said to the Search and Seekers, I would like to see bodies.'

'Ah,' began Morj tentatively, 'the thing is, you see, when I took this job it was on the condition that I would never have to do that sort of thing. Not unless it was a life or death situation, or in defence of the realm.'

'This is defence of the realm!'

'Yes, but I always imagined the threat as something more physical. Something that was going to kill me if I didn't kill it. A ravenous horde. A scaly monster. Not a dozen youngsters with petty theft in their hearts and pimples on their cheeks.'

'Well it's petty theft now, tomorrow; petty arson, the day after; petty murder.'

'Until that day comes my hands are tied. I'll find them though.'

The King was not happy, but bit his tongue. All things considered, he respected a man with a moral code. It's one of the reasons he'd hired Morj in the first place, despite his record.

'Very well. There is one more thing.'

'Yes, sire?'

'The Gate Closers failed to close the gate quickly enough and all but one of Aereon's friends escaped. A dwarf remained inside. He made short work of the Gate Closers apparently, rest assured they have been disciplined for their failures, and then disappeared. We searched every inch of Rjkovorg through the night and this morning before we opened the gates and there was no sign of him. He had to have escaped by other means. I would like you to discover those means Captain. But, tracking down the Night Bandits is your priority.'

*

Re-piecing together your squad after a raucous night could prove tricky, but for Captain Morj it was simply a matter of retracing his steps to collect the first eight and then on to the last three pubs to see if any had reached the end, and then there was Constable Bruts, who still hadn't turned up. Morj had picked up his armour from the Long House and then swiftly given it to Constable Yurgn when he found him still slumped over a table in the eleventh pub, exactly where they'd left him the night before.

He was beginning to get a little worried about Bruts, he was usually pretty good at shaking off knocks. He'd have to be with the mouth he had on him.

They passed the Curious Toad and before they even reached the Buggered Stoat (whose pub sign was something no one ever forgot) they found Constable Noak in a pile of – in the dirt.

After some convincing, they got him on his feet and continued to the Buggered Stoat. Only Morj went inside. He knew better that to bring them all in with him. It would only take one to say "Fancy a pint?" and others would say "Yeah, just one though", "Of course, just a quick one" and "I think I could force one down, sure". Then they'd all give him those eyes and say things like "Oh, yes can we Cap?", "Please please please" or "We'll þe really, really good". He was absolutely convinced that at the time of utterance they did really mean *just one*, but that was never what happened.

Constables Marius and Olle were not present inside.

Morj searched in the Wobbly Turnip as well, but he was informed that both the remaining contestants had finished their drinks and headed for the Burrow. He was assured that the night's consumption was catching up with both men and they were embracing the name of the game as they left on their hands and knees.

When they got to the Burrow, Morj found both Constables were still seated, it was just that their seats had tipped over to some extent. On the table were two tankards. Morj peered into them. Marius's was empty. Olle's was about half. The Captain smiled. It was a brave effort from the lad, but when you drink that much it *will* catch up with you. There was no shame in losing to Marius either. The man was built like an ox. The Greased Elbows' designated muscle and Morj's right hand man.

But the squad's youngest member didn't have to lose. Morj picked up the remains of Olle's pint and drained it on the floor.

'Oi! What the blazes do you think you're doing? I just cleaned that!'

Morj turned to the man bearing down on him. 'Uh, sorry. I was going for a kind of symbolic gesture. I guess I didn't think it through.'

'No, you bloody well didn't!'

Morj couldn't help himself. 'It's not really *that* big of deal though, is it? I mean, I practically have to grab my legs to lift my feet in here as it is.'

'Oh right, well. That's just fine then, isn't it?' said Mjcky, the landlord. 'Oh yes, let's just spill a few more drinks over the place, 'cos it's bad enough as it is! Oh yes. You know a couple of the chairs and tables are a bit wobbly too, why don't we just smash them up while we're at it? Oh yes. Let's do that. And you know, one of my kegs has only got a quarter left. Why don't we just throw that away and stick a new one in?'

'Seems like a poor financial move,' said Morj.

Mjcky made a noise like 'brruh!' then stormed off.

Morj went to Marius first.

'Feeling alright, Sergeant?' he asked after a couple ringing slaps.

'Been better, Cap.'

'Understandably.' Morj moved to Olle.

'Oh, let him sleep Cap,' rumbled Marius, leaning against the bar.

'That would be nice, but we have work to do.' Morj bent down and started shaking Olle's shoulder, 'Wakey, wakey.'

'I thought we were on the late shift today?'

'We were. There has been an incident,' said Morj without looking up. 'Come on, time to get up.' He shook a little harder.

'I could carry him, Cap? Just until he wakes up. He deserves it after last night's effort. Did he finish?'

'Check his mug.'

'He does look a bit green around the gills, Cap. But if he throws up on me then that's all in the line of duty.'

'A very admirable idea, but I meant his mug on the table.'

'Right you are, Cap.' Marius made his way to the table and peered into Olle's tankard. 'He finished! He can throw up on me all he likes, that's a very impressive showing from the young lad.'

'Very well, if you'll carry him, he can sleep a little longer.'

'No worries, Cap. I couldn't half go for some water before we leave though.'

'Water, Sergeant?'

'Yes. As long as it's got some yeast, barley and hops in it obviously.'

'Right you are. Two pints of your finest ale, landlord,' called Morj.

Amazingly, it was after just *one* pint when Morj and Marius emerged, with Olle slung over the latter's shoulder.

'Who won?' asked Constable Grunson.

'Both these fine specimens were victorious.'

Grunson looked past Morj at Marius. 'One look's in slightly better condition than the other,' he pointed out.

'The rules say nothing about what state you are in the next day, just so long as you drink your drink.' Morj returned his helmet to his head, 'Let's go.'

'Where are we going?'

'I suppose the best place to start is at the source. Where Constable Bruts was attacked. Attacked without any of you gents noticing, I should point out.'

'It was your idea to start singing, Cap.'

'Yes, yes, fine. The point is that we should do some proper policing. Inspect the scene of the crime for clues. That sort of thing. However, as it stands, Bruts's house is en route, so I thought we might just pop our noses in there first.'

Captain Morj had a good knock. It said "I am authoritative; I'd like to have a chat. Preferably over a cup of tea with a biscuit".

The door opened and revealed a plump woman. Grey was beginning to leach into the hair across her tied back temples, her face was stricken with worry lines and in Morj's experience she was almost always scowling.

'Hello, Melga. Is Bruts in by any chance?'

'One moment.' She disappeared back behind the door.

'Well that's good eh, Cap? He was here all along. All that worrying for nothing…'

The Constable's voice trailed off slightly at the sight of Melga rushing out the door wielding a rolling pin. The first strike caught Morj unawares.

He stupidly raised a hand and the second blow crunched his fingers.

His loyal men thought it better not to interfere without his specific instruction.

The third caught him on the back as he scampered away.

A fourth swing struck him behind the knee and he sank to his knees. He swivelled and managed to shield his face before the next blow came. 'Wait, wait! Can I at least know what I'm getting a beating for?'

The rolling pin looming overhead.

'I told you the last time'

'Ow!'

'I don't want you taking my husband out on you nightly piss-ups.'

'Ow!'

'They lead to nothing but trouble.'

'Ow! We weren't out with Bruts last night!' Morj rattled it out as quickly as possible.

The baton hovered threateningly.

'Oh really? Then why is that boy incapacitated?'

Morj looked over at the still comatose Olle. 'Well *we* were out last night,' Morj said in a way that suggested it should have gone without saying. 'But Bruts wasn't with us!'

'Then where was he?'

'I told her I –'

Bruts had appeared, cowering behind the frame of the door.

'You get back inside! You're in enough trouble as it is!'

Bruts's throat made a wobbly whimper and he scurried back inside.

Melga turned back to Morj. Behind her, Bruts's eyes slowly rose up above a window sill.

'Where was he last night?'

'I don't know the precise location,' began Morj, eyes on the raised rolling pin, 'but when I was in the Long House, I was informed that he had been struck on the head by Aereon Cusith.'

'And then what did you do?'

'I, well, we went to the – oh I see what you're getting at.'

If it wasn't for his helmet the blow would have caught him right between the eyes.

'You just left him there!' shrieked Melga, swinging again.

'He's a tough lad. Ow! I knew he'd be fine.'

'He was only in his under armour!'

'Ah, but look see, I brought his armour. Constable Yurgn, please!'

Before Yurgn could step forward and present said armour, Morj was forced to curl into a ball under the ferocity of Melga's blows, at which point the Greased Elbows decided it was probably time to intervene.

Eventually, Melga was tamed.

It was all thanks to Olle, who was woken by an accidental hit on the head when she was swinging for Marius. He offered her a sit down and a cup of tea. Everyone else waited outside, biting their fingernails while Olle and Melga had a chat.

Eventually he emerged wiping his brow. 'She's gone to have a little lie down. She's not pleased with you, but she says you can carry on your policing. She will speak with you tonight.'

'Not pleased with me? All I did was get hit on the head,' protested Bruts, quietly.

'Ditto,' added Morj, miserably.

'What do we do now, Cap?'

Morj rubbed one of the dents that was digging into his scalp. 'I suppose ask around and see if anyone saw where the youths went.

'Oh, that's the other thing. Apparently one of the dwarves was inside when the gates were shut. The King wants us to investigate how he got out. If the King suspects we knew about the hole in the wall and didn't tell him, I think he might be a bit peeved. So, I think I'll wait a while before I tell him that one. Now, who wants to cover what district?'

Within the Trees

L ars led the way and had instructed the others to drag
their feet as it would help to disguise his footfall from
anyone who may have picked up their trail.

On the second day, they reached a cold shallow stream.
Lars made them walk through it half a league upstream. When
they remerged on the other side he was confident that they
would have shaken any tails and he permitted the others to
walk normally again.

Lars drank in the air as Gwen snoozed on his shoulder. The
others were close to a similar state. Lars had not been
generous with their sleeping hours. He suspected that King
Victarian had sent adversaries to track them down which
provided ample reason to keep the party on the move.

'What's the plan here?' asked Edin, during one of his more
lucid periods. 'We just traipse through the woods until we
come out the other side?'

'Firstly, one does not traipse in a forest. Traipsing has a
tendency to draw attention and there are many creatures
within these trees that I would rather were not alerted to our
presence. Secondly–'

'What sort of creatures?'

Lars turned to the impudent interruption. 'Satyrs for a start. As well as–'

'What's a satyr?' asked Aereon.

'You know, a satyr, with the horns?'

Aereon looked around vaguely and spotted Volris who had his forefingers pointing out of his temples helpfully and was smiling encouragingly.

'Sorry no,' said Aereon.

'They've got furry legs?' continued Lars.

'Cousin to the centaur?' said Silvor.

'Nope,' Aereon assured them.

'Hooved feet?' said Lars.

'Nephew of the minotaur?' commented Silvor, who was absolutely convinced he was helping.

'Are you making these names up?'

'We had to face them in the ogre fighting pit, Aereon,' said Koel. 'Imagine a man with goat legs and a kind of goat-human face, with horns.'

Aereon gave this some thought, eventually he seemed to reach a conclusion. 'Ah,' he said waving his hand triumphantly. 'Trying to get one over on me, were you?'

'No.'

'Now, now. I like a good joke as much as the next person. But, you'll have to do better than that to – are you ready for this? – pull the *wool* over my eyes. The *wool*. Get it? Goats. Sheep. The *wool*.' The silence caused Aereon to cough uncomfortably. 'If this satyr did exist then how would it sit in a chair?' (Charlie Chum's *theory of relaxation* is a documented evolutionary concept).

'What?'

'Who says they use chairs?'

'Well, what are you suggesting?' scoffed Aereon. 'That they just sit on the ground with all those joints tucked in underneath them with their torso up straight? Or they stick their legs out in front of them and have their hooves tickling at their nipples?'

Since their escape, the ragtag youths had made themselves a camp. Camp may be generous. Den may be closer. Although they are usually associated with being at ground level, if not lower. Treehouse didn't fit either, because what they had constructed was nothing like a house. What they had was more like a tree-hammock-community.

A couple of the older teens had led expeditions back into Hudikvar to scrounge for what materials they could. Kajsha thought a lot about what Aereon had said. The farmers were not the problem. If you put a bad apple on top of the fruit bowl soon everything was rotten. As much as she agreed with Aereon that stealing from the farmers was a morally grey area, it was an idealistic view. They all still needed to eat. Only one among them knew his way around edible forest plants and could set a trap, that wasn't enough. For now, they were still dependent on theft to survive.

Sheep were one of the prime targets and were quite cooperative in the kidnapping process.

Thanks to the wolves in the area, farmers did not suspect youths for the odd missing cud chewer. Hudikvar had a lot of farmers and Kajsha's band were few in number. When Asta had conducted her raids, she had to feed every mouth in Hudikvar that needed feeding. Or at the least try.

The youths were surviving, but other than that they were a bit rudderless. They did not have a plan and most seemed to turn to Kajsha to produce one. She felt that surviving was a pretty damn good thing and should be enough for everyone.

But, it wasn't. Not even for her. They had all felt the rush of defying the King and now they craved more.

One night, Rjkaard gazed silently into the camp fire. He was a quiet boy and no one paid much notice as he absentmindedly spooned his dinner into his mouth. Thoughts were pooling at the back of his brain and forming a united idea that would storm Rjkaard's frontal lobes, which would quickly fall to the invasion and bow down to the epiphany.

Rjkaard missed his mouth and spilled his dinner down his shirt.

He placed his bowl down and wandered over to the older kids.

They were having, what Rjkaard perceived to be, grown up talk. He waited patiently for one to notice him.

'Yes?' said someone after a while. They hadn't looked up, but Rjkaard felt it was addressed to him.

'I've been thinking.'

'Gets you into trouble that.'

'Don't listen to him,' said Kajsha. 'What is it Rjky?'

'Do you remember when you told us what mister Aereon had said to you?'

Kajsha did remember. The details of her last conversation with Aereon had been prized out of her by expectant faces and brutally blunt questioning. 'Yes.'

'He told us all that King Victarian is the problem. He hinted that we should take our actions in a new direction from the Knight Bandit.' Rjkaard took a pause, 'With due respect, I think he was wrong. As much as I dislike the King, he is not the problem. He is merely an enabler. The ogres are the real problem. The King doesn't do anything to stop them, but they are the ones who kidnap and murder us.'

'What are you saying?'

'Mister Aereon advised us against alienating ourselves from other Hudikvarians. And going after their King is unlikely to be seen favourably. But if we can spark them to turn on him by exposing his weakness they may be more supportive. I suggest we do something that Victarian has never been able to. We should capture an ogre and show that they are not invincible. We need everyone to see that we can fight them and we can win.'

'In this plan of yours, have you considered how we are going to catch an ogre?'

'With a trap.'

'It's not like catching rabbits! Ogres are powerful creatures and massive.'

'Well, it will have to be a big trap then.'

There were a lot of tracks around lodge, but the Searches spread into an arc and soon located the trail into the woods.

'Excellent work, Bertil,' said the Captain to the youngest member of his team, who had found the trail. 'Now, what can you tell me about it?'

Bertil got to his knees and stroked the earth. 'The ground seems to be very agitated. There's definitely a dwarf track here though, and there's the other.' Bertil scuttled across the forest floor. 'Here's a man's gait. Another here.' He shifted on the spot. 'Ah, and there's the last one.'

'The last one?'

'If the Woodsman is not with them, then that should be everyone.'

'You said the ground was very agitated. I'd say exceedingly so. What do you make of that?'

'I'd say they were in a hurry.'

'Yes, they were, but this is more than that.' Captain Vander picked up a pitch of earth and watched it crumble in front of his eyes. 'This seems deliberate to me. This looks like they were trying to hide something. Trying to cover something up. Any ideas?'

'The Woodsman?'

'Did you hear that?' Vander whispered. 'That was the sound of a penny dropping.'

They stayed on the scent until they reached the stream.

'Well that's that then,' said the Captain, mockingly. He stepped into the water. 'I mean, it's not as if, without a little looking, we could spot which rocks have been moved.'

The water was crystal clear and the bed was silty but speckled with rounded pebbles. The Captain lifted one out the stream and inspected the line where the green of the algae stopped.

'Cover the river and see if you can find any stones that look as though they have been moved recently.'

'I just don't understand people sometimes,' said Vander. 'It's like they think water is this magical elixir that will just wash away any trace of them. It's insulting is what it is, that they think they can give us the slip so easily. Don't they realise we are professionals?'

They crossed the river and followed the bank on the other side upstream. In the late afternoon they found where the rebels had left the river and the tracks were clear.

'Dear, oh dear, Lars. You have been misbehaving.'

Moonrise

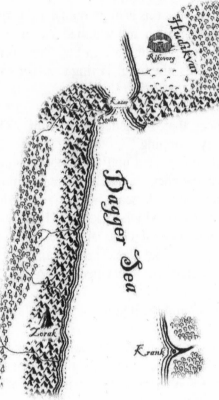

Hudikvar

Oak's Wood

Rikovorg

Kazar

Bolin

Dagger Sea

Sunrise

Sunset

Zorak

Krank

Moonset

Aftermath

Roughly two weeks ago...

Things were unclear. Things were so unclear that it was unclear what the things were. It felt like one of them might be pain, but it was a hazy pain, somewhere off on the horizon.

'Can you hear me? Come towards the light.'

Eyelids flickered. There was a light, it was bright and warm.

'Don't say that! You'll confuse her. Get out of the way.'

The light started to fade and shadows rose.

'Can you hear me sweetie? Say something. Anything.'

'Tell her to come towards the light,' whispered Codrich.

Things started to clear and the face in front of Lirna's eyes focused. 'Mum?'

'Oh, my baby's alright,' Mrs Hartilby embraced her daughter and it was a long time before she could be convinced to let go.

Her father was standing over her. King Codrich was just behind him and brandishing a torch. She was vaguely aware of other people scattered around in the background.

'What happened?'

'There was an accident,' said her father. 'There was some sort of explosion in the Creators' Shack. You were caught in the blast, but you got back up and tried to run inside. The King himself had to stop you.'

She tried to sit up, but her father rested his hand on her shoulder. 'What was I doing at the Shack?'

'You just rest now,' her mother told her. 'You need to recover your strength.'

'Everybody out,' Codrich blared, on cue, and started wafting people out the door.

'Thank you for rescuing her. Thank you for bringing her home.'

Codrich smiled to the trio. 'Just doing my Kingly duties.' He followed the last person out the door.

'Can I get you anything sweetie? Something to eat?'

'Some water would be nice.'

'I'll get it,' said her father. He let go of his daughter's hand and disappeared into the kitchen.

'You don't remember anything?'

'I remember dinner. I remember being at the table with you and dad, but after that it's just blank.'

'Maybe that's for the best,' said her mother. 'Sometimes it's better not to remember. You see this wrinkle here?' she pointed at her forehead and Lirna nodded. 'That's because I remember when you were two and you got on top of the kitchen cabinets.'

The next day Lirna was on her feet, but housebound. Her mother had shown strong resistance to any suggestion otherwise and she remained at home, so she could care for any and all of her daughter's needs.

112

It was almost lunchtime when Lirna discovered the piece of paper.

Lirna couldn't remember reading it before, but she knew she had. She realised, when she finished, that some part of her had already known everything that was written. Nothing on it had surprised her. She moved the paper to one side and glanced at it.

'Soup?' asked her mother, in an attempt to draw her attention.

'Oh, yes thank you.'

When she put the bowl down, Lirna's eyes seemed to refocus and her mother exhaled.

The two chatted between spoonfuls about nothing in particular. They gossiped and they laughed, it was like nothing had happened.

Mrs Hartilby could only ask Lirna if she would like another bowl so many times though and, all too soon, lunch was over. As her mother did the dishes, Lirna turned her attention back to the paper.

The heading at the top read *Arburella's nail polish formula*. Aereon had given it to her. She remembered thinking it was the most precious thing in the world. She recalled waking up with it clutched in her hand again and again. That had all been before she'd read it. It was last night when she had opened it for the first time. She didn't know what had made her look, but she knew she must have been disappointed when she did.

Since the day Aereon left, Lirna had taken the scrunched-up paper with her everywhere. The last thing he had said to her was that she should have it. It never even occurred to her that it might be for practical reasons. She'd spent hours thinking about what Aereon could have written. In the end, none of it had been done in his hand. Not even the little scribble in the corner, which had the necessary adjustments to turn Queen Arburella's nail polish into floyancy coating.

The floyancy. Over the last few weeks she had been working on it with Juta...

... Juta. She felt a stab in her chest. She had spoken with him the day before.

He had been to see the Queen. Arburella had demanded the completion of the floyancy from him. Juta had worked himself ragged through the night to finish, but Lirna and Juta could not locate any information on the floyancy coating. Juta was forced to return to the Queen without a result and Lirna went home for her dinner.

'Mum?'

'Yes, dear?'

'Did I read this at dinner last night?'

Mrs Hartilby looked at the piece of paper and frowned. 'No,' she said, tartly. Before adding, 'But you left after dinner. It's possible you could have read it then.'

'I think I did. I think I was going to take it to Juta.'

'Oh?' said her mother, innocently.

'But, I must have gotten hurt before I got to him. He had met with the Queen yesterday morning. She wanted him to find the solution for the floyancy. We searched, but it wasn't in the Shack. Don't you see? Aereon gave it to me. I had it all along.'

'I see,' was all her mother could manage.

'I should give it to him.'

'I'm not sure that is such a good idea.'

'Well you should give it to him then. He could be in

danger.'

Lirna's mother thought about how she could put it. 'I'm sure the Queen isn't going to harm him.'

'You can't know that. She could be torturing him right now!'

'We will discuss it when your father gets home.'

And boy was he in for a treat.

The conversation lasted right through dinner, and what was worse, there wasn't even any meat involved due to Krank's current food crisis.

Before he'd even sat down, his daughter was demanding answers from him and Mr Hartilby didn't have very many of those. She asked him if he would take the message to Juta. Her father said he couldn't. So she asked if he would take it to the Queen. He squelched up his face and shook his head. She asked why he would not take it to Juta.

For once he relished the opportunity to put something green into his mouth. Chewing gave him time to think. He agreed to take the note to the Queen. First thing in the morning.

Only when that time came, his daughter insisted that she give it to the Queen herself. Her mother still refused to allow her out the house and her father didn't have any food to hand so he was forced to whimper and agree to go to Arburella and ask her to take time out of her busy schedule of ruling to pay his daughter a vist.

There was more whimpering involved when he arrived at the Royal Abode.

Arburella couldn't stand whimpering but agreed, just to shut him up. She did have several other *shut up* methods at her disposal, but she was feeling charitable that day. She dismissed the whelp and left, while the King sat amazed at the lack of blood on the floor.

Arburella did not knock, she was above such things. She glided inside and gave the place a quick glance. As far as peasants went the Hartilby's weren't too badly off, but she still frowned at the state of the place.

Lirna was seated at the table and the Queen approached. 'I am not used to being summoned.'

Though, there were some within Krank who whispered she must have been summoned to get to the surface of the world in the first place.

Lirna's mother frantically offered Arburella a seat and something to drink. The Queen took to the chair like she owned it, but declined the offered beverage.

Lirna slid the piece of paper across the table. The Queen did not move. A quick glance at the grubby edges and strange stains was all it took to know that it was not something she was going to touch.

The paper sat sad and abandoned. Lirna reached across the table and took it back. She unfolded and started to read aloud.

'Oh good,' interrupted Arburella, as soon as Lirna finished the title. 'You found it.'

'I figured, you should have it,' said Lirna, holding out the paper.

Queen Arburella raised a palm, 'That won't be necessary.'

Lirna consulted the paper once more, 'It also has the dilutions to make floyancy coating. Perhaps you could take it to Juta? So he can complete the floyancy. I'd hate to think that something had happened to him just because I never opened this note.'

The Queen raised an eyebrow at Lirna's mother.

Arburella was not a cruel woman for the sake of cruelty. She was cruel, yes, but she operated with more logic than anyone else on the island. The parents had chosen not to tell their daughter what had happened and Arburella could see no benefit at this time to revealing the truth. 'Juta has been occupied. That is why he has not been to see you.'

'But he's alright?'

'I assure you, I haven't touched him.' That seemed to sooth the girl. 'Is that all? I am a busy woman.'

'I think so,' said Lirna, timidly. 'Are you sure you don't want this?'

Arburella glanced at the paper again. 'No. I shall leave that in your capable hands. I'm sure a charming young woman, such as yourself would relish the chance to brew my nail polish for me.' Arburella noticed the mother's face, 'Tomorrow. One more day of rest should suffice.'

Lirna's mother was still looking at the Queen. 'Isn't that stuff a little… dangerous?'

'Lirna may use my den. There is little flammable material in there. Would that be acceptable?'

It wasn't really a question. There was only one answer you could give.

When Lirna left her home the next morning it was amidst restrained trepidation from her mother, but it felt good to be out of the house and back on the streets. There was still the odd bruise and sore bone here and there, but she was too well to sit in the house all day and be cared for.

Krank didn't seem to have changed much in her absence. The streets were still lined with sand and filled with people. The sand scattered in the wind and the people wafted into their daily routines. In Krank this generally meant applying your trade. Fishermen fished, builders built, sellers sold, guards guarded, brewers brewed, butchers did not butcher.

Krank's dwindling mammals had been the main reason for the Creators designing the floyancy in the first place. But, they had famously forgotten their paddles and drifted unceremoniously away from Krank. Aereon was recruited to build a second, which had been briefly used to gather gobbles – a dim-witted bird that had been spat out by evolution – before he too left in search of the Creators. And so, the job to complete a third floyancy fell onto Juta.

In the weeks following Aereon's departure the butchers had come under increasing pressure. The gobbles that Aereon had been able to acquire lasted for a few days, but after that the butchers were squeezed more and more. They buckled one by one.

Lirna supposed the pressure would be off now. What with Juta's floyancy finished. That's where he must be, she thought. Lirna was slightly hurt. Ok, the King was a man likely to push Juta every day to ensure food was coming in and the Queen had said he was busy, but he could have spared a moment for a small visit.

But, if Lirna had been a few streets over she would have seen that the needs of the people were not being met. Hald, Krank's one remaining active butcher, was hunkered down in his shop with his two remaining boars. The place stank and tempers flared, as they often do when three mounds of muscle are forced to share a confined space. King Codrich had issued an instruction that Hald should only sell his produce to his majesty. Hald couldn't have refused. He sat within his dim walls, with a pig under each arm and listened to people swarming outside. The door was well barricaded, but occasionally someone peeled back one of the wall panels and Hald would throw a knife. Whether it hit or not, the hand would disappear and, for now, that was enough to keep the hoards at bay.

Inside the Royal Abode the King was having a doze while the Queen touched up her nails. She could afford to be frivolous now that the formula had turned up. Lirna stood quietly. The Queen tucked her vial away and spent a little longer inspecting and smiling pleasantly at her nails. 'Ok,' she said finally. 'Let's go.'

Arburella took them away from Codrich's snores and into a small outhouse next to their home. There was a guard outside the door, but he let them pass without a word. The Queen led the way down the steps deep beneath Krank.

In the centre of the room was a box containing Arburella's assortment of toys. Attached to the wall opposite the stairs were the various chains and harnesses she would use to accommodate her acquaintances. Arburella was an understanding person and she felt it would be inconsiderate if she conducted her business in a place where people on the surface would hear their discomfort. The room below the dirt was perfect for this function and Arburella used it often. Even so this was only the cellar's secondary purpose.

An entire wall of the cavern was taken up by the steel. Krankians had slowly been excavating it for centuries. With every clump extracted they lightened the lid of Gumpert's tomb.

'There will be adequate space here for you to replicate the solution,' said Arburella, while Lirna stared at the metallic presence. The Queen snapped her fingers and Lirna spun around.

'Yes. Yes, it will work fine.'

If the Creators had thought to invent sails for the floyancy, Arburella might have thought that she was not a fan of Lirna's jib, or the person who cut it. Without access to that playful turn of phrase, Arburella was resolved just to think that she did not like Lirna at all. Any of her. The entire vessel was a bad egg as far as she was concerned. She didn't like her smiling face. She didn't like her pleasant demeanour. She didn't like her blonde hair. But most of all she didn't like that she had people falling all over her.

'Good luck,' was all the Queen added.

Lirna tilted her head and watched the heeled feet disappear up the stairs. She took the paper from her pocket and consulted the ingredients.

Lirna found a few items within the cellar, but for most she would need to look elsewhere. When she rebirthed onto the surface, she found there were two guards outside the outhouse. The new arrival's name was Hule, and he was one of the more recognisable figures on Krank. A great brute of a man who, had he possessed any ambition at all, might have thought about staging a coup against Codrich. As it was, he was a defence to the crown and Arburella's chief intimidator, a job which he quite enjoyed.

'Where you go?' he asked Lirna when she emerged.

Lirna gazed up at his sun-eclipsing head. 'I was going to the Creators' shack?'

'To look for ingredients?'

'Um… yes.'

'Queen say you try do this. She say I go instead.' Hule reached down and plunked the paper from Lirna's hand with one giant thumb and one massive finger. She opened her mouth to speak. 'Wait here.'

Hule marched off and Lirna looked up at the sizable guard who remained.

She sat herself down on the sand and waited for Hule to return.

The rest of the day was mainly spent cataloguing the materials and liquids that Hule had been able to procure. Chief among the missing ingredients were the ladybugs. The recipe called for thousands of the devils, and Lirna had been secretly hoping that there would be a sack full of them lying around so she wouldn't have to do the culling herself.

Hule brought a large pot and several containers to put the nail polish in once it was made. All she had to do was make it, but it was time for dinner. Or so Hule thought. How he was managing to maintain so much body mass with so little food on the island was beyond her. There hadn't been any talk of missing people, but there were no depths the Queen wouldn't sink to keep her retinue fighting fit.

Lirna complained that she would like to inspect the Creators' Shack herself for the missing materials, but Hule was having none of it and even insisted on walking Lirna home.

Lirna was suspicious. Yes, she had taken a knock... somehow, but this was getting excessive. She doubted that she'd been watched this closely when she was a tiny tot. She had gotten onto the kitchen cabinets after all.

'Hule, how did I get hurt?'

Lirna waited, but he didn't seem to be a response forthcoming.

Something was definitely up.

They reached the Hartilby residence and, to Lirna's relief, that seemed to be good enough for Hule. She approached her door, but looked over her shoulder before she touched the handle. Hule already had his back to her. Lirna took her chance.

The island was quiet this time of night. Even if there wasn't anything on it, families liked to gather around the table in the evenings and be with each other.

It was a beautiful night, the stars above her were just beginning to wake and twinkle. The distant moon Endos was growing and brightening as the sun sank and faded.

Lirna moved quickly. She had questions that needed answers. Although, something twisted in her gut. Something inside her was screaming out that she didn't want these particular answers.

Lirna slowed down as she approached the Shack. The light of the sun was almost gone so she didn't notice at first.

The glow of the moon gave it away. The orb hung above the splintered and shattered walls of the Creators' once home. The roof was completely gone. The frame of the door was charred and black. The door was propped against the wall. She moved to it. Her hand stroked the handle. Her fingers moved up the grain and she pressed her cheek to the wood. Her eyes closed, she knew it had struck her.

Within the crisp walls everything was burnt.

She approached the channel. Wood and ash bobbed on the surface, but there was no sign of the floyancy. She searched, but she could not find any remnants of it. Someone must have gotten it out in time. That would mean... that would mean someone was inside when the fire started. Someone must have been inside when the door was blown off by the explosion.

Juta.

And she remembered. She remembered everything. She remembered reading the note Aereon had left her. She remembered running to the Shack to show Juta. She remembered the feeling of relief to see the lights from within and knowing that he was not being tortured by the Queen for failing to complete the floyancy. A feeling that was swiftly taken from her when the door burst from its frame and threw her from the Shack. She remembered screaming Juta's name as someone dragged her from the scene.

The feeling of dread was back, deep in the pit of her stomach.

Lirna ran through the streets of Krank as fast as her body would let her. Her eyes welled, but she blamed it on the wind. Her body ached and she knew now to blame it on herself.

She tried to take mollifying breaths before she knocked on the door. Though her heart was still rushing and her eyes wide when it opened.

Mrs Daas did not smile, 'You better come inside.'

Juta's mother led Lirna to a bed. Her husband was sitting next to the still body that lay upon it. Lirna couldn't feel her heart beat.

Juta's untameable hair frizzled against the pillow, but at the front a large clump was missing. Where his ginger curls should have been, a veiny burn rose out of his skin in its place. The red mottled mark ran down the right of his face, encasing his eyebrow and swelling his eye. It covered his cheek and disappeared down his neck and below the bedding.

'I think Lirna would like a moment with him.'

Juta's father looked up from his son through bloodshot eyes, but said nothing. Lirna lowered into his seat. Both Juta's eyes were shut.

'Is he…'

'No,' said the mother, kindly. 'He's just resting.' Mrs Daas moved to the other side of the room with her husband.

Lirna rested her hands on the sheets and looked at the boy's scarred features. 'I don't know what to say,' she whispered. 'I'm sorry.' She bit her lip. 'If I'd only looked at this stupid piece of paper the day Aereon left it, none of this would have happened. I could have been there with you. I should have been there.'

Juta did not move. Lirna looked up at his mother.

'Don't take it personally, dear. He needs his rest.'

Lirna stood up, 'Can I come back tomorrow?'

'Of course, I think he would like that. Even if he is not awake, I'm sure he would like to know that you are thinking of him. I like to think he knows we are here.'

Mrs Daas walked Lirna to the door and quietly shut it behind her.

Lirna ran. She ran until her legs burned and the salt crusted on her cheeks.

Ambushes in the Bushes

Days passed like trees. That is; numerously. With each, the Search and Seekers closed in. They especially enjoyed their work on days like this. Most of their pursuits occurred within the confines of Hudikvar. It was dull work, the Greased Elbows could have done it, but on the rare occasions when they had the opportunity to flare their nostrils and focus their eyes they remembered all the reasons why they liked outlaws so much. Proper outlaws. Real men didn't hide from justice, they ran.

Soon it was time for Captain Vander and Bertil to take their shift at the head. The Captain knelt next to the trail in the spongy moss and beckoned Bertil to join him. The sodden tracks led out in front of them, plain to see for both teacher and student.

'Can you see them all?' asked Captain Vander, while the rest of his troop mingled.

The boy nodded. 'The two dwarves are easy enough. And the three foreigners,' he said pointing to the marked moss. 'And there's the Woodsman in the middle.'

'Anything else?'

Vander and Bertil looked up over their shoulders at the

speaker behind them. The man was leaning against a tree and could not conceal the smug curl at the corner of his lips. His name was Rorj, and he was the finest tracker in the Search and Seekers but had always been overlooked when it came to promotions. There was not a mentoring bone in his body, or a fibre of his being that could understand the concept of him personally being wrong. Above all, he was a loner. Even by Search and Seeker standards, which was a itself a ragtag band of loners.

'He's not ready for that level of detail,' informed the Captain.

'What level of detail?' asked Bertil, curiously.

'Nothing. There isn't a sign of it here anyway.'

'Oh, there's a sign,' said Rorj.

Vander scowled at him. 'Never mind about it, it's not important. What can you tell me about the tracks? How old are they?'

Bertil looked at the tracks and his brow crinkled.

'Take your time.'

The boy reached out with his hand and gently felt the moss. He took a pinch and sniffed at it. Unsatisfied he dropped the foliage. 'How do I know *you* know how old the tracks are?'

Vander looked to Rorj, 'You see the habits you are teaching him?' Rorj shrugged. 'Arrogance is not a necessary quality in a Search and Seeker.'

'It has its uses,' said Rorj, nonchalantly.

'It does,' conceded the Captain after a moment, 'but we don't need two of them.'

'I don't mind a little competition,' said Rorj.

'Tell me how old these tracks are, Bertil. I know how old they are because I am your Captain and it is my job to know.

It is also my job to make sure that you do too'

Bertil moved his lips, but Rorj was faster, 'Seems like flimsy reasoning to me, Captain. Do you actually know?'

'For goodness sake.' Captain Vander extracted a small notepad and pencil from a pouch on his belt and handed them to Bertil. 'Write down your answer.'

Bertil looked down at the paper and pencil and his eyebrows lifted, 'Ok.' He turned his back and shielded the utensils.

'Do you want to know why I am such a good teacher?' Vander asked of Rorj.

'Not even a little.'

'Because I listen,' said the Captain, unimpeded.

Bertil turned around and gave the Captain back his pencil.

'We're about half a day's walk behind them now,' the Captain looked at Rorj smugly, who shrugged in return. 'Let's see the paper.'

Bertil looked down at the paper and then slowly gave the notepad back. The Captain took it from him, 'Half a day. Very good, although we'll need to do something about the state of your handwriting. I won't have that shoddy work within my ranks.'

'Sorry, Captain.'

'Lead on, young man.'

The mood of the company was merry, and Silvor and Volris were at its heart. Lars tried to quieten them, but his attempts were always half hearted and their joy brought a smile to his face. He watched them from the rear, observing their pushing and shoving and general boisterous nature. He looked down past Gwen and found that Aereon was next to him.

'Can I help you?' he asked plainly and without rudeness.

'I've just been thinking.'

'Yes?'

'Well, you know how Sunset from Hudikvar is the great water?'

'The Dagger Sea.'

'Hmm?'

'The water you speak of. It is called the Dagger Sea.'

'Oh?'

'When the moons work together to part it, it becomes the Broken Dagger.'

'Clever. So Sunset from Hudikvar is the Dagger Sea, and Moonset of it are the mountains and the ogres.'

'The Gorse Mountains. Yes.'

'And Sunrise leads to this forest.'

'Oak's Wood.'

'Uh, huh. So, my question is what is Moonrise of Hudikvar?'

'Not a lot. Walk far enough and you will reach water.'

'No people?'

'Not many,' said Lars. 'No one lives beyond the borders of Hudikvar in that direction, except for in the Citadel. But, there are only a dozen or so who call that place their home. And as far as I am aware they are all men, so I doubt their population will be on the rise anytime soon.'

'What's the Citadel?' asked Aereon. 'Who lives there?'

Lars scratched his chin. 'I suppose they would call themselves scholars and the Citadel the greatest place of learning in the known world.'

'You don't agree?'

'There is only so much you can learn from books. There

are a few amongst them who do travel. Those who realise even their great libraries do not hold all the answers or even all the questions, but most of them do not travel far from the Citadel.

'After that it's just water, as far as the eye can see. Peaceful and untouched. I suppose that's all going to change now.'

'How do you mean?'

'Once the world has one floyancy, how long do you think it will be until it has two?'

'Well, at least two have been constructed already, probably three.'

'That's precisely my point,' said Lars. 'Once someone, or someones,' he nodded at the Creators, 'comes up with something truly innovative and truly vital to their survival it is never long until someone else sees a different potential. Your once rescuer will become mutilated and someone else's destroyer.'

'But, it's tiny. It could barely make it across the Dagger Sea.'

'The principle is there now. The spark. The design will grow and change. Oh, it might get a rebranding, a new name perhaps, but what happens next is all going to stem from what those two did on that little island.'

'You sound resentful. Do you wish they hadn't invented the floyancy? Would you be happier if we'd all died?'

'Yes,' the word was a smack in the face. 'Of course I would. I would have never known you. I have not travelled that far Moonset in many years. You would have risen and fallen without my notice. But, now that I have met you, I do not wish you to die and I will do my best to help you return home. As it is, the best thing for me to do next is leave.'

'Leave!'

'Yes. Not for long. I'll head back a poronkusema –' measure of distance used to describe how far reindeer can travel before needing to urinate '– I will return in a day or so. I just need to retrace our steps and make sure we are not being followed.'

'Well, how will we know where to go?'

'They seem to be doing fine,' said Lars, gesturing to those in front. 'Just keep the mountains on your right and you'll be alright. Don't worry, if you do get lost, I will be able to find you.'

'When are you leaving?'

'I thought about now.'

'Now?'

'Yes, I thought so. Goodbye, Aereon. I shall see you again tomorrow.' Lars turned.

'Aren't you going to say goodbye to the others?'

'No use in worrying them.'

'I've never been completely sold on the Creators intelligence and the dwarves do seem to get absorbed in their own stories, but I still think even they will notice that you have gone!' Aereon stamped.

'I'm sure you will have some reassuring words for them when the time comes. Won't be long.'

Lars strolled away and the sleepy owl on his shoulder twisted her neck and opened an eye to Aereon. Nothing seemed to cause her alarm as she closed it and returned to her slumber.

Dusk was beginning to fall, but, thanks to Rorj, the Search and Seekers could track all through the night.

The Captain was upfront with Bertil too, although they remained a few steps away from Rorj to avoid any spattering of cynicism or narcissism.

'Come,' said Vander. He was crouched against a tree. Bertil crept to him and followed his gaze. 'You see the mark? By the fern?'

It was the Captain's policy to refer to every disturbance on the canvas of the world as a mark. With experience, you learned the difference between a natural brush stroke of life and a blundering blotch of the hunted.

'No.'

The Captain shuffled to the fern and pointed at the moss below.

'The spores have dropped,' said Bertil.

'Exactly.'

'Couldn't that have been a deer?'

'Could be, could be. What else do you see?'

Bertil squinted in the dying light. 'Nothing. Just plants.'

'What about those plants?'

'Nothing, I can't see any marks.'

'The absence of marks can still tell you something,' said the Captain. 'What do you know about these particular plants?'

Bertil considered them and all that he had learnt under the Captain, 'Several of them are edible?'

'Precisely. And yet, here they are, untouched. More than that, the floor is scattered with beech nuts, a favourite of deer, yet there is no sign of grazing. If it wasn't eating, what business would a deer have here? There is no running water nearby, and the ground is rough and riddled with roots. Animals always follow the path of least resistance.'

'So, by *deduction* –' a known buzzword that never failed to win the Captain's favour '– we can rule out animal life and count this as a mark from our quarry,' said Bertil.

'Yes. It is very important to look out for these solid markers.' The Captain rose and continued forward. 'Following tracks is excellent, but that is not always possible and signs like this help to keep us on the right trail.

'As your skills develop though,' began Rorj causing the Captain to seize up, 'it is important to learn to trust your instincts. After tracking for a few days, you pick up on the movements of the prey and the marks become less important. You learn the mind and follow that.'

Nobody said anything for a moment, 'Actually quite bad practice that,' said Captain Vander. 'As it is easy to make a mistake and lose the trail.'

'It's never happened to me.'

'It could!'

'Well, I hope that one day it does, Captain, and I shall learn my lesson and your marvellous teachings will continue to be accurate.'

Nobody said anything for a long time after that.

Bertil did admire Rorj's talents and felt that there was much he could learn from him, but he respected his Captain above all else. Vander had personally selected him and taught him everything he knew. It was just sometimes he seemed to get bogged down with the basics, the day to day tracking, and Bertil wanted to jump to the more exciting techniques. The advanced stuff. Rorj was the best man to listen to for that.

Or so Bertil thought. But Rorj wasn't someone many learnt from. He wasn't really someone who learnt things from other people either. The Captain had found that out quickly. When he first took on the aloof character he tried teaching him, but whenever he got halfway through a lesson the boy already seemed to know it. All the techniques were already somewhere in his head, they just needed stirring. It didn't take long for Rorj to find out that he knew more than the Captain. He didn't seem to take any time learning, one day he would just say something that he hadn't known the day before. It was all natural. It was in his blood. A born hunter.

This was Bertil's first proper hunt. He'd been involved with the Search and Seekers as they tracked down outlaws within Hudikvar before, but this was so different. So much more real. He swore he could taste blood in the air. It was the first time he had been involved in the tracking of more than a single person.

'You know how we are called the Search and Seekers? Well, what happens after that?'

'How do you mean, son?' asked Vander

'Well we're Searching and Seeking, right? What happens once we've done that? What happens once we've found them?'

'We bring what we find back to Hudikvar, for justice.'

'What if they don't want to?'

'Outlaws don't usually get much of a say in the matter.'

'Yes, but there are eleven of us and six of them. Plus, one of them is the Woodsman and I heard how the dwarves fought in Rjkovorg.'

'Well,' began the Captain slowly, 'our orders are only to return Aereon of Krank alive. His two countrymen can die, as can the dwarves as well as the Woodsman, now he has proven an enemy of the crown. His owl can go too.'

'Owl?'

'Yes, it must have been the bird that attacked Jorg when he was scouting the Woodsman's lodge for an opening. There have been signs of its loose feathers and owl puke along the trail. The King asked for the bodies of those we kill, obviously that will not be practical, so a token from each will be sufficient.'

'A… a token?'

'Yes, the head is customary in such scenarios. But, as you say, in a straight fight, they probably have the edge on us. There is not a warrior amongst us, prowlers and assassins that is what you will become within the Search and Seekers. Taking them unawares, that's what we do.' The Captain gave his pupil a look. 'Have you ever noticed that when commanders and kings draw their swords they make a *zing* noise?'

Bertil nodded.

'Well, that's because they want the attention. The attention is good; it rallies the troops. That's why heroes always have their sword scabbards made from metal. On the other side; it is important that scouts do not make a sound when we draw our weapons.' He gave a demonstration and in a flash, there was a blade in his hand. 'That is why all of our sheathes are made from leather. It keeps us silent.' Another quick movement and the knife was gone and the boy shaken. 'This is your first time, I will not ask you to kill on this occasion, but you will watch and next time you will and it will mark your inclusion into the Search and Seekers.' Bertil still did not speak. 'Here,' the Captain handed him the notepad and extracted the pencil. He almost handed it over. 'Could do with a sharpening this thing.' The Captain snatched his smallest knife from its place and put a point to the pencil. 'Here, once you've seen what you are going to see, I want you to write down what you feel. Anything at all, and we'll talk about it, ok?'

Bertil nodded vaguely, still clearly shaken.

Lucky for him he would never have to witness the murder of Aereon's party. Something unfortunate was going to happen to the Search and Seekers before they even got close.

It wasn't one of those things that they had time to worry about, it was something that just came out the black and blue and coloured them to match.

Their night vision had adapted well, and they could still follow, but no matter how well their eyes adjusted, there were always creatures within the forest that could see more keenly in the dark than men.

The Captain and Bertil were among the first hit. Rock slings came and knocked them to the ground.

'Did he say when he was coming back?'

'He was pretty vague,' said Aereon. 'He said he would be less than a day.'

Everyone groaned.

'How will we know where to go?' one of them demanded.

'He said we were doing fine. We just have to make sure that the mountains stay on our right.'

Aereon's opposition looked at the rising ground which marked the way to mountains. 'Well it's on our left now isn't it?' someone complained.

Aereon threw his arms up in a spasm. 'That's because you ingrates just stopped to complain. Turn back around and get walking. Lars said he will be able to find us.'

Begrudgingly the dwarves and the Creators did turn around

and they walked.

Aereon shepherded from the rear and they continued to create a trail across the woodland floor. All the way from Lars's lodge it was dotted with camp and rest sights. Where they slept was blatant to anyone, especially the craters left by the dwarves, but those with a keen eye could spot every seat they had taken along the way as well. They added another dot to the trail before sunset, as they collapsed onto the mossy forest floor.

The food they had taken from Lars's pantry had lasted as they supplemented it with hunting and gathering. But, they had not hunted that day and without Lars no one felt confident enough to gather strictly edible plants so they all tucked into their reserves and were able to produce a thick and hearty broth, for which everyone was thankful. Except for Aereon, who had a stick of celery. And then, because he felt he deserved it, had another one.

Volris added a few more logs so the flames would keep them warm through the night and agreed to take the first watch. With Gwen gone, it was important that someone was awake throughout the night. He found himself an uncomfortable perch looking away from the fire.

The other four each found themselves a mossy crevice between the roots and curled up.

A few hours later, Silvor was woken by a soft shake of the shoulder. He took Volris's report of nothing as well as his knobbly seat.

Later, Koel woke to what Silvor perceived to be a soft shake. Koel blinked at him, but Silvor would not move until he was sitting up. Koel propped himself up against the tree he'd been sleeping under and listened wearily to the tale of the badger in the night. When Silvor was finished he gave Koel a slap on the cheek and bumbled off to bed.

Koel woke Edin for his shift by flicking twigs at him until one bounced off his ear. He slowly rolled over and Koel waved goodnight. Edin grumbled and made himself slightly less horizontal.

Aereon eventually woke up. He rubbed his eyes and propped himself up on his elbows.

There were only the embers of the fire now. He squinted at the edges of the glow and tried to find his companions. 'Hello? Is it my turn to keep watch?' he asked the darkness. Someone must have fallen asleep.

He pushed to his feet and brushed some of the lichen off. One step was all he managed before the bag came down over his head.

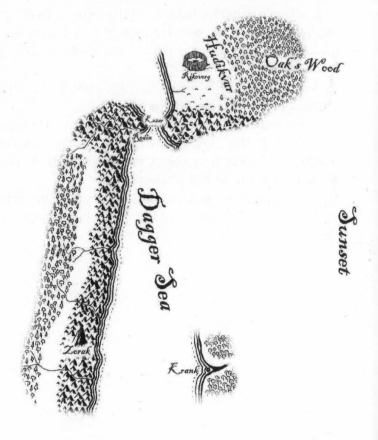

Moonrise

Sunrise

Sunset

Moonset

Hušhvar

Rikoverg

Oak's Wood

Kazar

Sedin

Dagger Sea

Lerak

Krank

Troublesome Youths

Captain Morj was in the familiar position of taking his dues from King Victarian. He stood up straight, letting it all wash over him, and caught the newly reinstated Captain Dagny looking at him. He gave her the eyebrows and shot a wink in her direction.

'When you have quite finished *goggling*, Captain!' The King's fingernails rattling off the arm of his chair.

'Well, actually–'

'Report!' snapped Victarian. 'What news of the youths?'

'Right, right. Well,' said Morj, clapping his hands, 'after some excellent detective work, we have discovered that the miscreants have entered the woods.'

'That seemed like a given, but continue.'

'We came across several individuals –' someone coughed behind him '– Most of them were found by Constable Noak –' another cough '– Alright, all of them! But, it's only because he got the luck of the draw and happened to cover the district that they passed through.'

'It was a team effort,' said someone else.

'Exactly,' agreed Captain Morj. 'A team effort. So, just shut up Noak!'

The King rubbed his face, 'Please continue, Captain. I am dying to hear what it was these individuals had to say.'

'They all said they saw Aereon leading the gang towards the forest. A couple were even able to point out where they thought the group entered the trees. We followed their guidelines and we did find a muddy track had been beaten into the wet grass, but it quickly disappeared within the forest.'

'Disappeared or is simply beyond your capabilities to find?'

'Are there any skilled trackers still within Hudikvar, sire?'

Victarian looked at the Captain for a long time, 'No.'

'Then it definitely disappeared,' said Morj.

The King's pupils vanished behind his eyelids while his lips formed some undiscernible words. 'Well then Captain, you will have to figure out some other way of finding them. Because, they will be found.'

'Yes, sire.'

'Any news on how that rat-dwarf slipped through the walls of Rjkovorg?'

'Not yet, sire.'

'Fine. I trust the youths will be found within the week and you will promptly turn your attention to that.'

'Yes, sire.'

'Dismissed,' said the King with the wave of a hand.

Outside, the Greased Elbows gathered around their Captain as he lit what he assured the King was a tobacco filled cigarette.

'I've been thinking, Captain,' said Constable Bruts.

'Uh huh?' said the Captain, behind cupped hands.

'Not so much thinking, more remembering, you know?'

'The two are more or less interchangeable in my

experience with you lot,' commented Morj.

'That night, when the dwarf escaped and I saw them all run past me.'

'Yip,' Morj leaned back and blew smoke into the air in sweet relief.

'I'm remembering now, they weren't just running they were talking as well. Mighty peculiar. The dwarf, the one who got locked in, he was saying there was a man, armed, knocking on doors in Rjkovorg. He said when people answered they also took weapons and joined him. I think he said there were six or seven of them and they all entered a house, all armed.'

Morj stopped mid puff. 'You're right, that is mighty peculiar.'

The youngest eight were making their way towards Rjkovorg. Digging a hole to capture an ogre was going to require man power. The rogue youths were uneasy about bringing adults into their operation though, so they had all agreed to settle for child labour. Kajsha's tent of companions had not been the only such residence in Hudikvar, in fact there were dozens. Almost all were near Rjkovorg, where the scrounging was at its best.

The eldest four were on a mission to gather tools and materials. Farms were the prime target. They would be able to pick up all the equipment they needed there, not to mention food, it was just a matter of not getting caught.

Both groups waited until the sun had set before they began.

Both teams wished each other luck and went their separate ways.

Rjkaard, the grand architect of operation *ogre*, led the

youngsters to the moraines Sunrise of Rjkovorg and issued instructions. He split everyone into pairs and made sure they all knew where they were going and their lines.

Not far away, he and his partner found themselves at their first tent.

Nine hungry faces looked up from a small bowl of vegetables they had managed to gather.

'May we join you?' asked Rjkaard. 'I promise we won't eat anything.'

The circle parted to make room for the new comers.

Rjkaard smiled to them all, 'We have an idea that we thought you might be interested in assisting us with.' He paused to look at the bowl again. 'We were like you not so many nights ago. Scared and tired, with Asta gone, not knowing where the next meal would come from. Asta was a great and kind woman, a pioneer. Her death was a tragedy to all the lost children in Hudikvar. Only because of her could so many of us survive. Life without her careful nurturing seemed hopeless, but then it came to us, that is not the legacy she would have wished to leave behind. Asta: the woman who saved the children of Hudikvar. That is no legacy. That dies with her. Asta: the woman who helped the children of Hudikvar save themselves. That has lasting power. Just because Asta is gone it does not mean the work of the Knight Bandit needs to stop.

'Join us and we promise you will never be hungry again. More than that, you will be remembered as the people who stopped Victarian. The people who ended his reign of tyranny. If any of you are interested, meet as at the old alder at the edge of the forest by midnight.' Rjkaard stood up. 'I hope to see you all there. Together we can do something great.'

*

'Are you sure this is a good idea, Captain?'

'Alcohol clears my head.'

'Yes, I know. Mine too,' said Olle, patiently. 'That's my point.'

'It's just one beer, Olle. Trust me, we'll be fine. I'm not going to let things get out of hand.'

Olle jumped up onto a stool and leaned across the bar, trying to catch his Captain's eye, as Morj waved ineffectively for the barmaid's attention. 'You know, there is no one I trust more that you, Captain. It's just, the last one was your second.'

Morj shrugged, still trying to flag down some more drinks, 'Well, one – a few, what's the difference?'

'Oh, another hour or so. Slightly more impaired judgement, meaning you will be more inclined to turn a few into a few more. I just think tonight will be a good time to look for the young troublemakers, if they have a fire within the woods it will be easy to spot.'

Morj looked down at his youngest Constable. 'You're a good kid, you know that. Come on, let's get the others.'

The Greased Elbows grumbled as they were herded out the Stoic Ram. Captain Morj did not mention that it was Olle's fault they would not be spending the rest of the night there.

'What's the plan, Cap?' asked Wilkinson.

The wind had picked up during the time they had spent inside, and they tucked their hands under their armpits.

'We go look for the kids.'

'The kids we took to the King?'

'That's the ones,' said Morj.

'Should be easy enough.'

'I wouldn't be so sure,' said Morj. 'It's a damn big forest after all. They could be anywhere.'

'There's one.'

'What?' snapped Morj.

'There,' elaborated Grunson with an incriminating finger.

Morj squinted at the two kids strolling down the street. 'Are you sure?'

'Positive, that's the girl I was in charge of when we took them before Victarian.'

'That's the boy I had, too,' said Marius. 'He had quite a voice on him. He was the only one that could hit the high notes.'

The pair were heading away from Rjkovorg and back towards the forest. The Greased Elbows darted from alley to alley until the boy and girl broke through the buildings of Hudikvar and entered the glacier-shaped land beyond.

Morj and his men followed at a distance and ducked into the long grass when the youngsters entered a tent.

'What is going on?' the Captain asked the world at large.

'Should we rush it?' asked Yurgn.

'No, I don't want to do anything until I know what is going on. Besides, do you remember the trouble we went through last time trying to find my helmet?'

'You went through trouble. We went through… something else.'

They waited and a few minutes later the two exited the tent accompanied by five others. They all turned to the forest.

'What is going on?' hissed Morj.

Morj told his troop to stay put as he climbed a rise for a better look.

'What the hell is going on!'

He could see scores of groups all heading towards the forest. There must have been almost a hundred of them. He'd never seen so many children moving in one direction. He'd never seen children so organised. He didn't like it. He didn't like it at all.

'Ok, I need to know what is going on here,' he said after a short descent. 'This is my city, and I'll be damned if there's organised youth happening under my nose. Olle what are you wearing under your armour?'

'My under armour.'

'Perfect, you'll fit right in. There is a group coming, not far behind us. I want you to join them and see what all these kids are up to. There's drones of the devils, all heading for the forest.'

'What?' asked Olle.

'Come on, come on. Get stripping.'

'But, they'll never think I'm that young.'

'Olle, you look about twelve.'

'I thought you was twelve,' said Wilkinson.

'I was. So were you once.'

'Yeah, he's actually got a point,' said Morj. 'We really need to sort out your grammar one of these days, Wilkinson.'

'How?' asked Wilkinson

'Well,' began Grunson, 'we'll probably just sit you down and –'

'He means *why*,' groaned Morj. 'Look, we don't have time for this. Olle, get your armour off.'

'I'll stick out a mile.'

Morj pitched the bridge of his nose. 'You'll be fine! Just find out as much as you can, then come meet us. Now, strip.'

Olle started unbuckling straps.

Marius shuffled his way over to the Captain's side. 'It occurs to me that we should probably stay in the one place while Olle is away. You know, so he knows where we are and can easily find us.'

'Did you have somewhere in mind, Sergeant?'

'The House of Amber isn't far from here…'

'Let me get this straight,' began Olle, aggressively unbuckling his belt. 'While I'm away, infiltrating treasonous ranks, who could do who knows what to me if I am discovered, you lot are going to the pub, to get drunk and have yourselves a grand old time?'

'That's about the size of it.'

'Thanks for taking one for the team, buddy.'

'We believe in you.'

'You're my hero, Olle.'

'Well what if there isn't an opening for me to come back tonight?' Olle protested. 'What if I am there for days?'

Yurgn rested his hand on wee Olle's shoulder, 'For you lad, we are willing to wait.'

Amber woke him gently. They'd been friends for years and something else before that. She'd had never been quite sure what, but it hadn't ended in a fight, which was a first for her. Being in her line of work, she came across a lot of drunks. She'd dated the bruisers and the jokers, even one or two of the abusive types, but she'd never met another who could have a whole crowd gathered in merriment thirty seconds after a comment on the weight of someone's mother.

He was funny, and well liked, and totally against violence, even before he'd taken his first job in law enforcement. Back when she first knew him he had not operated in conjunction with the law. Some upmarket criminals like to think they operate above the law, but Morj never deluded himself. His deeds had fallen well below that line.

She pushed his hair away from his face and spoke to him softly.

Morj's grey eyes blinked open from his cupped head and he looked up to the green ones staring down at him. 'That takes me back.'

She smiled, 'You're the one with knullruffs this time.'

'I beg your pardon?'

With some assistance, Morj sat himself up.

The House of Amber was much the same as the other taverns in Hudikvar: sticky, with a poorly enforced *no singing* policy. With the exception of Bruts, who still had a curfew, and Olle, the Greased Elbows were all there, though none stood at attention. Morj looked around over his shoulders at the officers scattered across the floor and chairs.

He dragged himself atop a stool and Amber sat herself next to him. Morj rubbed his temples and things started to come back to him.

He'd been sitting in that exact spot the night before when Grunson sat down where Amber was now.

'Captain?' he'd began. Morj scarcely looked up from his sad beer. 'Did you have any thoughts on what Bruts said? You know, about the guys with weapons wandering around Rjkovorg?'

'Well, Constable, I thought I might try to forget all about it.'

Grunson smashed his tankard against Morj's sending beer everywhere, 'I'll drink to that.'

There had obviously been several more drinks since then,

but the fact remained: 'It didn't work.'

The trouble with trying to drown your sorrows is the bastards usually have a life vest with a whistle to blast in your ear and a torch to shine in your eyes.

'Pardon?' asked Amber.

Morj's head rose. 'I've got work to do,' he negotiated himself off the stool. 'Do you mind looking after them for a while?'

'Oh sure, it's no trouble. Don't you want to take them with you?'

Morj looked about at his sprawled squad, 'Maybe just a couple.' He turned back to Amber, 'They can stay here as long as they like, but as soon as Olle returns one of them needs to come for me. If they're any trouble you can toss them out. I'll be in Rjkovorg.'

'I shall let them know.'

'Thanks, you're the best.' He gave Amber a peck on the cheek before turning to wake up Marius and Noak.

Olle was quite enjoying himself now he had gotten into the swing of things. Initially the back story had been essential, but once he'd got himself comfortable with it he could be playful with the details. His name was Odd Izzy and he was a lone wolf.

He sat against his tree on the edge of camp with one knee up and his arm resting on it coolly. In his mouth was a long blade of grass. He gnawed on it slowly and wished he had a hat with a nice big brim.

Most of the new recruits had stayed the night. He wasn't surprised, it had been a good speech. The Kajsha girl had given it. Olle had to admit, he had been moved. It had been all about everyone getting what they deserved and showing that the King should not be immune to suffering. He was no different to them, just a man born lucky. She hadn't revealed anything about the plan, but offered free food, which seemed to sway most people. That or the intrigue. Olle would have been surprised if it was really to do with sticking it to the man, but you never knew.

The ring leaders were gathering the new comers for the big announcement of the plan. The Captain had been right, they seemed to have amassed an army.

People were beginning to crowd and there was no way Olle would be able to see anything. However, Odd Izzy was an industrious little fellow. He spat out the grass and climbed a tree.

'Good morning everyone. Again, I must expressive how deeply appreciative I am that you have all agreed to join our little – well, growing – operation.' Kajsha smiled at the faces. 'You are all here because you're not happy with the way things are. You feel cheated, and we all have been. But, we've also cheated.

'We were dealt our cards, they perhaps were not the best, but we did not try to do anything with them ourselves. We, all of us, relied on the late-great Asta. It should not have been her responsibility. We are our own masters. It is time we learned to bet on ourselves. We have the means to look after each other. Together we could be much more. Together we could make it so no one ever has to live like us again.

'We need to expose the King for what he is. Over the course of his reign, he has done nothing to show he deserves such a position. Such power. Once the people see his true nature it will induce change. Sound simple enough? The plan is simple. The King has allowed the ogres to enter Hudikvar with impunity and take people, never to be seen again, splitting families and friends in the process. If we can show everyone that the ogres are not invulnerable they will begin to speak out. It is our plan to capture an ogre.' A gasp flushed through the youths. 'We are going to build a pit to trap one. The work will be tough, but I assure you, we'll be well out of the way when the ogres come. So, who is in?'

Odd Izzy looked at the silenced faces. Pansies, he thought gruffly. He swung from his branch and landed gracefully next to Kajsha. 'I am.'

Everyone seemed taken aback by his intrusion into the circle and Izzy puffed out his chest at the sound of the massed inhale.

'Me too,' shouted someone.

'And me,' said someone else. And then it became impossible to pick out individuals. Kajsha mouthed a *thank you* through the rabble. Olle thought about a wink, but decided a slight head bob was more fitting.

Less than twenty kids decided this wasn't for them and the rest were all treated to a fine meal unwittingly provided by the farmers of Hudikvar.

'Izzy, is it?'

'It is.'

'Would you like to help us look for a place to dig?' Kajsha asked. 'You seem like a savvy individual. I'm sure you will have some valuable input.'

Odd Izzy shrugged.

Noak, Marius and himself was a good team for the job. There was the charmer. The muscle, in case charm didn't work. And some brains to make sure both were distributed accordingly. All that was missing was the wild card. That's what Bruts brought to the table. Beauty, brawn and brains worked almost every time, but when it didn't, it was useful to have a maverick around to throw something extra into the mix. They swung by this house and picked him up on the way.

The four entered Rjkovorg without a real plan. That was the way Morj liked to play it, he liked to feel out a situation. Before they entered the gates, Morj had gone to inspect the hole in the wall and was now certain it was how the dwarf had escaped. The cover had been replaced askew, so he sent Bruts up Marius's shoulders to fix it.

He traced the map and plotted out which houses the dwarf would pass from the gate to the hole. He had a few routes in his head so there were quite a few different houses the armed individuals could have come from.

Tree Folk

The scratch of the earth underfoot was muffled.

His hands were tied behind his back. If he took too long a stride the rope around his ankles would snag.

In the dark of night, the bag, the rope and the hands had come. The hands had felt calloused and well used. There had been several of them, all working to get him restrained. They felt like the sort of hands that were connected to strong, knotted arms.

Aereon would have been delighted just to see a sliver of food, but none came. He considered, once or twice, the consumability of the bag over his head, but decided against it. The thought of previous occupants coughing and spitting into it put him off the idea.

They must have been edging around the side of a rise in the forest because, unannounced, out of the black came an explosion of light. A bright yellow glow that Aereon didn't think looked like fire, but couldn't think what else it might be.

Hands took him by his arms and guided him to the luminosity.

The light was a fluid thing. The glow shifted and grew within the trees. The glimmering split into paths and clusters, all connected into a vast network.

Beating drums bred with every step. Black figures within the light chanted and performed tribal dances. They moved as a massed group to the beat, with legs flinging into the air and hands slapping their knees.

Their captors steered them away from the sounds and down a dimmer path.

The glow shattered into a million pieces and Aereon looked at all the little stars drifting and floating around him. One landed on the cloth in front of his nose and Aereon's eyes crossed as he tried to focus on the pulsating light. At its brightest the light revealed the insect body it was attached too. It remained there for a moment and then fluttered away into the night.

The fireflies dispersed ahead, and the group were led into a cold, black cave.

Bertil pulled his legs up to his chin and tried to hug his knees. The rope pulled tight. Someone next to him grunted at the strain.

'Captain, is that you? Captain, what's happened?'

Captain Vander shook his head to focus himself, which turned out to be a near-vomitable offence. 'Yeah, it's me. Most of me anyway.'

'What happened?'

'It would seem we were attacked,' said the Captain, feeling a lump. 'Ambushed. I don't know,' he mumbled, 'call myself a Captain, must be getting old.'

'Ambushed by who?'

Vander looked out at the night. 'I have an idea. I'll be sure by morning, if we survive that long.'

'In case we don't,' said Bertil, slowly from the darkness,

'I have something to tell you. A confession of sorts. Yesterday when you asked me how old the tracks were, I didn't know. When you gave me the pencil I snapped off the tip by wedging it in my thumb nail. After you said the answer I quickly wrote it down. I'm sorry, Captain.'

The Captain was silent as he slotted all the evidence into place. 'That makes sense. Don't worry, lad. We deal in deception and a big part of understanding that is learning to do it yourself. I'm proud. It's a big step. Let's hope it wasn't for nothing. Is anybody else here?' he asked.

'I am Captain,' said a voice by his shoulder.

'Anyone else?'

The next person along announced his presence. They seemed to all be strapped against a tree. Everyone spoke in turn with the odd person regaining consciousness in the process until they made it back to Bertil.

'That only makes ten,' said the Captain. 'Where the hell is Rorj?'

Aereon was the first to wake. Years of being King Codrich's aide had cursed him that way. He pushed himself up against the wall of the cave and gave a despicable sigh.

The bars of the prison cast a cross over his face as he turned to the morning light. They looked like the roots of some plant growing from above.

Aereon sat up and tried to tug them apart, but it was no use, they were like cast iron. He slumped back down and almost sat on the food. He peered down at the pile of greenery within the leafy bowl. There were five of them lining the entrance to the cave. He picked up the nearest and ate everything within and then ate the bowl too.

He'd been finished a while when the others started the rise. The dwarves complained about the lack of meat, but they still eagerly ate all that had been offered.

When the last mouthful was swallowed, one of them appeared.

Aereon was almost dozing again so the feet were the first thing he noticed. They were a milky green and sprawled from her ankles and grew into a rooted pad.

Unwitting eyes shifted up the shape of her legs. The rest of her skin was the same pale green, but a piece of crusted bark grew out of her right thigh. Another curled up the left side of her torso and formed a shoulder pad. Her hands and wrists were also barked, with long fingers on the end of slender arms. Her face was sharp and intelligent and embedded with pure purple pupils. The hair was long and entwined with vines of ivy.

She regarded them all curiously as she walked by the cave.

'What. The heck. Was that?'

'An elf,' said Silvor.

'A what?'

'An elf. Tree folk.'

'How do you know about them?' asked Koel.

'Oh, they've been around almost as long as we have. Never met one myself though.'

'I bet you guys have some sort of age long feud, right?' said Aereon.

'What?'

'You lot been fighting for generations? Constantly bickering with each other, eh? They call you short arses you call them a bunch of long shanked fairies?'

'No. Nothing like that. Why?'

'Well you know, you're not exactly similar. Your thane, Fenrik, knocked me unconscious when he learned that I was vegetarian. He actually knocked me out on sight prior to that as well. These elves seem a bit more ask questions first, hit later. They seem very quiet indeed next to your boisterous nature. They're tall. You're short. I don't know. They have green skin. Yours is a sort of browny-black, at least the crust is anyway.'

'You think we would have a prejudice towards an entire race based on the colour of their skin? That's preposterous,' said Volris.

'I can't imagine anything more ridiculous,' said Silvor.

'I mean, sure, we have our differences,' Volris continued. 'But, they don't judge us for ours and we don't judge them for theirs. Why should we? The world would be a boring place if everyone was the same.'

'Huh,' said Aereon. 'Seems odd. I thought there might be some epic back story with famous battles speckled along the way.'

'Afraid not. We've fought together a couple times if that helps?'

'No, not what I'm after at all,' said Aereon, frowning slightly.

Everyone was hungry again when another elf returned with more leaves of food. As he disappeared into the trees the others were already digging in.

'Shouldn't we be asking the elves that come what's going on?' asked Aereon.

The dwarves didn't stop consuming, but Edin swallowed.

'Koel and I have been through this before. Trust me, Aereon, when they're ready, they will come and talk to us.

Either that or we will be taken to their leader.'

To Aereon's bitter disappointment Edin was right and shortly after lunch the big kahuna arrived. Or at least who they mistook to be the big kahuna.

More of his body was wooden and barked, but his hands were clear. His skin was a darker green than the other elves they had seen and his eyes were mottled white. Two wooden antlers grew from his forehead. He stood patiently beyond the roots until he had the full attention of everyone within the cave. Silvor, who had been snoozing, required an elbow from his brother.

'Hello, and good afternoon to you all. My name is Alnus. We apologise for the vines, but I hope that you have made yourselves as comfortable as possible. I am sure you have a reasonable explanation for your actions and we can have you released and sent on your way shortly.'

His voice was soft, with a whisper of song at the edges.

'Are you in charge here?' grumbled Silvor, who had been enjoying his dream. It had had ham in it.

'No,' said Alnus, calmly. 'We are above such things as Kings and Queens, and Lords and Ladies here. Requiring a ruler is a condition of the primitive.'

'How do you get anything done?' asked Koel.

'We have no need for rulers because we are all of the one mind and it has fallen on me to speak with you and assess your guilt.'

'What are the charges?' asked Volris.

'I would like to get to know you a little better first. Let us start with how you came to be so deep into the forest?'

'That is kind of a long story.'

'We have time,' said Alnus.

Aereon let the Creators tell the tale. They of course fleshed it out with much embellishment of their encounters with goblins and ogres. Aereon might have noticed his lack of involvement at any stage of the saga, but his mind had wandered. Somehow his eyes had drifted to the ground and Alnus's feet. The longer the tale rattled on the wider his feet spread and the deeper they bedded into the earth.

'Are you fleeing from justice or are you seeking your home?'

'A bit of both, I guess,' said Edin. 'We seem to have this habit of getting off on the wrong foot with everyone we meet.'

'The current evidence would certainly support that theory. What made you think it would be ok for you to come into our forest and cut down our trees?'

'Is that what we did?'

'I have got to say, that sounds a little extreme,' scoffed Koel.

'We didn't,' said Volris. 'We haven't cut a single tree since we have been travelling. We brought all the fire wood with us.'

The elf regarded him for a moment, 'Where did this wood come from?'

'Oh, I see what you're getting at. Well, I suppose we did do some chopping of trees at the edge of the forest. You see our friend Lars–'

'The so-called Woodsman?'

'Um, yeah, that's one.'

'I see.' He thought for a moment, 'Where is Lars now?'

'He left our company. He said he was going to back track to see if anyone from Hudikvar had followed us.'

'Well then, I hope for your sake…'

Something took Alnus's attention then and he turned to the elf running up the path. His roots retracted from the earth and he took a slow step to the tree fellow.

The gang could hear their conversation from the side of the cave.

'His eyes are opening. He is awakening. You must come.'

Alnus started to walk without another word to the elf or the captives. The group listened to their fading steps.

'Well, that was a little rude. Just disappearing in the middle of a conversation like that. Don't mind us. We're fine in here.'

'Did you see his feet?' mumbled Aereon.

Everyone nodded.

'Very impressive, those feet,' said Volris. 'They're what make elves the finest archers of all.' Everyone looked at him curiously. 'Sure, they are also the finest craftsmen of wood for making bows, but their feet give them unrivalled stability for the deadliest accuracy.'

'Do you know who they were talking about, Volris? Do you know who is awaking?'

'I do not,' said Volris. 'Fingers crossed it's someone nice.'

Moonrise

Sunrise

Sunset

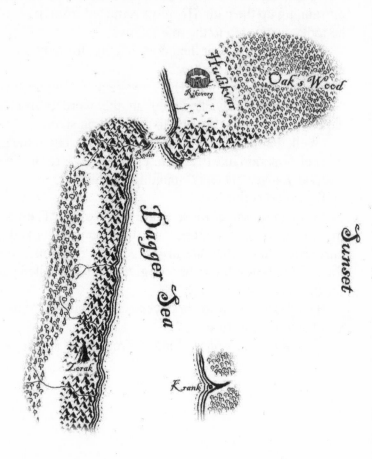

Hruškar

Oak's Wood

Rikovorg

Kazar

Rodin

Dagger Sea

Zorak

Krank

Moonset

Prophet Trees

There was no sign of breakfast. He scrambled to the cave mouth. There was definitely nothing outside. Aereon found a gap in the roots big enough for his head and wedged it through. He twisted his head from side to side, but there was still no sign of food or anyone who might bring it. He didn't feel especially hungry, just curious.

'What are you doing?'

Aereon jolted and smacked his chin off a root. He carefully tilted his head and prized his ears back through the bars. Behind him, Edin was awake. 'I was just seeing if anyone was about. Don't you think it's strange that no one is keeping an eye on us?'

Edin shrugged. 'When we were captured by the dwarves they didn't leave anyone to keep an eye on us.'

'Yes, but you were inside a mountain. You weren't exactly going to break out of that. All we'd have to do is get through these blasted roots and run.'

'Do you know how to get through the blasted roots?'

'No.'

'Then I suppose they don't really need someone watching us, do they?' said Edin.

'What about the food then? The elves seemed punctual and diligent to me. Seems odd they would stop bringing us meals. What are they playing at?'

A shadow fell across Edin and darkened the cell and Aereon watched his mouth slip open. His own lips moved very quickly and his eyes darted about as he thought of something to say. Being in continual company of the King and Queen of Krank, Aereon was used to having to use his brain to cover up for things his tongue had done.

But, when he turned around, he found he did not need to explain himself to an elf.

Lars was standing with one forearm propped up on the rock above the cave and craning his back, so he could see them all packed into the small space. He couldn't help but smile. 'I see you fellows are getting along just fine without me.'

Lars's deep voice roused the others.

'What are you doing here?'

'What do you think? Looking for troublemakers. What did you do this time?'

'Actually nothing. All we did was light a fire and they seemed to view that as a criminal act.'

'Ah,' said Lars scratching his chin through his goatee. 'I thought that might happen. You didn't cut any trees, did you?'

'No, we still had some wood in our packs from Hudikvar.'

'What do you mean, you thought that might happen?' whined Edin.

'It occurred to me that your day's walk might put you on the border of their lands and they might not appreciate a fire.'

'And you didn't think to tell us any of this?'

'I didn't want to worry you,' said Lars.

'We've spent the last two days worrying,' protested

Aereon.

'Mostly about food by the sounds of it,' said Lars.

'It was not mostly about food!'

'Oh well, no harm done,' said Lars.

'There has been plenty of harm done!'

'Ah, here comes your breakfast now,' said Lars. It was unclear whether he was ignoring their gloominess or was oblivious to it.

An elf carrying a tray of food stopped in front of Lars and almost stooped into a bow, but Lars waved it away.

'We are sorry, Lars, we did not know if their tale were true.'

'That's all right. No harm done. Do you think you could open the cell now?'

'Yes, of course.' The elf gracefully shifted the tray to one hand and touched one of the roots with the other. Nothing seemed to happen for a moment, but then the roots began to retract from the earth at the cave mouth and pull up the rock. Aereon stepped out first and the elf held the tray out to him.

'We apologise for the delay on breakfast,' he said.

Aereon picked up one of the leaves. 'No harm done, I suppose?' he said, looking at Lars.

'Correct.'

The others birthed into the light and took their breakfasts. 'Things have just been a little hectic around here since *Quercus* woke. I must get back there now. He is about to start speaking.'

Lars could see the anxious elf was raring to go. 'Off you pop then. We can find our own way.'

He said his thanks and skipped off down the path. Lars smiled after him.

'Come along, you lot. You heard the man, *Quercus* is awake.'

Lars led them back down the path that had been swarmed with fireflies two nights ago. Now, in the day, it was a pleasant winding walkway lined with moss covered trees. In the canopy above, birds of every colour flew from branch to branch.

'Where is Gwen?' asked Koel.

'Oh, she's around. She has friends here. She's probably off somewhere being fanned by someone with a really big leaf.'

Ahead the forest was opening. The ground disappeared in front of them and formed a bowl in the land. Lars stopped at the precipice and the others lined up beside him. The beginning of the feature was marked by the lushest and greenest moss Aereon had ever seen.

'Aren't we going in?'

'No,' said Lars. 'We must wait for invitation.'

Aereon looked at the trees growing out of the moss. The odd elf walked down the slope towards the obscured centre. Aereon didn't know much about trees. He knew they had leaves and branches and bark and roots. He could tell some apart, but he knew few of their names. Pine he could do. Aereon's, always informative, grandmother had described it to him well. He couldn't remember seeing one anywhere else in the forest, but there was one in front of him now. In all of granny's lessons she had not once ever mentioned a face.

Formed by the cracks of the bark, Aereon could see the two slits of its closed eyes. A lichen brow nestled above them. Below a long nose drooped over the seam of a mouth.

'Lars, my friend, are you not coming to see him?'

The group turned to the elf behind. She had beautiful olive

skin and twigs entwined through her reedy hair.

'Of course, Raddeana,' said Lars. 'May my friends come too?'

'They are welcome. I will show you the way.'

Raddeana moved between them like a breeze and drifted across the moss.

'Welcome to the Garden of the Primes, gentlemen,' said Lars. 'The home of the Greenmen.'

At the bottom of the basin, the slope started to level, and the crowd of elves appeared through the Greenmen.

Raddeana smiled over her shoulder and led them through a gap in the mass. Lars looked to follow, but something caught his eye and he marched off and started hissing angrily towards a Prime.

Aereon followed his gaze and found Gwen sitting in a commanding position on one of *Acer*'s highest branches.

She stretched her wings and settled back down. Steam blew from Lars's ears and he opened his mouth again.

'It is fine, she can stay there. It is no trouble,' said Raddeana.

'She should know better,' Lars grumbled, but allowed Raddeana to lead him away.

The tree ahead of him was colossal. Twenty people holding hands could not have wrapped the trunk. Once it must have been far greater, he thought as he took in the broken trunk-like branches. Lobed leaves from smaller branches tried to mask the damage. Aereon found *Quercus*'s high face and his amber eyes. His nose was cracked and homed an assortment of green and white fungi. His mouth was open, but silent.

The elves were sessile. All eyes were on *Quercus* and their ears pricked to hear him for the first time.

'Hhhhhh…'

The voice was quieter than Aereon had expected, but it rolled through the open air unchallenged.

The Creators were giving each other looks. The dwarves had, politely as possible, elbowed themselves to the front. Lars was still giving Gwen the odd stare. But, the elves never broke concentration. Aereon noticed that many of them were holding hands. Huge groups of them, hundreds, all connected; sharing the experience.

'…hhhheeeeeeeeee.'

Quercus's mouth slowly shut again, and silence returned.

The elves stood silent, waiting for the great tree to speak again.

There was a sound like bark snapping as his lips moved again.

'Hhhhaaaaaaaassssss.'

Aereon caught a glimpse of the dwarves in front of all the elves, closest to *Quercus*, sitting with their legs crossed and listening intently.

'Rrrrrehhh…'

Edin wasn't listening. He wasn't looking either. Well, not at *Quercus* anyway. He'd just been looking around vaguely, waiting for the talking tree to do its thing, when he saw the most enchanting creature he had ever seen.

The golden yellow skin was the first thing he noticed. It popped out from the other green and brown shades around her. Her own bark was a soft brown, tinged by green, and suited her skin well. A long streak of bark started on the outside of each forearm and grew up to her shoulder where it formed an elegant rise. Flecking started on her lower back and split across her hips into a long sinew down the curve of her body to her upper thigh. Her shins were speckled up to her knees. She had a soft and warm face with emerald eyes that sparkled. Her face was framed by a tiara that rose from her hair forehead to pointed wooden tips. Her short hair was spiked and filled with the greenest of oval leaves.

'…ehhhhtttt…'

Lars had figured out the word and what it meant. He was not surprised. He hadn't been expecting good news. The elves around him didn't seemed to have worked it out yet. They were all too busy listening to consider thinking.

Edin wasn't up to much thinking either. He was totally mesmerised by what was before him.

'… tttuuuuurrr…'

Why now? Thought Lars. After all this time, why now?

Why now? Thought Edin. After all this time, why do I have to go and start feeling things now?

'… rrrnnnnn…'

I wonder how many of them even know his name.

I wonder what her name is. I bet it's something beautiful that rolls off the tongue and makes flowers blossom.

'…nnnedddd.'

Quercus's words sank in and the elves began to talk.

'Do you dare me to go talk to her?'

'What?' asked Koel. 'Who?'

'*Who*? What do you mean *who*? Her.' Edin pointed.

Koel looked. 'Why?'

'What do you mean *why*? She's gorgeous.'

Koel tilted his head. 'Is she? She looks just like all the others to me.'

'What are you talking about?' exclaimed Edin. 'Her, there!'

Koel had another look and shrugged, 'If you say so. When did you need to be dared to go and talk to a woman?'

'I don't know. I feel a little nervous. Right, I'm going over. No I'm not. Yes I am.'

'Ok… good luck?'

Edin smiled and tiptoed across to the elf.

Silvor and Volris came barging back through the crowd.

'Wow,' Volris began. 'That was incredible.'

'I am glad that you enjoyed it,' said Lars.

'Does this happen a lot?'

'Usually one or two of the Primes speak every few years, but you would be very lucky indeed if *Quercus* chose to wake and speak during your life time. You two have been treated to something special.'

'You can say that again.' Volris was visibly beaming beneath his bushy beard.

Edin returned also beaming and grinning like an idiot. 'She said yes.'

'What? Who did? To what?' asked Silvor.

'See the elf over there – no not now! She's looking.' Edin peaked back across the Garden. 'Ok, the one with the golden skin? I'm seeing her tonight.'

'What's here name?' asked Koel.

'Damn! I'll find out tonight.'

'Aren't we leaving?' asked Aereon.

Everyone turned to Lars, Edin's hands came together in prayer. 'There is not much sense in us leaving now. It would be best to wait until morning.'

'Yes!'

'But, it will be a long walk so you will not be over tired through lack of sleep, will you?' said Lars.

168

'No. No I won't, I promise.'

'Good,' said Lars, with a lingering stare. 'Come on, I imagine you all have questions.'

They followed him away from the audience of elves and through the Greenmen.

It was the slowest Aereon had ever seen Lars move. But he looked happy as he strolled between the Primes.

Nobody really knew where to start. 'How do you know the elves?' asked Edin eventually.

'How does anybody know anybody?'

'That's your best effort at answering? Ok, how come you are on such good terms with them?'

'That is a more appropriate question,' said Lars. 'But you must first understand what an elf is. Volris and Silvor, I imagine you are aware of their origin?'

'I have heard stories and whispers,' said Volris. 'I would rather know the truth from you.'

'An elf is the spirit of a tree. They live and develop within and usually they never leave. It is only when their tree is fatally under attack that they are ripped from their vessel and forced to defend it. Only within this forest, where the power of the Primes is so strong, does this give the soul such a physical form to become an elf. Trees that grow further afield from the garden of the Primes can only produce a shadow of an elf. A phantom with varying physical presence. Sometimes they are a ghostly figure capable of inflicting vicious wounds upon the attacker. Other times it is a form which cannot be seen, but may leave a scratch on its victims from phantom claws. Whatever the form, these spirits are always known as dryads. Tree nymphs. Spectres of the forest. These creatures are possessed by the pain from the divide between them and their body.

'I work between the elves and the men of Hudikvar to ensure that no trees with their souls intact are ever felled. Sometimes I am forced to take a branch with an infection. Other times the infection has been so strong it has already driven the spirit away and I can cut the tree down. Sometimes the tree just gets old. The spirit is always the first thing to go.'

'So, your work reduces the number of elves in the world?'

'I suppose you could put it like that, but they are happier within the trees,' said Lars. 'There must always be some elves, of course. To care for and listen to the Greenmen, but I try to ensure that there are only as many as are needed.'

'There are thousands of them here.'

'The forest is vast and attacked by creatures more savage than men. I do all that I can.'

'Who are the Greenmen?'

'I am not sure how well I can answer that. They have been here a very long time. Some say before the mountains and the oceans. A lot longer than you and me, at any rate. They are the first of the trees and *Quercus* is the oldest of them all. Each Prime forged their disciples in their own image. Every tree in the world can be traced back to here.'

Aereon's eyes shifted over the trees. They passed a birch with a flaking face. Her name was *Betula* and often awoke to tell the elves stories of the land.

A linden looked out with open eyes of honey, deep inside the mess of branches. Twigs struck out her brow covered in green cordate leaves. *Tilia* had been awake for several years but was yet to say anything of much importance. Nevertheless, the elves devoted themselves to her word.

A rowan with an elf beneath its arrow-head leaves

collecting and examining the fruit as it fell. *Sorbus* was one of the most silent amongst the Primes. He chose to do most of his communicating through other means.

Lars stopped next to *Fraxinus*. The Woodsman placed a hand on his bark and looked at his face for a long time. 'The elves speak of a community between the trees. Their roots entangle to allow a seamless flow of information, which is particularly strong between trees that share the same Prime. The Primes always listen to their children but are almost always asleep. It is only when the Greenmen feel something is of extreme importance that they awake to speak with the elves. Some are more active than others and they have varying degrees of what they believe to be important. Usually it is only ever the elves who grew from a Prime's descendent who listen. Except for *Quercus*. He listens to all the trees and is the Grandfather of everyone. He is the least vocal of all the Greenmen and his last sleep was over a thousand years long. It is an occasion that an elf is lucky enough to experience once in their lifetime and all gather to listen to his words. It is rare that he says more than a sentence and he never wakes without reason.'

'How do you know all this?'

'Oh, you hear things on the wind,' said Lars, waving a hand dismissively.

'Who are you, Lars?' Aereon asked. 'I mean really?'

Lars smiled and gave *Fraxinus* an affectionate pat. 'No one important. Is anyone hungry?'

The dwarves asked Lars if they might have some meat for lunch, but he told them that the elves did not approve of it. Instead, they were found by an elf who provided each of them with another filled leaf and they ate happily.

They wandered aimlessly through the elven settlement and at every gap in the canopy Edin looked up and willed the sun to set. When he wasn't looking up he was looking at the elves they past.

Lars noticed him at his side, 'Yes?'

'You know what you were saying about elves coming from trees? Well, I've noticed that there are clearly... um... men and women. I've also... observed that the woman don't seem to have any... uh... you know?' Lars's expression was passive. 'Bits... and the men don't either.'

'You have *observed*? It is not polite to take notice of such things.'

'It's hard not to when they walk around without any clothes on,' Edin protested.

Lars scowled. 'Elves are only animated spirits, they are not capable of reproduction. Was there anything else?' Lars asked, wearily.

Edin scratched his head. 'No, I think that is it for now.'

Eventually the sun did set for Edin and the fireflies came out. He said goodnight to the others and skipped off towards the Garden of the Primes.

She was already waiting for him when his springing feet reached *Quercus*. She looked even more enchanting in the glow of the forest stars.

'Sorry,' said Edin, with feeling. 'Have you been waiting long?'

'No,' she said pleasantly. 'I just got here.'

'Oh good. Good. I feel shameful about this, but I realised I forgot to ask your name earlier.'

'My name is Kalei.'

Music. 'Hi, Kalei. I'm Edin. I can't remember if I said that or not.'

She smiled, 'You did.'

'Good, good. So, what did you think of what Quercus had to say?'

'*Quercus.*'

'Oh, yes, sorry. *Quercus.*'

'I am not too sure. Everyone has been talking about it. I do not know who he means.'

'Is *Quercus* your Prime?'

'No. His name is *Malus.*'

'Sounds like a vengeful fellow,' said Edin, after some consideration.

Kalei giggled, 'Not Malice. *Malus.* I can take you to him if you would like?'

'I'd like that very much.'

Kalei held out her hand and Edin took it.

He cursed his sweaty palms, but Kalei seemed not to notice as she led him between the Greenmen.

She untangled her delicate fingers in front of the smallest tree he had seen in the Garden. Its trunk was no wider than his head and branched low. Edin crouched down until he was eye level with the face. The smooth bark made it easy to pick out his mottled features. Edin stood back up and looked at the ruby and golden orbs.

'You were an apple tree?'

Kalei nodded.

Edin's mouth was open. 'This is amazing. There are very few trees where I come from, but apple trees we do have.'

'You do not cut them down, do you?'

'No,' Edin looked at her. 'We grow as many as we can.'

'That is good,' her voice sung.

'What's he like?' asked Edin.

'I do not really know. He's hasn't woken since I've been here.'

'How did you get here? If you don't mind me asking,' said Edin.

'There was a woman. A very old woman who lived in a rickety cottage in the woods. One day she found me. She dug me out the earth and dragged me back to her cottage. She stuck me in a hole and watered me, but my roots had been badly damaged. I felt ill, I could feel myself getting weaker, I had to leave my body. I wanted to scream and scratch the old woman, but I couldn't; she was so frail and defenceless. I hid from her and tried to build my nerve. The next day the leaves on my tree had lost their sadness and seemed greener. I watched as the woman nursed my body back to health and, after a while, sampled fruits from me. There wasn't anything I could do there, so I came here and started caring for *Malus*.'

'I think that's the saddest story I've ever heard.'

'There are definitely worse.' A handful of fire flies had landed on her tiara, making it sparkle. 'My body survived. It is sad that I am not there with it, but many elves have it much worse.' She flicked her hand out effortlessly as an apple fell. She held it up and the lights flew from her head and hovered over the fruit. It was red and striped with green. Edin looked at *Malus*'s branches. There were bright red apples, ruby ones, big yellow ones and small green ones. There were more types than Edin could count, every one seemed different. Kalei inspected the fruit. She turned it over in her hands and studied it all. Then she offered it to Edin.

He rolled his fingers over it. 'To eat?'

Kalei nodded.

Edin bit through its skin with a crunch. His eyes lit up. The flavour was tart, but there was a sweetness to it. The flesh was firm, but his voluminous saliva was merging with it to create a crescendo of flavourful juices. 'This is the best apple I've ever tasted,' he said, almost dribbling. 'Try some.' He held it out for the elf.

She shook her head. 'No, thank you.'

A band of elves marched past them and any tension in the air wafted away in their wake.

'Are you coming Kalei?' one of them asked.

'What is happening?'

'He has started talking again.'

The audience wasn't as large, but it was growing. *Quercus* was silent and there was a buzz in the air as new comers asked what had been said.

Elves were still trickling in when the Greenman added, 'Beeeeee.'

'*There will be*,' Kalei whispered to Edin as her fingers linked into his. Someone touched his other hand and he turned to the elf. The elf was looking up at *Quercus*.

Edin thought it a little peculiar, but that was before he saw the elf's other hand. He was holding the hand of the elf next to him, who in turn was connected to another elf. They all were. Edin felt it. He could feel it flooding across his arms and through his beating heart. He'd never felt a part of something so great and so important. He soaked in the warmth and looked up at *Quercus*.

And the All Father's final word came.

'Wwwwaaaarrrrrr.'

Make Like a Tree

Gwen gently beaked Lars until he opened his eyes. She didn't say anything. With a few flaps of her wings, she took flight.

He got to his feet and followed her through the trees. The tiredness shook from his eyes and his alertness had returned.

Gwen led him to the Garden of the Primes and landed on his shoulder. She hooted softly and Lars made his way to *Salix*.

The garden was quiet and the fireflies in short supply, but some had clustered onto a tree up ahead. Lars pulled back the curtain of glowing leaves and stepped within the drooping branches.

'This is not your concern, Woodsman.'

'Show me, and I will judge.'

The elves within led him over to a drooping branch and lifted the long leaves. The yellow lights danced so everyone could see the brown marks that speckled across the green.

'What does it mean?'

'It means someone has been cutting willow trees.'

'Cutting them down?' asked Lars. 'Have any dryads been drawn out?

'Not yet. If they do, it will not be a dryad that is ripped from its vessel. It will be an elf.'

'This is happening in Oak's Wood?' Lars was surprised.

'It is happening on the borders of Hudikvar.'

Lars understood why Gwen had woken him. 'Are you sure? I left ample supply for the people to use for fire wood and carpentry.'

'We are sure.'

'From what we can tell it is not wood for fires or carpentry that is being cut. It seems people are cutting long thin branches.'

'We cannot think what for.'

'But, we cannot allow it to continue.'

'As the elves of *Salix*, it is our responsibility to defend our brothers and sisters.'

'We will tell the others when they wake and we shall march on these ignorant peoples who have issued an unwarranted attack upon us.'

The elves' yellowish eyes flared in the glow of the fireflies. This was not the war *Quercus* had spoken of, and Lars was not just going to stand by and allow another into the mix. 'As you say, these people are ignorant. They are still young and learning. Let me speak with them.'

'How long can you go on guiding them Lars?'

'How long before you are no longer there to ensure the right trees are cut?'

'You have not been gone a week and look at what they have done.'

'You will not be around for ever.'

'Just let me speak with them. They are good people. They have made a mistake. This is not a time to start a war.'

The elves were silent, but Lars knew they were still communicating.

'Very well. You may go.'

'But if one spirit is drawn, we will attack.'

Aereon tried to tell them all that Lars had been rushed and was just doing what he had to, but it comforted them little. Aereon at least had Lars's last words to think about. He'd said he'd be listening to the wind for tales of Aereon Cusith of Krank. He had said he expected great things and did not have any fear of Aereon returning the Creators safely.

Lars had arranged for elven guides to point them in the right direction, but Edin refused to leave until he had said goodbye to Kalei.

He had no idea how to go about finding an elf, but he had a name, so he started with that and the first elf he asked pointed him in the direction of where she usually rested.

She was not there, but another elf said she usually woke early and told him where he could find her.

There was a rocky outcrop not far from the elves' main settlement. Edin spotted her atop and climbed up after her.

The boulders created a clearing in the trees and Kalei had her head tilted to the grey sky and her eyes shut.

He studied her and then copied. His head tilted back, his eyes closed and he turned his palms to the sky.

He didn't know how long they stood like that together. Long enough for the birds to begin their song and for the rain to start.

'Good morning,' she said.

'Good morning,' replied Edin, opening his eyes. They turned to each other. Edin lifted his finger.

'What is it?'

'You've got a… on one of your twigs.'

'Oh.' Kalei lifted her delicate hand to her head and the bird hopped onto her fingers. Edin stared, fascinated, as she lowered her hand again. 'Off you go.' The wren flew to a bush and disappeared. 'You have come to say goodbye.'

'How did you know I was leaving?'

'You have the look,' she said.

'I uh… I came to ask if you would like to come with me.' Edin cursed his cracking voice. 'I know you have friends here, but I just thought you might like to see what is beyond the forest. I thought you might like to see where I am from, and the apple trees that grow there.'

Kalei looked into his eyes. 'That is very sweet, but there are no other elves descended from *Malus*. There is no one else to listen and protect his children.'

'Before you, there was no one to listen to him and the apple trees got on ok.'

'If there had been someone here I may never have been dug up. I may never have left my body.'

Edin said slowly, 'That would have required someone else leaving theirs.'

'I know,' said Kalei, 'and I feel bad for thinking it, but I do think about it. If someone had left their tree before me and I learned they could have helped, but they were not around to listen to *Malus* I would have been… It is not our way. We must look out for one and other.'

'It is not fair that all that responsibility should fall on you, after you already lost so much.'

'It is the life I have been given.' She looked back to the sky. 'It is not a bad life.'

The rain slid down her face and body and she did look happy. Edin felt cold, but joined her in the experience. He tried to forget about it and feel the world instead. As Kalei did. As the elves did.

She took his hand unexpectedly and led him back down the rocky rise.

The others had retrieved their confiscated gear and weapons. Two elves were also waiting and trying to look patient.

'Come on. It is long since sunrise. We need to get going,' said Aereon.

'I don't see why we can't stay a little longer. It was Lars who wanted us to leave today, we could stay another day or more.'

'No, Edin. It is time for us to go.' The others agreed with Aereon. 'We do not belong here.' Their two elven escorts nodded.

Edin looked to protest. Kalei spoke first. 'It is ok. We will see each other again.' She looked through his eyes at what was beneath, 'I am sure of it.'

'But, I don't want to leave,' said Edin.

'You must. How else will you learn to come back?'

Gently, Koel took his arm and peeled him away. Kalei smiled as Edin's fingers slipped from hers.

They were led Sunrise from the home of the elves. The trees they passed had new meaning for all of them, but none felt it so keenly as Edin. Every trunk was a new wonder. All its branches and all its leaves, everyone was individual. Everyone was an individual.

Aereon was just a couple paces behind their guides, hoping to hear a little of their conversation and find out where they were going and how far the elves would be with them, but they weren't talking. One foot landed in front of the other and they wound through the trees in silence.

In the full sun of early afternoon, the elves stopped at the beginnings of a dying path. Life was squeezing it to death. Here and there clusters of paved stones huddled together.

'Stick to the path,' said elf one.

'That seems manageable,' said Koel.

'It will lead you from the forest and beyond the reach of the mountains,' said elf two.

'Nice and straight forward. I like it.'

'Do not leave the path,' said elf one. 'If you do then–'

'Yeah, yeah. We get it, guy. Only a bunch of idiots would wander off after explicit instructions not to.'

'How long will it take reach the edge of the woods?' asked Aereon.

The two elves scoffed. 'That's just typical of you humans. To call a forest: a *wood*. It just seems to be your natural instinct to refer to things as whatever you can get from them. Where does it stop? You might as well refer to a mountain as treasure cove, or a jewel cavern, or a gold mine.'

'I didn't mean any offense.'

The elves exchanged bitter looks. 'It will take you not more than three days.'

The elves walked back the way they came. 'Thank you,' Aereon called after them, but there was no response.

'Bravo, Aereon,' said Koel. 'You've established a good lasting impression there.'

'Oh, don't mind them lad,' said Silvor. 'Some people are so touchy. One wrong word can be all it takes to set them off.'

They continued through the woods – I'm the narrator, I can

say whatever the bloody hell I like – but now upon the ancient untrodden path.

Despite their best efforts, everyone was listening to Edin who was talking again. Talking *still* may be more accurate. He hadn't shut up about that elf all day.

'Can we talk about something else for a while?' Aereon asked at breaking point. 'I've had just about enough of Beastaphilia for one day.'

'I'm in lust!' said Edin. 'Just let me have this, ok?'

'What in the world does that even mean?' asked Aereon.

'It's the deepest emotional connection Edin is capable of having,' informed Koel, solemnly.

'Exactly,' said Edin. 'So just lay off.'

'Yeah, leave him alone, Aereon. Let him have his moment,' said Koel. 'Besides, if anything he's a dendrophile.'

Lars was making good time. Without the need to babysit he could increase his gait and stride through the growth. This did affect his stability though and Gwen had an intermittent sleep for which she was none-to-pleased.

She squawked in his ear.

Lars frowned, 'I know.'

He sampled as he went. Pulling up roots and picking mushrooms and eating on the move.

A small fruit-bearing bush caught his eye. He went to his knees and picked himself a handful of berries. He ate a couple and tucked the rest into his pouch.

'You can come out now.'

The forest was silent.

Then a figure stepped from behind a tree. He wasn't exactly close, but closer than he should have been. The man walked forward and stopped in front of him.

Lars clocked several knives on his person.

'I am impressed. I did not leave much of a trail. How close to the elves did you get?'

'I saw the fireflies.'

'Very impressive. The elves are vigilant people. Although, I fear you grew a little bold when following me. Overconfidence, I fancy,' said Lars.

'It makes things tricky when there are a set of eyes pointing in either direction.'

Lars smiled at Gwen. 'Yes, the revolving head does help, but I spotted you myself. Why follow me so closely? You're clearly an accomplished tracker.'

The man shrugged, 'I like a challenge.'

'What's your name, son?'

'Rorj.'

'Of the Search and Seekers, I would imagine. What happened to the rest of you? The satyrs get them? I saw the evidence of a scuffle a while back, although I confess I did not see your tracks. How did you escape?'

'Yes, the rest were taken by the beasts.'

'And you didn't remain to help them? You chose to track me?'

'That was my diktat,' said Rorj, flatly. 'Anyway, I followed the satyrs to their camp first. There was nothing I could do.'

Lars gave Rorj a long hard look. 'There may be something *we* can do.'

Rorj gave Lars a measured stare. 'You'd be willing to rescue the same people who were tasked with killing you just a few nights ago?'

'A favour for a favour seems fair. I help your friends –'

'I wouldn't use that terminology.'

'– and you all will do something for me.'

The tracker shrugged, 'Might as well. I've got nothing else going on.'

'Good. Oh, and Rorj, please do not think about doing anything stupid. I do hate having to kill when it can be avoided.'

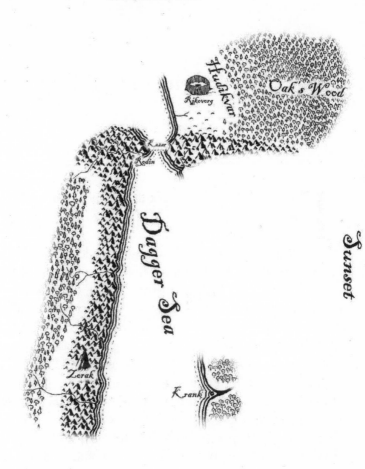

Moonrise

Sunrise

Sunset

Moonset

Hudkvar

Oak's Wood

Rikoverg

Knaur

Rodin

Dagger Sea

Zorak

Krank

The Legend of Odd Izzy

'That one there looks good. No, no, that one. Tulgan, look at me. Now look at where I'm pointing. Yep, that's it.'

Rjkaard's plan was coming together nicely, largely due to his overseeing of it. He wasn't involved in much of the hole making, he'd left Kajsha in charge of that, but it had occurred to him that even an ogre was unlikely to just wander aimlessly into a gaping pit. So, he came up with a means of disguising it. Willow branches were the first stage. He had a flock of kids in the trees working on it now. Selection was critical. They needed to be long enough to reach over the precipice and strong enough to hold the weight of the twigs, mosses and grasses that would cover it, but weak enough for an ogre to snap. This final specification was not a difficult one to meet. Another branch came crashing down and a few orderlies scuttled forwards to add it to the pile.

The sun was sinking behind him. The diggers would be back soon. Back and ready for dinner. Rjkaard himself was getting a little peckish. Through the trees, he could see a fire and the shadows of the cooks. His stomach made a gurgle.

He cupped his hands over his mouth, 'I think that's enough

186

for one day. Finish the branch you're on and then go and get yourselves ready for dinner.'

There was a pleased rumbling chorus from above.

They weren't sitting long before Kajsha returned with the others. It was mostly the oldest that went, except for that Izzy fellow. Rjkaard wasn't sure how old he was, but he looked like the youngest among them. He always sat with the oldest at meal times too, or they sat with him. He tended to sit down first, usually against a tree and the others would migrate to him. He seemed to have a knack for stories and making people laugh.

He was talking again and Rjkaard edged around the fire for a better listen.

'… the old man saw me.' His voice was gruff and thick. 'That's when he called for the others. Had no choice but to throw the keg at him. It hit him in the chest and planted him flat on his back. I looked him dead in the eyes and said "have a drink on me".' Odd Izzy paused and waited for the gasps and laughter to stop. 'I climbed to the window and jumped out.'

'That is amazing.'

'You really said that to him?'

Izzy shrugged, 'Him or someone else. I got so many stories, it's hard to tell them apart sometimes.' Everyone just gawped at him. 'Tell you what, all this talk of tales of drink, I could do with a beer.'

'Oh yeah! Why don't you go get yourself one?' scoffed Darjl. 'Or better yet, why don't you steal a keg, so everyone can have a drink?'

'Alright.'

'What?' squawked Darjl.

'I said *alright*. I'll go get us a keg.' Izzy stood up and walked from the group.

'Can we come with you?' asked Kajsha.

'If you want,' Izzy called over his shoulder. 'To watch,' he added. 'I don't want any of you coming in and getting in my way.'

'Where are we going?'

'There's a tavern not far from here. The House of Amber. We'll be able to get what we need from there.'

It had been a hard few days for the main body of the Greased Elbows. The nights were good fun, but the days were a struggle.

Amber herself was working around the clock, tending to their needs and cleaning up after them. She was making good money and they were a decent bunch, entertaining too. And as for the cleaning, it wasn't her favourite part of the job, but she preferred questionable stains on her floors, that she could convince herself were beer, to ghastly red ones.

The hangovers seemed to be gone again and tipsiness was returning.

Grunson bounced over to the bar. Amber smiled, another couple hours and it would be a stumble. 'Another round, Grunson?'

'Another round please, Amber.' He slapped a fist full of coins down on the table. The Greased Elbows had stopped counting days ago and Amber shortly after. If she was a few quid short by the end of this venture it was no big deal, and if she was a few coins to the good she probably deserved it.

'Coming up. I'll bring them over.'

'You're the best.'

The Greenmen

Grunson made his way back to the table, with a slight wobble. Maybe less than two hours, thought Amber. She picked up a tankard and turned to the kegs behind the bar. She'd just finished filling a couple glasses when the door burst open and swung back and forth on its double hinges.

Everyone turned to the figure in a power stance at the entrance, hands on hips and ankles a mile apart. Wilkinson opened his mouth, but Odd Izzy raised a finger until the door had finished swinging.

'Olle! Good to see you. Pull up a chair.'

'No can do,' said Izzy. 'I'm here on business. Any man who gets in my way will soon learn the price.'

'That voice is amazing.'

'I know, right?' said Olle.

'Seriously cool.'

'Yeah, I've got this whole character thing going. That's why I'm here. I need beer.'

'Well you came to the right place,' said Amber. 'What'll it be?'

'Actually, I need it to go,' said Olle. 'A keg, please.'

'What for?' asked Yurgn. 'You're not planning on selling beer to underagers are you? Not that I would object. It's just, not talking about such things to authoritative figures is tiresome work. Thirsty work too,' he added.

'I'm not selling anything. Besides it won't be beer. Amber have you got any kegs that are about half full?'

'Yes,' replied the barkeep, sceptically.

'Great. Could you refill the rest of it with lemonade for me? I have some money in my coin purse, but I might need to owe you a little. Guys what did you do with my armour?'

'It's in the corner,' said Wilkinson, 'but I seem to

remember that when we got here the first few rounds were on you.'

'Yeah, they were.'

'What?' spat Olle.

'Cheers, Olle.'

They all raised their glasses and toasted to him. Olle just stood with a gaping mouth.

'Weren't you supposed to tell Morj when Olle came back?' asked Amber.

The Greased Elbows stared at one another and slowly their eyes narrowed.

'Last one to finish has to go!'

They all threw back their heads and started quaffing. Wilkinson's tankard was the last to hit the table and he swore bitterly and got to his feet.

'When you see the Captain tell him I can't stay just now, but I will try to be back for midnight,' said Olle. 'Also, could you do me a favour?'

'What?'

'Could you sort of dive through the door like you've been thrown and then run away?'

'Why?'

'It would really help my character, and it would be good if you looked over your shoulder in fear too. I've got people watching.'

Wilkinson shrugged.

'Excellent. Amber, how's that shandy coming?'

'That's actually happening, is it?' she asked.

'Yes please. And these fine gentlemen shall be paying for it. Now, Wilkinson, if you'd be so kind.'

Wilkinson ran for the door and smashed into it head first

sending splinters flying. He landed on his shoulder in the dirt outside. He got to his knees and looked at the swinging door with convincing terror and ran towards the city.

Izzy propped open the door with his shoulder. 'Yeah you better run!' He turned his head back inside. 'Oh, you want some too?' Izzy moved back inside and the door closed.

'What is happening?'

'It's a long story,' said Olle. 'Just go with it.'

Amber had dutifully taken the keg down and was busy pouring jugs of lemonade into it.

'Right, Grunson. Take your sword belt off and put mine on.'

'Why?'

'I think my character would suit a sword, that's why! Just do it ok?'

'Alright, alright. No need to get titchy.' Grunson stood up and started unbuckling his belt.

'That's it full,' said Amber as she banged the cork back in with her fist. 'But you're not getting it until you tell me what is going on. What do you need this for?'

'Well, I've developed this character right, he's this cool lone wolf kind of guy and has all these amazing stories of fighting against the system and stealing kegs of beer and stuff. So, I told a story and this guy Darjl – bloody Darjl, he's the worst – was like "oh yeah? Why don't you go get us a keg then?" Acting like my story wasn't true.'

'It wasn't true.'

'That is not the point,' said Olle. 'Anyway, so I said "ok. I'll go get a keg then." That shut him up, should have seen the look on his face.' He looked at Amber's face, she was not smiling. 'But, I'm still a responsible citizen, so I wasn't going to give youths alcohol. Well, not proper alcohol. Hence the lemonade.'

'Won't they notice?'

'Nah. My guess is none of them have ever tasted beer before. They won't get drunk off this stuff, but they'll think they should so hopefully there will be a sort of placebo effect and they'll be none the wiser.'

'I have to say, Olle, that's actually quite diabolical.'

'Why thank you, Amber. How's the belt coming, Grunson?'

'Ready. So, what's happening?' asked Grunson, cheerfully.

Olle started rolling the keg. 'Ok, I'm going to push the keg out the door. Then you will stumble out backwards and trip over the keg. Then I'll come barrelling out – ha barrelling – and jump on top of you. Pretend to punch you a few times and then steal your sword.'

'Which is actually your sword.'

'Right.' Olle pushed the keg out the door and before Grunson knew what was happening, he pushed him too and ran out after him. Izzy landed hard on his chest.

'Steady on!'

'It has to look real,' rasped Olle, taking a swing.

'Ow! That *was* real!'

'Sorry, I get excited. Hit me back.'

Grunson caught him in the jaw and Olle was knocked from him. Both men stood up and stared at each other. Olle reacted with a swift kick to the giblets and Grunson went down.

'You little bugger!' wheezed Grunson. Olle gave him a fake hit on the head and started unbuckling his sword belt. 'That really hurt.'

'Shut up. You're supposed to be unconscious.' Olle got the belt and put it on. 'See you tonight,' whispered Olle. Then Izzy spat.

'What the f–'

'Copper scum!' shouted Odd Izzy. He grabbed the barrel and started rolling it towards the woods.

Grunson squinted as a gang of youths emerged from a bush and joined Izzy. One patted him on the back, another offered to push the keg and a third told him how amazing he had been. Grunson curled up with his hands cupping his goolies and thought about how unjust life was.

The trail was cold. Frozen. Frozen at a dead end. Frozen at a dead end with a stale scent in the air. No one was talking, that was the big problem. Although it would help if he could suss out a motive. Morj fumbled with a match and lit his roll up. He breathed in deep. Initially he had assumed that it was a simple case of vigilantes, militia, who had heard about Aereon and his friends' escape and just wanted to help. As they'd gone from house to house he'd ensured that if this was the case he would be understanding. He'd possibly wag a finger and remind them of the rules about armed citizens within the capital, but he promised he would not tell the King. People knew him well, he was an honest man. Well, honest in the sense he didn't lie. Not often anyway. No one came forward though. No one admitted to it and they'd been through almost every house now, so they must have spoken to the people who had taken up arms. Even if they had done something else, Morj thought they would have owned up to the militia idea, that way they knew they were out and the investigation would stop. The fact that no one had said anything worried him. It suggested that what had really been going on was far more sinister. Morj exhaled, he could do without anything sinister just now.

'Oi! Captain Morj!'

Oh, what fresh hell is this? 'Yes?'

It was one of the King's Guard. 'The King requests your presence, immediately.'

Of course he does. It's never "whenever suits best" is it? 'Then I shall go to him presently.'

'I will escort you,' said the pompous twit.

Marius, Noak and Bruts tried to make themselves as small as possible, but there was no way Morj was going into the lion's den alone if he could avoid it. 'Come along chaps.'

All three glared at their Captain.

King Victarian was in his usual pleasant mood. 'You have been working in Rjkovorg for several days now. I trust you have not been frivolously wasting your time, which is in fact my time, and have some information for me.'

Morj had told a slight fib on that score. He'd decided not to worry the King with the incident of armed citizens wandering around Rjkovorg and instead told him he was searching for how the dwarf had escaped.

'Nothing solid yet sire, but –' the fastest *but* that ever was uttered '– I do have one of my men working undercover among the youths.'

'Ah huh, and what does he have to say?'

'Nothing yet, sire. He is yet to report in, but I am expecting him soon.'

The door opened to the long house and a figure strode in.

'Ah, right on time,' said Morj. When he turned though, it didn't look like one of his men. He squinted at the tall figure, but the torches on the walls provided little light.

The man stopped in the dim glow offered by Volris's ceiling hole. Morj looked up at him, he recognised him alright.

'Captain, I believe you have met my son.'

'On occasion, my liege.'

'He's a strapping young lad isn't he.'

Morj had his doubts. The Prince was older than him for a start. By a good few years, too. He'd heard from various chatty grannies around town that he was the image of his father. Morj did see the similarities. His eyes were thin and cold. His cheeks high and gaunt. His hair wasn't as wispy as the King's but it was certainly going that way. Both carried an air of authority as well as superiority.

'He certainly is, sire. Charming too I'll bet,' said Morj, giving the Prince a wink.

'Do not patronise me,' he spat back. 'You wished to see me father?'

'I thought we might have a lesson. Nothing too formal. Just a chat concerning the duties of a king.'

'Father, I have not had a lesson since I was fifteen years old.'

'All the more reason to have one now then. Wouldn't you say?'

'No.'

'Are you going somewhere, sire?' asked Morj.

'Slowly, yes,' said the King. 'What do you think, Captain? Do you think the Prince should resume his lessons? There is much a king must know after all.'

Morj looked from the King to the Prince and back to the King. 'Uh… before I answer that, sire, do you think you could give me a rough time line for when it is you think you will be *going somewhere*?'

Thin eyes thinned further.

'Never mind, not important. I think that it can never hurt to learn something new and I am sure there is much you could teach, sire.'

'I was asking Captain Dagny,' said the King slowly.

'Ah. Yes, that makes sense.'

'The day I ask you for advice will mark the day that I am as good as *gone* somewhere.'

'Yes, sire. Very good, sire.'

The door opened and everyone watched Wilkinson walking as fast as he could towards the throne. 'Captain,' he said, 'Olle has returned from the youths.'

Where the hell were you five minutes ago? 'Excellent. My liege, if you would permit me, I should make haste and speak with him'

'Actually, he said he had to go so there's no need to–'

Marius slapped his hand over Wilkinson's mouth. Morj smiled at the King.

'Go, but next time I see you I want you to tell me exactly where those treasonous youths are hiding. No excuses.'

'Yes, sire.'

Marius harried Wilkinson towards the door and Bruts, Noak and Morj filed in behind.

'Why do you have him?' asked the Prince when they were gone.

'He has his uses,' replied the King. 'We shall add that to the list of things you are yet to learn.'

People were offering Izzy praise and trying to shake his hand, he refused to take either.

The keg was mounted on a table and the first drink was poured. The grail was passed from hand to hand until it was placed into Izzy's. He lifted it slightly in thanks and strolled off.

He found himself a seat away from the fire and took a sip. Olle licked his lips. It didn't matter how many beers you'd drank in our life. You were never too good for a shandy.

The usual suspects approached him with their own drinks in hand and sat themselves down.

People were still trying to compliment him. He did his best to ignore them until one asked to see his sword. Izzy looked at the boy. They hadn't spoken, but Izzy knew him. This was the boy who'd come up with this great scheme to capture an ogre.

In a swift movement, Izzy drew the sword. He tilted it and offered the hilt. 'Here kid.'

Rjkaard reached out with shaking hands and grasped the handle. He stood up and gave a few experimental hacks.

'Careful. It's not a toy.'

'Sorry,' said Rjkaard. He lowered the weapon and inspected the pommel. Everyone else seemed to relax. 'Who is Olle Vymer?'

'What?' said Olle.

'It says here on the handle *property of Olle Vymer. If found, please return to the recruitment and equipment office in…* I guess he ran out of room.'

'He must be the guard I stole it from.'

'I bet he's someone important. He's got a last name and everything.'

'He sounds like a twerp,' said someone. Others laughed.

'Oh, well now,' said Olle, 'I don't know about all that. I mean he's just a guy trying to do his job after all. As for the writing on the handle, that seems like good sense to me. Just in case it got misplaced.' Everyone was staring at him. 'It's misplaced now, no amount of thoughtful name labelling is going to help him get it back.'

The rest of the night went off without further trouble. Kajsha had issued an age cap on the keg which meant some of the older kids could even have two drinks, which put them in a right giddy mood.

With the moon high above and everyone dancing beneath, Olle was able to slink off through the trees.

Captain Morj's head was in his hands and he was propped up against the bar. Not because of any form of severe alcohol abuse, it was life that was giving him the headache. 'Still no sign of him?' came his muffled voice.

'No.'

'I still don't understand why you let him leave.' Morj lifted his head. 'I mean, I expected it from these nitwits, but Amber,' he held is hands up pleadingly, 'what happened?'

'He was very persuasive. He had a plan and everything.'

'Oh, yes,' said Morj swivelling on his stool to inspect Constable Grunson's face. 'It looks like a humdinger.'

'Lay off me, Cap. I'm in enough pain as it is.'

'Yes. Remind me how a five-foot-nothing pipsqueak managed to do that to your face?' The rest of the Greased Elbows chuckled.

'Caught me unawares, didn't he? It was meant to just be for show. I got a couple good hits in, but the boy's got a jaw like an anvil. My wrists agony. I think it might be broken.'

'You punched him in the face and broke your own wrist?'

'Did you have your thumb on the inside of your fist as well?'

More laughter at Grunson's expense.

'Now look here,' began Grunson. 'All of you. I know how to punch. You'll see when he comes back I'll show him.'

'You'll show me what?'

Grunson froze. Everyone else turned to Izzy. 'Come on,' he said. 'What were you going to show me.' With a zing Izzy had brandished his sword.

Everyone's brows hit the ceiling. Grunson stepped off his stool and drew his steel. 'If it's a duel you want it's a duel you'll get.'

'Alright. This bout of willy wagging is over,' said Morj, stepping between them. 'Put those things away before you hurt yourself. The pair of you, do you hear me? And you, quit it with that voice.'

Slowly the swords were sheathed.

'Sorry, Captain.'

'Sorry, Cap.'

'It's not me you should be apologising to. Now shake hands.' Hands grasped. 'Now what do you say Grunson?'

'Sorry Olle.'

'And what do you say Olle?'

'Sorry Grunson.'

'Good. Now, will someone please tell me what is going on? Olle, let's start with you. Why are you doing that ridiculous voice?'

'It's all part of my alias I've been working on. He's called Odd Izzy… get it, because I'm on a bit of an adventure?'

'Yes, yes. Very amusing. Has Odd Izzy found out anything

useful?'

'You better sit down,' said Olle.

'Get the drinks in Amber,' said Grunson.

'Please!'

'Sorry, Captain. Please, Amber.'

When everyone was seated, Olle told them his tale. Even Amber sat herself down to hear the story.

'An ogre?'

'Yes.'

'Like an actual ogre?'

'Yes.'

'Why?'

'I think they want to prove a point. If they show that we can stand up to the ogres, then there is no reason we can't stand up to the King.'

'We?' questioned Morj.

'Speaking figuratively, Captain.'

'You better be. The last thing I need is a member of my squad going rogue. You're not getting in too deep, are you? Do I need to pull you out?'

'No, sir.'

'Alright.' The Captain rubbed his head. 'So, they're not planning on actually doing anything to the King or the people of Hudikvar.'

'Don't think so, no.'

Morj's head was in his hands again. 'That poses a bit of a problem. Hard to pin a crime on them. When the King gets his hands on them he's not going to be lenient. Especially with the ones Aereon helped, the ringleaders. He's going to kill them. I've tried to hide from it, but that is what's going to happen. I thought I'd be able to suck it up when the time came if they were plotting against the crown. If they're not actually doing anything illegal... I can't, I just can't.'

'You told the King that next time you see him you would tell him where they were hiding. No excuses,' said Wilkinson.

Morj resurfaced. 'Then I will have to go to great lengths to make sure I do not see the King. Noak, Marius and Bruts, I want you to continue the enquiry in Rjkovorg.'

'What are you going to do, Cap?'

'I'm going to find this hole they're digging and ask them to bury me in it.'

'Come on, Cap. Don't be like that.'

'It's not all bad.'

'I suppose you're right,' Morj conceded. 'I'll get to sit back and watch you lot do the work for once. Olle I want you to bring me more reports. Let me know when the trap is set. You three, let me know if something comes up in Rjkovorg.'

'What do we do if the King asks to see you?' asked Noak.

'I'm sure you'll come up with something. The rest of you, you've been holed up in here for too long. Go out and mingle. Do what you guys do. Keep Hudikvar running. Go on, off you pop, the lot of you.' The Greased Elbows got to their feet and slowly made their way out, downing any remaining beverages before they left. 'Amber would you care to join me in a drink?'

'I'd love to.'

'I'll get them.' Morj swiped their mugs from the table and took them to the taps. He left the appropriate change behind the bar and sat back down next to her.

Morj had himself a long sip and collapsed against the back of the bench.

Amber ran her finger over his temple. 'All that stuff you

have to think about. It's wearing you out.'

'All for a few extra pennies every week.'

'Well I'm glad someone is thinking about it. You just need to find a way of getting yourself a little stress relief.' Amber gave him a look and bit her lip.

Morj raised his eyebrows at her. 'We haven't done that in a long time.'

'We'll take it nice and slow then. I'll walk you through all the steps. You were never very good anyway.'

'I wasn't that bad!' Morj protested. 'Alright, fine. You're on.'

Amber felt under the table and pulled out her copy of Karplaw. 'Who would you like to be?'

Out of the Ashes

irna went to see Juta every morning, but he was never awake. She would have stayed all day if his mum had allowed it, but she told her it was not good for someone so young to be cooped up all day. She sent Lirna on her way and told her to go and enjoy herself. That's where the trouble was for Lirna.

Aereon was the first person she had ever felt she could open up to. When he left, she had started directing that energy onto Juta. With him incapacitated she felt lost and empty again.

She couldn't occupy herself with work either. Arburella's nail formula had hit a dead end when Lirna had gone to green growers to enquire about obtaining some ladybugs. All of them had shooed her away.

First the Creators had promised to solve the meat problem on Krank with their invention. The orchard owners had reservations about this, as is to be expected when money is concerned. But, then they left with the first floyancy and things looked up, with less food on the island their business was booming. Then Aereon had been tasked with building the second and he did so, just when the green growers were beginning to struggle with the amount of mouths that needed feeding. The device was used a couple of times to bring edible gobbles to the island, but then Aereon stole it! The gobbles lasted days, not weeks, and the pressure was back on green food. Juta had constructed the third, but then presumably blown it up along with much of his face. All of this meant that the farmers were very protective over their crops and if the ladybugs helped to keep the aphids at bay then nobody was getting their hands on the polka-dotted beauties.

Lirna had gone to the Queen with their attitudes expecting an explosive response, but Arburella waved away her issue and dismissed her. Lirna supposed Arburella had conceded that people eating was perhaps more important than her nails being red, for now. She asked Lirna to finish the formula without colouring.

It hadn't taken Lirna long to make a batch of formula, so she had her days free again. She still had Hule with her most of time, but he tended to stalk behind her and not say much.

Hule waited outside while Lirna was in the Daas home.

She sat in the seat by his bed. She'd like to say she thought only of Juta the entire time she was there, but she did wonder about Aereon. He'd probably know what to do in a situation like this or have something helpful to say, at least. Juta's hand twitched. She smiled at his face and wondered what he might be dreaming about. His fingers started to tighten around hers and he squeezed hard. His cheeks were stiff and his jaw clenched. Juta's arm was shaking and his chest throbbed. Lirna turned to his parents, but they weren't looking. He was mumbling incoherently as his body shook.

He stopped when his eyes opened.

He just gazed up at the ceiling. His breathing stopped and

he was still. Lirna's mouth was open. Slowly he turned to face her. 'Ow.'

Lirna threw her arms around him and started to laugh and sob.

Juta's parents hurried across the room.

'Why are you all looking at me like that?'

Lirna let go and let his parents take over. She stood up and Mrs Daas took her seat. Juta's father stood over him and smiled brightly. His mother started talking and told him about the accident. About the explosion. Mrs Daas told her son it had been Hule who had found him washed up on the beach, not far from the shack. Lirna slowly made her way to the door, she could see this was a family affair.

She slipped outside, Hule was still there looking vacant. She hadn't known it had been him. Juta must have been thrown from the Shack in the blast. Or else struggled out and then collapsed with exhaustion. She felt new admiration for the brute.

'Where to now, Miss?'

She honestly didn't know. Gone were the days when she would be content to spend the rest of the day sunbathing on the beach. Aereon had spoiled all that. 'I don't know, Hule.'

'You look happy, Miss.'

'I suppose I am. Juta just woke up.'

'That good news. He remember what happened?'

'He seems a little confused right now,' said Lirna. 'I'm sure it will come back to him though. His mum said that it was you who found him. I didn't know that. You're a bit of a hero, Hule.'

He shrugged his tectonic shoulders. 'Just doing my job. If you excuse me Miss, King say I should tell him as soon Juta wake.'

'Yes, of course. I understand.'

'Thank you, Miss.'

Lirna was sad to see him go. Conversation with him may not have been terribly intellectual, but it was genuine, which was more than what she was getting from anyone else.

As she wandered, she saw people she knew and just about made it through pleasantries. That was all she could muster though, and quickly told them she had things to do and hurried off. She found her way to what was left of the Creator's Shack and stepped over the wall.

The place was still very black. She flicked various bits of debris with her toes trying to make sense of it, but everything was unrecognisable. She thought that the floyancy would have at least been an identifiable pile of ash, but she supposed if it had been covered in a highly flammable coating it may have all burned away. The floyancy channel had cleared. With its door to the river Juta burnt away, the water's flow had cleaned all the ash away.

The sun had not started to set when she found herself back at the Daas residence. She was beckoned inside and offered the seat next to Juta.

Someone had propped up his pillows so he could see who he was talking to. He turned his head from Lirna and smiled at her with the corner of his mouth.

'How are you feeling?' she asked.

His skin still looked waxy and he was pale, but it was good to see him awake. 'I'm surviving,' he said, still not looking directly at her.

'You look well,' she said.

'I've looked better.'

He was hiding his burns from her, she realised. 'You don't have anything to be ashamed of,' she said, delicately. 'What you were doing was very honourable. You were trying to help us all.'

'So was Aereon. He didn't blow himself up in the process.'

'No, he didn't, but he did leave and put all that pressure on you.'

'Most people think what he did was courageous,' retorted Juta.

'It *did* take courage. He also abandoned us though.'

'That's no worse than what I did,' said Juta, bitterly. 'How is the floyancy? Still in one piece?' he asked for hope's sake.

Lirna didn't have a good answer for him, only the truth. 'Your floyancy did not survive the explosion.'

'You see. At least what Aereon did will help someone. He left to rescue the Creators. He stood up to the Queen. He'll probably be paraded around when he returns. He's a hero. What did I do? I was given an opportunity to help everyone and I blew it. Now everyone is suffering because of me. Don't try and deny it. Everyone was desperate before I destroyed the floyancy. Now they are beyond hope. Is anyone even bothering to build another one?'

'No,' said Lirna quietly.

'Everyone's given up. I was their last hope and I failed.'

'You can never give up on hope. Aereon could return any day with the Creators and two floyancies.'

'Oh, brilliant. Yes, won't that be just great,' said Juta. Lirna didn't say anything. 'Sorry. That would be good, obviously. I'm just tired.'

'You don't have to apologise. You've been through a lot. I'm just glad you're back with us.' She smiled.

207

*

It was almost noon when Lirna got up. She'd been awake for hours, but there was no reason to be out of bed. She made herself a small breakfast and got dressed. When she closed her front door behind her, she spotted Hule standing not far away.

'How long have you been standing there waiting for me?'

Hule tottered his head back and forth, 'As long as had to.' He took a step towards her, not threateningly, but purposefully. 'King like speak to you.'

'The King?' she asked. She had possibly spoken with him a couple of times in her life, but it was more offhanded hellos in the street, he'd never actually asked to speak with her.

'Yes.'

Hule waited outside the door when Lirna entered the Royal Abode.

'Ah, Lirna,' bellowed Codrich. 'Just the young lady I was hoping to see.'

'What can I do for you?'

Arburella was sulking in the corner. Lirna guessed that whatever the King was up to it was something she did not approve of but was powerless to stop.

'An excellent question. Oh, don't mind her. Here, come with me.'

The Queen's eyes lifted to remind Lirna that she should definitely be mindful of her.

'My dear wife, bless her,' began Codrich, after closing the door. 'She is a passionate woman and does get herself in a strop on occasion. She'll bounce back though, you mark my words.' Lirna had no doubt. 'Hule tells me that Aereon-two has woken up.'

'Juta? Yes, just yesterday.'

'Juta! That's the one,' said the King, leading her around the building. 'How's he doing? Does he remember anything from the accident?'

'He is ok. The best he can be really. He seems be suffering a little memory loss. I'm sure it will come back to him with time.'

'Oh yes, of course. Let's hope so. Not too quickly mind,' added Codrich. 'This is us here. After you.'

Lirna opened the door to the outhouse and descended into the cellar. The porcelain jars she'd filled with Arburella's nail polish were sitting in the middle of the room next to Juta's red floyancy.

It had a few scorch marks, but it looked largely intact. She edged round it just to check there were no gaping holes. There were none.

'I don't understand.'

'Good,' said the King. 'I want everyone to be surprised. Especially Juta.

'After I had taken you away from the Shack, I passed you on to one of my men and told him to take you to your parents. I felt it was important for me to remain at the scene to keep everyone calm and help if I could. Hule told me Juta was inside. As you would expect, I did not hesitate to enter the burning building.'

Lirna conceded it did seem exactly like the sort of thing Codrich would do.

'I could not stay inside for long, with the smoke and the heat, but I saw no sign of him. The floyancy was also gone. I gathered Hule and some of the others and told them to search the beach for him. Hule spotted the floyancy and Juta was inside, out cold. I had the idea right then. One of my better ones, if I do say so myself. Hule took Juta home and the others discreetly concealed the floyancy. I myself went to go check on you.'

'I'm still not sure I understand. Don't we need the floyancy for food and resources? Why hide it?'

'You sound just like my wife. She also failed to see the big picture. My vision! Here's this boy. Yes, he made a mistake, but once the mistake was made he did not think of himself. Many others would have, there's no shame in it. If you find yourself inside a burning building, survival instincts are sure to kick in. His did not though. Juta thought of the people. He thought of Krank and he rescued the floyancy at his own peril. An act of extreme bravery. An act that deserves reward. He deserves a ceremony and he deserves to be the one who takes this floyancy on its maiden voyage across the river to the lands beyond. Don't you agree? I can see in your face that you do.

'Of course, it would have been too much to ask for the floyancy to remain undamaged in the fire. It is – or rather was – covered in flammable coating. It was all burned away before he could submerge it, although the charred red colouring remained, it is no longer watertight. I cannot think of anyone else more suited to recoat it than yourself. What do you say?'

Lirna was equally excited by Codrich's plan as she was impressed by it and nodded vigorously.

'That's the spirit. I'll leave you to it. I've left a brush out for you. Oh and Lirna, let's keep this hush-hush, yes? Not a word to anyone. Not even Juta.'

'Yes, of course.'

'Good. One last thing, be careful with the torches. The coating is highly flammable,' the King flashed her a wink. It wasn't exactly in good taste, but if you can't make tasteless comments when you're king then what's the point?

Lirna took her time, carefully applying every brush stroke. When it was drying she went to see Juta. He was still very upset, but she found it easier to deal with knowing he had something to look forward to. Even if he didn't know it yet.

The final coat was applied a couple days later and the King was pleased with the result. The ruby red gleamed strikingly and the darker areas gave it a nice texture.

Soon after, Juta was on his feet and out the house. On the streets he got looks like the ones people give puppies that have peed on the floor. He would have preferred it if they were just angry with him. It was the sympathy he couldn't stand. The pity. The unshakable feeling that somehow, they found him adorable for his failure. He was so pathetic it was cute! Lirna could see him hurting and every time she saw Codrich she asked if they could tell him about the floyancy, but he always refused her.

It was little over a week when Juta got his wish and the people started to turn. Most people were running on fumes and they no longer cared to be sympathetic. The looks turned to piercing stares and the solicitous eyebrows turned to heavy frowns. Only then did Codrich concede that it was time for Lirna to invite Juta to the outhouse.

'What is this?' asked Juta. The last few days had made him cautious and fearful, he was not in a place where he could willingly accept the floyancy for what it was: good news.

'This is you lad,' said Codrich. 'Your work. Your bravery. When the accident happened, this is how you escaped. You saved it and it works.'

'Did you know about his?' Juta questioned of Lirna.

'I wanted to tell you, but the King had a plan and wouldn't let me.'

'I did not think it was right for someone else to pilot this contraption after it was you who buried your soul into it and risked your life for it. For us,' continued Codrich. 'I decided to wait until you had recovered. And you made a good job of it, with a few days to spare before the rioting starts I reckon.' The King scratched his head. 'I tell you, the Queen has been all over me about that the last few weeks. But here we are, at the finale and all is well. What do you say sport, are you ready for your moment?'

The King departed and took Lirna with him, to go and make the arrangements.

Juta ran his hands over the floyancy. He remembered applying the red. He supposed he remembered the explosion too. Or at least the events immediately leading to it, but he couldn't remember leaving the Creators' Shack, with or without the floyancy.

Juta sat down in the floyancy. One of the paddles the Creators had made was lying inside, Aereon had taken the other. He picked it up and gave a few experimental strokes at either side of the hull. 'Nothing to it,' he assured himself. 'You've done this before.' At first with Aereon, but he'd even ventured beyond Krank on his own several times, before Aereon had taken the floyancy away. For whatever reason, this felt very different.

The door opened and he bent down so he could peer up the stairs. Codrich came bouncing down and smiled. 'What a natural,' he said, palms framing Juta. Codrich looked over his shoulder at the two burly individuals coming down behind him. 'Look at him, already in position and everything. Well almost, lie down.'

Juta did as he was told. The cronies approached the floyancy and threw a thick blanket across.

'That's it,' Juta heard Codrich say. 'Make sure it's all covered. Right, now lift.' Juta felt a sensation as the two men picked up the floyancy. 'Good. Follow me.'

Going up the stairs was a little bouncy and Juta's head smacked off the wood several times, but after they surfaced the ride was remarkable smooth. Codrich led them somewhere at a steady pace and the pair plonked him down quite gently.

'Ladies and gentlemen,' boomed Codrich. 'And the rest of you.' A light chuckle rippled through the crowd. It sounded like a lot of people. 'Thank you for coming on such short notice. Today I am going to do something that I do not do very often. Perhaps not enough. Someone amongst us is worthy of praise. If I do not do this sort of thing very often it is because I am waiting for something truly exceptional. Something selfless that is for the good of the people, each and every one of you. Off the top of my head I cannot think of another incident such as this. Exempting the Creators of course.' The King would never fail an opportunity to praise those two. 'So, without further-a-do I give you Juta and his floyancy!'

The sheet was ripped from above Juta and the shining light struck him. The applause was flattering when he got to his feet. He returned a shy wave. The clapping and cheering continued so he raised his hand again and offered a sure wave. He even cracked a smile.

It went on and on. Eventually Codrich had to call for quiet. He placed his big hand on Juta's bony shoulder. 'As you can see. The accident has left its mark on Juta. Much of his body was scarred in the blast.' Juta tried to hide himself again. 'He must have been in tremendous pain, but did he give up? Did he run for salvation? No. This boy kept is head and knew that we needed this device intact. He somehow was able to get the flaming, and no longer watertight, floyancy into the Juta. If he had lost consciousness then, he would have gone down with it. But, that is not what happened. He did his part. He reached the shore and collapsed with his energy spent. I am sorry for my part in the deceit and for hiding it from you, I had my reasons, but let me assure you this boy had no part in it. He is too good and honourable for that sort of thing.'

Everyone started to clap again, and the King allowed it to continue as long as it needed to. Someone shouted, 'Take it for a spin!'

The King turned to Juta, 'What do you say? Are you up to it?' Juta leaned down and picked up the paddle. The crowd roared. 'That's the spirit. Do the honours lads.' Codrich's men pushed the floyancy down the beach. As Juta took his seat, it entered the water.

He paddled out a little way. A chant was forming behind him, not the most exciting, just his name over and over, but it was intoxicating. He gave them a bit of a show, edging this way and that. Then he returned to the shore and the floyancy drifted softly against the sand. Codrich came down the beach to him and offered a hand. Juta did not take it. 'Do you have a knife on you?' he asked.

'I might have' – Codrich was always prepared in case a steak happened to materialise in his vicinity – 'Why?'

'I'm going to get us some food.'

Codrich chuckled, 'I like your enthusiasm, but are you sure that's a good idea? You're still on the mend after all.'

'I've never been surer of anything.'

Codrich reached into his belt and flicked out the long blade. 'Don't lose that. Wait a moment while I jazz this up a little.' He turned to his people with palms raised and silence fell again. 'It would appear our hero of the hour is not quite finished. Juta has just informed me that he will be leaving us for the afternoon to bring home some dinner.'

'How does everyone feel about gobble?' tempted Juta.

Almost everyone cheered, and the others only didn't because they were too busy licking their lips.

Juta took the floyancy to the Moonset bank of the river, where he and Aereon had first found the gobbles, but when he arrived at the forest there was no sign of them.

On his way to the forest, he passed the grazers. Great brutes of animals. With thick hides and dangerous horns. One of them probably still had the knife Juta had taken last time sticking out of its rump. No, he would not be trifling with them again any time soon. He took one last look at the plain for a sign of anything more manageable before entering the forest.

Small birds and squirrels darted about. He could not catch any of them, and they would be too small even if he could. He searched with his eyes and listened with his ears, but there was no sign of gobbles.

He continued cautiously into the forest, keen not to get lost. It wasn't long before he came across markings in the earth. He knew the print. Juta inspected the trees nearby until he found the tell-tale grooves in the bark. Tusk marks. He smiled and picked up the trail.

He walked with his nose to the ground, making sure he did

215

not lose the tracks but not paying attention to what they were leading him to.

Juta was lucky enough to hear the boar before it saw him. The steaming mass pulled its nose from the hole and chomped away on something. With his olfactory sensors freed the boar picked up his scent. The beast's muscles swelled and it started hopping in circles, trying to fix on him.

Juta edged himself behind a tree and raised the pitiful looking knife. This all felt very familiar. After a deep breath he stepped out from behind the tree. The boar turned to him instantly and squealed angrily. Juta roared. Both bowed their heads and charged.

Whether they had remained the whole time, or regathered, Juta didn't know, but the crowds were chanting his name upon his return. He was still panting and his shirt was stuck to him by sweat and blood. Not all of it his, but definitely some of it. He did not feel pain, only the breeze and the euphoria.

As the floyancy was dragged up the shore, Juta tried to explain about the gobbles, but nobody cared.

The boar was hoisted out the floyancy and Codrich declared there would be a grand feast in the name of their guest of honour. The King oversaw the cooking, but offered the role of taster to Juta.

When the food was ready he was given a large piece. After he'd swallowed, he gave a thumb's up, which was met with great applause. He found himself a seat. It wasn't long until Lirna was next to him with her own dinner.

'Good day?' she asked.

'Yes. That was… that was a good day.'

The Favour

T his one was quiet. Not necessarily a bad thing, Lars
mused, just stark in contrast to the company he had
been keeping of late.

'How are you with hunting?' asked Lars as they filled up
their canteens by a river.

The Search and Seeker shrugged. 'I do ok.'

He knows that he is good, he's just fishing for a
compliment. 'And how about the rest of your merry gang?'

'Ok too, I suppose. But, I'm not sure how merry they'll be.
The satyrs have had them for days. They might not be
anything anymore.'

If he was capable of remorse he did not show it. 'The satyrs
will not harm them,' said Lars. 'That would spoil their value.
Still, we do not have long.' Lars returned the lid of his canteen
and crossed the stream.

Rorj wasn't far behind him. He never was, but never
alongside.

Lars did not slow for the man. The tracker was always
there though, and never looked uncomfortable with the pace.

They arrived at the sight where the Search and Seekers had
been taken. Lars had a closer look at the scene. 'They came at

217

you from all sides.' Rorj made no comment. 'It is very impressive that you were able to avoid being taken. You must have seen them coming.'

'Heard.'

'Yet there was no time for you to warn your companions?' questioned Lars.

'I assessed the situation. Our odds of prevailing in a fight were not sufficient.'

He wasn't lacking brains, this chap. Even if he was morally bankrupt.

'Can we stop for food?' moaned Edin.

'You heard the elf. We can't leave the path –' well Aereon never actually got beyond *or*, because Koel interrupted him.

'Once you've been told you can't do something you don't really need to know why not, do you? Because you're not supposed to be doing it anyway.'

'How very judicious of you,' said Aereon.

'If I don't eat soon I don't think I will ever eat again,' groaned Edin.

'I am also in need of sustenance,' informed Volris.

'And me.'

'I could eat.'

'We are not supposed to leave the path,' Aereon reiterated.

'We are not supposed to lose the path,' said Volris, thinking out loud. 'We have the ropes, we could tie ourselves together and one of us stays on the path. It might give the person at the end a hundred feet. It's not much, but it's something.'

Aereon still had reservations, but he knew they would all have to eat at some point.

He agreed to stay on the path and tied himself to Edin.

'Shouldn't Volris or Silvor go on the end with the crossbow?' Aereon asked when he saw that Volris had tied himself to Edin.

'Never been the most accurate, myself,' conceded Volris.

'Not my weapon. I prefer to get stuck in,' said Silvor.

Koel took his crossbow off his back, as his stomach groaned, and hoped his lessons would not fail him.

It was amazing how dense the trunks could get, thought Aereon from the path. He could see Edin and the odd glimpse of Volris, but the other two were completely lost in the trees and the undergrowth.

Aereon sat twiddling his thumbs. When he looked up, Edin was gone. The rope was still there and steadily tightening. 'If you carry on like that you're going to run out of space,' he called. No one answered. The rope pulled straight as a pole and tugged Aereon from the path. 'Hey wait!' He called dragging his feet. 'Wait! We're going to lose the path. Stop!'

Lars was leading Rorj towards the mountains and the ground was growing rocky and steep. Still the man behind him did not slow or complain.

The peaks were beginning to appear through gaps in the thinning canopy. Finally, Lars started to slow. Gwen woke. She stretched her wings and took flight to survey the situation ahead.

Lars was careful with each step. They were close now.

He stopped by a tree and Gwen dropped from above. She hooted in his ear. 'seems very heavy handed. Even for them,' Rorj heard him say as Gwen took flight again. Lars turned to him. 'You're in for a sight today. There are a lot of them.'

'Did she tell you about the four behind us?'

Lars smiled. 'I trust you can make yourself scarce.'

'Woodsman!' Lars turned to the satyrs behind him. 'You should not be here. This business does not concern you.'

'Oh, but it does.'

It was a strange language, thought Rorj. Must be very harsh on the throat.

'Where is your friend?'

'She is around,' said Lars. 'I will speak with Throx.' He turned his back on them and walked through the remaining trees onto the low mountain slopes.

Rorj watched Lars bark at the great beast.

Slowly the minotaur turned his horned head. A gold ring hung from his thick nose and his red eyes burned into Lars. Behind him the Search and Seekers were tied to an obsidian obelisk.

'You have no business with these people,' said Lars in beast tongue. 'These are men of Hudikvar.'

The minotaur took a step towards him. 'They were within my lands, they are fair game. You do not scare me Woodsman.'

'Someone does,' said Lars. 'Since when did the great Throx offer sacrifices to the ogres? When did you become fearful of what they would do if you didn't?'

'Careful now, man. Remember with whom you speak. I am looking after my people. From the minotaurs, to the centaurs, to the satyrs.'

Lars could see a couple minotaurs lurking in the forest. There were a lot of satyrs around as well. No centaurs though, he could work with that.

'These are your lands. No one knows them better. Why not

fight the ogres off? Your people are strong and fierce. Or at least they used to be. Can you not defend yourselves?'

Steam blew from Throx's nostrils. 'You dare to call us cowards?' he took another step.

'Prove me wrong.'

Throx sneered, 'With pleasure.'

Lars caught the mighty fist with both his hands, pushing Throx off balance. With one swift twist the beast was on his back.

Gwen burst from the trees and harried the fast reacting satyrs. Lars was on the Search and Seekers and fumbling with their binds.

Throx rose and charged. Lars dropped the ropes and ran for the mountains.

'After him,' roared Throx. All the satyrs flooded into the rocky pass. Gwen attacked the front runners and Throx tried to beat her out of the air whenever she came close, but she was too quick for him.

Only the two minotaurs remained. Rorj picked up a stone. This would be easy enough.

'What's going on?' rasped Aereon.

'I don't know,' said Edin. 'But I strongly suggest you lower your voice.'

The rope to Volris slacked as those in front slowed down and Edin and Aereon caught them up. 'What is going on?' Aereon rasped again.

'Shh!' echoed Silvor and Volris.

Koel pointed at a cottage ahead. 'A woman just walked inside.'

'What do you mean a woman?' asked Aereon.

'You know, a woman-woman. Pretty old. Had a crooked back and dressed in rags,' said Koel.

Edin wasn't looking for her.

'Why did you chase after her?'

Edin wasn't even looking at the house.

'I thought she might have food.' Koel pointed, 'And look, an apple tree.'

Edin was looking at the apple tree.

'What are you suggesting? That we steal from this poor old woman?'

'Well,' began Koel, 'look at it; the branches look ready to snap. There's no way she needs that many.'

The apples were rich red and as big as a fist.

'We can't eat them.'

'Thank you, Edin,' said Aereon. 'At least somebody is talking sense.'

'It would be... invasive,' said Edin, still staring at the apple. He really hoped no one had seen him lick his lips.

'Invasive, yes,' Aereon agreed.

'We are all hungry,' said Volris.

'Let's take a vote,' suggested Koel. He did not pause for agreement. 'All those in favour of grabbing some apples – just as much as we need to keep us going – raise your hand. Right so Silvor, Volris and myself makes three. All those not in favour of eating the apples raise your hand. Come on, let me see those hands. Thank you, Edin. Aereon?'

'This is stupid.'

'Raise your hand. That's it. Ok, that's two against and three for. Now I'm no mathematician, but–'

'Just get it over with,' Aereon snapped across him.

They untied themselves from one another and crept out the

undergrowth and across the clearing to the fruit tree. Each kept a watchful eye on the squint window of the rickety lodge for a sign of a moving shadow, but it was black inside and they saw nothing.

Silvor was first to the apples and quickly started filling his bag with the golden orbs that pleasantly reminded him of home for some reason.

Aereon did not want any part in it. He stood guard, watching the door.

The rest of them crowded the tree, picking as fast as they could. Except for Edin. He lifted his hand to the nearest apple as everyone else blurred around him. With little grip, he gave it the slightest twist and it fell willingly into his hand. There was not a speckle to be seen. It was pure and rich. Inviting. Tempting.

'Go on, take a bite.'

The harvest halted and everyone looked at the tooth-challenged woman who had appeared next to them and then they all turned to Aereon.

'I thought you were watching the door?'

'I was!'

The old woman's expression remained impassive. 'I see you have been helping yourselves to my tree. And me; just a poor old woman. You should all be ashamed.'

Koel gulped and took a step forward after several quite painful pinches in the back of the leg. He scowled down at Silvor who looked up with what he must have thought was an innocent expression. 'Sorry,' Koel began. 'We just thought that one woman couldn't have use for all these apples. Especially one with so few...' his tongue fluttered around his mouth but the word wouldn't come '... uh.'

'Why don't you boys come inside?' She smiled.

It was ironic. Koel couldn't remember being more aware of teeth in any other smile.

'Oh, well, I don't know about that. We really should be going.'

'Koel!' blurted Volris, in shock. 'I think hearing what this nice lady has to say is the least we can do after we were caught with our fingers in the cookie jar.'

'I have cookies inside, if you would like?'

'You see?' bellowed the dwarf. 'She has cookies inside. What's the worst that could happen?'

'Are you going to explain what just happened?' asked Vander.

'Just shut up,' said Rorj as he peered round a tree behind them. The minotaurs were there, but they were nowhere near their trail, stupid beasts. 'Come on, carefully. Don't make a sound and don't leave a sign.'

Rorj led them silently until the minotaurs were out of sight. 'Ok, now we need to move.'

'Not until you tell me what is going on. I am the Captain, and I demand to know what is going on.'

Rorj groaned. 'You're being rescued, isn't that enough?'

'No. What was the Woodsman doing there?'

'He was helping. A big man with an owl always makes for a distracting spectacle, wouldn't you say?'

'He was working with you? Why?'

'He wanted to exchange a favour for a favour. That's why we need to get moving. We need to make it back to Hudikvar before he has a chance to tell us what it is.'

'You roped us into a verbal contract without consulting

224

me?'

'Yes. I thought metaphorical ropes might be preferable to physical ones, easier to slip out of,' said Rorj.

The Captain looked stern. 'Not always.'

Rorj moved like a phantom through the forest, swift and silent, but with the care to leave little mark of his presence. Some of the Search and Seekers were equally good, but there were those in the forest with even greater talent.

The Captain almost bumped into the back of Rorj. 'What is it?'

Rorj stood frozen on the spot. 'Time for the fruition of that favour.'

Lars was growing increasingly noticeable as he waded through the undergrowth towards them.

'You got here very quickly,' he said. 'Almost as though you were trying to get away from something. It couldn't have been the satyrs, they were all chasing me.'

'I thought it would be best to get to you as soon as possible,' said Rorj.

'Job well done then. Funny that, I didn't even think to organise a rendezvous point,' said Lars, while giving Rorj a deep look. 'On to introductions I suppose. These must be your loyal men, I do not believe we have met.'

'Hello, I am Captain Vander of the Search and Seekers.'

'Captain?'

'Yes. Rorj didn't tell you he was Captain, did he?' questioned Vander, giving Rorj a look.

'Oh, no. He didn't say he wasn't Captain, and I just assumed. Seeing as he was offering deals I thought that he must have been in a position of authority.'

'Well, now you know that he wasn't –' began the Captain.

'Nevertheless,' interrupted Lars, 'the deal has been made.'

'What is the deal?' asked Vander.

'Your services,' said Lars. 'There are a number of youths – I am unsure of how many yet but we shall soon find out – who are operating out of Hudikvar. I imagine out of the law. They have been cutting trees and, I can only assume, pillaging farms. They know little of the wild, of the forest. I would like you to teach them.'

The Captain wasn't saying no, although he was certainly thinking it. 'For how long?'

'Indefinitely.'

'Why don't you do it?' scoffed Vander.

'That is a good question,' said Lars. 'I guess because I did not find myself in a situation where I required you to save my life.'

'The King will not be happy.'

'The King will never know. He will never learn of your return. He will think you were killed within the forest and I will not suggest otherwise.'

Vander was pretty sure that Lars knew what he was suggesting was treason, so he did not bring it up. 'What do you get out of this?'

'Peace of mind,' said Lars. 'As you are all aware I am a woodsman, and I am sure some of you know that I watch over the forest. These youngsters are causing a problem that needs fixed. I cannot think of anyone more suited to the job than you fine gentlemen. You will teach them how to hunt and gather, so they do not need to pillage the farms in Hudikvar. I will show you how to tell which trees can be cut and you will teach them.'

'And if we don't want the job?' asked one.

'Then I have two problems instead of one. I would prefer to have none,' said Lars.

'What you are asking will completely change our lives,' said Vander.

'Without him you wouldn't have lives,' said Rorj, to everyone's surprise.

Lars saw through to his motives, though. 'Do not forget your part in this,' he said. 'You had the chance to be free at any point, but you chose to help your fellows. You are in this as much as they are.'

'I understand the repercussions for you, but what happens to us if we refuse?'

'A valid question,' conceded Lars. 'Believe it or not, the satyrs are not far from us. Gwen would leave to attract their attention and lead them directly to you and you would be back where you started. I am offering you a chance at a new life. Well, actually I'm just giving you a chance at life, which is far better.'

The light was dim within the cottage. The grimy window left the crooked corners black. The old woman sunk into a rocking chair, which started to creak effortlessly. She offered her guests stools and access to a jar of cookies. There was no one else inside and there was no other way in or out. Koel knew he had seen the woman enter the cabin and Aereon knew she could not have left it, but seeing neither of them knew both these facts they could happily assume the other was mistaken.

'What brings you all to the forest?' her voice cackled around the walls.

'Just trying to get home,' said Koel.

'Home, yes. Back to the island,' said the woman.

'How do you know that?'

'That is not the question for now. The question is how are you going to get out of here?' a few yellow teeth flashed in the darkness.

'Poison?' blurted Volris, sending cookie crumb projectiles across the room.

'Don't be ridiculous,' said the witch. 'You think I spend my mornings baking poisoned treats just on the off chance that I will have apple thieves in the afternoon?'

Volris relaxed and took another bite. Aereon tried the door. The hinges were rusted and look ready to snap, the wood was brittle, but the door would not move. 'What have you done?' he asked.

'Less than you'd think I'd have to.' She grinned again. 'The good news is I am going to let you go and keep your stolen apples. All I require is something from one of you.'

'Which one of us?'

'That would be spoiling the fun.'

'Are you are going to harm whoever is picked?'

'I swear his skin will not be bruised, nor his bones broken, nor his blood spilled. I won't even cut his hair. And that includes beards,' she added for the dwarves' benefit.

The gang looked at each other and slowly conceded a nod in agreement. 'Alright,' said Koel.

'Good,' the witch smiled. 'You can leave.'

'All of us?' said Koel, hopefully.

'No. This has not been an elaborate test, I regret to say. Although, you can take Volris with you, I suppose.' She leaned close to the dwarf and added, 'And you can take as many cookies with you as you like.'

Volris's hand fumbled into the jar and he grabbed another

two. He hopped off his stool and waddled to the door. Koel opened it with ease and they walked out.

The witch fixed the remaining three with her beady eyes, each in turn. 'Silvor,' she said at last, 'you can also go.'

The dwarf gave her a long hard look. Aereon thought he might go for his axe. The witch just sat back under her quilts with a faint wisp of a smile playing on her lips. The dwarf turned his back on her and walked out.

'What are you looking for?' asked Aereon.

'Something powerful,' she said. 'Something burning.'

'Did you know?' said Edin. It was the first thing he'd said since they found the cottage.

'Excuse me, deary?' His eyes were red and his hands were shaking. 'Oh, and I think I've found it,' she added.

'Did you know about trees and their souls? Did you know about elves?'

'Ah, so that *is* the girl. Interesting. Very interesting.' She pulled at the hair growing from a mole high on her cheek. 'Of course, I knew. I'm not an idiot. The tree is better without her. All that communicating takes up energy. And for what? Just so what's-his-face...' she snapped her bony fingers. '*Malus*, that's the one. Just so he can keep informed about what's going on? It's slavery is what it is. You've seen my tree. Have you ever seen a happier apple? One so fruitful?'

'It harmed her,' said Edin as calmly as he could.

'That it did,' she agreed, 'but you show me a man or woman who cares more about the condition of their soul than they do about their body and I'll apologise.'

'I do,' said Aereon.

Her hand sprang away from her cheek as the hair came free. She held it up to her eye and squinted through it at

Aereon. 'Oh, you do don't you.' She threw up her hands theatrically, 'I'm sorry,' she cackled. 'Curse that mouth of mine. You both have so much to offer, I wish I could have you both. Aereon your determination, I don't mind telling you, it's intoxicating. Edin your lust, oh my, your lust…' she leaned to him and licked her cracked lips. 'I can taste it.' Her eyes closed. 'Oh yes, that's the one. Fitting really,' she said opening her eyes, 'seeing as I am the one who gave it to you. Without me you never would have met the little she-elf and gotten yourself all hot and bothered.' Her eyes were fixed on him now. 'Aereon, you may go.'

Aereon stood up slowly and walked to the door. He should have been grateful. He should have been relieved. He turned around with his hand on the handle. 'I am in love,' he told the witch. 'Why does his lust trump my love?'

The witch looked into him with clear eyes. 'No you're not sweetie. There is much to you, but not love.' She turned back to Edin. 'This next part is going to get a little personal. So, I think it is only fair that you know my name.'

Aereon slammed the door behind him and marched to the others. Koel couldn't help but look upset when he saw it was not Edin walking towards him. Aereon didn't care. He threw himself down by a tree and fumed. He had half a mind to go and knock on the door and tell her he was angry now too. Anger was all consuming, but it was temporary. It wasn't like Silvor's fury. The witch could have used that, but she was going for the big prize. In that little hut, at that time, Edin's lust had been the strongest.

They were inside together for a long time and the wood was silent. Aereon's anger burned out as concern leeched into his mind. She had wanted his determination. She wanted

Edin's lust. But how could you take such things? And at what cost? Would they ever grow back, if she did?

The door swung open, seemingly on its own accord because all that was revealed was the blackness within.

A shadow flickered by the window and Edin stepped into the door frame and across the threshold.

He looked much the same. His shoulders a little hunched, perhaps, and staring into the dirt, but he seemed unharmed. His hands fumbled around, not knowing whether to seek the concealment of his pockets or fold across his chest for security. Koel tried to catch his eye, but Aereon was looking back at the house.

A pale hand slithered from the darkness and the fingers placed elegantly upon the door. The hand slid up the wood, feeling every knot and groove. A woman stepped out like a weasel leaving its burrow for the first time. Curious, with a look of wonder, but there was a presence; with every step, instinct told her she belonged at the top of this food chain.

She glided towards them. Still looking up to the trees and the animals they homed.

She was quite striking, Aereon thought. Dangerously so. You couldn't call it a mole anymore, it was a beauty spot and enhanced her delicate features. The salt was gone from her hair. The black shimmering hair was short over her neck. She still wore the rags, but they draped over her body elegantly instead of bulging in unflattering places.

She stroked Edin's face, who twitched to the touch. 'Thank you for releasing me,' she whispered and smiled a full set of pearly whites.

'You were inside that horrible old woman?' Koel asked.

'In a way,' she said simply and unoffended. 'It was me, but

231

now am not imprisoned by that tired body.'

'... How?'

'I took Edin's lust and did something useful with it. In the end he agreed that it was only causing him pain. He was happy to be rid of it. Weren't you my darling.' Her finger and thumb tried to lift his chin, but he pulled away. 'Oh, so sensitive.'

'What happens now?' asked Koel.

'I am a woman of my word.' Most witches are. Trickery comes naturally to them, it's their bread and duck liver pâté, so they like to give themselves a challenge by only using clever word play or subtle deceits. Lying is just too easy. It takes all the sport out of it. 'You may leave. All of you and you may keep the apples.'

'How will we find the path?' Aereon protested. 'The elves said–'

'The elves!' she scoffed. 'Those little fuss pots. Nemophilists! Always telling others to be careful while they lead a whimsical lifestyle. Hypocrites, the lot of them. Just follow your feet and you will find the path.'

As soon as they were out of ear shot Koel asked, 'What happened?'

'We will never talk of it,' was all Edin replied. He still had her last words to him rattling around his skull "I will be in touch". She had been right about them finding the path again, he hoped she was not right about that too. Unless he was old, on his own death bed, then maybe she could return the favour. He tried to push the thought from his mind. That only reminded him of his hunger. He took the apple from his pocket and looked at it quizzically. He tried to focus on it, to see something else, but it was just an apple. Nothing more. He took a bite.

Moonrise

Hudkvar

Rjkoverg

Oak's Wood

Kazar

Rodin

Sunrise

Dagger Sea

Sunset

Zorak

Krank

Moonset

Weed

The fire was ahead. The glow of impending destruction and the evidence of crimes already committed. Those behind him remained ill at ease with the situation, but what choice did they have? They had a few. Lars had played his hand, but now he was relying on them to make the right choice. They could go to the King, reveal this location and send for a force to bring in the Woodsman. His work would stop, and the youths would be found.

Odd Izzy was sitting in a tree with his legs dangling over a branch. It was the rabble that brought it to his attention. Almost all the children knew Lars, most of them through reputation rather than experience, but he was not a man often confused with anyone else.

Olle was far more concerned with those behind Lars. He recognised the uniform. It didn't have the big breast plate or as much chainmail as the other guards, but there were similar motifs. 'The Search and Seekers,' he whispered. They've tracked us down. Weren't they supposed to be going after that boy and his friends?

Lars stopped near the fire and allowed people to gather. He recognised Kajsha and gave her a nod.

'What is going on?' she asked.

Lars turned to the forest at large and raised his voice, 'Hello to you all and congratulations on your new-found independence. I assume most of you know who I am. Good. That will save some time. Do any of you know what I do?'

'Chop wood for Hudikvar,' said a small boy around Lars's knee.

'Good. What is your name?'

'Rjkaard, sir.'

'Don't call me sir. Does anybody know why?' Lars found his voice was becoming louder and gruffer than he intended, but he did not attempt to reel it in. 'Has anybody even spared a moment's thought to it? No. Of course you haven't. I do it all because I do not trust anyone else to. You cannot just walk into a forest and start hacking away at things. Those are lives you are playing with. Cutting at trees doesn't just take from one life. Think of the birds who nest in the branches or the squirrels who need the trees nuts to survive or all the life which flourishes in the undergrowth.' His voice had ascended to a roar. Gwen stretched her wing which may or may not have intentionally smacked Lars in the ear. He took a pause before continuing at a lower decibel. 'You have taken great initiative in your quest to carve out a life here, but it cannot continue in this manner. I would like to help you with that. These men behind me are the – are formally of the Search and Seekers.' A gasp fled through the youths and several took a step back. '*Formally* being the operative word. Over the last few days we have gotten to know each other quite well. I know that they are capable of teaching you all to track, hunt and gather so you do not have to steal from the farmers anymore and,' he turned to face the men behind him, 'they

235

know what sort of man I am. I have had a chance to give them a brief education on which trees can and cannot be cut. It is a discipline that would take a life time to understand, but you have forced my hand, and they now know enough of the basics. They will teach you these skills and you will all listen. Understand? Anyone who will not listen *or* anyone who will not teach will have me to answer to.'

From his vantage point Olle watched and bit his nails as the youths offered Lars and the Search and Seekers a seat by the fire. This was probably exactly the sort of thing that the Captain would like to hear about.

As it turned out, the witch's cottage was very close to the edge of the forest and there was still daylight when they spilled out the trees and onto the plain. It was primarily silty dirt that covered the land, with a balding glade of sprouts and shoots poking through here and there. To their right, in the distance, were the fading red peaks of the Gorse Mountains. Ahead of them was the path. It remained, resolutely, and was growing stronger. Without the bane of forest life, all its paved stones remained. It had little chance of being overgrown out here.

The next day they found signs of people. Farms cropped up and the path cut through them. There didn't appear to be anyone around. The group were not above theft, but seeing as how their last attempt had gone, and they still had some of its ill-gotten apples, they left the produce untouched.

At dusk, with a smattering of apple cores behind them, the stones beneath their boots turned to cobbles and buildings came to greet them out the dim. A sign was swinging from two posts over the road.

Welcome to Weed.
Where the unwanted thrive.

Another sign sticking out of the ground at the side of the road to read:

An Unfairtrade Town.
Have your wits about you.

Heads turned as they continued into the town, faces peered from houses. Dwarves were not a common sight anymore. Generations had come and gone without anyone in Weed seeing one.

But blood remembers. The Crow Inn had been in the Durst family for centuries. Buried somewhere inside its current owner was the knowledge that dwarves had money. Lots of it.

'Thirsty? Hungry? Tired?' he stepped forward and angled himself to create a path to his door. 'Whatever it is you need, we've got it. You look as though you've been on your feet for a fair while. Time for a seat?'

'Do you have meat?' asked Silvor.

'Yes, yes. All sorts, we've got –'

'I'll have one of everything,' said Silvor, as he brushed past him and into the tavern.

'Same for me,' Volris told the owner, as he slapped him on the arm.

'I'd like to see a menu please,' said Koel. Edin nodded in agreement.

'Do you have anything that isn't meat?'

'Oh yes. We've got chicken.'

'Sounds delightful,' said Aereon, as he followed the others inside.

Even for being a smutty little town, the buildings in Weed were a step up from those of Hudikvar. The walls of the tavern were stone and the floors weren't covered in sawdust. Most things seemed to operate at right angles and the tables didn't wobble.

Urnun Durst offered them the best booth in the house and waited until the dwarves were wedged in, 'Drinks?'

'Start us off with a flagon,' said Silvor.

'Excellent,' said the landlord, purely on reaction. 'I'll just go see about those menus.'

He returned with a flagon, goblets and a couple menus for Edin and Koel. 'So, that was two of everything for you two, wasn't it?'

'Yes. Although, did I hear you say something about chicken?' asked Silvor. 'You can hold that. Nancy food if you ask me.'

'Same here,' said Volris.

'What's wrong with chicken?' asked Aereon.

'Red meat. That's what you want,' said Silvor, smacking his fist against the table.

'I mean, it's bird,' said Volris, with a shudder. 'Who eats bird?'

'Bird? Oh, no I don't eat bird. Sorry, sir,' said Aereon turning to the still grinning owner. 'What I meant was; I don't eat animals of any kind.'

'I know, it's preposterous,' Silvor said to the landlord, 'but we've been through it a dozen times, he won't change his mind.'

'I suppose I could just bring you a plate without the meat?'

'That will be fine,' agreed Aereon.

'Whoa, whoa, whoa!' said Silvor. 'They come with vegetation? You can just forget about that.'

'As you wish,' Urnun said with a smile. He turned to the Creators, 'Have you gentlemen made a decision?'

Olle snuck away at the first moment that arose. It wasn't difficult, everyone was too occupied with the new arrivals.

Captain Morj wasn't drunk when he reached the House of Amber, but he'd been drinking. Probably had been for days. Say what you will about the Captain, but he was one of the best slow burners in the business.

'Hallo,' he said when Olle sat down across from him. He didn't seem terribly focused. Just sitting there, leaning over his drink. Probably thinking again, thought Olle, he does that.

'I have news, Captain.'

'Oh?'

'Lars is back. With the Search and Seekers.'

The Captain's eyes seemed to defog a little. 'When you say *Lars is back…*'

'He's alive,' said Olle. 'Came strolling into the camp bold as brass.'

'With the Search and Seekers?' asked Morj, who was bolt upright now.

'Yes!' said Olle. He was really glad the Captain was concerned about this development as well.

'This is bad.' The Captain took a swig, to no effect. 'This is really bad.'

'They say they are no longer the Search and Seekers. Lars has made some sort of deal with them. They've denounced the King.'

Morj scratched his thickening stubble. 'I've never known the Woodsman to tell a lie. Not one that wasn't to help people anyway. But the Search and Seekers are a tricky bunch. You're going to need to get close to them, Olle. Figure out what they are up to. Any movement they make, come to me. They can't get to the King before we do. It would be best if they didn't get to him at all. I want you on them like a sticky-willy.'

Olle's mouth was hanging open. 'What? I can't do all that. I need to get out Captain. You need to pull me out.'

'What for? I thought you were enjoying all this undercover stuff?'

'That was before. It's all gotten very real. I could be recognised. They could blow my cover. The youths will eat me alive if they find out I'm a copper,' protested Olle. 'I can already picture Darjl's smug face.'

Morj didn't care to ask who that was. 'Don't worry about it. You have a very forgettable face. Don't take it personally, it just means life hasn't beaten you around too badly yet.'

'I don't like it Captain, it seems like a big risk.'

'I need you in there, Olle. Do this for me. You'll be fine, they are not going to figure out who you are.'

'Incorrect I'm afraid, Captain.'

Morj looked up to see Rorj standing smugly next to the door.

The food was not on the plates. It was on the floor, in beards and bellies, but not on plates. There wasn't much beer in the flagons either. It could be found pretty much in the same places as the food.

Both had been consumed in vast quantities by the dwarves.

Vast didn't really do it justice. Simple volume physics shouldn't have allowed it. One might think chemistry and biology would have something to say about it too. The Creators had also enjoyed their meals and had a few goblets worth. There was alcohol on Krank, but it tended to be overripe fruits which had been squeezed into an alcoholic smoothie. The mead was totally different and had certainly done the trick. Aereon had never tried alcohol before and he wasn't about to start. He hadn't entirely grasped what was to be gained from being slightly louder, less coherent and constantly needing the loo.

Urnun was behind the bar, busy with mathematics. He hadn't done this sort of thing in ages; that's what underpaid and overqualified employees were for. Combined with the poorly constructed stories involving highly exaggerated historic tales that were being uttered back at the table, there were several school subjects that were taking a battering in the Crow that night. Include Aereon's attempts to work out their geographical location in relation to Krank and collectively they'd pretty much failed the lot.

Sweat beaded on Mr Durst's forehead and his tongue licked at his moustache. He was of the persuasion that maths was only worth doing yourself if there were big numbers involved. His three waitresses leaned against the end of the bar watching him with mild curiosity, the way cats watch people redecorate.

He brought his crinkled and scored paper over to them and smiled encouragingly.

'That's wrong, for a start,' said the one in the middle, pointing a lame finger.

'What!' Urnun snapped up the paper for further inspection.

'Yeah,' continued another, 'you've times'd their drinks instead of adding them.'

'Well that sort of mistake doesn't matter,' said Mr Durst waving his hand dismissively. 'There's been no undercharging, right?'

All three glanced at the bill again. 'No. You've been quite thorough in that respect.'

'Good,' he said. '*Good*.'

The three stuck their tongues out at him as he headed over to the table.

'Ah, gentlemen, how was everything?'

'It woz ver good,' said Koel.

'It hic... hic... hit the spot,' said Edin

'I am pleased to hear it. I have here the–'

'Did I hear you say that there were beds available?' asked Volris.

'Yes... you have to go back outside and through the other door to the left. Shouldn't be too much trouble for some wild folk such as yourselves.' He laughed, but before he could continue, his profits were pushing past him towards the door. 'Um... I know it's a little inconvenient, but I prefer to run the Inn as a different establishment. If it's not too much to ask, could you pay for your meals here,' he added, raising his voice.

Silvor paused at the door. 'Pay? What do you mean pay? There was no mention of payment prior to consumption.'

The bill flopped pathetically in Mr Durst's hands, 'It was implied.'

'It was implied? When we were walking down the street and you went out of your way to offer us a meal it was implied that we would have to pay for it?'

'Yes.'

'Maybe this is just the way they do things here,' said Volris.

'It is outlandish to assume such a thing without first establishing a formal contract,' snapped Silvor.

'Lars didn't ask for any payment. He welcomed us with open arms.'

'He did hic... hic... make us chop all that wood.'

'Ah,' Silvor wagged a finger, 'I knew you were going to say that. That was in exchange for helping us get through the forest. Not for food. Even the ogres offered us something to eat, free of charge.'

'As inedible as it was,' added Volris.

'Are you saying you won't pay?'

'I'm saying we can't pay,' said Silvor. 'Got no money.'

'I'm sure we can come to some arrangement where we can offer our services and be of use to you. We are quite handy,' said Aereon.

'I want my money!' stamped Mr Durst.

'We don't have your money,' said Volris, diplomatically.

'This will take forever to sort out,' said Silvor. 'We're all a little tired, why don't we get some rest and come at this first thing in the morning. I'm sure there is a middle ground. Out the door and to the left?' he said, but didn't wait for an answer.

'Hey! Wait!' shouted the landlord. He waved his hard-earned receipt in the air and ran out after the dwarf.

Aereon was the last back onto the streets and the first thing he did was trip up over a particularly high cobble, which had been the bane of the Crow's customers longer than it had been called the Crow.

'Watch where you're going, you bleeding drunk!'

243

Aereon turned around to the speaker, but there didn't seem to be anyone there.

'What do you mean we can't seek lodgings in your Inn? Are you saying that all your rooms are full?'

'Well, no.'

'Then what's the problem? You've got beds, we need beds.'

'Yes, but you have to pay for the beds.'

'What?' roared Silvor. 'Even though you have empty beds? The food I can almost understand, but turning away weary travels at your door. That I cannot abide. Get out of my way, you foolish man.'

Silvor pushed the man aside and strode through the door into the Crow Inn.

A forth underpaid staff member was standing behind the reception desk. She watched as the dwarf marched up to her and then disappeared under the edge of the desk. A hand shot up and brandished a finger.

'Now you listen here,' said the hand. 'I am right good and tired and all I would like is a bed. Give me a bed!'

'Do not give him a bed!' shouted Mr Durst, as he came marching down the hall.

The hand disappeared as Silvor moved round the desk and scuttled through the pass under the receptions flip door. 'Give me a bed!'

The receptionist folded her arms and looked down at him.

'Are those for the rooms?' He was looking up at the dangling keys above him.

'Do not give him one of those!' snapped Mr Durst, who had reached the desk.

Silvor was springing for the keys now. Up and down he

went, to no avail. Volris was trying to get through to help his brother, but Urnun Durst had grabbed onto him and the Creators in turn had attached themselves to Urnun.

Ding.

Everyone froze and slowly turned to Aereon who had his finger on the reception bell. 'Hello, Magda, is it?' he asked tilting his head to read her name tag. 'My name is Aereon. I was wondering if it would be possible to have a room for myself and my four, very rude, companions, please.'

'I am afraid we only do double rooms. But, I could set you up in eight and six. Six has a couch one of you could sleep on.'

'That would be lovely, thank you.'

All eyes were on Magda and several open mouths as she reached behind the desk and plucked two keys from the wall and handed them to Aereon. 'The rooms are upstairs.'

'Thank you, very much. Come along everyone, bedtime,' said Aereon, as he started to climb the first few steps.

The rooms were easy enough to find and he had them both open by the time the entourage ascended the stairs. The dwarves led the way and bustled into room six. The Creators stumbled past him and grabbed the key for room eight from his hand as they went. The door slammed without so much as a goodnight.

The snoring inside room six was unbearable. The dwarves had collapsed on top of the bed. Clothed, booted and armed. After considerable effort, he was able to prize a pillow from underneath them.

He twisted and turned on the couch, but no matter what he did with the pillow, the sound would not be silenced. Aereon swore that the walls bowed with every snore.

*

'Can I offer you gentlemen something to drink?'

Captain Morj and Rorj hadn't said a word since the latter sat down. Olle wasn't even sure either had blinked. The Captain was breathing at least, he couldn't hear anything coming from the Search and Seeker though.

Slowly Morj turned his head to Amber, his eyes remained on Rorj, 'A top up would be great, thank you.'

'I'll have one too, please,' said Olle.

'None for me, thanks,' said Rorj.

'Two beers coming up.' Amber disappeared behind the bar.

'It is bad form not to drink in company. Am I to expect this is not going to be a friendly meeting?'

'What is your game here, Captain? Why are you spying on the youths?'

'Spying is a little harsh, that implies some sinister motive. Besides – thank you Amber – you are the one who has questions to answer. Lars is a trustworthy man, so I believe him when he says he is trying to help. You on the other hand, I have my doubts about.'

'Listen Captain, I am not the one who has been caught under incriminating circumstances. I did not have to come here. I could have stayed and exposed Olle to the youths, but I didn't. I decided to give you the benefit of the doubt. All I am asking for is some answers to prove that I was right to do so.'

Of all the guards in the King's employment, the Search and Seekers were Morj's least favourite. He'd heard what they were capable of. Never first hand though, only whispers. That's what scared him. 'I am simply keeping an eye on them.'

'So, the King has not asked you to find them?'

'He did, and I have. Job well done, wouldn't you say?' said Morj.

'You do not plan to tell the King?'

'You catch on quick, Rorj,' said Morj. 'Which leads us to you. You can understand my concern now that you, a member of the guard, have appeared on the scene.'

'We have renounced our title as the Search and Seekers and will play no further part for the King.'

'That is all very fine and well to say,' Morj retorted. 'How do I know it's true? How can I trust you?'

'Honestly, I don't think you have a choice,' said Rorj, almost grinning. 'I do not think you are going to harm me, Captain Morj. I am sure you have heard plenty about me and I know my fair share about you. I think I could walk out of here right now and all that would happen is your knuckles might get a little whiter. Maybe you'd throw your drink against the wall and instantly regret it. Maybe you'd weep as your would-be stupefaction trickled down the wood. I would prefer if that didn't happen. I would like if we could come to some understanding, but at the end of the day, your only option is whether or not you chose to lose sleep over me.'

'It is not just you,' began Morj, 'there are ten others. Can I also put my faith in their silence?'

'Probably not,' conceded Rorj. 'Most of them want out.'

'Why don't you?'

Rorj smiled, 'You obviously don't know as much about me as I do about you.'

The Search and Seekers loved to talk in riddles. 'What's stopping them going to the King then?' asked Morj

'I am.'

'Brilliant. So, what's stopping them going to him right now?'

'What do you suppose I told them I was doing right now?'

'I see. I am to trust a man who lies to his own squad?'

'I already told you, you don't have a choice.'

Moonrise

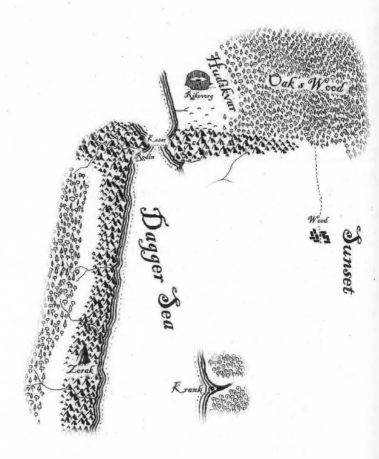

Hulskur

Oak's Wood

Rikoverg

Kazar

Bodin

Dagger Sea

Weed

Sunset

Sunrise

Zerak

Krank

Moonset

Waking to a Bad Dream

It was probably the best night's sleep of Aereon's life. The winds had howled outside the thick walls, the bedding was warm and the mattress much softer than anything he had ever experienced. The sun had spread across his double bed when he finally did wake, and he felt so fresh he didn't even entertain falling back to sleep.

The sun was warm on his skin. The storms of the night had moved on to terrorize other lands, it was going to be a good day. He put on his clothes, flattened his hair and went for the door.

He was sure the landlord would see reason. A simple favour and all that tension of the previous day would be water under the bridge.

The hallway was still. Dust hung in the light-beam from the window. There were some strange noises coming from somewhere, he couldn't quite place them though.

He locked the door to room eleven and swung the key round his finger as he whistled down the hall. Around the corner, he found the Creators' door open. He peered inside, but there was nobody there. He thought about it for a moment then shrugged his shoulders and began whistling again. The dwarves' room was also open with no one inside. Aereon did not continue whistling after that, the noise from the stairwell would have drowned it out anyway.

He stood atop the landing and took in the scene. Halfway down Silvor was sprawled on his back with his arms above his head. Volris was spread across the bottom three steps with his face pressed against the stone on the ground floor. Both snored deeply.

Aereon teetered his way around Silvor then hopped over Volris and took in the scene from this new position. It still looked peculiar.

He tried ringing the bell at reception, but nobody came. He turned back to Volris. Nothing for it.

He gave the dwarf a prod with his foot. Nothing happened. He moved his light prod to Volris's head. Still nothing. He gave a kick and jumped back a step, but still the dwarf did not budge.

Aereon looked at his hand, it was a good hand with a nice flat palm he noted. He recalled being knocked unconscious twice by Lord Fenrik. Slowly he nodded his head, warming to the idea.

In a swift swing, he struck Volris loudly on the cheek. The dwarf's eyes opened like a shot. He tried pushing himself up, but he hadn't accounted for the stairs and he just ended up sliding further down on his face. He rolled over and looked up at Aereon.

'Sleep well?'

'Uh… yes,' said Volris, quite pleasantly. 'Um… why am I on the stairs?'

'I was hoping you could tell me,' said Aereon.

Volris struggled to his feet. He looked around puzzled.

'Maybe he knows?'

Aereon had his doubts, but he watched anyway as Volris climbed the stairs and started bellowing and shaking his twin until Silvor opened his eyes. Aereon's doubts were confirmed. Neither had any idea why they were on the stairs and neither had seen the Creators since they went to bed.

Edin and Koel were not picked up in Aereon's quick scan outside, so he entered the pub, maybe they were in there having breakfast. It would not entirely surprise Aereon if they had gotten up early to smooth things over with the landlord. It wouldn't surprise him if they succeeded either, they had a charm that seemed to work on people.

Aereon spotted Mr Durst, cleaning the bar and humming to himself, maybe he knew something. Perhaps the Creators had sorted everything out. He marched up to the bar flanked by the dwarves. 'Excuse me–'

'We ain't open yet,' said Mr Durst, without looking up.

'I was wondering if you had seen my friends?' On either side of Aereon was a dwarf desperately trying to climb a barstool so they could be part of the conversation.

Mr Durst raised his head, 'Bah!' he screaked, leaping back. 'What are you three still doing here?'

Volris was grinning manically with his chin on the cushion of the stool. Slowly his weight started to tip the chair and he landed on his back with a clatter.

'Am I to understand that you are aware what has become of Edin and Koel then?' said Aereon, continuing the conversation as if nothing had happened.

Mr Durst's eyes were fixed on the wobbling stool as Volris tried to right it while uttering all manner of dwarvish obscenities. His face adjusted as if just realising what Aereon

252

had said. 'What? No, of course not.'

'He's lying!' barked Silvor, who had his fingers on the bar and was using it to pull himself up.

'Thank you, Silvor. I can handle this.'

'Volris! Volris, get over here!' Silvor had his shoulders above the bar now and was wagging his legs around, trying to find the stool beside him.

'Where are Edin and Koel, Mr Durst?'

'That's it! That's it!' shouted Silvor as Volris rammed the stool into the back of his legs. Silvor flopped into it and grinned at his new-found loftiness.

'I notice there is only one way out of that bar, Mr Durst,' Aereon pressed. 'Do you think you could make it there before my friend, Volris?'

Volris took a step back from the bar so the landlord could see him. He smiled and waved, 'Hello.'

'They're in the Sheriff's office,' conceded Mr Durst.

'There you go,' said Aereon. 'You see, we're all reasonable gentlemen here. And where is the sheriff's office?'

'Follow the street down to the square, it's the big building. You can't miss it.'

'Thank you. Come on Silvor, we're leaving.'

The dwarf sighed. He'd been enjoying playing with all these new toys at counter top level. There were coasters. And limes. And Peanuts! He hadn't mastered cracking them without sending shell everywhere, but he was enjoying the experience nonetheless. He wasn't entirely sure how to get back down so in the end he just tipped himself backwards and landed with a wince from Mr Durst.

The Sheriff's office was the grandest building in the town. Or at least had been built to be the grandest, but time tends to have the final word about that sort of thing. The whole square must have been quite impressive once. Several of the buildings had pillared fronts and there was a stagnant fountain in the centre. Aereon gave it close inspection. The figures had turned a murky blue, which distracted from their image, but he could still pick out several characters. There was a valiant looking man in the centre, a host of adoring men and woman at his feet. The big man in the middle had a jaw as wide as his neck, but all the other statues were thin faced and gaunt. He read the plaque.

DEDICATED TO THE UMBRA, WEED'S FINEST SON.

Aereon shrugged and moved off to the sheriff's office.

'What's the plan?' asked Volris.

'I thought we'd walk in and ask for Edin and Koel back.'

'I like it,' said Silvor.

'Good.' Aereon strode through the double doors and did just that.

The Sheriff slowly placed his quill down and removed his glasses. 'Ah, so there are five of you,' he said simply.

'Where are Edin and Koel?' demanded Aereon.

'They are not here,' said the Sheriff, as he folded his fingers together.

'Forgive me if I do not believe you,' retorted Aereon. 'Silvor, keep an eye on him. Volris, you make sure nobody comes in.'

'I assure you, there is no need for this,' said the Sheriff.

Aereon could see a row of cells in the back of the building

and marched to them. 'Edin!' he shouted. 'Koel!' he called. His stomping steps grew quieter and then louder again as he made his way back to the front desk. 'Alright, where are they?'

'They left first thing this morning.'

'Where are they going?' breathed Aereon.

'Oxfort.' The Sheriff was a practical man. He had to make quick assessments in his line of work. He had his ears to the ground the moment two dwarves rocked up in his town. When Mr Durst had come to him and told him they had refused to pay and smuggled themselves into his rooms, he had reacted.

'Am I supposed to know what that is?'

'Follow the road out of Weed,' he pointed vaguely out his window. 'Should take you – oh – two days on foot. Maybe three,' he added, looking at the dwarves. This lot were trouble; he could smell it. A job for people earning more than he did. He had intended to send them all as prisoners, but the dwarves had been bloody heavy, it wasn't worth the effort and the other one hadn't been in the room he was meant to be. He supposed it didn't matter how they arrived at Oxfort, just so long as they weren't here.

'Am I just meant to take that on faith?'

'What's your name, son?'

'Aereon.'

'Let me put my cards on the table, Aereon.' The Sheriff leaned back in his chair. 'I want you out of my town. All of you. The lot of you have the stench of paperwork about you. Two of you are gone and when the three of you leave I will send a pigeon to the capital to inform them that you are on your way as is my duty. In all probability, there will be a trap waiting for you. That is up to you to deal with, I do not care one way or the other how that turns out. I just want you away from here and you just want to find your friends.' The Sheriff raised his hand to the door and smiled.

Aereon turned on his heel without another word and took the pesky dwarves with him. The Sheriff went to his window and watched them down the street until they were out of sight. He sat back down, returned his glasses to his nose and picked up his pen. He read what he had so far.

To the honourable Lord Visma,

Two law breakers, who refused to pay for room and board, are being escorted via horse and cart by my men to Oxfort and should arrive with you within the day. They were not alone in their crimes. A young man and two dwarves were also involved.

The Sheriff dabbed his quill into the ink.

These three, highly dangerous individuals, have been dispatched to you, but unfortunately it was not possible to apprehend them.
I suggest you assemble sufficient numbers to deal with them. The boy, who goes by the name of Aereon, does not carry a weapon, but the dwarves, Volris and Silvor, carry a hammer and axe respectively. Shields also. They should arrive within three days.
Yours dutifully,
Gilad Hornsworth
Sheriff of Weed

Gilad went to the cage next to his desk. He plucked the old

and worn bird from within and attached the scroll to its foot. It cooed in his hand as he opened the window. It took some seeds from his hand before he threw it out into the world.

Sobriety Brings Clarity

The three of them were prattling on. They were worried. And tired. But, most of all useless.

'You were not supposed to come back to me with more problems,' said Morj, cutting through them. 'I told you if the King asks about me to deflect him.'

'We did,' said Marius.

'And what did you tell him?'

Bruts looked around sheepishly.

Noak grinned like a scoundrel.

Marius cleared his throat, 'We told him you were investigating a possible contamination of Hudikvar's water supply.' Morj fixed his grey eyes on Marius and willed him to continue. 'We um... We said you were doing this by...' Marius shifted in his chair. 'By um... going around all the taverns and checking the beers were ok...'

Noak leaned forward. 'The King's not too happy with you Cap,' he tutted.

'Shut up, Noak. You realise what you've done, don't you? You've completely jeopardised my hiding place and all the other taverns. Where am I supposed to go?'

'Oh, jee,' said Bruts. 'We didn't think of that, Captain.'

Morj rubbed his eyes. 'At least tell me you didn't come straight here after the King spoke with you.' There was silence and Morj's head shot up.

'We wanted to keep you informed,' said Marius, defensively.

'Idiots! The lot of you,' Morj exclaimed, although louder than he felt he should have. He rushed to the bar. 'Amber, I need somewhere to hide.'

The King's Guard walked in with trademark pomposity. They were Victorian's errand boys. Tasked with sticking up wanted posters, spreading his word and arranging meetings. Finding people who did not want to be found didn't usually fall into their purview, but with the Search and Seekers missing in action, they were rising to the occasion.

'Hello gentlemen,' said Roak. 'Didn't expect to find a bunch of shiny armours such as yourselves in a place like this. Why don't you join us?'

Not one paid him any attention. They fanned out and peered round corners for any sign of Captain Morj.

Their leader walked up to the bar and Amber smiled at him, 'Can I get you gentlemen anything to drink?'

'Are these your only customers?' the Captain nodded to three members of the Greased Elbows.

'Yeah, early doors yet. Well, apart from Raat.' She pointed to the darkest corner. 'Don't let his name put you off, he's really a lovely fellow.'

The leader of the King's Guard did not take his eyes from her. 'You have never heard of a Captain Morj?'

'Oh, yeah. He comes in here all the time.'

'But, he's not here now?'

Amber gestured to the bar at large, 'What you see is what you get.'

'We will have a look around,' informed the Captain.

'By all means,' said Amber, with another smile.

This is fantastic, thought Morj, as he grabbed his glass.

The King's guard set about peering under tables and marching into the back room. The Captain made a bee-line for the so-called Raat. The Greased Elbows would never turn on their Captain, but perhaps this drunkard would.

'Excuse me sir,' he offered. There was no response. 'I said, excuse me sir.'

'I wouldn't touch him,' said Amber.

The Captain paid her no mind. The man was fully awake. At least his eyes were open and he was sitting more or less upright. He'd asked twice for his attention and he hadn't given it. A prod on the shoulder was not hugely offensive.

'I said, excuse meaahhhh!'

Raat grasped the Captain's finger with lightning speed and slowly tilted his hand, forcing the guard to his knees.

'Ger off! Ger off!'

'I told you not to touch him,' said Amber.

'Tell him to let go of me!'

'I can suggest it.'

This really is fantastic. Blissful solitude.

Amber made her way around the bar.

A little cramped, perhaps, but that is a minor inconvenience.

'Raat, I don't suppose you would consider letting this gentleman go? He is an officer of the law. I'm sure he didn't mean any trouble.'

Raat cast his heavy eyes over Amber, before shifting them

to the Captain in his grasp. His hand peeled open and the Captain pulled away.

'Assaulting an officer!' spat the Captain, once he was back on his feet. 'I should have you taken before the King. Have him deal swift justice to you. He'd probably take a couple of fingers for that. Ironic, isn't it?'

'That would involve touching him again,' Amber pointed out.

The Captain glared between them both, before carefully taking a seat across the cask Raat used as a table.

'I have a few questions for you.'

Raat grunted.

The Captain waited to see if anything else would be added, it wasn't. 'What does that mean?' he asked Amber.

'"Fine",' Amber translated,

'Ok, then. Have you seen a man in here known as Captain Morj? You would recognise him, because he would be cavorting with these layabouts.'

Cavorting? I don't cavort, do I?

Another grunt.

'Fine again? How can it be fine? That doesn't make any sense.'

'No that was *maybe*. It is a very subtle dialect,' said Amber.

'I will take it as a yes,' said the Captain. 'When did you last see him?'

Grunt.

'What was that?'

'"A day or two ago. He said he was on some mission to test all the beer in Hudikvar for contamination".'

This story gathering traction does not bode well for me.

'You got all that from one grunt?' asked the Captain.

'He's been coming here for years,' Amber put forward.

The Captain leaned back and sighed. This line of questioning was getting him nowhere.

If I'm really honest, my legs are starting to hurt a little.

The King's Guard had finished their raid and were lined up next to the door. One approached the Captain.

'We didn't find anything sir.'

'Not even a spoon, Sergeant?'

'No, sir.'

'Very well. I don't suppose there's one place you haven't looked?'

Ahhhh! This is torture. Need to move. Need to move. Need to move.

'Don't think so, sir.'

Mustn't move. Mustn't move. Mustn't move.

'Damn.' The Captain rattled his fingers on the cask before slowly getting to his feet. He gave everyone a final look as he made his way outside, knowing in his bones that something was amiss.

Bruts eyed them through the window until they were out of sight. He gave Amber the nod.

'Alright, you can come out now.'

The lid shot off the cask table and Morj spilled out like champagne. Raat sat back, still looking unaffected by the evening's events.

'Never again,' Morj muttered to himself as he shook his legs. Amber replaced the lid and Raat put his drink back down. Amber stood over Morj expectantly. 'Thank you,' he said.

'No problem, at all. Would you like a hand up?'

'That won't be necessary.' Morj got to his knees and then his feet and smiled at Amber. 'See? Still some spring left in these bones.' He winced as he hobbled over to his men and gave a comfortable sigh when he sat down. 'So, you three are telling me you have found out nothing about the armed civilians in Rjkovorg.'

'Nothing yet, Captain.'

Morj was beyond the realms of anger and into the vast wastelands of confusion. Why was no one talking? It didn't make any sense. 'Alright, just keep at it. Something will turn up.' Morj wasn't convinced, it had gone on too long for that. It was at the stage were someone was going to have to figure it out.

'What are you going to do, Captain?'

Not figure anything out, I suspect. 'I'm going to go to the only place that's still safe for me.'

'Where's that?' asked Noak.

'I fear telling you would make it less safe.'

'Good point, Captain,' said Marius.

'Smart,' agreed Bruts.

Morj got back to his feet.

'You're really not going to tell us?' asked Noak.

'No. If I need you, I'll reach out to you. If the King asks for me again, tell him you've found where the dwarf got out of Rjkovorg. Show it to him. If that happens though, you can't stay in Rjkovorg. They'll be no preface for you to be there. You can't tell the King you've known about the armed citizens, it's gone on too long. We'll have to abandon the case.'

'We'll figure it out before then, Cap,' said Bruts. 'You can count on us.'

'You're the finest men I've ever met. I'll see you anon,' Morj walked over to Amber and embraced her. Both ignored the wolf whistles coming from the table. 'Thanks for having me.'

'You're welcome.'

Morj headed for the door, but turned just before he reached it. 'Oh, and Raat, sorry for disturbing your evening.'

'It's no trouble, Captain.'

Morj knocked on the door. It wasn't his usual knock. It wasn't bustling with authority and punctuality. This was a citizen's knock. From one man to another.

The door opened, 'Ah evening, Sergeant.'

Captain Morj did not flinch. 'I have something to ask you.'

'Aereon isn't here if that's what you're after.'

'Ah ha. Very good. No, I am here wondering if I could stay with you. Just for a little while. You understand?'

'Not really,' said Lars. 'But, far be it from me to turn away someone from my door. Come along in.'

'Thank you.' Morj climbed the steps into Lars's lodge. 'It will just be for a day or two. Just until I figure out where I'm going to go next. Or preferably a situation presents itself so I can go back.'

'Nonsense, you'll stay as long as you have to.' Lars closed the door and got a whiff of the Captain. 'Goodness man, you stink of the sauce.'

'Oh yeah, I had to hide. It's a long story.'

'You cannot use alcohol to hide from your troubles.'

'No… I know… It wasn't like that… I was in a cask… There was…' Morj tried to continue, but Lars's face was flat.

'This is a dry household I hope you know. There will be

no *booze* consumed within these walls or by anyone sleeping under its roof. Is that clear?'

This was bringing back some disturbing preadolescent memories for Morj. 'Your house, your rules.'

Lars moved quietly for his size, but Morj was a light sleeper.

'The stories are true,' said Morj, with grog. 'You really do rise early. A glökotta through and through.'

'My apologies, I did not mean to wake you. Would you like some breakfast?'

'That'd be grand.'

Lars busied himself with his trademark porridge, notable for its uses as paving. It was a bit of trick getting it into the bowls, but somehow, he managed. Lars folded his arms and studied his guest. Funny the way things work out, he thought to himself. 'You mentioned last night that you were happy living with my rules if you were sleeping under my roof?'

'Yes,' replied Morj, struggling to pull his jaws apart.

'Another of my rules is that any guest does not receive free room and board. You will have to work. When Aereon and his company were staying here, they helped me with the trees. I am guessing that you would prefer if no one knew your whereabouts?'

'Preferably, yes.'

'Something inside would be best then. Keep you out of sight. Can you cook?

'It's just throwing things in a pot and stirring, right?'

'Can you clean?'

'That's just moving dirt from one place to another.'

'Good. I shall leave you to clear away breakfast then.'

*

Captain Morj looked ridiculous. Lars had confiscated his smelly clothes and provided him with a shirt. It was two torsos too big for him and down to his knees. Sometimes, when he leaned in a certain way, the neck would slip down over his shoulder. The apron didn't help either. Lars only had the one and it needed to be folded several times so Morj wouldn't trip over it. Lars had clearly seen the funny side as he'd taken wholeheartedly to bellowing "Honey, I'm home" whenever he came in for a meal.

'Oh, well this looks lovely,' he said as he sat himself down for dinner. 'How was your second day sober?'

'Less headachy.' Morj thought it best to leave out the part about the shakes.

'Good,' said Lars as the pair tucked in.

'And you? Another successful day chopping?'

'Yes, indeed.'

After dinner Lars offered Morj a game of Karplaw. He'd lost six on the trot against Amber and the wounds were still fresh. He didn't understand why he couldn't get his head around the tactics of it. He wasn't really in the mood to play again, but he could see his landlord really wanted a game.

As they played Lars asked what sort of trouble it was he was in and Morj couldn't see a reason not to tell him all of it.

'What are you going to do about Amber?'

Morj almost spat out his bovril. 'Excuse me? Aren't you more concerned about all the other stuff?'

'You seem like a man well suited to his job,' said Lars. 'I don't worry so much about you screwing that up.'

'Don't you worry about me. I know what I'm doing.'

'I do not think even you believe that,' said Lars, moving a troll forward.

*

'We've tried this door at least three times already,' moaned Noak.

'You never know when the time will come you get the answer you need,' said Marius, after a booming knock.

The door opened and the man sighed. 'I told you. I don't know anything.'

'Look,' began Marius, 'we just thought that your memory might have changed after a little reflection.'

'I haven't thought about it at all. I don't need to. That night was a night like any other. If you'll excuse me, my lunch is ready.'

'Oh? What's on the menu?' asked Bruts.

'Sandwiches.'

'Sandwiches! I love sandwiches! What's on them?'

'Uh... cheese and pickle.'

'An absolute classic and my all-time favourite. Oh, sure, why not? I could eat,' added Bruts, as he brushed past the man.

The man looked horrified as he chased after the squat Constable, but Marius just smiled. You had to love the wildcard. He and Noak went inside and shut the door.

Noak inspected the coat hangers by the door, but there was no sign of weaponry. Together they followed the flustered voice of the resident to the kitchen. They scanned for incriminating evidence or a place it might be hidden. Noak checked the cutlery drawer, but nothing within struck him as especially formidable.

Bruts was sitting with his boots on the kitchen table and had just bitten into the middle of triangular sandwich. He wiped the crumbs from his chest onto the floor and gazed out the window. 'It's a nice place you've got here. Good view of the strip. I bet you've seen all sorts, sitting right here.'

'I told you, I didn't see anything that night. Nothing out of the ordinary.'

'Really? Not even when all those youths broke out of the Long House and escaped through the gates with two dwarves.'

'I thought only one dwarf escaped?'

'And where did you hear that?' asked Bruts pleasantly.

'I… um… I can't remember. There have been a lot of people talking about it.'

'But no names spring to mind? Funny that, how lots of people saw the breakout, but no one stayed up just a little longer to see what happened to the dwarf. Very odd. I bet the information would have been useful too. And valuable, of course. I bet the King would have paid a pretty penny for it. It's a shame that no one had the foresight to keep a look out. I guess you must have all been very tired. I mean, what else could it have been?'

Marius could practically see the cracks beginning to appear on the man's face. Sweat beaded on his brow.

'By my reckoning,' Bruts continued, with his mouth full, 'there must have been something, or someone, that got you all worried about looking out your windows that night. Or too scared to say anything about what it was you saw. Who was it?'

The man licked his lips and shifted his eyes pleadingly from face to face.

'Give us a name.'

'Hey!'

Everyone jumped. No one had noticed the face appear at

the window.

The Captain of the King's Guard grinned, 'The King wants a word with you three.'

'Where is the rebel base?'

'The what, sire?' asked Constable Bruts.

'The youths. You mutt. The youths!'

'Oh, them. Haven't heard yet, your highness.'

'Where is your Captain?' shouted Victarian. 'Where is Morj. I want to speak with him. I am sick of dealing with you fools.'

'I'd prefer if you didn't paint us all with the same brush,' said Noak.

'I don't care what you prefer,' spat the King. 'I care for what I want. I want to deal with someone of moderate intelligence. Failing that, Captain Morj will do.'

'He is… indisposed, sire,' said Marius.

The King stared at him before shifting his weight. 'You do realise that hints he is unwilling to come and suggests you have been in correspondence with him?'

'Oh, well, he certainly isn't that then,' confirmed Marius.

'You see, this is what I mean,' complained the King. 'It's like talking to monkeys. You three have absolutely no idea how to conduct yourselves.'

'Thanks, sire.'

'That was not supposed to be taken as advice. It was an insult.'

'It's your honesty we appreciate, sire.'

'It's uncanny,' muttered the King to himself. 'I presume you are going to tell me that he is still getting himself blind drunk for the benefit of the country?'

'Yes, sire,' said Marius.

'I've been wondering about that,' said Bruts, conversationally. 'How do you go about poisoning a water supply anyway?'

Noak shrugged. 'I don't know. Dissolve a witch in it or something.'

'Do the three of you at least have an idea about how that half-pint hooligan got out of my city?' asked Victarian, who was desperate to keep the trio focused.

'Yes, there's a hole in the wall,' said Marius. 'Been there for years.'

Noak coughed.

'Looks like it has anyway,' Marius added. 'I wouldn't know for sure.'

'Show me this hole in the wall.'

'Uh… are you sure that's a good idea, sire?' asked Dagny.

'Yes, Captain, I am. I have considered it. You are not here for your condescension.'

'Another scrumptious meal.'

'I am glad you enjoyed it,' said Morj, getting up.

'No, no. Leave those for now. I thought we could have another round or two of Karplaw.'

'Don't you have to get back outside?' asked Morj.

Lars shrugged and picked up the board. 'The forest isn't going anywhere. Who's your race of choice?'

'You know what? I'll go man. I haven't been them in ages,' said Morj.

'I shall go elves. Would you like to set up first? Or shall I?'

As the armies made their way across the board, the couple

talked about Lars's adventures since he'd left Hudikvar and his pleasant greeting after he returned. The King's Guard had been to see him. They had questions which came directly from Victarian. Lars made a face to show how he felt about all that hoity-toity. They both laughed. Before Morj knew what was happening, he'd lost.

Lars had hidden his elves within the wooded areas of the board and offered fleeting attacks at Morj's bulky force until a gap in the line offered an opportunity for him to pierce through and strike down Morj's General.

'Damn,' exclaimed Morj. 'It doesn't make any sense to me that rule. Why is it only for the race of men? Why should they lose just because their commander has been killed? In real-life if a leader was killed his successor would have nicked his symbol of office and be ordering people about faster than you could say *thou shalt be avenged.*'

'Now, now. Nobody likes a sore loser.'

Morj's face had gone to stone, his whole body stiff. 'Oh, you great big lummox!'

'Hey! What did I just say?'

'Not you,' said Morj, slowly starting to break out of his cocoon and reveal a moth that spun fury on wings of competence. 'Me! I know why there were armed people in Rjkovorg that night. I know who was behind it. Stupid, stupid, stupid. I should have seen this sooner.'

'It's amazing what three days sober does for a man.'

Morj ignored the comment. 'Lars, do you think you could send Gwen on an errand for me?'

'No. But, I could ask her and I'm sure she would say yes.'

'Whatever,' Morj waved his hands. 'I need her to go to the youths' camp and bring Olle here.'

271

'Do you think Olle will recognise her?'

Morj thought about it, 'Probably.'

'Do you think he will know to follow her here?'

Morj thought about this as well, 'Probably not.'

'If he is with Rorj, he may be able to figure it out.'

'Do you think he is clever enough to know she is there for Olle?'

Lars thought about it, 'Probably.'

'Do you think he is honest enough to send Olle back with her and not just come himself?'

Lars thought about this as well, 'Probably not.'

'Me neither,' said Morj. He sighed, 'He might actually be better suited for the task, but I'd rather I had someone I trusted.'

'Forgive me Sergeant, but it seems to me you have quite a lot in common with Rorj.' Lars ignored the sharp inhale. 'Both of you were asked to bring Aereon before the King, and both of you failed when you ran into me. The pair of you have since renounced your loyalty to the crown and are essentially in hiding. I'm not sure what he's done to warrant such hostility from you.'

'He's a schemer,' rasped Morj. 'A sneak.'

'And you're a drunk.'

Morj scoffed, 'If he can go three days without plotting, I'll ease up a bit, but I don't see that happening, do you?'

'Nothing wrong with having a few plans up you sleeve. It would certainly help your Karplaw game.'

'Fine.' Morj, threw his hands up. 'Send for Rorj, but that git is getting turnips for dinner. You hear me? Turnips!'

The entire Royal Guard had been assembled. There were three

teams that worked in shifts around the clock to keep King Victarian protected. Captain Dagny wasn't taking any chances. This was the King's first public appearance since he'd shouted at Aereon from the doors of the Long House. She couldn't even remember the last time he'd ventured down the steps onto the streets. It might have been before she'd been made Captain. Since he'd been stabbed on her watch she had been on high alert. Something was wrong in the city, she could smell it. God, strike Captain Morj down for turning his back on the crown at this time, when he was needed most. She did not agree with the way Morj conducted his work, but she could not argue with his results. He had a way with people and picking out the truth in rumours that was valuable to the King. She never enjoyed that area of policing. She was a wall, a shield, and so were her men. Together impenetrable.

'How many deep?' she barked.

'Two!' they roared.

'Show me defensive formation!' she stood in the middle of the circle and they all took a step in towards her. Two pushed her to her knees as the shield shell came down and blocked out the light. 'Good,' she said to everyone inside. 'What are the rest of you doing out there?' she shouted.

'Locating the threat and neutralising it,' her best fighters shouted back.

'Good! And break!'

The shields change position and the swords and spears came out, but the tight circle remained. It wasn't bad, she thought as she shifted her eyes. 'Shield, Colson!'

'Yes, Captain!' said Colson, raising his shield. 'Sorry, Captain!'

'Don't apologise to me. Apologise to your dead King.'

*

'Good evening Rorj,' said Lars, as he opened the door.

Rorj stepped inside and wiped his boots.

'Oh, that's very courteous of you.'

'I was raised good and proper,' said Rorj.

The pair laughed, neither noticing the mockery Morj was making of them both.

'Come and sit down. Dinner should be ready soon.'

'Well it smells lovely,' said Rorj, taking the offered seat.

'It's turnips,' said Morj sourly.

'Oh, my favourite. And may I add, that outfit is very becoming on you.'

Morj stuck his tongue into his chin as he slapped down a dollop of the mash on Rorj's plate.

'So, what is the occasion?' enquired Rorj, once everyone was seated.

'Morj has something he would like to ask you,' said Lars. 'A favour,' he added, Morj felt needlessly.

'The day Aereon's band left Rjkovorg, you will recall one of the dwarves was trapped inside but found a way to escape.'

'Through the hole in the wall, presumably,' said Rorj.

'How do you know that?' asked Morj, through his teeth.

'It was my job to know these things.'

'It was also your job to report them to the King.'

Rorj shrugged. 'You didn't.'

Morj, gave Lars a look. He did not like this comparison. 'My men may have by now. The night the dwarf escaped he saw some armed men in the streets of Rjkovorg. I've been using the mystery of the dwarf's escape as a front so I can investigate this odd occurrence.'

'Very underhanded of you. I must apologise, I did not

realise you had access to such wealthy stores of guile. Have you ever considered a career in the Search and Seekers?'

Morj pressed on. 'I think I've figured out who those people were, but more importantly who they get their orders from.'

'Well, by all means Captain, spill it,' said Rorj.

'Prince Victarian,' said Morj.

'Prince Victarian?'

'Yes. I think he is plotting to kill his father. A big no-no in my book. As I've said before, about as treasonous as you can get.'

'Do you have any proof?'

'No, which is why I can't go to the King, but it feels right. I know it.'

'No need to explain,' said Rorj. 'I've been there before. What do you want from me?'

'Three of my men are operating within Rjkovorg, or they should be. If they've halted their investigation tell them to find another excuse to be inside Rjkovorg. I need you to go to them and explain the situation. Tell them to keep an eye on the King and especially on the Prince. I would go myself, but there are people looking for me.'

'I shouldn't need to remind you Morj that I am also in hiding.'

'Yes,' agreed Morj, 'but people aren't actively looking for you, are they? Lars told the King's Guard that you were dead. Besides, I'm sure you are more than capable of covering yourself from prying eyes.'

'Speaking of which,' said Rorj, 'at this angle you are revealing a considerable amount of nipple.'

Outside a crowd had amassed. King Victarian was imminent.

The Royal Guard had formed a protective square with a small opening at the door to the Long House for the King to step into. Captain Dagny stood outside the formation next to Marius, Noak and Bruts. Several of her men were dotted around to keep any civilians from approaching the main guard.

Two armed men held the doors open and Victarian birthed into his Kingdom for the first time since he'd been stabbed. The wound was well concealed by his mottled fur cloak, but those who were looking for it might notice the stiffness in his arm.

The King found his way to the centre of the guards and stopped.

Dagny turned to the Greased Elbows, 'Alright gentlemen, lead the way. Slowly.'

She kept up ahead, with the trio, but was continuously looking over her shoulder and peering down side streets. Curious eyes stared back at her. With every alley, the crowds grew, cutting off her escape roots and housing a greater risk of threat. The quicker this was over the better.

Silvor had concealed this side of the tunnel well. The two-hundred and seventy-fourth post looked just like any other.

The front of the guard split and allowed the King to join the guides at the base of the wall. Victarian fingered the bark and turned to Morj's men. 'What am I looking at?'

Marius grabbed Bruts by the ankles and shoved him up the wall. A few hard thumps and bark gave way to reveal the hole. Marius placed his palms under Bruts's soles and pushed him the rest of the way. The sea of gasps roared against the cliffs below as Bruts disappeared into the cave.

'And if I just push this,' his echoed voice came from above,

'It leads outside.'

Bruts's face reappeared with a clear breeze ruffling his hair.

'This doesn't make any sense,' mumbled the King.

Within his private room at the rear of the Long House were his most prized possessions. His grandfather's sword. The shield that had broken Skortan's hammer. His ancestors' memoires. He'd read them all, cover to cover, a dozen times over. They went back to before Rjkovorg existed. Back to the days when there were a dozen clans living in Hudikvar. They told the tales of his family's rise to power. It had taken him years to learn the old script. He knew those pages as well as he knew the back of his hand. Nowhere within them did it mention anything about this hole. This abomination. Had his ancestors done this to him? Had they known of this passage and kept it a secret? Were they laughing from the heavens at his ignorance?

No. He would not believe that his blood could betray him.

Someone else must have built the tunnel. He always felt that having people to rule was one of the cruxes of being a ruler. Things would be much simpler if they didn't exist. All anyone ever did was complicate things. What was the point in putting a hole in a perfectly good wall?

No one in his family would do something so stupid. He looked at the hole again. It looked old at least, something that had not occurred on his watch. It seems odd that it could have occurred on anyone's. It was massive.

'How did you find it?' he demanded of Marius.

'The covering on the outside had not been replaced properly and we spotted the hole.'

'When was this?'

Marius had a little think, 'This morning,' he concluded.

'Why didn't you come to me straight away?'

'Excuse me, your highness?' said Marius.

'Captain Turjl tells me he found you in a residence within Rjkovorg. What were you doing there?'

'Um...'

'We were inspecting which houses people could see this post from,' said Noak, 'and questioning those, to see if any could be suspected of foul play and protecting the dwarf and his secret.'

'And?'

'Nothing yet, sire.'

The King looked back to the hole. 'You should have come to me immediately. Find out who could have known about this. Find out who has been lying.'

'Yes, sire.'

Elsewhere, at the rear of the masses, the Prince dwelled. He'd found himself a wall to lean against and could still gaze over the heads of the common folk thanks to his family's long build. His eyes were fixed on the back of his father's head. His scalp was beginning to show through his fading hair. A clear sign that an end to his reign was long overdue.

The time was ripe. The scenario, on the other hand, left a lot to be desired. Curse that antagonist, Dagny! She'd done an impressive job. There was still an opening for an archer on a roof, but he did not have anyone in his entourage he trusted to make that shot. He could, but he couldn't be seen to have an involvement in the murder. Gone were the days when people actually respected you if you committed treason and actively got behind you because of it. Now everyone was obsessed with that *long live the King* nonsense.

The Greenmen

As much as he hated to admit it, his followers were precious to him. It had taken years to discover their loyalty and slowly feed them his plan. And they were still outnumbered two-to-one by the Royal Guard. Not to mention all the other guards and citizens wandering around Rjkovorg. If things went wrong, they'd never make it out. Who knows how long it would take him to assemble this many servants again.

What choice did he have though? The Long House wasn't exactly accessible, especially now the roof had been fixed. Who knew how long it would be until the King left his fortified home again. He knew his father looked ill, he probably was ill, but he'd been that way for years. For all he knew, he could continue struggling on like that for another decade. The Prince would not wait that long. He refused to.

What was it his mother had said to him as a child? *It's better to have tried and failed than to have never tried at all.* Crazy old bint that she was, at least that had made sense.

Slowly he lifted his hand with two fingers raised. He exhaled slowly.

'Now is not the right time.'

The Prince was not a man easily startled, but there was a shadow of a jump.

He looked at the hooded figure next to him. 'Who are you?'

'A friend.'

Generally speaking, anyone who has to tell someone they are a friend is usually an acquaintance angling for a promotion. Occasionally it's a complete stranger who is pushing their luck a bit. But, more often than you might like to know, it's an enemy who thinks you've got turnips growing out of your ears and you should probably invest in some cotton swabs if you don't smell the skulduggery afoot.

'Well *friend*, this is not something I have much practice in saying, but what can I do for you?'

'Take my advice,' said the hoody.

'And what wonderful advice I am sure it is, but I do not take advice from strangers.'

'I am a member of the Search and Seekers. Rorj is my name.'

Victarian's lips moved as he pieced a few things together. 'I heard the Search and Seekers were killed within the forest.'

'We were not killed. We are living within the woods and have unofficially, but very realistically, renounced our allegiance to the current crown.'

'I see. And what is this advice?' asked the Prince, still somewhat sceptical.

'Today is not the day to strike. Look at these walls. Look at all these guards. Almost all of which are fiercely loyal to the King, because they have been trained to be. Of course, if the King were to die they would be loyal to you, but the King needs to die first and seemingly without your involvement.'

'What makes you think I want to see my father die? What you are speaking of is treason.'

'Do not treat me like an idiot, my lord, and I will grant you the same privilege,' said Rorj.

Victarian gave the part of face he could see a long hard look, 'Why should I not strike today?'

'Because you'll lose. You may even be killed yourself. Certainly imprisoned.'

Victarian laughed. 'I was not planning on leading the charge myself.'

Rorj did not smile. 'I am sure your men are fiercely loyal. Willing to die for you, I would imagine. Otherwise you would not even be considering this. Dagny is not stupid though. She has the numbers necessary to take a select number alive. Willing to die for someone and willing to suffer for someone are two very different things. They'll talk.

'You need to level the playing field. The Search and Seekers are not alone within the woods. You will remember the youths that escaped from the King's clutches thanks to the infamous Aereon of Krank. They have not been idle. They've gathered numbers. Over half of the homeless children of Hudikvar have joined them in their plan. In a few days, it will come to fruition and King Victarian will be forced to leave Rjkovorg and go after them. That is when you strike.'

'That is a lot of faith to put in a gang of youths.'

'Not a gang, an army. And no, it's not. You're trading one suicidal chance for my word that this will be a better option. Do you remember the heirlooms the youths took from the Long House? That is their lure. They will issue an ultimatum and the King will follow.'

'He does like his heirlooms, my father.' The Prince seemed to reach a conclusion. 'Very well.'

'Good. One final thing. Captain Morj, of the Greased Elbows, knows about you. He has no proof, but he knows. He has formed an alliance with me. It is my job to tell his men over there to keep an eye on you, and I will. I do not wish my dear Morj to receive word of my infidelity. So, keep your little group meetings to a minimum until the King leaves Rjkovorg, then assemble the troops.'

Rorj bowed his head and turned to leave.

'Wait. How do I know I'm not going to receive the same

treatment as everyone else you've pledged allegiance too?'

Rorj turned his hood, but did not show his face. 'When I do someone a favour, I like to have interest. You, I suspect, can offer me the biggest return.'

'But, what do you want?' Victarian called after him.

'Use your imagination.'

Breaching Oxfort

That'll be it then, thought Aereon.

It was indeed *it*.

They'd passed through small towns and villages since they left Weed, but nothing that could have been construed as *it*. Nothing like this.

The trio stood atop a rise and gazed across the land before them.

A great river dominated the view; cutting through the ground and lifting it away to be flushed downstream. The hills did their best to tame the water, but they were of little consequence to the river.

A settlement sprawled in the shadow of a vast cliff. Much of the town was submerged in the mist that spread out from the waterfall's splash.

It was incomprehensible to Aereon that there could be so much water in one river. Surely the waterfall would run dry? Was there a valve or a dam that they used and only turned on the water occasionally? Maybe it was just for show, for when they had visitors.

The three of them looked up to the centre of the falls. A massive turreted wall commanded everything below. It stood over everything with absolute surety. Even the relentless water that fell beneath could not drag it over the cliff or undermine its presence.

'That'll be it then,' said Aereon.

Both dwarves nodded in agreement.

'I think you two should stay here,' said Aereon, nervously, while trying to add an air of authority.

'What?' breathed Silvor.

'You heard what the Sheriff said. They are going to be waiting for us. I have a sneaking suspicion it will be you two who are the giveaway. It will be safer if I try to go in myself.'

'What?' roared Silvor. 'You do not know how inconspicuous we can be!'

There were many words that sprang to mind when Aereon thought about dwarves; inconspicuous was not one of them. Cantankerous, yes. Inconspicuous, no.

'This is not the same as Rjkovorg. We don't know where the Creators are being held. We don't know how many guards will be waiting for us at the gates. How many more will be inside. Consider the Three Little Pigs. Look at that wall. Stone. Rjkovorg was wood. We have gone up a whole piggy level. And if you'll recall, the Big Bad Wolf could not huff and puff the third pig's house down. No, we need a new approach. We need reconnaissance. If I can get inside and find out where they are being held I can come back, and we can come up with a plan.'

'If we're the Wolf, does that make us the bad guys?' asked Silvor.

'You know, I've always had a bit of an axe to grind with that story,' Aereon began. 'I mean, for all those pigs know, he was just after some sugar.'

'How do you explain the huffing and puffing?' Volris asked.

'Hay fever,' said Aereon. 'When the Wolf was at the first pig's house, all that straw got him sneezing and he couldn't get it out of his system for the rest of the day. Meanwhile, he's painted out to be the villain of the piece.'

'… When really he just wanted some sugar?'

'Look, I'm not saying that's exactly what happened, I'm just saying we should consider the facts and approach it rationally, instead of jumping to conclusions.' Volris and Silvor remained unconvinced. 'It doesn't matter. The point is, I think it best that I go in alone.'

'Fine. Fine,' said Volris. 'You go and do your reconnaissance mission. We'll stay here.'

'Thank you. I'll see if there is a way for me to get them out myself. If not, I'll come for you. You two will stay here?'

'Oh yes,' said Volris, with a smile. 'Right here.'

Silvor's expression was contorting. No one noticed though. That's what happens when you have a doormat growing out of your face.

'Ok, I shall report back when I can. Wish me luck.'

'Good luck,' said Volris.

Aereon gave a solute and turned up the hill, which rose and curved up and around the cliff to the lands above.

Silvor waited until Aereon was out of earshot. 'Are you serious?'

'Of course not,' said Volris. 'Come on.'

Silvor followed Volris down the slope towards the settlement at the foot of the falls.

Aereon ate away the ground and the flat plain above came into view. The castle was the first thing to appear. Stamping its authority on the land. Coned turrets cornered its square walls.

Buildings spilled from beyond the walls. Nice buildings too.

As the river spread over the vast precipice, its waters thinned, and black rock jutted out of the calm water. Every rock had its own building, or more. All connected by a labyrinth of wooden walkways.

His feet took him to a platform at the end of the water. As he approached it looked like the end of the world, but at the edge the land below could be glimpsed through the great smog the falls created. His eyes followed the river as it stretched out into the distance. It seemed to know where it was going, but didn't care too much about how it got there. The blue twisted and wound through the green until Aereon lost sight of it in the hills below.

The town below was in stark contrast. The realm above sapped all the wonder from the land and drained everything it did not desire over the falls. The mist covered everything and everyone in little dank droplets.

'We've come to the right place.'

'Are you sure?' grumbled Silvor, who's beard was plastered to his face.

'Yes. This is the right place. We just need to find the right person.'

'Who's that then?'

'I'm not sure yet,' Volris conceded. 'An upstart, certainly. In all probability, he will come to us. Best thing for us to do is find a place where we'll get noticed. What we need is somewhere people gather. The more people see us, the quicker word will spread to our mystery man. Or woman, of course. Let's not rule that out.'

'Surely there is a centre to all this rabble,' stated Silvor, pointing out a few buildings that had loomed out of the fog.

'There will be pubs and taverns, but we need something bigger. We need somewhere we'll stand out like a sore thumb. We both know that dwarves blend into taverns like an octopus in paella.'

'What then?'

'I don't know. We need a...' Volris waved his hands about, just as raised voices started to echo through the thick air, a stall appeared ahead, '... market.'

'Apples? Check. Pears? Check. Plums? Check. Garlic necklaces? Check. Tea leaves? Check. Ornamental elephant book ends? Check. Terrifying dolls that look at me no matter where I stand? Check. Horse shoes? Check. Pigs' ears? Check. Bird feeders? Check. Bird feed? Check. String to attach to birds so they cannot fly away? Check. Flowers? Check. Scarves? Check. Lizards to control fly infestation? Check. Curtains? Check. Carpets? Check. Cats to scratch curtains and carpets? Check.'

Lurdic vob Pooshwiggle was particularly chuffed with that last one. The castle was already choc-a-block with cats. In fact, you couldn't swing a cat without hitting two more, but those ones didn't have a little sign in front of them reading *perfect for eating your neighbour's birds and lizards*.

Today was the first time Lurdic had been invited to the Oxfort market. Fifteen years he'd been selling on the doorstep. He was an outsider, a foreigner, and despite Huranland's very liberal attitudes, he could not shake the feeling that it had counted against him. Here he was though, his day had finally come and he was determined it would be a success. He looked over his cart and challenged anyone to do the same and not find something they needed.

Feeling quite good, he tilted the cart off its legs and pushed it along. The squint wheels bounced along the cobbles as he went.

Aereon found himself deeper and deeper within the city. The buildings were denser. Stone bridges had been built to allow for more ground to build on, but pleasant arches curved between the stones to allow water to flow beneath.

He was making his way in the general direction of Oxfort's gates, but he wasn't in a huge hurry. Would it really be worth missing all this culture just so the Creators would have twenty fingers between them when he arrived, rather than seventeen?

Of all the places Aereon had been since he left Krank. This one seemed to smack him in the face more than anywhere. Speaking strictly figuratively, the dwarves had done quite a bit of the literal sort.

Brightly dressed people walked by him in loosely fitting clothes. Many wore impressive headgear and bore intricate paints on their faces. Hair came in all shapes, sizes and colours. So, did the people.

Some were absolutely enormous. He passed one man, sitting and fanning himself, and he doubted the man could get back up.

There were slim people as well. Tall people. Short people. Strong people.

Skin colour was less of a monopoly too. Back home everyone had a base coating of sun and dirt. The people of

Hudikvar were pale with a clear quality to their skin. Here people shone golden brown or sported vast networks of freckles, others' skin offered a dark refuge to the noon sun.

The magnificent people were joined by animals. Monkeys leapt from beggars' sides to perform unwitting transactions. Birds of every shape and colour rested on merchants' shoulders and clamped their bills onto coins to determine their authenticity. Great cats strolled behind their powerful owners and commanded respectful space in the crowded streets. A spotted yellow one, sniffed at his hand as it passed, but Aereon moved a whole walkway away to avoid a black-striped orange beast.

No one challenged him as he made his way to the front of Oxfort. Outside its gates there did seem to be a bit of a party waiting. Thirty guards, or so, but they seemed at ease. People were walking in and out the gate without much fuss. There didn't seem to be anything to it.

On his approach, he found his eyes wandered to the foundations. The structures were thick. Built to reinforce the bedrock of stone the walls had been raised upon, but the entire structure was porous. The river made its way beneath Oxfort and cascaded out the other side. If it weren't for the metal bars the castle might have given the impression that it was floating above the river.

Most of the guards were leaning against the open gates or propping themselves up on their weapons. Aereon smiled to the people exiting the walls and positioned himself behind a group making their way in.

Two guards stood up straight and cast a vacant look across people before allowing them to pass. The eclectic group ahead of Aereon shuffled inside, their slippered feet flicked over the flagstones.

Aereon's pleasant smile was harshly put to an end by two spears, which came down to block his path. Both wielders looked down at him sternly.

'Yes, hello. I'd like to get inside please.'

'Move along, Meanderfall,' spat one.

'Come on, you know the law,' said the other.

Aereon's mouth hung open below his quizzical eyebrows, but he worked out that it was probably better to act as though he did know the rules. 'Yes… uh… sorry.'

Aereon turned on his heel. Time for a rethink and, if possible, find out what in the world a Meanderfall was.

Volris and Silvor had approached the stalls and pointed at things. They hadn't said a word to anyone and no one had spoken to them. Volris was not panicked. He knew that just meant the right person had not been alerted to their presence yet. Silvor was less confident. If he had his way, they would have grappled halfway up the cliff by now.

Volris was standing in the middle of the market and trying to look lost, but nobody seemed to be biting.

The dwarves retreated to the edge of the market and Volris stuck his hands on his hips.

'Should we try somewhere else?' ventured Silvor.

'This should be our best bet. I don't understand why –'

'That's a fancy axe you got there, mister.'

The dwarves turned to the boy standing next to them. Much of his face was covered by a mop of black hair, which had tried to be contained by an overburdened brown flat-cap. He was looking down at Silvor's axe, which had somehow found its way off the dwarf's belt and into the boy's hands.

'Hey!' barked Silvor, snatching it back.

'Sorry mister. Din't realise it was a sacred axe. How bouts that hammer? That goan fall ti bits ifs I hold it?'

Volris was smiling when he unclipped his weapon and handed it to the boy.

'Otcha! That's got a bit o' weight ti it. Take a man's 'ead clean off I reckons. Wotchas doin' 'ere? Never seen dwarves in these parts.'

'Is there somewhere we can talk?' asked Volris.

'We's talkin' now,' said the boy.

'I was meaning somewhere that we can speak more privately.'

'Sounds like you twos is up to no goods. I wants no parts in it if that's the case.'

'Oh, right,' said Volris, matter of factly. 'You better be going then. I thought you looked like an adventurous individual. Someone who might know a way of getting into Oxfort without being seen? Obviously, I have misjudged you.'

The boy ruffled his hair and fiddled with his cap. 'Ain't easy,' he said finally and quietly.

'I wouldn't expect it to be,' said Volris. 'Otherwise everyone would do it.'

'Foller me.'

The dwarves disappeared into the mist, away from the market, towards the roar of the water.

Whereas the river above the falls was slow and blue, here it was fast and brown. They followed the turbulent waters upstream until they reached the monstrous plunge pool. Their guide stopped in front of the waters. He was only a few strides ahead, but he was shrouded in mist.

'You sure you's wantin' to do this?' the boy almost shouted.

Volris nodded, although a small issue was waving its flag in the recesses of his brain.

'We need to swim across. There's a cave at the other side that will lead us inside the rock.'

The issue started blowing trumpets.

'How far is it across?' asked Silvor.

'A fair swim. Twen'y minutes or so.'

Symbols smashed together inside Volris's head.

'Are yous two ready?'

'Um… Now, don't get me wrong here,' began Volris, 'dwarves can swim. We can definitely move through water laterally. However, we have a habit of moving vertically as well.'

'I see. How long can you hold your breath fir?'

'Not twenty minutes.'

'What do you mean he's gone?'

'He left first thing this morning. He said something about it being a big day.'

'It is a big day,' complained Lurdic. 'It's my big day. *Our* big day. We've been talking about it for weeks.'

'I'm sorry,' said the woman. 'You know how uncontrollable he can be. Most of the time he's here he just sits in his room, doing god knows what. Half the time he isn't even here. He's out doing god knows what.'

'What am I supposed to do?' moaned Lurdic. 'If I show up to the market without a worker I'll never get asked back.'

'I tried to explain to him this morning, but he was adamant. You know how stubborn he gets. I suppose this means he's fired?'

Lurdic crumpled his face. 'When he's actually there, he's the hardest worker I've ever had. But, some days he doesn't even turn up for the market out here. The boy certainly is a maverick. Don't tell him he's fired, but I will be having words with him tonight.'

'Yes, as will I. And sorry again.'

'Not your fault, Barabara.'

Lurdic picked up his cart and continued to wind his way towards Oxfort.

Aereon couldn't get his head around what had gone wrong. He watched from a distance as everyone else was permitted to walk freely in and out the gates. He was sure that if the guards had suspected he was part of the party who had caused the trouble in Weed they would have arrested him on sight, but they hadn't. What exactly was it about him that had made him so objectionable?

His feet scuffed off the stones as he started making his way across the walkways. Now he thought about it, the people in general were giving him funny looks.

Aereon looked down at himself. His adventures had come at a price. He'd crossed seas, climbed mountains, been on the losing end of a few scuffles, the brambles and twigs of the forest had had their way with his clothes too. Tears and rips littered his shirt and trousers. One of his pockets had a hole in the bottom, he had no idea how that had happened. Back in Krank he never would have let this happen. His clothes were always clean. So was he for that matter. Other than rains and the odd splash on the face Aereon hadn't washed since he'd left. He shuddered at the thought.

Home seemed a distant memory. He had to remind himself to think about what he'd left behind. He supposed one of the reasons his mind might be trying to block it out was because of all the stuff he was going to have to deal with when he got back. He had not left on the best terms. In fact, he'd stolen Krank's floyancy, the one that had been constructed to benefit the people. Another floyancy was in construction at the time at least. Still, the Queen was not happy. Technically she had banished him.

He hadn't even had a chance to say goodbye to his parents before he left. He did feel bad about that, but with the Queen chasing him down, there had been no time. It would be forgiven though, eventually. They were his parents after all, they had to do that sort of thing.

Who knows how Juta will have reacted. He did say that he wanted some space from his father and the fishing industry but would Juta really thank him when he was having to deal with the royals on a daily basis and all that pressure Aereon had left him.

Perhaps Juta wouldn't have coped. Maybe they'd all be dead. What then? Simply carve a life out of the ruins with two dwarves and the Creators for company?

No one was dead. He trusted Queen Arburella to keep herself alive. And he trusted her to keep her subjects alive too. She may not have liked them, but she couldn't live her lifestyle without them. He trusted her to explain the price of failure to Juta. He'd understand that they would all die, but he might not fully grasp how slow his death would be.

More than anything, he trusted Lirna. She had said she was going to wait for him so that is what she would do. The two of them had a connection. No matter what that old crone had said.

Aereon swung his foot at a pip of some exotic fruit which bounced further than he expected and struck, loudly, into the side of an oncoming cart.

'Watch it!'

'Sorry, sir. I'll be more careful,' said Aereon.

'Yes, well, you just better.'

Aereon mumbled another apology as he went by. Lurdic shook his head and picked the handles back up.

A thought occurred to him. 'Hey kid, wait!'

'What's all this then?' asked Silvor.

'It's a load of logs,' confirmed his brother.

'They come over the falls,' continued the boy. 'Them that don't get washed away end up here.'

The dwarves looked down at the pale wood bobbing in a slow spiral within the calm pool.

'Do you have summin useful in all those pouches, like some rope?'

Volris pulled out his rope from a pocket at the rear of his belt.

'This'll do. Help me line 'em up.'

The dwarves did not completely grasp the concept of a raft, but as logs were tied together and the structure's weight capacity increased, they seemed to get to grips with it.

'What's your name?' asked Volris, as he passed another piece of wood.

'Blade,' said the boy.

'*Blade?*' scoffed Silvor.

'Yes,' said Blade.

'Your mother calls you Blade?' questioned Silvor.

'My mother's deed,' said Blade.

Dwarves do not have mothers themselves and therefore do not grasp the gravity of statements like that.

'Well what did she call you?'

'I don't know, never met her.'

Silvor gave him a look, 'How do you know you're called Blade then? Who said that was your name? Who told you?'

'I don't know. Do you remember who first named you Silvor?'

'My Thane named me.'

'All I know, is I've always been called Blade.'

'That's not all you know,' said Volris. 'You knew his name was Silvor.'

Blade finished the knot he was working on, 'Oh that. I jus' over'erd you two talking earlier.'

'I see,' said Volris. 'In that case you'll know my name is…'

'Volris,' said Blade.

'Exactly.'

'Are you two ready to climb on?'

The dwarves negotiated themselves onto the raft. Blade pushed them away from the bank with a conveniently long plank. Volris picked up one for himself and began to paddle. Silvor, found his axe worked a treat.

The raft drifted into the mist and towards the roar of the falls.

Within moments they were completely soaked.

They struggled against the waves as they closed in on the waterfall. They couldn't see it, the dwarves were particularly impaired as their thick eyelashes were sticking together, but they could feel it and they could hear it. The mist did not part or thin, but all of a sudden, the wall of water loomed.

Blade guided them along it until a small gap in the curtain showed. It was a struggle to keep the thing straight and Volris feared it may start to fall apart, but the kid knew his knots.

On the inside, it was even louder. Blade steered them to the cliff where he found a suitable hole in the rock to tie the raft.

'Do You Have Any More Rope?'

Silvor handed Blade his length of rope.

'Your Hammer, Please.'

Volris handed Blade his hammer.

'The Cave Entrance Is Thirty Feet Down,' shouted Blade as he began attaching the rope to the hammer. 'The Rope Won't Reach That Far, So Make Sure You Hold On To It And Keep It In Sight. I'll See You Down There.'

Blade dove in with the hammer and disappeared instantly.

Silvor tapped his brother on the shoulder. 'I DON'T THINK I MENTIONED YOUR NAME SINCE WE'VE BEEN HERE!'

The rope started to unravel on the raft.

'I KNOW! I HAVEN'T MENTIONED YOURS EITHER!' replied Volris.

Dwarves really are fantastic shouters.

'HOW DID HE KNOW THEN?'

'I DON'T KNOW!'

Volris grabbed hold of the rope and vanished with a splash.

'This is ridiculous. I *look* ridiculous!'

'Nonsense, you'll be fine,' said Lurdic. He smiled at passers-by as he held up one of his carpets as a screen, in front of a wall.

'I will not be fine. I'm in a skirt! Worse than that, if the

297

breeze catches it right you'll be able to see all the way up my leg. I really wish you'd let me wear my trousers underneath.'

Lurdic looked down at Aereon's heap of wafting clothes on the floor, suspicious they might begin to crawl away. 'No,' he said firmly.

Aereon sighed, 'Alright, fine. I'm ready.'

Lurdic lowered the delightful fabric.

The first thing he saw was big and it was purple. As the screen dropped the turban became clear, just above Aereon's miserable mug.

A silk scarf had been elegantly draped over his neck, but other than that, there was nothing covering this torso.

A coarser selection of scarves had been used like lappets to make the skirt. Aereon had folded them in half and tucked them into his underpants. They covered his knees, but when he moved his skinny thighs popped between them.

'They're never going to let me in looking like this!'

He did look peculiar, Lurdic agreed silently. He'd probably get laughs, but it was the looks of disgust it was important to avoid. 'You look zippy. You fit right in.'

'I'm covered in dirt,' complained Aereon. 'At least my clothes hid most of it.'

Lurdic couldn't argue with that. He took another glance at Aereon's clothes. 'It's fine. It makes you look tanned. Give me those,' said Lurdic, snatching Aereon's fermented sock stuffed boots. 'Here, put these on.'

Aereon took the sandals and slipped them onto his feet.

'Good, now come here and take the cart. I have got to give the right impression.'

Lurdic marched towards Oxfort with one arm folded across his belly and the other swinging loosely at his side. The wheels of the cart rattled behind him as Aereon pushed it along.

A guard at the gate halted them.

'Merchant's name?' he asked.

'Lurdic vob Pooshwiggle.'

The guard consulted his list, 'License.'

Lurdic produced a card from the recesses of his toga breast.

'Just the one worker?' asked the guard.

Lurdic swallowed some words. 'For now, yes. You've got to start somewhere, right?'

'Oh, indeed,' said the guard. 'Fine day for it too.'

'Oh, yes,' said Lurdic. He gestured to Aereon, but the guard's hand was planted on the kart.

'Of course, that's assuming you enjoy the heat,' the guard continued. 'Personally, I like things a little cooler.' Lurdic smiled weakly. 'It's days like this when you really need to keep hydrated. Liquids are good, but I've always been partial to fruit.' The guard's eyes locked with Lurdic's.

He understood. A few of his associates had come across this sort of thing. Their advice had been to pay up in exchange for safe passage. Lurdic wouldn't stand for it. This was *his* merchandise and it wasn't for sale.

'Yes, always important to keep hydrated,' he said. 'You must be very lucky to have the river so close to your place of work.'

'Yes, that is true,' said the guard, scratching his chin. He'd dealt with first timer's before, sometimes they missed his subtle approach. He tried again. 'Those plums look good. Very refreshing are plums.'

'Oh yes,' said Lurdic. 'They are the best money can buy. I pick them myself.'

Both guard and merchant stared. It was a long stare. Aereon's eyes shifted between the two, wondering who would blink first.

'How much are they?'

'Five pence per fruit.'

'I'll take one,' said the guard.

'Certainly, sir. Are you sure you wouldn't like to buy some for your fellow guards?'

'Don't push it, Pooshwiggle.'

When the transaction was complete the guard waved them through with juices dribbling down his chin. No one even looked at Aereon.

Dwarves are well suited to the dark. Volris liked to think he could also handle all types of weather, but water was something different. Rain he could handle, but being surrounded by nothing but water was not an experience dwarves were used to. The black seemed more crushing when experienced through dulled senses. It wasn't that dwarves were claustrophobic, they weren't. You wouldn't survive in the mines if you were.

He sank like a stone, no bottom in sight. That was the scary part. Not the drowning. Drowning was like suffocating in many ways, and he'd experienced that deep in the mountains. It was the falling. Not the hitting part either. Climbing up mountains there was always a risk of a fall. On the mountain, a fall was always followed by an impact. In the water though, he didn't understand. He could fall for ever. Never seeing another soul and no soul ever seeing him. The loneliness in the black.

Volris reached forward and pulled himself down the rope.

Something below caught a sliver of light. He shifted his weight and fell into the cave mouth. He landed on the rocks next to his hammer.

He tucked his weapon into his belt and looked up. A pale light trickled down through the water. He grasped the wall and started to climb.

He'd scaled mountains that pierced through the tallest clouds, but dwarves were very well adapted to extracting oxygen from thin air. They were simply useless at getting any out of water.

With every reach his arms ached more. With every pull the glow on the rocks increased. Above him he could see the ripple of the surface.

His head breached and Volris sucked in as much of the cave's stale air as he could.

He dragged himself up onto the slippery rock and tugged at the rope.

The rope went tight. Volris reached forward and pulled up again. His arms were white hot. Still he heaved hand over fist at the rope.

Silvor erupted from the pool, huffing and panting.

'Well done,' said Blade. 'Very well done.' He was on a landing above them, next to a stash of torches. He held one aloft and illuminated the cave. 'When you're ready.'

Aereon thought outside was bizarre. Inside was a circus.

Not just the animals either. The people were, if anything, even more colourful and more of them per square foot. More of them per cubed foot as well. Children sat on shoulders or ran through people's legs, nobody seemed to mind, it was all just part of the experience.

Smells concocted into a rich and confusing blend. Aereon couldn't place any of it and he wasn't sure if he enjoyed the overall combination. You couldn't ignore it though, he'd say that much for it.

He pushed the cart through the streams of people that quickly became a rabble.

Lurdic was leading him towards the densest mass and noise.

The merchant shooed people away and told Aereon to park.

Lurdic pulled levers, which unveiled compartments and drawers filled with merchandise. He kicked the side of the cart and a parasol sprang out and unfolded itself. He busied himself shifting various products, making sure everything looked just right.

'The market looks as though it's been going on for some time,' said Aereon.

'Hmm? Oh yes, since this morning.'

'How come you're only just getting here?' said Aereon as he fixed a few of the flower heads so that they looked their best.

'The market always starts at sun up. But those of us who do not have permanent stalls within the walls are only ever offered half days. I drew the afternoon slot. Now, come on, are you ready to start selling?'

'What? No. I don't know what anything costs, nothing is priced.'

'Well, nothing we sell is priced,' said Lurdic, stroking a kitten. 'It's the customers that are priced.'

'What?'

'Everybody has their own price they are willing to pay for

this geranium for example. Our job is to find the right person. Ideally you want someone with a blank look of wonder, with just a hint of confusion. Yip, that's the one. You'll be fine. I'll show you the ropes. Lesson one: keep your voice level and clear at all times. Roll Up! Roll Up! You Need It! We've Got It!'

It was a dank little tunnel. The walls were slippery and their feet were wet, but the dwarves were feeling quite at home. Slowly they were shaking off the ordeals of the water. It had been a long time since they'd been in a cave system. It was comforting.

They bore deeper into the rock, always on the rise. Occasionally Silvor's rope was taken out to traverse a particularly steep and sheer section, but it was mostly a simple climb. In truth, they didn't really need the rope. The dwarves had been climbing for the best part of a century, but thought it would be polite to offer Blade assistance. And Blade had made this passage a hundred times, but thought it would be impolite to refuse, especially since he felt the dwarves were probably just making the suggestion because they themselves needed the security of the rope.

Dwarves know a lot about caves. They know when they've been formed at the hands of dwarves, can spot the inconsistencies of men's work, easily know when water has grinded its way through stone, detect the scars left by ice that has cracked away the insides of rock over time, or realise the signs left by ice that has cracked its way through the rock in the hands of a yeti. Walls told stories.

Volris suspected the cave was not the only thing that was not what it seemed. This Blade character was not entirely who he had been expecting. When the boy straight out of teuchter-ville had shown up he'd thought things seemed about right. A little scampering sprog, who knew the ins and outs of a mighty castle. That was how these things were supposed to go. That had a touch of the fairy tale to it.

Blade had slipped up though, and now Volris was on red alert. A common dwarvish phrase ever since some hapless miner struck magma.

'How long did you say you had been following us?' he asked, in a conversational tone.

'Just a few minutes,' said Blade, without turning.

'How did you know we were in whatever that town was called?'

'Oh, you know, word travels pretty quick when there are dwarves afoot. You're not exactly common around here. And it's called Gredol. Although, the topsides call it Meanderfall.'

'Why?' asked Volris. He wasn't particularly curious, but he wanted to keep Blade talking. Keep him talking until there wasn't a shadow of a doubt. Until there was nothing for him to hide behind.

'We're currently making our way up the Meanderfalls. So called because they occur in the Juta's lower course. The topsides use the falls as a way to look down on those below. They call those who live beneath the torrent Meanderfalls. They spit the word.'

Volris was hugely interested in culture. Particular that of other races. Back in Oth-Rodin and Oth-Zorak, he'd read as many tomes on men as had been available. Their class systems had always amazed him. In dwarf society it was simple: the oldest dwarf of the Oth, the Thane, was the leader. When he moved on to settle, the next oldest was in charge.

Within the mountain everyone was given a chance at what humans would call royalty. Until only the very last dwarf remained, and he was usually hugely respected by dwarves of other Oths just by being.

'I cannot help but notice,' he began, 'that your accent has changed.'

'Oi ey. This accent Oi've got 'ere guvna?'

'That's the one.'

'We're getting close to Oxfort, an accent like that wouldn't do up there. As I say, they frown upon Meanderfalls. They are not allowed within the castle.

'Where are you from?' asked Silvor.

'Dwarves are renowned for their silence and discretion,' ensured Volris.

'Ok, my name is not really Blade.'

'Shocking.'

'It's true. And I'm not technically from below the falls. I spend a lot of my time there though. I find the people are more honest.'

'A bunch of bare faced liars up top, are they?'

'That's not what I mean. The people are a lie. That's what I'm saying, I think. Down below everything is simpler, the people know who they are and they know what they like. Say what you like for the wonders up there, the people down below live twice as much.'

'Is that not a little backwards?' asked Silvor, who sort of understood the basics of human society. 'Shouldn't they be trying to become more like you, rather than the other way around?'

'So, the poor can strive to climb the social ladder, but those better off can't take the chute back down? You're elitist, you are.'

'So, if you're not Blade from Gredol, who are you?'

'What do you care? I'm the guy who's helping you. I could be the King of all of Huranland for all it matters.'

Market was hoaching. Aereon had to admit, he was thankful for the flow of air across his legs even if it did reveal them in all their pasty white splendour.

He had taken to mercantile like a cuckoo to a nest. Things were going so well that Lurdic had given himself a little break.

Aereon didn't know how long he'd been gone. Time was consumed by the cart. By the haggle. By the sale. From behind the stall Aereon distributed everything. People coming for birdfeed to attract birds left with birdfeed, bird feeders and cats to control their new bird infestation.

Lurdic returned with his moustache covered in some sort of orange sauce that clashed spectacularly with his purple side burns.

'How are sales?' he asked, wiping his face and drumming his stomach.

'Good. Offloaded a few more cats.'

'Keep it up, I might just have to employ you on a more permanent basis. Even if you are a Meanderfall. No offence meant.'

'Ah ha, none taken,' said Aereon, who was yet to get to the bottom of that little mystery.

'Here,' Lurdic picked out a few coins from the profits Aereon had earned him, 'it's your first time in Oxfort, right?' Aereon nodded and Lurdic slapped the coins into his hand. 'Take this and enjoy the market. Get yourself some food, it doesn't much matter what, it's all good. There are a few touristy things to do. I'm sure they'll find you.'

'Thank you. I'll be back soon.'

'Take your time.'

Aereon could smell food. Where the smells got stronger, so did the crowds. He moved away from the centre of the market in search of a quieter place where he could find himself something to eat.

The last row was against a wall of houses. The bazaar reminded Aereon of home. In Krank people often collapsed walls to turn their homes into stalls, here things seemed a little more thought through, with counters and display cabinets, but the principle was the same.

The smells were here too. Aereon's new sandals flopped across the flagstones as his nose pointed and his stomach pulled him towards it.

''ello, little one.'

Aereon's feet scuffed to a halt. He looked around over his shoulders. Nobody seemed to be paying him much attention.

'Yes you.'

There was a space between two houses, Aereon was sure the voice had come from there.

'Come closer.'

It was only a whisper, but he could hear it clearly over the bustle of the market. He took a few steps through people and entered the alley.

The roofs above kept the light dim, but he could just make out a banner draped between the two walls.

The Three Hags

The sound behind him faded, as though he was underwater.

Below the sign were a table and stool. He sat down.

'What'll it be?' a pair of long hands appeared in front of Aereon, one was holding a deck. 'A game of cards?' One card at a time, the deck flew from one hand to the other.

'Or wid ya like to know yir fortune?' A hand to Aereon's left placed a stack of cards on the table.

A third pair of hands, to Aereon's right, fanned out another set of cards. 'Or, will it be a magic trick you seek?'

Aereon looked at the three decks, but his mind was on the voices. There was something familiar about them. 'How much do they cost?'

There was a cackling from all three, clearly some sort of an inside joke.

'The fortune's twen'y cents per card.'

'A dollar for a trick.'

'An' whatever you've got to put on the table for cards.'

Aereon tried to look at where he thought their faces might be, but saw nothing. 'I do not have enough money for the fortune telling or the magic and I'd rather not waste what money I do have on a game of cards that I'll inevitably lose.'

'Oh, don't you worry about thats. I'm really bad at cards.'

'You've got a dollar and fifty-five cents on you, that's more than enough for a trick.'

'I am sorry, but I need my money for lunch and possibly a present if I can find one,' said Aereon.

'Oh, there's a girl!' the one on the right cooed.

'I'll give you a freebee then. How's that? On the house?' offered the fortune teller. The other two made approving noises.

Aereon thinned his eyes. 'You three wouldn't happen to be witches, would you?'

'Of course we is!' said the Dealer, somewhat offended. Her finger shot up towards the sign. 'What part of *The Three Hags* din't yer unnerstand?'

'I met one of your friends recently.'

'Did you?' asked the Trickster, curiously.

'Yes, in the Oak's Wood.'

'Oh, Jillian,' said the one in the middle.

'I don't think so,' said Aereon.

'Lives in a little cottage at the edge of the woods?'

'Yes.'

'That's her,' said the Dealer.

'Her name is Jillian?'

'Yes.'

'*Jillian?*' exclaimed Aereon.

'How is the old bat?'

'Not so old, last time I saw her.'

'Oh, dear,' said the fortune teller. 'You didn't let her take anything from you, did you?'

'Not me, my friend.'

'What did she take?' asked the Dealer.

'His lust.'

Aereon heard three sharp inhales.

'Nasty thing for a man to lose.'

'How about that free fortune?'

Aereon's looked at the cards on the table. He could feel himself leaning forward, like an invisible force was sucking him in. He snapped himself back. 'No. No, I don't think so.'

He got to his feet. 'I need to go.'

The cards and the hands disappeared.

'We will see you again.'

The witches watched as Aereon stepped back into the

market street and disappeared.

'He's got a touch of destiny about him, that one,' said the Dealer.

'Aye. He's got a date with her, I'd say,' said the Trickster.

'And she's ordered the lobster,' said the Teller.

They could hear the gurgle of water entering the tunnel. One final corner and the cascading water appeared. Light danced across it as it fell. One by one, they climbed up and out the cave.

Blade had trained himself not to stand up, but if Silvor and Volris were any taller they would have hit their heads. They shuffled away from the mouth and slipped into deeper water. The Juta flowed all around them, interrupted here and there by rock and mortar. The floor of Oxfort rested above them.

'Come on, this way,' said Blade. 'Try not to make too much noise.'

The dwarves waded after the boy, who found the bag he had been looking for and started unbuttoning his shirt.

'Do you two mind?'

'Mind what?'

For dwarves, there was nothing on their person they would be embarrassed to show, other than their chin. Clothes were for protection, not hiding bits and bobs under.

'Averting your gaze,' said Blade. 'I need to get changed out of these clothes. They won't fit in up there.'

'Who are you?' asked Volris again.

'I'm incognito!'

'Hey, Volris, come look at this,' said Silvor.

Volris turned his back on Blade and joined his brother, who was standing in the bars of light, cast by a grate. 'What?'

'I can see up this woman's skirt.'

'So? What's it to you?' asked Volris.

As mentioned, dwarves are lacking in the finer points of what lurks under the clothes of other races. Dwarves' libido generally consists of drooling at the sight of steak done rare.

'I don't know,' said Silvor. 'Just a conversation point.'

Volris tilted his head and took another look. 'My goodness, those are the smoothest legs I've ever seen. That can't be natural, can it?'

'Why would they want to get rid of it though? Keeps you warm on cold nights does good leg hair,' said Silvor.

'To improve aerodynamics?' suggested Volris.

Behind them, Blade had pulled up his jade, sultan trousers and started buttoning half the buttons on an effortlessly baggy white shirt.

'Wait a minute,' said Volris, still looking up at the grate. 'That's Aereon.'

'Is it?'

'Yes, look.' Volris grabbed his brother's face and shifted it so he could see.

'So it is.'

Volris poked his finger up through the bars and pressed down on the foot.

'… Volris?'

'Yes!'

'What are you doing down there?'

'Coming to lend a helping hand.'

'I got in as a market worker,' said Aereon. 'I'm going to see if I can stay behind tonight. Once the place has quietened down a bit, I'll be able to have a look around. Why don't you two stay down there, while I figure out where they're keeping

311

Edin and Koel?'

Volris slapped his brother in the face. 'Yes. Good plan, we'll be waiting.'

'Brilliant, ok. I've got to go just now. Just finished my bur-ri-to. It was quite good actually. It's amazing the vegetarian options they have here. Got to get back to work. I'll be back later.'

'Bye,' said Volris.

Blade was dressed to impress. He'd added a pair of curled slippers and slicked back his hair.

'Well, well, well. Don't you look nice.'

'Thank you.'

'Where are ours?' asked Volris.

'I'm working on it. I think I should be able to throw something together,' he said, pulling more clothes out the bag. 'There are just one or two issues I need to sort out.'

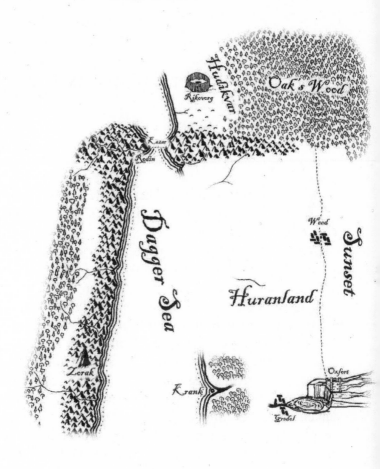

Moonrise

Sunrise

Sunset

Moonset

Huskvar

Oak's Wood

Rikoverg

Kazm

Bodin

Dagger Sea

Wood

Huranland

Zorak

Krank

Oxfort

Grodol

All is Right with the World

Another glorious day. The river was quiet. Hule sat in the front with sturdy axe lain across his lap and a smile on his face.

Ever since the first day Hule had been volunteered by Arburella and he'd come back looking like a dog with its head out the window, word had spread and now volunteers were lined up around the corner. A rota had been required so everyone had their turn. It had been a couple of days since Hule had left Krank; he was rested and ready.

Juta, the man in charge of the rota, sat behind him. He liked having the big man along. He was a hard worker and Juta had not forgotten that it was Hule who had rescued him from the sunken wreckage of the floyancy. Well he *had* forgotten, completely. Concussion will do that to a man, but he had not forgotten finding out that Hule had rescued him from the sunken wreckage of the floyancy.

Juta's paddle found the water and pushed the floyancy upstream. If there was one drawback of having Hule in the front it was that Juta had to lean quite far over the edge before his paddle found river.

The novelty had not worn off and crowds still gathered to

see them off. Juta left from the Sunrise point, as he did every day. After the first couple days, he'd made the decision to continue exploring the Moonset bank. It had provided food, such as boar and bison, resources, like nice big trees, and interesting things that Codrich was convinced should have one floppy ear and love their belly being rubbed. The wolves in the area were not yet aware of this.

Even on a calm day the river was a handful. Again, having Hule at the front did not help, but Juta carved their way upstream and ploughed the floyancy onto the bank.

Hule hopped out and dragged the craft up the beach. Clutching his axe, the great man jogged off to the forest. He passed a man burdened with a sack. Hule scarcely seemed to notice, he'd found a new passion in chopping things.

'Morning, Juta.'

'Good morning, Denn.'

'Lovely day for it, isn't it?' said Denn, studying the sky and the land.

'It sure is. Is that from last night?'

'Yes. Another successful catch.'

Less than a week ago, Denn had stood in a loop of rope that was thinly hidden in the sand outside his house. The rope had constrained around his ankle and he'd fallen on his face. He couldn't really be angry, he'd put it there. That'd been a few weeks ago, when things had looked very shaky on Krank. Before Juta's recovery. Before the floyancy had been unveiled in all its glory. Finally, what was promised, a device for the benefit of all in Krank. So, Denn had dug up his traps, obviously he'd missed one. After the initial embarrassment, it'd turned out for the better. A little modification and he had an idea both King and Queen agreed was a good one. A very rare thing, indeed. Now, Denn was the first out on the floyancy almost every morning.

'What've you got?'

'Some of those grey bouncy thingies, a handful of those tree grey bouncy thingies and one of those ones that looks like a tube on legs.'

Juta returned the floyancy to the Juta. 'Excellent. Traps reset?'

'Yes.'

'Well, would you like to jump in?'

'I think, if it's alright, I would prefer to stay here for a little while.'

Juta supposed there was no harm in him staying across a little longer. 'Sure, fine. Just toss the sack in then.'

He'd only just set off when heard Hule roar, '*Timber!*' somewhere off behind him.

'I'll take that,' boomed Codrich, snatching the sack from the hull. Behind him, a goring of butchers were eagerly awaiting their rations. 'Yes, yes,' said Codrich, slapping their fingers away. 'Just wait your turn.'

The rest of the morning was primarily concerned with taking more people out, but as the afternoon wore on Juta was forced to start pulling people away from the new-found land. Codrich had a firm rule that everyone must be back on Krank before sunset.

The floyancy landed for the last time and those on the beach clapped Juta home. The King was there again and he grabbed Juta's arm and yanked him to his feet. Codrich enveloped the boy and ruffled his hair.

'Another success.'

The King took Juta's shoulder and wheeled him away from the beach. Behind them, the Queen had overseen the hoisting of the floyancy by two of her loyal servants and was shadowing them all into Krank. Every night the floyancy was taken down into the outhouse and put under guard.

Juta was led into the Royal Abode and offered something to eat. It was small and cold, and he was not given a seat, but simply to be invited inside was a great honour.

Codrich extracted a skinned squirrel from his pocket and skewered it over the fire. Arburella had resumed her usual seat in the corner and the King plonked himself down at the table.

'So,' he began, 'how do you think things are going?'

'Good,' replied Juta. 'Very good.'

'I agree, but are there no improvements to be made?'

'Not that I can think of, sire. Everyone is operating at maximum efficiency.'

'Very well,' said the King.

Arburella rolled her eyes. She was disappointed with Juta. She had previously hoped that with a little effort he might make a very nice lackey. She felt she'd done her part. Let's not forget it was her who had encouraged Juta to finish the floyancy, with a few threats and just a hint of what one might call unconventional encouragement. Now Juta was getting all the praise for it. She was not bothered by that. What bothered her was that she had received nothing for her efforts. Even a *thank you* from Juta would have been something to work with, but he hadn't even given her that. Ungrateful sod that he was. Ok, fine, so he'd gotten a little charred here and there, but that was nothing compared to the admiration he was receiving now. If anything, the scars added to it all. Was it fair that she should lose out just because she had pushed him?

The King's new-found joy for Juta was not helping matters either. As long as he was getting a steady food supply, he was happy to just sit and let Juta get on with it. Which meant it was up to her to probe a little deeper.

'Are you *sure* that there is no way to improve things?'

The two boys looked at her. Everyone reverted to children when Arburella adopted that tone.

'I suppose another paddle would help,' Juta said, slowly. 'Mostly for when I am going upstream. It takes very little effort at all coming back, but if my passengers helped paddle when we travel to the Moonset shore it might help speed things up and enable me to ferry more people.'

A reasonable suggestion. 'Anything else?' she asked.

Juta scratched his head where the hair no longer grew. 'I suppose it is a bit inconvenient that we have to cut the wood so much before we are able to load it into the floyancy. There are many houses which need long panels after materials for the three floyancies were given up, but all we can bring back are logs that can be used for fire or patchwork at best.'

Another valued point. No hint of a solution though. With the King's current good mood, Juta would probably get away with that slander.

'I suppose we could get started with that second paddle for now,' said the King. 'You can get started on that tomorrow.'

Juta worked a six-day week. Through the King's good will, he was allowed custody of the floyancy for the seventh, to do with as he pleased. He had plans. 'I am out tomorrow, I'm afraid, sire.'

Fool, thought Arburella. You ignorant fool. The tide will change. Aereon knew better than to have plans when it was inconvenient to the crown.

'Oh, yes of course,' said Codrich. 'I shall send for one of the carpenters tonight, he can take measurements and get started on the rough shape tomorrow.'

You're an ignorant fool as well.

'Thank you, sire.'

'Well, I think that's all for tonight,' said Codrich. 'Run along.'

Yes, run along, Juta. Make the most of those legs.

Juta was lying on his back, snoring softly, with his feet dangling over the edge of his bed.

He had an amazing sense of time. It had been built into him over the years by his father, who had a strict philosophy of the early bird catches the worm which in turn catches the fish. Before Juta had started working with the floyancy, his father had been adamant that he would join the family business of angling. Every morning, at the crack of dawn, he'd wake his son up with a sharp prod in the ribs.

At the crack of dawn, Juta opened his eyes. Legs flung over the side of the mattress and his feet slapped the ground. He put his elbows on his knees and rubbed his face. The burn wasn't painful anymore, but it was still tender and hot. His fingertips slipped over mottled skin.

Krank was not naturally an early rising nation, so Juta was alone in the young mist.

He quite enjoyed being alone. He enjoyed people too, but there were times when solitude had its attractions. Like getting yourself psyched up for a big day. He was not in a rush, he'd woken himself up early, specifically so he had enough time to get himself worked up to a nervous wreck and then pass straight through to the other side by the time the day properly started.

He was feeling quite calm again when he found Hule outside the outhouse, looking formidable.

'Morning, sir. You here for floyancy?'

'I certainly am, Hule.'

'I go fetch for you.'

'Good man.'

Hule returned from the depths with the floyancy and dropped it onto the sand.

'You like me carry for you?'

Deductive reasoning. Arburella had Aereon to thank for that. Prior to a few choice comments from that menace, Hule would have happily received the order *stand guard here* and remained there until the next order came. Now though he was able to deduce that if the floyancy wasn't there; he didn't need to be either. It was a nuisance, Arburella didn't want her people thinking for themselves. That's what she was for.

'That would be great, thanks.'

'To Moonset beach, sir?'

'No, today I'll be leaving from the Moonrise shore.'

Hule was left to look after the floyancy. He may have only recently discovered his love of chopping, but standing with his arms crossed with important things behind him had long been high on his list as a good way to spend a day.

This was going to work. There was no reason why it shouldn't work. It was going to work, right?

Juta took a deep breath and knocked on the door.

It was Mr Hartilby who opened it.

'Uh, hello sir. I was wondering, is your daughter in?'

'Lirna! Someone to see you,' Lirna's father called, before

muttering, 'At least this one had the decency to knock.'

'Hey, Juta,' said Lirna, with her usual bounce.

'I was… um… er… wondering if you might like to… see I've got the floyancy… it's my day off today… to the Moonset bank… together… with me?'

'Sounds lovely,' she grabbed her shoes and stuffed her feet into them. 'Dad, I'm off out.'

Mr Hartilby didn't look up from his breakfast as the door shut.

'What, and I don't get a goodbye?'

Mr Hartilby froze, mid chomp. He looked across at his wife. Slowly he resumed chewing and swallowed. He could see Mrs Hartilby was upset. After eighteen years of marriage he'd got that down to a tee. He lifted his hand to her.

'Bacon?'

Maybe in another eighteen years he'd figure out what to do to fix the look. He took back the unappeasing bacon and bit off a chunk. The grease oozed across his mouth. That's what marriage was all about. Attrition.

'Ah, excellent work Hule,' bellowed Juta, noticing the floyancy was still present and in one piece.

'Tis my wheelhouse, sir.'

Juta didn't doubt the truth of that.

'Do you mind helping Lirna in so that she doesn't get wet?'

Hule pushed the floyancy into the water with one hand and hoisted Lirna inside with the other. Somehow, she even managed to make being manhandled by Hule look graceful, Juta waded into the water and climbed in behind her. Hule handed him the paddle.

'Are you excited?' Juta asked, once they were on their

way.

'Yes,' said Lirna.

'I just thought that it would be nice if we went to the Moonrise bank today.'

'I'm sure it will be very nice,' said Lirna.

'Just think, we could be the first two people ever to see it.'

'Yes,' said Lirna.

Juta smiled at the back of her head. Things were going well.

Lirna quietly admitted to herself that there were some benefits to Juta. For one she hadn't been dragged out of bed at a ridiculous hour. She didn't have to paddle. And so far, she had not needed to provide one of her socks to plug a leak.

'I have sandwiches,' said Juta.

Presumably not vegetarian thought Lirna, whose animal rights movement had lasted less time than it takes to say "Mmmm, gravy".

The floyancy struck sand. Juta jumped out with a splash and pulled the bow up the beach. Lirna stepped out onto the sand and breathed in.

There was less salt here. On Krank, the two forces of the river and the sea colliding churned up a strong aroma. On the bank, the smell was still there, but it was a smell Krankians were used to. A smell they barely noticed anymore. What Lirna breathed in was the smell of the land. The rich smell of the earth. The delicate to pungent array of flower fragrance. She'd forgotten how much she enjoyed it here.

'Shall we go?' asked Juta.

'After you.'

Juta climbed the slow slope of the sand and splashed into the sea of grass. The glade was overflown with flowers, and

Lirna loved them all.

'Here's good,' said Lirna after a time.

Juta stopped and looked about. He supposed it was good. He removed the sandwiches from his pockets and sat himself down. He held one up for Lirna, but she wasn't paying attention. He watched her soft dress blow in the wind until she tucked it behind her legs and sat down. She plucked the offered sandwich from him and took a bite.

Juta didn't know what to say. He tried catching Lirna's eye in the hope that she might say something. In the end, he gave up and tried to enjoy his sandwich.

'What do you think of it out here?' asked Lirna, once she'd finished hers. 'Is it different from the Moonset side?'

Juta prematurely swallowed the bite he'd been working on and choked then coughed. 'It's more peaceful,' he answered, as soon as he could. 'It seems purer, in a way.' He thought about it a little more. 'It's hard to explain. Over there life seems to have more pressure on it. The animals feed on the plants or themselves, while the plants desperately regenerate to replenish themselves. Here there seems a bit more give and take. Like an equilibrium is in place. The plants grow, the bees and butterflies pollenate and little guys like that live off the shoot, but do not exploit the grasses.'

'Tingo!'

'Sorry?' asked Juta.

Lirna froze, but recovered well. 'He looks like a Tingo, is all.'

The so-called Tingo was grey, with floppy ears and fluffy white tail.

Juta assessed the situation well and decided it was probably best not to mention that something that had once looked very similar to Tingo had gone into her sandwich.

'I suppose he does look like a Tingo.'

Tingo's nose twitched as it picked up something promising. He took a few experimental bounces towards them.

'Juta, could you pass me a piece of your lettuce, please,' said Lirna quietly.

Juta did as he was told.

Tingo was practically on Lirna's feet. She tore a strip of lettuce from the leaf and offered it. The greenery did not dangle in the air for long. The rodent's teeth chattered enthusiastically.

The rabbit put its paws on Lirna's shin and looked up expectantly. She fed him another bit of lettuce. As Tingo chewed, she slipped her hand underneath him and scooped him up. He didn't seem to notice until he had finished munching. He looked around curiously, but then his eyes fixed on the foliage again and he remembered what was really important.

Lirna gave him the rest.

'Oh, I wish I could keep him.'

Juta had been watching the interaction intently. 'Why don't you?'

Lirna opened her mouth to explain, but then slowly shut it when she realised she didn't know how. 'I can keep him?'

Juta shrugged his shoulders. 'I don't see why not.'

They both turned to Tingo. He looked back. The lettuce was gone. He twitched his nose at them. Something was going on, he could feel it.

She placed him on the grass. 'Thanks Ju. I'll pick him up when we leave.'

Tingo took a few hops into the grass, but remained close to Lirna.

'Nobody has called me Ju since Aereon left.'

Juta could have bitten his tongue off. Stupid. Stupid. Stupid.

Lirna took a painfully long time to say anything. The silence was pregnant with possibilities. 'It's strange, Krank doesn't even seem to notice he's gone.'

'Do you miss him?'

What did you ask that for? Juta demanded of his brain.

Look, sunny Jim, you started us down this path, his brain retorted, I'm just trying to clean up your mess.

'Yes,' said Lirna.

It stung and Juta didn't have anything to say to it.

'It must be hard for you too,' continued Lirna. 'You two were good friends.'

'Yes, we were friends. Good friends I suppose,' said Juta. 'Very open to sharing things. He would share some of my things and I would share some of his things…'

Your level of tact astounds me.

Shut up!

'A little unfair of him to leave us here wasn't it,' said Lirna.

That's something we can work with. Keep her talking! shouted Juta's brain.

'I suppose you're right,' said Juta.

'It's all fine and well for him. He's off, out there, somewhere, having a great time of it and we're stuck here expected to sit and wait for him.'

Ask her if she is tired of sitting. Ask her if she is tired of sitting!

'Uh… are you tired of sitting?'

Lirna's eyes flicked up under her long lashes as she lifted her hand and felt Juta's scarred face. 'If it wasn't for him this never would have happened.'

'That's true. But if it hadn't happened then you wouldn't be touching my face just now.'

Oh, very good. I have to admit, that was smooth.

Lirna's head moved in a little.

And Juta's head moved in a little.

They both closed their eyes. Past the point of no return.

Lord Visma and Prince Elijah

It had been an interesting few days. Aereon had returned to the drain the first night, but the dwarves had gone. He wasn't surprised. He just hoped they didn't get themselves into too much trouble and if they did, he hoped trouble had something to shield itself with.

Lurdic's usual worker hadn't turned up, so Aereon had been asked to stay on. He didn't really have an excuse that wouldn't draw attention. Besides, he needed to eat.

He nodded to the guards as he entered Oxfort at sun up for another nosey around. They barely seemed to notice him. Aereon was pretty sure that back on Krank a man in a skirt on would draw a few stares. Nobody here seemed interested in him at all now he was clean. Well, almost nobody.

He strolled down the side of market. Many of the stalls were yet to arrive or were in mid setup. The smells were there though; you'd need an industrial cleaner to get rid of them.

'Fancy yer fortune t'day, laddie?'

The voice reached his ears like it was whispered from lips an inch away.

'No, thank you!' he told the alley. 'Every-blooming-time,' he mumbled to himself.

He followed his nose. It was not a very decisive nose. Turning this way and that. Leading his feet all over the place. They did not find the cobbles outside the prison, but eventually they found the wall overhanging the falls.

The wall was four times as thick as the other three and from what Aereon had been able to pick up on the grape vine it housed the royal apartments.

He walked under a great arch. The wind swept up his skirts, but he didn't notice. He was looking at the view.

He passed through the wall which opened onto a balcony. Swifts darted up and around the roaring mists. Aereon stepped close to the edge.

The platform was held in place by a rock that strutted out, defiantly, from the falls.

He watched the birds hunting for flies. Finding prison cells seemed meaningless in comparison.

He shook himself from the daze and stepped back.

There was plaque attached to the railing at the head of the platform. Aereon began to read.

The underbelly of the palace was well into its flow by early-morning. Lord Visma had been up for several hours, most of the night, in fact. He was one of those people who seemed to live on an hour of sleep a day.

He was on his way to the kitchens. An interesting place for information to lurk, but it certainly did. The chefs and servers were remarkably perceptive though. Intruders in the kitchen were quickly shown the door, especially if they were feline. Visma was light on his feet, so if he had time, he might gather a morsel of information, but he didn't have time for all that today. In any case, not all his eyes and ears were attached to his head.

He glided into the kitchen and quickly found the serving platter. He lifted the silver cover and inspected underneath. Everything seemed to be in order.

Visma was a tall man, even with his arched neck and stooped back. His head sprouted not a single growth, but ironically, his scalp was so shiny that other people would use it to adjust their own hair. His nose was long and pointed, perfect for looking down at people. He wore a long set of robes which disguised his slippered, silent feet.

Unlike most people, he relished bad news. Bad news prompted bad decisions and that created elbow room. Visma had now elbowed himself to the top and it was relatively simple maintaining that position, nobody seemed overly eager to stage a coup against him.

The only trouble with delivering bad news to people was they had a tendency to shoot the messenger. That's the thing with princes and kings and queens and dukes and whoever else, their anger rarely extends beyond their own field of vision. It doesn't matter what the news is or where it came from, if you uttered it, you got it in the neck. Often that meant literally, although not for Visma. He knew the manoeuvres, most of them wriggly and unethical, to ensure he was never in the firing line. Still he found it a bit tiresome having to perform his dance to avoid the unfortunate threat from pompous prats every time there was bad news to spill.

That's why he'd worked considerably hard to land himself the position of Prince Elijah's advisor. For the most part, he was a calm man and they had established a good rapport. Of course, there were power struggles. The trick was not to let your opponent know they were losing. There is no room for ego when competing with someone who could have you decapitated, or your meals poisoned.

Visma carried the tray up the many winding stairs and corridors of the castle, until he reached a tall set of doors. He knocked, and slipped inside without waiting for an answer.

The Prince was performing his morning routine.

'– Seventy-six, seventy-seven, seventy-eight –'

Lord Visma made his way across to the table on one of the room's two balconies. This one faced Sunset. The Prince liked to look out over the falls when he ate.

'– Eighty-four, eighty-five, eighty-six –'

Visma was long past the point of rolling his eyes. He'd stood outside the door one morning and listened to Prince Elijah do his full workout routine. It was natural to assume that the whole thing was for show, but it wasn't.

'– Ninety-eight, ninety-nine, one-hundred.'

The Prince got to his feet and stretched. He wandered over to the Sunrise balcony and stretched some more. His body glistened with sweat.

The Prince sat down next to his breakfast on the ivy cupped balcony and gazed down to the lands below. 'So, what news have you for me today?' he asked, tucking into a sausage. As with many people, the Prince enjoyed catching up with the news over breakfast. And Visma proved even more effective at this than a paper, as he didn't require hands.

'I'm afraid I've got some bad news,' Visma reach into his sleeve and produced a scroll. He unravelled it with complex dexterity, as the Prince tested the bacon. 'The reply from Bergrond has come.'

'And?' demanded the Prince, while shovelling beans.

'Well, sire, I'm afraid it's checkmate.'

'Damn and blast!'

'If you remember sire, I did advise against your last move. As well as the four before that.'

'I don't pay you to advise.'

'Actually sire—'

'Alright, alright, alright.' The Prince delicately shovelled yolked bread into his mouth.

Visma returned the scroll to the folds of his robes. 'There is another matter.'

'Yes?' the Prince said, as he soaked his bread in the various juices still on the plate.

'Five days ago, I received a pigeon from Weed. The Sheriff there had a peculiar story to tell. Five travellers had reached the town and were fed and bedded in one of the Inns, but refused to pay.'

Prince Elijah lifted his tea and took a sip. This was a bit small fry so far, but he knew Visma well, there would be more.

'He was able to apprehend two of them,' continued Visma, 'which he sent along to us. They are currently in the black cells. The Sheriff said the other three would be along in a day or two. They have not yet arrived.

'Have the two been tortured?' asked the Prince.

'Not yet, sire. I deemed you would wish them sit for a while,' said Visma, in a tone like velvet. 'As is customary in these situations. There was one other thing in the letter that was sent, Sheriff Hornsworth mentioned that two of the remaining three are dwarves.'

'Dwarves?'

'Yes, sire. I know of the man; he is pragmatic, efficient and without creativity. I don't think it likely he would make something like this up. He has nothing to gain, not unless he's gotten tired of having ears over his shoulders. Still, it is quite a striking claim.'

'Yes,' agreed Elijah. 'This is a diverse city, but there hasn't been a dwarf inside these walls for a thousand years. The next step would be to speak to these prisoners, presumably?'

'Yes,' said Visma. 'Soon their lips will be ready to tell us whatever we need to know. If not, then torture. And if they tell us a lie, then torture. And if they tell us something that we don't like the sound of, but is probably true, then torture. And once I have extracted every scrap of information they have and their usefulness is complete, then torture.'

'That's a lot of torture.'

'They are treacherous thieves and squatters. Fear not my liege, they will feel your full justice before the end.'

'What happens if they don't do anything which you deem as torture worthy?'

'Trust me sire, that never happens,' said Visma, tucking his hands into his sleeves.

The Prince rose and entered a side door to get dressed 'This happens now?' he called.

'I have several matters to attend to prior to interrogation. Once I have finished those, the two prisoners will have my full attention.'

'What do I do? Should I make an appearance? You know, put the fear of god in them type of thing. Do some shouting, you know the drill.'

'Ah,' began Visma. The Prince was a good man, and good men were no use in an interrogation. Visma actually had an incident where a bleeding prisoner apologised for making the Prince sick. No, never again. 'No, sire. Best not. The dungeons are no place for the likes of you. You carry on with your ruling. I shall return this evening with good news.'

'I look forward to it.'

Visma lifted the empty breakfast tray and departed.

Aereon was *in a rush*, a tried and tested sales technique. People hated the idea of a deal missed. He had been sent off with as much merchandise as he could carry and had now whittled it down to a few handfuls and a helpful gentleman was in the process of purchasing most of Aereon's remaining goods.

'Will that be everything, sir?'

'Oh, yes. I think so,' the buyer replied with the look of a man who hasn't quite figured out how he is going to get all this stuff past his wife.

'Can't interest you in a cat?'

'What? Oh, uh, no. I don't think so. Thank you.'

'Are you sure?' asked Aereon plucking the dozing kitten from his shoulder by the scruff of its neck. The cat seemed not to notice. 'Specially bred this one.'

'Is it?' asked the customer, transfixed by the kitten.

'Oh yes. Every cat in his family for six generations has hunted only vermin. If you do the maths that's over seven-thousand cats, and a heck of a lot more rodents. No birds, you understand?'

'Yes, uh, very impressive,' said the man. 'But if there's are over seven-thousand of them, I guess I can wait a few days. You know, think it over.'

'Ah,' said Aereon. It was a good *ah*, he'd learnt it watching the other merchants. 'That's where you'd be making a big mistake, see. Last one this, isn't it.'

'Is it?'

'It is.'

'What happened to them all?'

'Plague, wasn't it. What from all the rats.'

'I don't want a plagued cat that's going to keel over any second!'

'Ah,' there it was again, 'this one's immune, see. This one's special,' he added, pointing to the kitten.

'He doesn't look like the most alert cat I've ever seen, I must say.'

'What?' said Aereon. 'You must be joking. This one's a born killer. Only this morning he took out an entire colony. He's just resting that's all.'

The mark looked unconvinced.

'Perhaps you're right, best not to be hasty,' said Aereon. 'It would be terrible for something to happen to wee Roland here. What with him being the last of his family. Maybe it's best not to push him into the life of a cleansing cat. It would be better to preserve his legacy, you know, get him breeding.' Neither noticed Roland's ears prick up. 'Then we could sell his offspring.' Aereon retracted the cat a little. 'I think I'll just go mention that to my boss actually. There must be some money in it. What do you reckon, am I'm in for a promotion?'

Aereon pulled away to leave.

'No wait! How much to you want for him?'

Less than half an hour later, Aereon had shaken his remaining produce and gained a considerable amount of coin in the process.

He found Lurdic and placed the purse into his hand.

'That you done, is it?' asked Lurdic, pulling open the strings for inspection.

Aereon nodded.

'You were quick,' the merchant raised his bushy brows at the bag, 'and persuasive.'

Lurdic took a pinch of coins from the purse and dropped them into Aereon's hand. 'Off you go then, lad. Good work today.'

Aereon skipped and hopped across the bridges and walkways of the town and didn't even bother to smile to the guards at the gate when he paced into Oxfort.

He had something to look for now. Something big. A lot bigger than the Creators. Something that should be easier to find. He may have even seen it already. But that was before he needed it. Before he knew to look for it.

The best part was, he could ask about it and it wouldn't appear suspicious. He started towards a woman not far away when his neck started to prickle in the way it does when the eyes have seen something peculiar, but the brain hasn't quite received the message. In those instances, the neck steps in to say "hey guys, shouldn't we be giving that a second glance?".

Aereon stopped and turned.

There was a man walking towards him. He wore a long grey coat with the arms tucked into his pockets. He walked like he didn't have any legs at all. Just a pair of feet that had to frantically shuffle forwards. On his head was a brimmed hat and a pair of glasses.

He stopped in front of Aereon.

Aereon squinted up at the bearded face.

'Silvor?'

'Down here.' Aereon looked at where the man's stomach should have been. The slit between two buttons pulled apart and Silvor appeared. 'Hello.'

'… Hello,' said Aereon.

Silvor disappeared and Aereon looked back up at the face. 'Volris?'

'Got it in two!'

Aereon's mouth opened, then shut, then opened again, 'What in the blazes are you two doing?'

'We're incognito,' said the head.

'That's right,' said the stomach.

'Shut up,' said the head.

Volris smiled down at Aereon.

'Someone is going to notice you!'

'Oh, I don't think so. We've been at this for three days. They're none the wiser.'

'They do give us the odd look,' came Silvor's voice.

'True,' agreed Volris, 'but it's more out of curiosity than suspicion.'

'What have you been doing for the last three days?'

'Oh, this and that. Had one of those burrito things you were talking about. It was quite good.'

'It wasn't in here,' complained Silvor.

Volris and Aereon ignored him.

'Haven't you been looking for the jail?' Aereon asked.

'Which one?' shrugged Volris, causing Silvor to tense. 'We've found three so far.'

'Oh… um… good. How did you find them?'

A boy, smaller than Aereon, appeared at his side.

'Aereon, this is Blade,' said Volris.

'Don't ask,' mumbled Silvor.

'He's a local that's been helping us out,' Volris continued. 'Put together this fancy get up for us.'

Aereon took in the outfit again and decided it was best to

say nothing on the subject, he was hardly in a position of fashion superiority. 'Have you guys been into the prisons yet?'

'No,' protested Volris. 'You told us to stay put.'

'I know what I said,' said Aereon, dismissively. 'I'm surprised you do. Ok, I have a plan,' declared Aereon. 'You two, keep up the good work, the disguise is excellent, and find where they are keeping Edin and Koel. Blade, you're coming with me.'

'What are you going to do?' asked Volris.

'We're going to the library.'

In hindsight, it was not the dramatic line he had hoped it would be.

Edin leaned against the bars.

One cell over, Koel was on his back.

'I've been thinking,' said Edin glumly.

'Oh, yeah? What's that?'

'Have you noticed that ever since we left Krank all people do is throw us in jail? The dwarves. The ogres. The elves. Now this.'

Koel was silent for a moment while he considered this. 'Huh, now you mention it there does seem to be a bit of a pattern.'

'A bit of a pattern! I swear, somebody needs to come up with a new plot device for us, because this is getting ridiculous.'

'It's almost worth going back to Hudikvar,' said Koel.

'Yeah,' agreed Edin, bitterly. 'That is a bit of blip on our record. When we get out of this mess, we'll go and give King Victarian the finger.'

'I am pleased to learn that we are not the only ones who have had trouble with you two.' Visma stepped out from around the corner and approached their cells.

Koel sat up.

'You must be the big kahuna,' said Edin.

Visma stood in front of him. 'I don't know about *the*, but certainly the biggest you are going to be in contact with. My name is Visma, but you can call me Lord Visma.' Visma looked between them both. Edin and Koel were slumped against the bars, dejection in their eyes. 'Shall we start with some questions?'

There were mild nods of agreement.

'Do you work alone?'

Edin and Koel shared a look. 'Define work.'

Visma gave them both a look. 'Who did you pull the Crow Inn heist with?'

'*Heist!*'

'That's a bit strong, isn't it?'

'Alright,' said Visma, calmly. 'Have you been travelling alone?'

'If we were to say no,' began Koel, 'what would happen?'

'I will ask you who they are, so they too can be apprehended.'

'Ah huh,' said Edin, 'and if we say yes?'

'I will be forced to have you tortured to confirm if that is true.'

'Well what sort of choice does that give us?' complained Koel.

'Ah, so have we established that you have not been travelling by yourselves?' asked Visma.

Koel and Edin looked at each other again. 'We could lie

338

about who are companions are?' suggested Edin.

'Now there's a plan,' said Koel.

'Sorry to butt in,' said Visma, 'but, I'm afraid anything you tell us will be given excruciating research to find out its truth.'

'Oh, come on,' complained Koel.

Edin opened his mouth.

'And before you ask, silence will also be met with torture.'

Edin shut his mouth.

'Now, there are certain answers that I am expecting from you, so if you give me those answers the research will not be as thorough. Shall we try that again? Who have you been travelling with?'

Edin gave Koel the nod. Koel slumped some more, 'Aereon, Silvor and Volris.'

'And they are?'

'Aereon is our fellow countryman–'

'Where is that? I'm having trouble placing your accent. It almost sounds like–'

'Krank,' said Edin.

Visma tapped his chin. 'Krank... Krank... nope, never heard of it.' The Creators mouthed the words with him. They'd travelled to many places and seen many lands, but it seemed no one in the world had heard of theirs. 'And I know most. That will definitely need researched *deeply*.' He pulled a scroll from his sleeve and made a little note. 'And Volris and Silvor, was it? Who are they?'

'Dwarves,' said Edin.

'Dwarves,' echoed Visma. 'I bet there is a pretty tale behind that.'

'Is it ever,' said Edin. 'Have you got enough paper?'

'Oh yes.'

'Would you like a seat my Lord?' asked Koel. 'There is a prefect good bench in here.'

'No, I'm quite fine, thank you.'

'Suit yourself,' said Koel.

'Right,' said Edin, rubbing his hands together. 'Where do I begin?'

'At the beginning?' suggested Visma.

(See Divine Invention: chapter 1)

'Is that it?' asked Aereon.

'No,' said Blade. 'That is a church.'

'Is that it?' Aereon pointed at another building.

'No,' said Blade. 'That's also a church.'

'Oh, ok,' said Aereon. 'Hey, what's a church?'

'What?'

'What is a church?'

Blade gave him a funny look. 'Uh… it's a house of god.'

'Really?' asked Aereon, with genuine enthusiasm. 'Is he in?'

'What? Oh… um, no. No, it's not really his house. More like a house that he owns and lets out, only the rent is worship and belief.'

'He must have a lot of worshippers to have so many houses.'

'Oh, they're not all for the same god,' said Blade.

'Wow,' said Aereon. 'How many gods are there?'

'Depending on who you ask, somewhere between none and several,' said Blade.

They continued through the streets, every now and then Aereon would point at a building.

'What about that? Another church?'

'Technically a temple, but basically the same thing.'

'Woah. Whose house is this? It's the biggest one yet!'

Blade stopped at the doors of the building. 'Some people would say this is the house of knowledge,' he said. 'This is the library.'

Aereon approached the steps.

'What do you need to go in for?' asked Blade.

'You said this is the house of knowledge, right? Well, knowledge is power,' Aereon took another step.

'Wait,' said Blade. 'If you want to look at the books you'll need this.' He reached into his pocket and took out a card. 'Just don't tell anyone, alright?'

Aereon took the library card and read it. 'Anything you say, Rhys.'

'Well,' said Visma. 'That certainly is a long tale. I hope, for your sake, it is not a tall one as well. This... um...' he looked down at his notes *'floyancy* seems particularly farfetched.'

Edin and Koel felt quite chuffed that after everything that had happened to them, their creation was still the most unbelievable part.

Visma looked at his notes again. Some things were quite troubling. 'Do you know where you are, gentlemen?'

'Somebody said this place was called Oxfort?' Edin ventured.

'Yes,' said Visma, 'and do you have any inkling as to where Oxfort is in relation to the rest of the world? You saw the river when you came in. Do you know the name of that river?'

Edin shrugged. 'No. Is that important?'

Visma understood faces. A good thing too, as they were often more reliable than voices, but in Edin's case both seemed to be saying the same thing. 'And you, Koel? Do you know the name of this river beneath our feet? If you listen very closely you can hear it through that drain over there.'

Koel listened and he heard it, but he wasn't sure what he was supposed to deduce. 'Sorry, no idea.'

Juta. They had definitely mentioned it. That's where this Krank was apparently. A brigade had been sent towards Sunset once, but they hadn't found anything. There was nothing down there. But, why lie?

'Gentlemen, there is somebody I would like very much for you to meet.' Visma jingled a little bell on the wall. After a moment, footsteps answered it. 'This is Mister Goodman,' said Visma as the figure, flanked by two orderlies, came around the corner. 'He is the one who will be carrying out my research for me. I'll leave you in his capable hands.' Visma handed Mr Goodman his notes. 'Something for you to work on.'

Lord Visma gave the Creators one last troubled look and then left.

'Hello folks, I will be your torturer for the foreseeable future,' declared Mr Goodman with a toothy grin. 'You just tell me when you've had enough.'

'We've had enough,' said Edin.

Mr Goodman laughed more than Edin felt was necessary. A wispy, wheezing laugh. When he finished, he wiped his eyes, 'Oh that is delightfully droll. Do you know, in all the years I've been doing this, I've never heard that one. Very good. Yes, I think I'll start with you.' Mr Goodman unlocked the cell. 'Tie him up boys.'

The orderlies sprang into action and suspended Edin as if he was mid-star-jump.

Mr Goodman walked into the cell and dropped his tool bag in front of Edin. 'I'm going to make you wish you'd never been born,' he said, inches from Edin's face.

'I doubt that,' said Edin.

'Yeah,' Koel agreed, knowingly. 'I think you're facing an uphill battle there, chief.'

Aereon placed his stack of books down and pulled out the chair. The table was long and dark. And old. Venerable was the word. The dark wood gave the impression of unwavering solidity and permanence. The entire library did. The light within was dim and the shelves a black mystery. He had been directed to the second floor where the bookcases rose to the high rafters.

He'd found the right section and selected a stack of promising titles. A cold lantern sat not far from him. He picked up a box of matches from the table and lit the wick. The glow of the flame found the cover of the first tome.

Kings and Queens of Huranland and their deeds
Volume Four
Two-Hundred-Seventy-Three B.S. to One-Hundred-Twenty-One A.B.

Aereon flicked through it. There were many passages on the great deeds of Kings and Queens and the spaces between the lines told the story of the back stabbings as well as ill-advised decisions made, but it didn't have what he was looking for.

He closed the book and picked up the next one. Again, Aereon was sure it would make fascinating reading, but he had no time to be leisurely.

He got to the bottom of his stack without a result. There had been hints of it, enough to keep him reading, but nothing conclusive. Aereon blew out the lamp, put the books back exactly where he found them and went to hunt down the librarian again.

The greying woman looking up from her desk. 'Yes, dear?'

'I was wondering if you had anything on Princess Elina and Prince Avery?'

'Oh, is that what you were after? You should have said so, dear.'

She got up from her chair and led him away. As they walked between the shelves, she gave him a look over her half-moon glasses. 'Aren't you a little old for that story?' she asked.

'Sorry?' said Aereon.

The librarian stopped and gave herself a small tap on the forehead. 'Silly me. You'll be wanting the memoires, not the fairy tale.'

'Yes. Oh…uh, hang on. I'll take a quick look at that fairy tale first, if that's all right?'

'Oh course,' she said. 'It's just down here.'

The books on these shelves were more colourful than the rest of the library and much shorter. The librarian picked up a book and handed it to Aereon.

'Well, you're not in short supply,' said Aereon, looking at three shelves stocked with identical books.

'Oh, no. We keep plenty of stalk. It's a very popular children's story. I can show you to the memoires now if you like?'

'No, that's fine. I think I'll give this a quick read first.'

'No problem, dear. You know where to find me.'

The librarian shuffled back towards her desk and Aereon found a nearby table with a lamp and observed the cover.

The Juta's Love

A bright picture depicted the happy couple sharing a kiss atop the Meanderfalls.

Aereon smiled. 'I had a cat, and his name was Roland.'

Aereon's pragmatic mind occasionally had difficulty with the subtleties of common phrases.

A Night of Hunters

It was a night for wolves. A night when clouds are low and each touched by moonlight. A night where mist drifted across the moors. A night wolves howled.

A pack of ogres broke through the mountains in search of men.

Or women. Say what you will about ogres, they do not discriminate on that point.

A couple carried clubs, occasionally one would lift a rock just to make sure there were no humans hiding underneath.

Not far away some humans were hiding. They were part of Kajsha's ragtag fleet of rough necked youths and they were ogre spotters.

Rjkaard was amongst them and first to spot the fog rise as the ogres pushed it aside.

He turned to his second fastest runner and gave the orders.

The ogres lumbered across the landscape, because that's the kind of thing they do. The lights of Hudikvar ahead pierced through the mist.

Ogres have a grand gift of a vacant stare. It comes naturally to them, like a mohawk to a cockatoo. Ogres are not as dim-witted as they appear, though. It is true, they are a little linguistically challenged, but that does not impede their malice.

Not mindless malice either. Some creatures are just violent for the sake of violence. Ogres on the other hand, do it on behalf of religion, which is much better.

Endos's moon cycle ended monthly with a solar eclipse. At the blotting of the sun the ogres set alight a great pyre of bodies from a number of species and races. And every time they do, the sun returns. The ogres have been carrying out this ritual for so long that no one really knows for sure whether it is the salvation of life or simply an abomination upon it.

Around the ogres, the young rapscallions were taking up positions. The stomping feet had missed the hole, but Rjkaard had anticipated this and come up with a contingency plan.

He wiped his brow and turned to his fastest runner. 'Are you ready?'

The ogres were almost on top of them now.

'I was born ready,' said Odd Izzy. 'Just give me the torch.'

Rjkaard placed the wood into his hand and struck a match. Izzy took flight.

Rjkaard watched the flame engorge as Izzy passed through the methane filled air between the first ogre's legs.

Olle patted his hair frantically and kept moving. He wasn't at full pace yet; he was giving the ogres a few seconds to assess the situation. Once they'd reached the necessary conclusions and had turned themselves around they gave chase.

Ogres are not fast.

That is, no part of their body moves very quickly. But they are big creatures: twice the height of a man and *complicated equations* greater in mass. The result was that they did have a bit of pace about them.

Olle glanced over his shoulder. There was a zip of air as club passed where his head had been. He lifted it back up from between his shoulders and looked desperately at his legs.

He wasn't entirely convinced that he was going any faster, but his head did not go sailing into the night and he took that as a good sign.

The topography ahead was quite distinct. The Gorse mountains jagged in the distance. Bronze in the light of the moon. The foreground was dominated by moraines and Olle had been studying them for days. He made special effort not to *look* like he was studying them though, because Odd Izzy would not study. He aimed for a gap between two of the rounder formations.

The ogres charged in behind him.

Olle noted the change underfoot and he raced across the willow branches.

Behind him there was a noisy crack.

'Oh crumbs,' said Olle.

The hairless heads of the ogres shone in the night, Kajsha's band in their path.

'Shouldn't we be doing something?'

'We have to wait for Izzy,' said Kajsha.

'I don't see him, do you?'

'Isn't he supposed to have a torch?'

'Look, we can't wait forever. They're almost on top of us!'

'We're not abandoning him,' stated Kajsha.

Light rippled as it bounced off different sections of wobbling flesh. There was a lot of it, size was something the ogres held in the highest regard, and there was no use having any at all if you weren't going to throw it around.

'Bollocks to this,' said Darjl. He struck a match and flicked it to the ground.

The flames roared in front of them and into the ogres' eyes. The fire spread in a long line through the moraines towards the mountains.

Ogres are not naturally afraid of fire, but like most, they do not appreciate it springing up under their feet seemingly of its own accord. They roared and shielded their eyes.

'You were supposed to wait for Izzy,' rasped Kajsha. 'You were supposed to give a signal!'

The youths peered through the flames, but the second fire had not gone up.

The ogres turned and fled from the flames and ran back towards the pit. Eventually the second fire was lit and just caught the heels of the last monster as it disappeared into the night.

The flames roared and raced after the other line and formed a well-planned corridor away from Hudikvar and away from the hole. No ogres were inside.

There was, however, an ogre inside the pit, a fact that Olle was becoming increasingly concerned about.

It was still a little dazed from the fall and hadn't quite come to terms with what had happened, which gave time for Olle to find a good location beneath the wreckage to see this one out.

'Gurrrr.'

The beast stomped to its feet and patted the walls just to make sure they were real. It scratched its head with a fat finger.

'Ere Wot Choo Oing Down Der?'

Olle peeped through his cover. The other ogres were standing over the hole. This was not the plan.

'Unno,' replied the ogre.

'It Is A Bit Illy Int It. Eing In A Ole.'

The trapped ogre considered this. 'Es,' he agreed.

'Why Oou O In Den?' asked one of the ogres.

Olle rolled his eyes. This could go on for a while.

'Unno,' replied the ogre in the hole after some more head scratching.

'Eems Oo Me Dat – Hey! Wot Choo Oo Dat Or?' Demanded the ogre.

The ogre next to him looked around in a way that was probably about as innocent as a ten-foot hooligan can look. 'Me?' he asked, pointing at his chest.

'Es, Oou!'

The offended ogre gave a shove.

'Ot Is Oar Oblem?' asked the shovee.

'Oou It Me Wif A Rock! I Want A Apple... Apol... I Want Oou Oo Ay Orry!'

'I Ever Dun Noffin!' the ogre pushed back. 'Cept Dat And I Aint Orry For Dat!'

'Dis Is All A Ittle Illy,' commented third.

'Shut It!' shouted the other two in unison.

'Ont Ell Im Oo Shut It. Oou Shut it,' said one.

'No Oou Shut It,' said another and threw a fist.

A fight broke out amongst the heathens, punches were missed and struck bystanders, soon all the ogres were sucked into the fray. Leaving the ogre in the pit still scratching his head.

A stone came down and bounced off his head. He had a think for a moment before coming to the conclusion that it hadn't been his finger. This made him angry.

'Grrragh!' he roared. 'Oo Frew Dat!'

The ogre swivelled on the spot trying to find someone to shout at.

'Hello.'

He ogre tilted his head to the flame that was flicking from right to left. 'Oooohh,' he said.

'Yes, it's very pretty, isn't it?'

'Es.'

A pebble hit Olle in the ribs and made him start.

He lifted his head as a rope came down from above and landed not far from him. With a glance to the distracted ogre he pulled himself from under the debris and grabbed the rope.

'Tie it around your waist,' said the whispered voice.

Olle did what he was told. The rope tugged at his skin and he started to climb.

The dirt had been packed in tight and it was hard to get a hold, but he was a born climber.

'Here, give me your hand. I've got you.'

'That's it. Thanks… *Rorj?*'

'Surprised?' Rorj smiled in the moonlight.

'N-no. No, of course not.'

'Good,' said Rorj. 'I'd hate to think that people didn't see me as a charitable figure.'

'Uh, no… of course not.'

'Good. That is good.'

'Izzy!'

Rorj smirked as Olle turned to the approaching youths. It was amazing, it was like everyone else's sensors weren't wired up quite right.

'What happened? We thought the ogres might have got

you,' continued Kajsha.

'He was hiding under a pile of willow branches.'

Everyone turned to Rorj.

'Don't be ridiculous,' said one of the youths.

Everyone turned to Olle.

'That's right,' said Izzy. 'I wasn't hiding. I was just luring them into a false sense of security. It's lucky you came along when you did, because that ogre was about to be in for a world of pain.'

Everyone nodded in agreement.

'Oh, I see,' said Rorj. 'I suppose you'll have a plan for dealing with this lot then?' Rorj pointed a thumb at the squabbling ogres.

Olle looked at the rolling masses.

'... Yes. Absolutely.'

'Terrific,' mused Rorj. 'Care to fill us in?'

Everyone was looked at Olle again.

'Well... what I'll do is... I'll just –'

'Chase them off!' shouted someone.

The suggestion was met with raucous reception.

'I'll chase them off!' agreed Olle, adopting the voice of Izzy and regaining some of his confidence. He drew his sword and basked in the admiration of the youths.

Rorj noted Olle's eyes flicker as he looked back to the brawling brutes. He leaned in close, 'Better go get 'em, boss.'

Olle couldn't even afford to give him a glare, although there was a little rattle from his sword. He gave what he felt was a reassuring nod to the youths and paced across to the ogres, sword raised.

'On guard!'

The ogres did not look up. Although, the one receiving a

noogie really didn't have much choice.

Rorj cupped his hands over his mouth, 'Oi!' The ogres stopped what they were doing. 'There's someone here who thinks he'd have your guts for breakfast,' he called, helpfully.

The ogres looked down at Olle. One stuck out a sausage finger. 'Im?'

'Me,' said Izzy. He sprung forward and jabbed the nearest ogre in the stomach.

'Ow! Ee Abbed me!'

'Ight! Ome On Lads.' The ogre raised his hands over Izzy menacingly. 'Let's Et Im!'

Izzy stabbed him in the foot and ran for it.

The ogres chased.

Sometime later, Izzy returned triumphantly. Followed by Rorj, although nobody knew where he had been.

Privately he was quite pleased with himself. It would have been relatively easily to distract the ogres from Olle and then give them the slip at a point of his choosing. Far more difficult, however, to do it without Olle noticing.

Rorj sidled over to the rest of the Search and Seekers as Kajsha looked to make her speech. Someone had found her a box to stand on, but still people were crammed up the surrounding slopes.

'Well done, to you all,' she began. 'This is your night and it belongs to all of you.'

There were a few whistles and shouts which she smiled at, but she wisely chose to ignore the "Ank Oou" from the ogre in the pit.

'Long weeks of hard work have gone into this plan and you've all done brilliantly. Give yourselves another round of applause.' She waited for them to quieten. 'There is one person here though, who I feel deserves a special mention. One person who put more work and more thought into this plan to ensure that everything worked out. Everyone, give a huge hand for the brains behind this operation: Rjkaard!'

And there was a huge round of applause. Many wolf whistles and roars of excitement. Again, everyone did their best to ignore the ogre.

Rjkaard waved to them all in thanks as he stepped forward. 'Thank you all,' he said in his mousy tone. 'Thank you all for working so hard on this. We are now so close to the finale. The next part falls on me, but I am sure you will not hesitate to wish me good luck. Aha. Thank you. I will now go to King Victarian. I will tell him we have something that demands his attention.'

Definitely Not Barrels Out of Bond

Mr Goodman was an artist. People looked upon his work and saw a body, living and functioning. Some keen-eyed individuals might spot a bruise or a small pin mark on the skin or under a nail, but only a select few understood his art in all its gory. Edin was being given a first-hand lesson.

Mr Goodman twisted his implement. 'Do you wish you were dead yet?'

'No! I wish *you* were!'

'Ha ha ha. That's very witty, sir,' said Goodman. 'I could listen to your sharp jibes all day, but alas I have other people to attend to.' Edin breathed a sigh of relief. 'Let me just add some salt here.'

'Aaaarrghh!'

'Excellent. I will be back to see you again this afternoon.'

Mr Goodman left the cell, an orderly locked it and followed him down the corridor.

'Can I open my eyes yet?' asked Koel

'Oh yes, god forbid you see anything which causes you trauma.'

'You know I have a weak stomach,' protested Koel.

'That's true, we mustn't upset your sensibilities,' jerked Edin.

'How are you feeling?' Koel tried.

'Well, I'm not throwing up,' said Edin, like a dog with a bone.

Koel didn't know what to say. Edin didn't want him to say anything. So, Koel stood in silence while Edin hung. This went on for a while until Edin said, 'Did somebody just throw a pebble at me?'

Beneath the bowels of Oxfort, Aereon splashed through the streamlets and ponds of the Juta, open mouthed in the secret shallow chamber under the city.

'What is this place?' Aereon rasped.

'Helpful,' said Blade.

'You're not,' said Aereon. 'How did you find it?'

'I was on the run and I came down here.'

'Why were you running?' Aereon rotated his hand encouragingly, 'Keep going, you're doing great.'

'I get myself into places I'm not supposed to be, you could say,' Blade said. 'That's how I knew you were coming.'

'You knew we were coming?'

'I read the letter from Weed's Sheriff. It said when you were coming and contained all your names. The dove went to Lord Visma's aviary, so it's not exactly an easy place to get to. Right on top of the battlements, as you'd expect, in one of the towers. Only one staircase up with lots of locked doors and only one set of keys. And–'

'Wait, wait, wait. Who is Lord Visma? Is he in charge here?' Aereon asked.

Blade's head went to one side, 'Sort of. Technically the

Prince is in charge, but Visma does more of the day-to-day running of things. I guess you could say the Prince is the above all and end all, the buck stops with him, he makes the decisions. It's just that he only makes ten percent of the decisions. Granted they are the big important ones.' Blade paused for a moment. 'Visma's also very good at laying traps. The corridors are filled with–'

'So, this Prince character,' began Aereon before Blade could pick up any sort of momentum. If he'd known that getting Blade to talk would have led to self-indulgent bravado, he wouldn't have bothered. 'Where would I find him?'

'There are a few places. I know all of them, because I must. Seeing as I spend a lot of my time avoiding him…'

'Ah huh.'

'I suppose the place he spends most of his time is within the palace,' Blade continued, with disappointment. 'In his apartment.'

'How do I get in there? And let's keep these answers concise.'

'Tricky. I've never actually been in, myself. He stays in the King's apartment, which is at the very top of the Sunset wall.'

'How does the King feel about that?'

'What?'

'Nothing, just a little joke,' said Aereon.

'I thought we were going to try and keep this conversation concise,' said Blade.

'You're absolutely right, *Rhys*. In future, a laugh may help to speed the process along, rather than additional questioning,' said Aereon.

'Oh, I see… ah ha ha ha, *How does the* King *feel about*

that? Very good.'

Aereon said nothing.

'Tricky,' said Rhys. 'That distraction so the guards come running stuff doesn't work in real life. Would be nice if it did, but the world doesn't work like that. The guards on duty get even more resolute and reinforcements are called in from elsewhere. Sneaking in won't work either. There's just one small corridor, filled with guards.'

'I thought you said you climbed up to the highest point of the battlements and inspected pigeon droppings or something?'

'Carrier pigeon messages,' said Blade.

'Yeah, those.'

'The wall is very heavily guarded. The aviary is not. Visma relies primarily on traps for the protection of its knowledge. A foolish notion, even if he does have little trust in people.'

'So, coming in from above is out?'

'Yes.'

'That makes things easy.'

'Easy?'

'Well, simple, at any rate,' said Aereon.

'Simple?'

'We'll just have to go through the front,' said Aereon, plainly. He noticed the look. 'You'd be surprised how effective an authoritative voice can be. And, if all else fails, I'll have two wrecking balls with me.'

They rounded a structural pillar and the two wrecking balls came into view. One was standing on top of a rock and talking into a grate, the other was below and looking furious about not being on the rock.

Aereon and Blade were given a signal to come slowly and

quietly.

Aereon looked up through the small square of metal bars and found Edin.

'Hello,' Edin said. 'Don't panic Koel, Aereon's here.'

Aereon tried to pay no attention to the distant groan of derision.

'Go on then,' said Edin, 'tell us you're going to cut through this bar and rescue us.'

'Uh…'

'Go on, we're all waiting.'

'I have a different plan,' said Aereon.

'This ought to be good.'

'I am going to seek audience with the Prince and secure your release.'

'There's a Prince?' asked Edin.

'That must have been the biggest kahuna, that baldy lordy was talking about,' said Koel.

'Why do you always have to plan?' demanded Edin, thrashing in his harnesses. 'It's perfectly simple, just take Silvor's axe and cut through that metal?'

Aereon sucked in through his teeth. 'Thing, is I've put a bit of time and research into this. I'd kind of like to see it through. Besides, smacking away at that water drain is probably going to get noticed.'

'Uh, that's not for water,' said Blade.

'I was wondering that,' Volris contributed. 'Why would they need a drain inside a building?'

Blade searched for the words. 'It's for the prisoners… if you catch my meaning.'

'Ah,' said Volris as the penny dropped with a splat. 'Is that why I appear to be sinking into this stone?'

'Yes,' said Blade.

'Ha!' taunted Silvor. 'It's a stalagshi–'

'Thank you!' said Aereon, swiftly.

At arms' length, Aereon and Silvor pulled Volris out the mess and dropped him in a shallow pool.

'Do we get to hear this master plan?' asked Koel.

Aereon tapped his lip, 'No, I think not. Volris and Silvor will come with me and together we will get you out of here. That's all you need to know.'

'What if it doesn't work?'

'It's going to work,' said Aereon.

'Are you so arrogant that you won't even consider a backup plan?'

'Alright cry-babies. How about this: Blade can acquire a saw to get through these bars and the ones in Koel's cell.'

'I'm not touching those bars,' said Blade.

'I have utter faith that you will be able to find yourself a pair of gloves, which you can dispose of afterwards,' said Aereon. 'If things don't work out, we will meet down here.'

'How will we know if things don't work out?' Koel asked.

'Oh, we'll tell you,' said Aereon, simply. 'You'll have to stay in your cells of course. If they notice they are empty, then the grates will be the first thing they'd check and they would find you down here.'

'I know you have been incarcerated, Aereon,' said Koel, 'but, I must be going crazy because you are acting like someone who has never enjoyed the experience.'

'You'll be fine,' Aereon said. 'Have some faith. And on the off chance that the plan doesn't work then, I don't know there must be some casks or something that we can get into.'

There was some silence until Blade said, 'To what end?'

'To go over the falls in,' stated Aereon.

'Are you mad?'

'We'd be smashed to pieces!'

'That's what the barrels are for,' said Aereon dismissively.

'There is a passage that leads down to the bottom. You can take that,' said Blade.

'Oh, well that works too I suppose,' conceded Aereon. 'Are you sure?' he added after a pause.

'Yes!'

'Because I've just thought of a really good alliterative title for what we could call it.'

Silvor and Volris were feeling self-conscious. That tends to happen when everyone is looking at you for no reason, other than you being who you are.

'Are you sure about this?' Volris rasped.

'I'm fairly confident,' said Aereon. He led the dwarves without their disguise towards the palace.

A tall set of wooden doors marked the entrance. A brigade of guards highlighted the first obstacle. They had already spotted the dwarves and begun the frantic whispering Aereon had expected.

He stopped in front of them. 'Hello.'

That silenced them.

'We're here to see Prince Elijah, he's expecting us.' Aereon added a smile to enforce that nothing funny was going on.

The guards retreated into a huddle to discuss this. Occasionally they would look over their shoulders to find Aereon still grinning pleasantly.

'Do you have papers?' asked the boldest.

'I have papers,' said Aereon. 'What sort of papers would you like?'

This answer did not give the guard anymore confidence. 'Personal papers. Stating your identities.'

'Oh, how rude of me. I'm Aereon Cusith of Krank and this here is Volris and Silvor, both of Oth-Rodin.'

Every guard looked between the dwarves. 'That's not exactly official, is it? How do I know they are Volris and Silvor from Oth-Rodin? I'm just having to go on your word, you see?'

'Look, when was the last time you saw a dwarf?' There was no reply. 'So, is it reasonable to assume that these are the only two dwarves in Oxfort? Probably the only two this side of the Dagger Sea. So, what benefit could I possibly have for giving you false names?'

'That's a fair point.'

'Of course, it is. The truth always makes sense. And don't you think that if there were two dwarves in the city, the Prince would want to have a meeting with them?'

'I can see that,' said the guard.

'Glad to hear you're seeing sense. Now, will you let us through? I would hate to keep the Prince waiting.'

The palace was not huge, but it wasn't small and it was certainly luxurious.

Rooms broke off from the corridor on the ground floor, nothing too fancy, the kind of place guests' servants would stay or not very important guests. They passed the guards at the foot of the staircase with less trouble. They reasoned that if two dwarves were in the palace, then they had a legitimate reason for being there.

The next floor was similar, perhaps a little grander. And

the two floors after that were even grander, the last floor had a vaulted ceiling. The stairs stopped in front of a landing occupied by two guards in front of a fancy looking door.

'Hello,' said Aereon, with accustomed pleasantness. 'We're here to see the Prince.'

'What for?' said guard Alpha.

'We have something very important to discuss with him,' said Aereon.

Guard Alpha studied the dwarves. He had the look of a man who was not used to being intimidated by things smaller than him, but the half-pints were certainly having an effect. 'He's not in,' he blurted out.

'What?' said Aereon, with equal shock.

'He's out,' said guard Foxtrot.

This was not how this was supposed to go, he wasn't supposed to be out. 'Out where?'

Knock, knock.

'I don't know,' said Foxtrot.

'It may interest you to know,' began Alpha, 'that it is not our job to know every detail of the Prince's schedule. It is our job to guard this door.'

Knock, knock.

'Well, can we go in a wait for him?' asked Aereon. 'I assure you, we are stand up individuals.'

Knock, knock.

'Absolutely not,' declared Alpha. 'You could be anybody.'

Knock, knock.

'Oh,' said Aereon. 'If that's the issue, I'm Aereon Cusith and the dwarves are both of Oth-Rodin.'

Knock, knock.

'I don't care who – I'm sorry, what is he doing?'

Everyone turned to Silvor, who was in the process of wrapping another brick in the wall with his knuckle.

Knock, knock.

'What are you doing, Silvor?' Aereon asked.

'I'm looking for the secret tunnel,' he said offhandedly.

'The what?' asked Aereon.

'It's simple,' said Silvor, continuing with his work. 'If the Prince is out, but none of the guards downstairs knew he is out, then he can't have gone out the main entrance. Ergo: secret passage.' He reached guard B's leg. 'Excuse me.' The bewildered guard took a step to the side to allow Silvor to continue.

'There is no secret passage,' said guard Alpha. 'I can assure you.'

Aereon noted the slight crack in his voice, but his attention returned to Silvor who had begun snorting like a warthog.

'What's he doing now?' said guard Foxtrot, who had started hyperventilating himself.

'Silvor?' asked Aereon coolly.

'Searching for the air pocket,' said the dwarf. 'There'll be a crack in the mortar here somewhere. Find that, and you find the door.' He breathed in deeply.

'There is no passage!'

'Look,' said Aereon, 'just let us wait inside and we can forget all about it.'

'No!' said Alpha.

Aereon lost patience. '*Shields!*' he commanded. Everyone gave him a funny look. He slapped his head. 'Oh right, that was the last one.' His tongue twisted in his mouth as it wrapped itself around the dwarvish word Silvor had insisted he use. 'Hodrik... Hodrisk...'

'Hodrisqlak,' said Volris, helpfully.

'That's the one,' Aereon snapped his fingers. '*Hodrisqlak!*'

A couple swift moves later and Alpha and Foxtrot were both in crumpled heaps at the top of the stairs. Aereon stepped over them and opened the double doors.

There was a rustling and the sound of a drawer sliding shut.

'Ah, Prince Elijah, I was just – who the hell are you?' asked the bald figure who had stepped out from around the corner. The dwarves joined Aereon and the picture fell into place. 'Aereon of Krank, I presume? And you must be Volris and Silvor?'

'*I'm* Volris, *that's* Silvor.'

'My mistake.'

'You wouldn't be Lord Visma by any chance?' said Aereon.

'I would,' said Visma, circling his way towards a chair. 'And may I ask how you knew that?'

'You can ask all you like.'

A frail smile traced Visma's lips.

'We've come to speak with the Prince.'

The smile vanished. 'As I'm sure the guards outside would have told you, the Prince is not in, but, seeing as you are here anyway, is there anything I can help you gentlemen with?'

Aereon's plan was built around a conversation with the Prince, he wasn't sure it would work on a Lord. Particularly this Lord. For this plan, someone patriotic would be needed. Someone with beliefs. People with beliefs could be rattled. Lord Visma did not look like be believed in a whole lot except himself.

'I would prefer to wait for the Prince,' said Aereon.

'Oh, come now,' said Visma. 'We're all friends here. I imagine you would like your companions to be released. I am a man who could help facilitate that. So, come on, convince me.'

'I would really prefer to talk with the Prince.'

Lord Visma sighed, 'I can't change your mind?'

Aereon shook his head.

'How dull.' Visma reached over his shoulder and tugged on a rope. The action was received by a gong.

'What did you do that for?' Aereon complained.

'I'm not spending my time babysitting you three for nothing. If you have nothing to offer, then it's to the dungeons with you.'

The dwarves were already drawing weapons and heading out the door.

'No,' said Aereon. 'We're not going to fight our way out.' He ignored their faces. 'If you want to make yourselves useful, you can pull that chest in front of the doors.'

'What are you going to do?' asked Volris.

'Something I'd hoped I wouldn't have to,' Aereon replied.

Visma watched, with some amusement, from his chair as the scene unfolded. The chest was dragged in front of the doors, as well as some additional furniture. A decent barricade, he felt. It wouldn't hold the troops back for long, but perhaps for long enough. He turned his attention to Aereon, who had unravelled the scarf from his head and was in the process of disassembling his very fetching scarf-made-skirt.

Aereon stood in his undies and began tying the various materials together. Volris and Silvor had stopped to observe as well.

Once he had completed the makeshift rope, he headed to the Sunset balcony and secured it to the railing, just in time for the first bang on the door. It wasn't a bang of someone trying to smash a door down. It was a bang of someone expecting it to open and walking into it when it didn't. There was a muffled 'Ow' before a second bang, with a full assessment of the situation.

'Volris, you first,' said Aereon.

Visma watched the dwarf walk across the room and peer down over the falls.

'Are you sure about this?' asked Volris

'Oh, yes,' said Aereon. 'Trust me, I'm quite good with knots.'

Volris had another look. 'How are you with structural integrity of scarves?'

'Quietly confident,' Aereon declared. 'Come on, come on. We haven't got all day.'

Reluctantly, Volris climbed over the railing and grasped the rope. He had a quick prayer as Aereon told him to aim for the platform below. The public one, where he had found the plaque dedicated to Princess Elina and Prince Avery, the place where this crazy plan had started.

Aereon watched the dwarf shimmy down the rope until he was all the way down. Then he called over to his brother. Silvor was sceptical about leaving his position, as he was now an integrated part of the barricade, but Aereon shouted and he came.

The doors started to rattle and the furniture started to shake, but still Silvor felt he had time to turn to Lord Visma and bellow, 'Swivel on it, punk!'

Visma looked up at the ceiling, where the dwarf's trigger

finger had pointed, and couldn't help but think something had been lost in translation.

Silvor vaulted the railing and slid down the rope.

Aereon had really hoped he wouldn't have to do this, but there didn't seem to be anything for it. He shuffled over to the table next to Visma and shyly pulled out a small square of paper which had been lurking somewhere within his underpants. In a mousy voice, he asked, 'Could you pass this on to the Prince, please?'

Aereon returned to the balcony and disappeared over the edge. Visma picked up the piece of paper and walked to the banister. He watched Aereon descend as quickly as he dared. Visma probably had a knife of some sort on his person, but that would have such a finite conclusion. Such a swift end. He liked possibility.

Aereon's feet touched down, just as the first guard reached the balcony. Others joined him and peered over the edge. Visma took a step back and unfolded the paper and read the top entry, '*The Juta's Love*?'

Silvor yanked open a drain and they landed heavily onto the rocky ground beneath the castle. Aereon reached up to shut the grill, when he turned around he was staring at Edin.

'What are you doing here?'

'Escaping?' Edin suggested.

'I told you to wait in your cell,' stated Aereon.

'I thought we only needed to be there if things went well?' asked Koel.

'*So?*' Aereon protested.

'So,' echoed Koel, 'did it go well?'

'That is beside the point. You didn't know if it was going

to go well or not, you were supposed to stay in your cell.'

'Can we just get on with escaping, seeing as we're all here?' enquired Volris.

'Fine,' said Aereon. Edin really wanted to ask why he was only wearing underpants, but he bit his tongue.

'Where's Blade?' asked Silvor.

'He took off,' said Koel. 'He did a good job getting us out, but after that he said he was done.'

Volris and Silvor took the others to the watery tunnel and showed them into its depths.

No one had a torch, so it was a slippery and claustrophobic experience. Rock jabbed at groping hands and stabbed clumsy knees. When they got to the bottom, Silvor almost fell into the pool. The rest heard the slash and froze.

'It's ok, I'm alright. We're here.'

'Ok, this part is going to be tricky. Tricky for you lot to begin with and trickier for me and Silvor at the end. We are going to dive into the pool behind me. It's deep and dark so you are going to want to turn back, but what you have to do is not let go of the rope. Whatever, you do *don't let go of the rope.*'

'What rope?' It was Aereon's voice.

'This rope,' said Volris, finding him in the darkness.

'Where was this when I was stripping clothes like an overzealous teen?'

'In my pouch,' replied Volris.

'Why didn't you tell me?'

'You seemed like you had everything in hand.'

Silvor tied the end of the rope to his belt and took a deep breath. After a moment Aereon felt the tug and the cold of the water.

Aereon's eyes burned so he shut them. His fingers screamed and he hugged them. His head throbbed, his toes cracked, his limbs went stiff, but there was nothing he could do about it.

Volris had undersold the weight of the dwarves. Getting down was not a problem at all, the rope went tight and Aereon was dragged towards an icy glow.

His eyes picked up the entrance to the cave and his feet barely grazed the bottom before he felt himself being dragged up towards the shimmering surface. He felt bad, but his body was frozen, all of it tucked around the rope, every part of him clinging on with whatever strength he had left. He'd done his part, they'd made it. They were out. He still had the Creators. Now he just needed to follow the Juta and take them home.

Long Live the King

'My wise Lord,' began Erling, taking a knee, 'your words have come true. Captain Dagny has gathered her forces. The King is set to leave Rjkovorg.'

I shall have to begin devoting some time to the reward for that Rorj fellow. 'Notify the others. I want them armed, but not *visibly* armed, you understand?' said Prince Victarian. 'We need to be smart about this.'

'Yes, my Lord. Thank you, my Lord.'

Herm led the loyal servant to the door. On his return, he noticed Prince Victarian's smile.

'Something amusing, Master?'

'Oh, I was just thinking,' began Victarian, 'that maybe the last time anybody ever calls me *Lord*.'

Herm seemed to consider this. 'When the moment arrives, would you like me to continue calling you Master, Master?'

'Oh, yes, I think so,' said Victarian. 'Seeing as we're old friends.'

'Very good, Master.'

'Are you sure this is really necessary?' asked King Victarian.

'Yes,' said Captain Dagny. She ducked under his arm and resumed fastening his breastplate. The King's armour was one of the few things on the walls of the Long House that hadn't been pillaged by the youths. 'And I'd really like it if you reconsidered the helmet.'

'Absolutely not,' declared Victarian. 'The people need to see their King. It will be good for them.'

Dagny had been with the King for a long time. She'd been the fifth woman to join the guard and had done so as soon as her age allowed. She was the first woman to reach the rank of Sergeant. The only one to be given command. Command of the Royal Guard, no less. A position known as First Captain. The highest rank within Hudikvar. No one knew the King better. His wife had abandoned him (Dagny did not value death as an acceptable excuse for desertion) and his son was... his son.

King Victarian's will was like bamboo. Once it was of a mind it quickened its growth on the subject, strengthened its belief.

What Aereon had done was chop down one of Victarian's thickest stalks.

For years, the King had seen the Long House as impenetrable. The knife wound had changed all that. The roof had been repaired and the doors reinforced, but the seed had been planted. A new grass grew.

Fear can do strange things to men. It can make cowards out of them. It can make them paranoid. It can also give them strength. For King Victarian he felt that if his home could not be invulnerable, then he would need to be.

'I'll take my sword,' he said.

Dagny glanced at his arms, but said nothing. She finished

372

attaching his armour, tied his sword belt and returned his arms to the sleeves of his coat and his furs to his shoulders.

Outside, those nearest, were clad in even more armour than he and armed with bows, swords and shields or spears.

There was a boy standing by the door.

'I'll take that, thank you,' said Victarian, swiping his sword out the boy's grasp. He inspected the edges. 'Undamaged,' he said and sheathed the weapon.

'Why did you return it?' Dagny asked, with sharpness.

'As a show of good faith,' replied Rjkaard. 'Everything that was taken from you will be returned so long as you follow me and do not harm any of my people. Or me,' he added hastily.

'They are not your people. They are my people.'

'And we will not follow you. You will tell us where we need to go,' said Captain Dagny. A pair of hands came down on Rjkaard's shoulders. 'Keep him close.'

Morj was still in drag, a point which Lars had made a conscious decision not to comment on. He had washed Morj's clothes, but for days now they had been sitting in a neat pile next to Morj's bed.

Lars didn't allow weapons or armour in his household. The only reason the dwarves had gotten away with it was because it was their national dress and Lars liked to accommodate different cultures, but he thought Morj would have been more comfortable in his under-armour clothes. This did not appear to be the case.

Lars made his way to the table and pulled out a chair. Morj was cooking omelettes for breakfast.

A loaf of fresh bread was placed on the table. Lars picked

up the knife and cut it into slices in time for an eggy plate to arrive in front of him. Morj sat himself down opposite Lars.

They both smiled at one another.

Someone knocked on the door.

Morj sighed.

'No, that's alright,' said Lars. 'You just start. I'll get it.'

'It's not a matter of who gets it. We only get so much time together a day, I'd prefer if we did not get interrupted.'

Lars gave him a long, hard look before conceding that it wasn't all that odd of a thing to say for someone who had been confined for so long.

Lars opened the door.

'Hi… uh, is Morj here?'

'For goodness sake! I've just sat down!'

'Come inside, lad,' said Lars.

'And wipe your feet!' shouted Morj. 'I just finished cleaning that floor.'

'Better do as he says,' said Lars. 'He's in a bit of a funny mood.'

When Grunson reached the table, he found that this was indeed correct.

'Ah, Grunson, what news have you got for me?'

Grunson had no idea.

'I'm afraid I don't allow weapons to be carried in here,' said Lars.

Grunson undid his sword belt and handed it to the Woodsman. His eyes did not move from his superior officer.

'I usually don't allow armour either,' Lars added conversationally, 'which goes some way to explaining Morj's current attire.'

'Oh, yes, I forgot all about this,' said Morj.

Morj was now wearing one of Lars's vests. Or, at least, what had once been one of Lars's vests, but having little to do all day Morj had taken up sewing.

The vest had been taken in at the sides and would no longer fit around Lars's torso, indeed it fitted quite snuggly on Morj. For unknown reasons, it had also been shortened. Lars was always sure to avert his gaze whenever Morj was dusting on his tiptoes. But, perhaps most alarming was the colour. Morj had informed Lars that he had intended to dye it red. Whether that was true or not, the fact remained: it was not red.

'What do you think?' asked Morj, slouching in his chair.

'Uh... airy, Captain.'

'Yes, it is quite,' agreed Morj. 'How did you know I was here?'

'Figured it all by myself,' Grunson smiled.

Morj looked.

And a crack appeared. 'Well it was more of a group effort I suppose. We weighed up the options one night and concluded that this was the only logical place you could be.'

Morj looked at the great fissure opened across from him.

'Alright that Rorj feller told us, ok?' Grunson conceded.

'I told you, you should trust him,' said Lars.

Morj raised his eyebrows to him briefly. 'Well whatever lies and deceits it may have been which led you here –'

'I told you it was Rorj.'

'Exactly,' said Morj. 'Now you are here, what news have you got for me?'

'The King is preparing to leave Rjkovorg. A messenger, one of the youths, came this morning.'

'That must mean they've captured an ogre,' mumbled Morj under his breath.

'Captain Dagny found me, sir. She has assembled quite a force. She was very… direct with her language. I think she might be ruddy annoyed if you aren't there, Cap.'

'Do the others know?'

'The Sarge is rounding them up now.'

Morj got to his feet. 'Lars, are you finished with my clothes yet?'

'Oh, yes, just finished with them. I put them at the end of your bed,' said Lars, who really was a very accommodating man.

Morj walked across the room.

'Watch your eyes, son,' whispered Lars, looking at the ceiling.

'What?' said Grunson. '… Oh *jeeze!*'

The dress was tossed aside and Morj began returning himself to his own clothes. He found his armour and strapped himself in.

'Ah,' he exclaimed, 'feels good to be back in the old uniform again.'

'It looks very good on you, Cap,' said Grunson emphatically.

'Will you join us Lars?' asked Morj.

Lars put up his hands. 'Nothing to do with me, I'm just a woodsman.'

'And a terrific host,' said Morj offering a hand. Lars took it.

'You're a good man *Captain* Morj. I'll miss having you around.'

Captain Dagny nodded to the Gate Openers. Her force had halted at her command beyond the walls of Rjkovorg. Along with most of its residents. They all wanted to see what happened next.

'Do we really need to do this?' asked the King.

'I think it wise, your highness,' said Dagny. 'For all we know this whole thing could be a ploy to get us outside the capital so they can move in and take over.'

Victarian clucked his tongue in disbelief. 'I'm sure you know best, of course. I just wish we'd had the foresight to leave someone in charge. My son perhaps.'

Dagny might have clucked too if she weren't ever the professional. 'I think this will work out,' she said. 'As well as the Gate Openers, I've also placed a unit to guard the hole in the wall, one to protect the Long House and two to patrol the city. Everything will be fine.'

The gates slammed shut.

'Hmm,' said the King.

Dagny waited for the sound of the wood beam being wedged into position on the other side.

She barked her commands and the armoured soldiers marched off, with King Victarian secured amidst their ranks.

The Greased Elbows waved pleasantly. Morj and Grunson waved back.

'Hallo, Captain. Good to see you again,' bellowed Marius.

'Good morning, Marius. How's the hangover?'

'Not too bad today. Was a quiet one last night. And you?'

'Lars doesn't allow alcohol, I'm twelve days sober.'

'Dear, god!' said Wilkinson.

'Do you need us to go anywhere, Cap?' asked a concerned Marius. 'Just for a nip or something?'

'No, I'm fine,' said Morj. 'We should catch up with Dagny

before she gets too mad at me.'

'Captain, we've been over this, you don't have a chance in hell.'

'You don't know that,' snapped Morj.

'She's miles out of your league,' declared Noak.

'Shall we go, now? You know, just if you've all finished,' said Morj bitterly.

'Oh, I've got more.'

'Me too.'

'The pair of you together would be like a butterfly and a caterpillar hooking up. I mean, technically you're part of the same species, but one of you has spent too much time consuming and forgotten to turn into something beautiful.'

'I am prepared to lower myself to a caterpillar,' said Morj, before he stormed off.

Going on what Grunson had seen in the Woodman's lodge, he was inclined to agree that Morj was indeed a butterfly.

The Greased Elbows walked after him and soon calmed him down.

It was late morning when they caught up with Captain Dagny's force. Morj composed himself, put on his best smile and went to find her. This had nothing to do with flirting, just survival.

'Where the bloody hell have you been?' demanded King Victarian.

Dagny gave him a steely eye.

'I've been busy?'

'Busy doing what?'

'Working,' said Morj. 'As my men told you,' he continued, sourly, 'I have been privately investigating a possible contamination of Hudikvar's water supply.'

'And is it?'

'... No.'

'Forgive me, Captain, but it sounds to me as though you have been frivolous wasting the hours I pay you for, to support your drinking affliction.'

'No, sir. Not at all. I haven't touched a drop for almost two weeks. Look, smell my breath... ahhhhhhhhh.'

'I will not be doing that, Captain,' said the King. 'And even if I did, it would not constitute as what I believe you would call reliable evidence. No, I'm afraid once this is all over, you and I are going to have a little chat about your work ethic.'

Dagny hummed in agreement.

Morj loathed little chats. 'I've also been on constant communication with my man on the inside. I can tell you what they have. What they want to show you.'

'Well, Captain, that would be a fine start. So, what is it these rapscallions want to show me?'

Nothing had gone wrong, but it was getting to the time of day were lots of things could.

Kajsha paced, nervously. The King would soon arrive. With an army.

She hadn't seen Izzy. He'd probably have something inspiring to say at a time like this. Instead she had to listen to Darjl drone.

'– I mean this just seems like the worst plan ever, doesn't it? What are we supposed to do when they get here? Just ask them nicely not to arrest every single one of us?'

'They'll never get all of us,' said Kajsha. 'No matter how many men they bring, we outnumber the guards, and we have a plan in place so they don't catch any of us.'

379

'Are you sure that's going to work?'

'We don't really have a choice anymore, do we?' said Kajsha.

'We could run,' said Darjl.

'No, we couldn't.'

The tinmen of Dagny's force approached. Stomping in unison. The people of Hudikvar climbed the mounds around them.

With one last chorus of boots the ranks stopped.

'So,' shouted the King from within the formation. 'I understand you have something to show me.' There was a smugness in his voice.

'Yes,' replied Kajsha.

'I recognise that voice. That wouldn't be Aereon's girlfriend, would it?'

King Victarian was too far away to see Kajsha go red.

'If you step forward to the pit, you will see what we have brought for you, *King*,' she said, trying to regain the upper hand.

It didn't work. 'Oh, I am well aware of your ogre. Tell me how do you plan to use this weapon? How will you train it? What is stopping me from killing it right now?'

Captain Morj may have failed to mention the symbolic lesson the youths were trying to teach the King and the people of Hudikvar. He could always plead ignorance later. Pleading ignorance was a strong part of Morj's game. It came naturally. It was believable.

'The weapon has already been used. It's already killing you!' screamed Kajsha. 'If you could kill this ogre now, then why have you done nothing about the others? Why haven't you put a stop to the thousands of people who have been taken during your reign? If we can strike fear into the ogres, even capture one, why can't you? The ogres are not invulnerable and neither are you!'

The youths roared in excitement. The guards shifted in their armour. The crowds around them were beginning to murmur.

Captain Dagny had chosen her position well. There were vantage points around the force, but they were a long way off. It would take an exceptional skill for someone to get something anywhere near the King from there.

On a rise, in the distance an arrow was nocked.

The ogre took this moment to roar. The crowd stirred and the murmurs turned to whispers.

'I have not tangled with the ogres, because I did not want to draw further interest from them,' shouted Victarian. 'Who knows what terror they will reap down upon us now?'

'Scuse Me,' the pit acted as an amplifier for the deep tone. 'I Oont Urry Bout Dat. Ogres Arnt Oo Soppy Bout Dat Ort Uv Hing.'

'I thought you said you weren't going to train it?' barked the King.

'We didn't,' protested Kajsha, as shocked as everyone else.

'Thas Ight. Ust Tryna Elp,' bellowed the ogre cheerfully.

The King flapped his arms about. 'How do we know you didn't get him to say that?'

The bow string pulled tight.

'We plan to leave him with you. And he is a he. Known as Glat… wait, I can get this… Glacht.'

'Ver Ood Iss.'

Take aim.

'Thank you… Glacht. As I was saying, he is yours to do with as you please. If you kill him that is on you. We are just showing that they can be killed.'

Adjust for wind.

'I see,' said Victarian. 'So really you are no different than any other children. You get a cute little idea into your head, without fully thinking it through, and then ask daddy to clean up your mess. Well I'll tell y–'

People screamed when the arrow thudded into the King's chest.

'Protect the King!' shrieked Dagny.

The nearest guards backed around the heaped body and linked their shields. More joined and created a roof. The testudinal grew with every edition until it reached capacity, just like they'd practiced.

'Woz Appnin?'

Nobody seemed to have an answer. The youths were perplexed. The citizens stunned. The guards flustered.

Dagny darted around the structure checking for any gaps and searching for any signs of threat.

The voice was muffled and not as commanding as it had been, but still most heard the King say, 'I'm alive.'

Dagny reinforced the issue. 'The King lives!' she turned to the youths. 'You hear me? Your petty assassination attempt didn't work and now you will feel the King's full retaliation.'

'That wasn't us!' shouted Kajsha. 'Was it?' The kids around her shook their heads or shrugged. 'That wasn't us!'

'Guards of Hudikvar, Advance!'

The archer lowered his bow and looked down over the scene.

'I can't believe you missed,' said someone behind him.

The archer turned to face the man. 'There may be another opportunity,' he smiled with his mouth.

Someone threw a punch.

Down below the armoured men marched on the youths.

'Run!'

Dagny's head snapped to her left. Her eyes beaded. 'Who said that!'

Captain Morj's head was low and his shoulders high.

'Who said that?' she roared.

The youths had taken the advice and were scattering towards the forest.

A brigade split from Dagny's main force to see them off. They didn't need to catch them all; just enough to send a message.

Glacht roared once more. It was his loudest yet. It was not a roar that said "hello I'm still here". It was a roar that said "It would be foolish to forget about me".

Everyone felt it in the ground. They all stopped and turned to his hole.

Rorj was standing next to it with a blade to Prince Victarian's throat.

'Thank you, Glacht,' he said calmly. 'Hello everyone, I'd like to speak to the King please.'

What the hell is he doing? thought Morj.

Captain Dagny marched towards Rorj.

'That's close enough,' he said. 'And I would add,' he spoke, looking behind him, 'that if you have any archers in position make sure they are an *extremely* good shot.'

'What is the meaning of this?' demanded Dagny. Prince Victarian was on his knees and with a growing bruise around his eye.

'Bring forth the King and I'll tell him all about it.'

'Certainly not,' said Dagny.

'Glacht,' Rorj called over his shoulder.

'Es?'

'Anything that finds itself down there with you, I want you to rip in half, ok?'

'I An Oo Dat,' replied the ogre, cheerfully.

'Good,' said Rorj.

'What's going on?' it was the King from inside his armoured cocoon, which had ambled its way over to the conversation.

'Ah, that's more like it,' said Rorj. 'Good afternoon, sire. I have your son here, he has some very important things to say to you.' Rorj kicked the Prince in the stomach, 'Come on, say hello to daddy.'

'Father… he's crazy…'

'Oh, how original,' said Rorj, rolling his eyes with disappointment. 'Your son has some explaining to do, your highness, and seeing as he currently has a knife to his throat, I think it's a good time to get started.'

'He's what?' shouted King Victarian. 'Let me out, let me out of this prison, this instant!'

'I strongly advise against it, sire,' pleaded Dagny.

'Shut up. I do not care for your advice. Show me my son. Call off your men.'

At Dagny's command the troop changed formation so the King could see the Prince. Victarian stood up, the shaft of the arrow was sticking out of his breast plate and a dark patch was spreading across his clothes beneath. He strode forward.

'Ap, ap. That's far enough,' said Rorj lifting his blade slightly.

'I'm inclined to agree,' said Dagny.

The King froze. 'Just what exactly is going on here?'

Rorj was impressed with the King. He must have been functioning on adrenaline. The arrow may not have found a killing mark, but it looked like a painful wound through the ribs. Victarian, to his credit, held himself tall and resolute.

Rorj bent down next to his captive, 'Would you like to tell the story, or shall I?'

'Don't believe anything he says!' screamed the Prince.

'That sounds like a vote for me,' said Rorj. 'I'll start with that arrow sticking out your side. It was shot from that rise, using this bow.' Rorj lifted a bow from his shoulder and tossed it in front of Prince Victarian, 'his bow. Any lies so far?'

'He stole it from me!' shouted the Prince.

'Plausible. Very plausible. As you know sire, I am a master of stealth. However, one thing that I can assure you of is *I* would not miss.' His smile was full of teeth. 'The Prince fired the shot. An attempt on your life, sire. *Treason* I belief is the buzz word in moments such as these. It was his hope that in the commotion he would be able to make his escape and if he missed, he would have men available to finish the job. Yes, they are among us now.'

'This is lies. Lies and slander. *This* is treason!'

'How do you know all this?' the King asked.

'It's my job to know,' shrugged Rorj.

'It was him who fired the shot!' shrieked the Prince. 'He's been plotting for weeks. He told me you were going to leave Rjkovorg!'

Rorj rolled his eyes.

'He's been working wi–'

Rorj's heel caught Victarian in the chest and the Prince tumbled into the pit.

Nobody on the plain dared move.

'Ello…'

'No! What are you doing? I'm the Prince! I'm the Aaaaarghhhhhhh!'

There was a horrible sound of squelching blood, bladder and bones as Glacht ripped apart Prince Victarian's body. 'Der. Dats In Alf.'

The King's face was grey. 'What have you done?'

'Saved you from a spot of bother,' said Rorj. 'He was a terrible son. He tried to kill his father. If he'd been King, who knows who he'd have tried to kill. *I* may have even been on his list.'

'You're on mine,' growled the King.

'He would have tried again. I just saved your life. How about a little gratitude?'

'*Gratitude?* You just murdered my only son. The sole heir to my throne. Captain Dagny, seize him.'

One step forward was all she got, before Rorj started twirling his knives and made her think twice.

'Leave him to us.' Captain Vander strode out of the crowd with the rest of the Search and Seekers on his flanks.

As the Search and Seekers advanced weapons appeared in their hands as they tried to circle Rorj.

Morj couldn't say who attacked first, they moved too fast, but Rorj was first to find his mark. A Search and Seeker went down and he would not rise again. A silent death as the crimson spouted from his throat. Others were knocked into the pit and given the Glacht treatment.

Soon only Captain Vander, Rorj and a young boy who

Morj didn't know the name of remained, but he had had enough. The fight was eclipsed by the Greased Elbows.

Rorj stopped and looked at Morj.

Morj breathed deeply. 'Enough. Give me the knives.'

Something in Morj's eye convinced him. Rorj took a step to Morj and placed his blades into the Captain's hands.

'Put him on his knees,' said the King.

Morj stepped back and allowed Marius and Grunson to lower the apprehended to the ground. King Victarian stepped forth with his sword drawn. 'May the gods be purer and wiser than I. May they be forgiving. May they be merciful.' He raised his sword.

'Oh, crumbs.'

Olle, sprang forward to meet the blade of damnation. A flick from his wrists and the King was sent reeling. Rorj's hand reached behind his back to one of his many concealed knifes. The blade came to a squelching halt in Captain Vander's throat, and he fell with a gargle, clutching his own knife, too slow on the draw.

'No!' screamed young Bertil. His throwing star gouged into Rorj's shoulder.

Rorj's face contorted into a sneer and he turned to face Bertil. 'I should imagine you will live to regret that. *Live* may not be the right word, but you catch my meanugh...'

Rorj went down. Behind him, Morj shook his wrist, painfully.

'Now, I am not a man who condones violence,' Morj began, 'but that felt really good.'

'Well done, Captain,' said the King.

Dagny stepped forward.

'He's not going with you.' Morj observed their faces.

'Marius.'

'I'm on it.'

The Sergeant lifted the limp body onto his shoulder.

'I've always had a question mark over your dedication,' Dagny began. 'You're often late and hungover, drunk, or both. You put off certain tasks which do not appeal to you, or ignore them entirely. But, I never thought your loyalty would sink this low. I never for a moment thought you would betray the King or throw your lot in with him.' She gestured to Rorj.

Morj looked hurt by her words, but then he smiled. 'Oh Dagny, we could have had something special.' Morj pulled Rorj's head up by his hair and wagged a finger at it, 'You better not have been lying.'

'What makes you think that we will allow you to leave, Captain?'

Morj called over his shoulder, 'On my mark…'

'Protect the King!' shouted Dagny.

Her troops sprang into formation around the King and encased him.

The Greased Elbows were already on the move.

'Sir,' began Wilkinson, 'we don't have any archers.'

'I am well aware of that, just run!'

'After them! After them!' the King shrieked. 'Let me out of here!'

'I'm sorry, sire, but you are our priority. Hold Your Ground!' Dagny commanded her troops.

By the time Captain Dagny had deemed it safe to release the King he was in a foul mood. They followed him to the forest. No one, not even Dagny was of a mind to stop him. He walked to the tree and ripped the note from its bark.

Dear King Victarian

Please accept my apologies for the events of the day, but I am sure you can understand a man's gotta do, what a man's gotta do. I hope this formal resignation finds you well.

~~Yours faithfully~~

Best regards,

~~Capt~~ Morj

P.S. Please don't chase after us, I would really appreciate it.

P.P.S. Writing on bark is chuffing difficult.

Pages of History

Prince Elijah was not happy, but he wasn't particularly upset either. He was busy weighing up the situation and hadn't quite worked out his emotions yet. In terms of damage, there didn't seem to be too much other than a couple of dented guards and doors, but the damage needed to be contained. Words were danger.

'They escaped?' the Prince asked.

Visma answered, 'Over the balcony, yes. Before they entered the sewer and escaped down the river cave, as best I can see. They must have broken their friends out before they came here. Either that, or they had help, which I have not yet ruled out.'

'Help? Who would give them assistance?'

'Blade, for one. It would explain how they knew about the sewer and the passage behind the falls.'

'Him again?' said Elijah. 'Are you sure we can't do something about him?'

Lord Visma teetered his head. 'I'd still advise against it. He doesn't usually do any real harm and the people love him. If you were to act I feel the backlash would be worse than his current actions.'

'I suppose you're right,' said the Prince. 'I do quite enjoy hearing about his escapades. He seems very good at evading detection. Maybe we could use him for something?'

'Perhaps, someday,' was all Visma was willing to commit to.

The Prince looked back at his crooked door, 'And that's it?' he asked. 'There was nothing else?'

That put Visma in a bit of a dilemma. He knew better than any *knowledge is power*. He liked to keep his cards close to his chest, but he was very careful not to overplay his hand. His finger tucked into his sleeve and flicked at Aereon's note.

'There was also this, sire.' Visma extracted the paper from the depths of his sleeve. 'The boy, Aereon, asked if I would give it to you.'

The Prince took it. Read it. Turned it over. And read it again.

'Library books?' he asked.

'It surprised me too. He was an interesting character. He seemed to have the command over the dwarves.'

'Did he make any mention as to what was the meaning of this?' asked the Prince.

'He was mute on that point,' said Visma. 'He seemed very reluctant to give it to me at all. I believe he hoped to speak with you personally.'

The Prince glanced at the paper again. '*The Juta's Love*… it's a children's story. I remember it from when I was a lad. Have you read it?'

'Haven't found the time,' said Visma. 'I was thinking now might be a good opportunity.'

'A fine idea. Take a look at the others too. Let me know what you find.'

'Of course.'

The magic was over and reality had returned like a prodigal son. It was time to face the music.

Blade knocked on the door to his house.

He heard the latch move and the handle turn. His mother's face appeared and he saw relief flicker across her features until she remembered that she was furious.

'Get inside this house right now Rhys Rowds and tell me why I've spent the last week wobbly-kneed with worry?' Head bowed Rhys stepped past his mother. Before the door closed, bystanders on the street could just overhear her mutter loudly, 'Lord knows this better be good. Oh boy, you better pray this is real good.'

Rhys had a good excuse. He'd helped people. He'd potentially saved lives, he was confident he could swing that argument; his mother was not the biggest fan of Lord Visma anyway. She didn't trust grown men who wore dressing gowns out and about, she said.

It wasn't an excuse he felt comfortable with though. Revealing that would expose all the work he did. His mother would be impressed, maybe even proud. Then the worry would grow, he was determined not to add more to her plate than she already had.

He stood on the exposed carpet and his mother sat down in her seat.

'Well?'

'I was seeing some friends,' Rhys said to his feet.

'Ut uh. You'll look me in the eye when you tell me your whimsical tales.'

Rhys looked up, 'Sorry mum.'

'Who? Where?' she demanded.

Rhys resigned to tell a little truth. Always a good strategy to tell as much truth as you could. Liars always told the truth. 'I was in the Meanderfalls…' Rhys began ominously. 'I thought it might be good to take them food…'

'For free?' his mother asked threateningly.

'Of course,' answered Rhys.

'Where did it come from?' eyes beaded.

'Not the Meanderfalls.'

His mother could make a good guess what that meant. 'Where did you get an idea like that?' she asked.

Rhys shuffled his feet for dramatic effect. 'From Blade.'

'From…' her voice trailed off. 'When did you have a chance to make acquaintance with him?'

'I haven't ye– I haven't.'

'You better not!' his mother stamped. 'That boy is nothing but trouble and is not to be fraternised with!'

'Yes, mum.'

'Don't you *yes mum* me, unless you mean it.'

'I mean it, mum,' said Rhys. 'I will never try to find Blade. I promise.'

'Those are not the same things,' said his mother, acutely.

'And if he ever finds me, I won't speak to him,' said Rhys. 'I'll run away.'

'Good,' she said, after studying him for a long time. 'Now, who are these *friends* of yours? How do I find their parents?'

'You don't know them,' said Rhys, quickly.

'You'll tell me their names, right now.'

'You don't know them,' Rhys protested. 'They're from the Meanderfalls.'

She'd never had much luck with love. She had it to give,

393

plenty of it, but she'd tried and failed to find anyone worthy of it. Then her little Rhys had come along. Out of the dark and in a man's arms, he'd been given to her. They told her to keep him safe. She didn't know what else they thought she would do. She'd cared for him, named him and raised him as her own. The boy knew, everyone knew, but he never asked. He seemed happy with her love and she was glad to receive his.

Barabara Rowds, fixed him with a stare and sighed, 'A mother should not have the burden of knowing when her child is lying.' She sat up and struggled to her feet, 'But I can understand why you made it. Loyalty is important. Just remember, that your old mother should be number one.'

'Yes, mum.'

'Now come here and give me a hug.'

Prince Elijah raised his head to the bang and he looked at the stack of books that had been dropped onto the table. 'That's a lot of big books,' he said.

'Yes,' said Lord Visma, who did not pant or seem out of breath. But academics never felt the burden of books. 'Luckily, Aereon left a helpful key of which pages to focus on, so I did not have to read cover to cover as it were.'

'You found what he was trying to communicate then?' asked the Prince.

'Oh yes. He was not, shall we say, subtle about his message.'

'Should I be sitting down?' asked the Prince.

Visma studied him, 'You are sitting down.'

'Yes, thank you. I would like to pace if it is an option, is what I mean.'

'By all means,' said Visma. 'You're the Prince.'

Elijah got to his feet and strode to the window.

Almost instantly, Visma was in Elijah's seat with one leg crossed over the other. He pulled the top book towards him. '*The Juta's Love*,' he read aloud, 'covers the basics.'

'It does?'

'Yes. It's a good starting point,' Visma declared, 'and if needs be, we can dive in deeper, but everything should be clear to you once we're through this.'

'Proceed,' said the Prince.

Visma tapped the book with his finger. 'What do you remember about the story?'

Elijah looked down over the falls. 'The basics,' he said. 'Boy meets girl. Boy falls in love with girl. Girl falls in love with boy. Both tumble over the edge of the falls and are one forever. I never could work out if it was a happy story or not.'

'That's the gist,' agreed Visma. 'Do you remember where the story came from?'

'The author's name escapes me.'

'Rymond Tulse,' said Visma, without looking down, 'but he did not create the story.'

'Stole it off someone else, did he?'

'Yes,' said Visma. He glanced at the stack of books, 'He plagiarised from the pages of history.'

'It's true?'

'Well, there was a Prince Avery and a Princess Elina, and one day they did disappear. Reports claim that they were last seen together on the platform over the falls...'

'The dais of desire...' said Elijah, clicking his fingers.

'Yes, or the podium of passion, or the scene of sex. It is a bit of a *hot spot* amongst the people, sire. They try to recreate the love of the Prince and Princess, without the danger. Or maybe with the danger, but without the peril. There is actually a plaque there dedicated to the lovers and to discourage some of the more adventurous citizens.'

'So, who were they?'

'If you're going to sit down, now would be the time,' said Visma. Prince Elijah returned to the table and sat down in the slightly less cushioned chair. 'Prince Avery was heir to the throne,' said Visma. 'They were pretty well liked too, from what I can make out from Aereon's research. Loved by all. People couldn't wait for the old King to kick the bucket.'

'Pity about them falling off the cliff then.'

Visma raised an eyebrow. 'You do realise you would likely have never sat the throne if that had happened. When the Prince died, his younger brother took it and you descend from him.'

'Still a shame, nonetheless.'

Lord Visma, was not sure he shared the sentiment. 'I do not think they fell over the falls, sire.'

'What?'

'Well, I believe the point Aereon is trying to make is that he, and everyone else from Krank are descended from Prince Avery and Princess Elina. I've read the accounts, no one saw them go over the falls, it was just assumed as that was where they were last seen. They could have easily snuck below the city and used the cave behind the Meanderfalls to escape.'

'Why escape?' the Prince asked. 'They were loved, you said. Heirs to the throne.'

'They were young. They cared only for each other and did not wish to have their love burdened with the pressures of rule.'

'Seems a little farfetched.'

'I am not saying I believe it,' said Visma, 'but it is the kind of thing that captures the imagination of people.'

'Did this Aereon say if he planned to tell anyone?'

'No,' said Visma. 'If it was his plan to, he would have done so already. The only reason he would have told us is because he wants something.'

'What do we do?'

'We steal the initiative, take that opportunity away from him,' said Visma.

'How do we do that?' the Prince asked.

'We march on Krank, with an impressive force. Strike a bit of fear into them. And then sire, it is time for that little thing we talked about.'

The Prince's eyes faded as he tried to remember. Then they came back sharply. 'No!'

'Oh, yes.'

'No, I won't.'

'I am afraid, you must.'

A Warm Welcome

There had been a bit of tension involved in the build up to the raft being revealed. The dwarves had explained the premise of the floating device they and Blade had made, which had gotten the Creators a little wound up, but once they actually saw it, they burst into laughter at its inferiority to the floyancy.

Getting unto the raft had also been a bit of an issue, each of them shivering to the bone. And once they were on, keeping it afloat was no picnic. They untied it and drifted through the water screen and out across the plunge lake, past the town of Gredol and into the flow of the Juta.

The first day was slow, but the Juta picked up pace as the water headed into the hills on the second. None were comfortable, but sleep found all as the raft was carried down the winding river. Occasionally they would guide the raft to the banks to forage for food. They enjoyed the land beneath their feet and relished a chance to stretch their legs, but Aereon never let them linger long. He was so close.

The sun was setting on the fourth day when they broke through the hills and the river slowed as the land flattened. Trees sprouted along the banks and in the black of night, the lights of Krank shone ahead.

Aereon woke the others and they all sat in silence as the flickering grew. Noise spread like music across the calm water as shadows flowed around the fires. They used their hands to push themselves towards the island. The wood found the sand with a soft crunch and the exhausted occupants slid off the raft and climbed the beach.

There was indeed music playing and a gathering with general merriment. There were a number of fires and torches fluttering not too deep inland. People congregated around the flames and the party swelled.

Aereon and the Creators stepped into the light...

... and...

... the music did not stop. The merriment did not diminish. There were no gasps or stares. Everyone carried on their business of talking, laughing and eating. It wasn't that they weren't noticed, several people walking past told them what a splendid evening it was, it was just that there seemed to be nothing worth noticing about them.

Silvor and Volris stepped forward and still there was no *twang* of a snapping fiddle string.

Finally, a head turned. Then the legs stopped and the jaw fell. An elbow found a rib and the cycle repeated. As flailing appendages found the sides of musicians the music fell away and only the crackle of fire remained.

Everyone stood far from the dwarves and it did not appear to be by accident. The crowd – a few heckles and a trip to a garden centre short of becoming a mob – took in the three figures who bizarrely seemed quite comfortable next to the dwarves. A breath or two escaped tight lungs as faces were placed and a murmur began to spread.

One brave individual stood forward with his torch and illuminated their features. More gasps rose above heads in wisps, as feet stirred and curiosity encouraged them to take a closer look.

'Alright, alright. What's all this then?'

Codrich waded his way through the people and onto the scene.

'Ah, Aereon,' he said. 'What seems to be the meaning of this?'

Aereon did not answer.

Without one, the King's brain was forced to think on its own and, on this occasion, came to a reasonable conclusion. '... Aereon?' he said. 'Edin... Koel... can it really be?' He grabbed a torch from an unresisting hand and stepped closer. 'Well, I'll be... Aereon... why are you in your underpants?'

Aereon looked down. When he looked back up, everyone else was looking at him. 'Would you prefer I wasn't?' he said.

Codrich cracked a grin, which became a chuckle, before flowing effortlessly into a hearty laugh.

'Shall we sit down by the fire?'

'Yes, yes, of course,' Codrich boomed. 'Are they safe?' he asked, referencing the dwarves with a stray finger.

Aereon observed the dwarves watching Codrich's finger, with beady, cat like, eyes. 'Probably not,' he concluded.

'Good, I hate dull evenings,' said Codrich.

When everyone was seated, Aereon cleared his throat and started to speak. Someone grabbed his ear and tugged him to his feet.

'Ahhhhhhhhh!' he exclaimed.

Nobody got up or did a thing.

The circle faded as Aereon was pulled through the crowd.

Beyond the audience his ear was released, and he straightened up to see a tear stricken face. His mother's.

He couldn't think of what to say and she wouldn't speak until he had.

'... I'm back,' he tried.

'*You're back?* That's all you have to say to me?'

'No, not all,' said Aereon. 'I brought the Creators back with me. Did you see the Creators? I brought them back, just like I said I would.'

'Good for you,' she said, rigidly.

'I am sorry if me leaving upset you, mum. I hope you can understand why I had to do it.'

His mother took a step towards him. 'I am not upset because you left.' She hit him. 'It terrified me, but I was proud to support you.' She hit him again. 'I am upset because you never even said goodbye!' The blows came in a fury, pounding into his chest as his mother began to sob. 'You never even considered how your father and I would feel!'

His father was there, emerging from the dim, he grasped his wife's wrists and pulled her away from their son. She stopped struggling. Husband and wife looked at their son.

'It's good to see you,' said Daron, levelly. 'Congratulations on returning the Creators.'

Aereon observed their interlocking arms and protective embrace. Guarding each other from... me, he realised. 'Thanks,' he mumbled. 'Look, I am sorry I didn't tell you I was leaving. There was just no time. Arburella was on my tail. If I'd gone to the house, she never would have let me leave. I had to leave. Look, will you stop looking at me like that! I said I was sorry, alright!'

'We hear you, son,' said his father. 'Your mother and I

have talked long about the day you would return. Wished for it, even. But, we can't let you back in the house. We need time for you to appreciate what you did.'

'You're kicking me out?' asked Aereon, leaving his jaw open.

'No,' said Daron, 'you left. The lock has changed. The walls have been repaired.'

'What are you trying to achieve?' Aereon didn't wait for an answer. 'To make me feel your pain?'

'We hope that you will learn the consequences of your actions. That you cannot just paddle off into the blue without a moment's thought of how it will affect others.'

Aereon was almost breathing as deeply as his mother now. 'I know the consequences of my actions. I have been experiencing them for the last five months! You seem to have some notion that I've been off gallivanting; having a ball. Well, I haven't. I've seen things you couldn't even imagine. I've faced death. I've argued with Kings. I've climbed mountains. And I've done it all as part of my duty. I would have thought my loving parents could understand that.'

'Please don't use that tone,' said his mother. 'We will always love you.'

'You have a funny way of showing it.'

'Love should not be a one-way flow, Aereon,' said his mother. 'One day you will look back and thank us.'

'One day I'll look back and wonder how I could have been spawned by a bigger pair of idiots.'

His father struck him then and Aereon hit the sand.

'Don't you dare talk to your mother like that, you little brat!'

It was his mother's turn to grab her spouse and push him

back. 'No!' she screamed. 'Please, Daron.'

Aereon fingered his cheek bone and felt the burst skin and the blood.

'You disgust me,' his father spat. 'You didn't just turn your back on your family. You turned your back on all of Krank. Everyone here who needed you. Who needed the floyancy. You left us to suffer and starve while you went off to play at being a hero. You're no hero. When all was dark, it was Juta who stepped up and saved us. Ask your little girlfriend. She knows the truth. She knows he's the real hero. You're nothing, but a fraud.'

His mother was on her knees now, with both hands over her face.

'Where is she?' Aereon asked his father.

'She'll be on the Sunset bank,' his father replied. 'They tend to enjoy some privacy in the evenings.' Aereon ran. 'That's right,' his father shouted after him. 'Run away. Run away like you always do!'

Aereon did not slow until he reached the Moonset shore. He stopped and scanned the slope until he found the two figures and moved behind them.

He stood just on the edge of sound and listened to the voices over the soft brushing of waves on sand. He watched the moon shimmer the sea between them. Then the shades moved together, and he could no longer see the waves as their silhouettes became one.

It could not be unseen. Could not be unheard. As the heads parted the couple laughed together and pulled each other close.

He stood and watched them for a while. He wanted to stand there until something happened. Until the pain started to fade as anger filled his gut and shoved it into his chest. He hoped they would turn and see him, that way he could enjoy their struggle as they stumbled over apologies. None of that happened. They just sat there, absorbed in one another's company. It hurt, but all he saw was two happy people.

Slowly he turned his body and walked up the beach and back into town. He approached a building and slouched his back to it. He remained there for a time, lost somewhere in his own head.

Lost with what he'd given up and what he'd received back in return. Did it seem a fair trade? Not to mention everything he had needed to do in between the giving and receiving. But it does not do to dwell on ones fortunes.

He straightened himself up, took a breath, almost took a step forward and then remembered that he had nowhere to go. He waved the thought away. That didn't matter right now, he just wanted to walk for a while. He stepped around the corner.

'Didn't I banish you?'

At first there was just the voice. Then the glaring white eyes rose from the darkness. And the red lips. Her face caught the light of the pale moon and accentuated her sharp features.

Aereon did not answer. It wasn't as if he'd even said "well at least things couldn't get any worse" or "it's only up from here". Sometimes life was just cruel.

Arburella's glowing eyes shifted from his largely naked body to the point where his flesh had burst on his face.

'You've looked better,' she said.

Aereon agreed.

'I wouldn't worry too much about it,' she said. 'I've always found parents to be an overrated aspect of life. After the initial part, obviously, that is quite essential. And you shouldn't be concerned about your clothes. You aren't going to need any for what I've got planned.' She laughed at his expression. 'Take that either way you like, I'm not sure which terrifies you more. No, that won't be necessary Hule.' Aereon became aware of the hulking presence behind him. 'I believe Aereon is ready to come quietly. Am I right?'

Aereon nodded.

Arburella placed her arm across his shoulders. 'Look on the bright side, at least you'll have a roof over your head.' She laughed at his expression. 'What? Too soon?'

Before the Creators were being shown to their Shack, there had been much laughter and enjoyment. At the end of it all, Codrich had hoped he might be able to slip the Creators into the Shack without them noticing it didn't have a roof or most of its walls.

'What in the world happened!' stamped Edin.

'Oh, it's noticeable, huh?' said Codrich. 'Just a minor event, you'll patch that up in no time.'

'*Patch it up?* We'll have to start the whole thing again from scratch,' Koel protested.

'No, no,' assured the King, 'A bit of wood here, a lick of paint there, it'll be good as new.'

Koel felt he had the right to be doubtful, because what he was looking at was basically a door frame, with no door, and a large square of debris scattered around it.

'Who did this?' asked Edin.

'Juta had a little mishap.'

'That goober!'

Codrich leaned into Edin, 'You can't say that. He's a national treasure.'

'He's a what? That carrot-topped stick insect?'

'Yes, that's the one,' said Codrich.

'What was he doing in our Shack?' asked Koel.

'He was working on a new floyancy...'

'This is why children shouldn't play with grown up toys.'

'... which he finished,' continued Codrich. 'At severe harm to himself, I might add. Then he took the device beyond Krank and brought us food when we needed it most.'

'Oh, sure. Anyone can *use* a device,' said Koel.

'It's inventing them that's the tricky part,' added Edin.

'Yes, of course,' said Codrich. 'Don't you lads worry. I'll make sure your valued contributions are not forgotten.'

'Thanks, Coddy. But this isn't on. Where is he?'

'We will deal with it tomorrow,' the King whispered back. 'I suppose you two – ah, sorry, you four will be wanting to get to bed. You've been through a lot of travelling after all.' Codrich ruffled Volris's hair. 'I've got to tell you, I just love these guys.'

Volris could have swung his hammer at Codrich's ankles until the longshank fell over, then he could start beating away at something else, but dwarves had something of a blind spot to any discrepancies from anything with a beard longer than their own. Something that was heavily built into their society and had served them well so far.

Volris smiled up at the King.

The Creators wished Codrich goodnight, as well as the mass of people that were still following them around.

After some yapping with a member of the crowd, Codrich stepped inside with a roll of blankets. 'I was able to acquire these for you,' he said, handing them to the doe eyed Creators. 'I wouldn't worry too much, lads,' he added. 'It might be uncomfortable for a few days, but we have access to the forests on the banks now, you'll have it repaired in no time.'

'I've slept in far worse,' said Volris.

'That's the spirit,' said Codrich. 'Listen to the half-pint.'

For what it's worth, Aereon slept pretty well. Arburella opted to start things anew in the morning. She had her prize and was in no mood to rush the treat. He was tied up, locked up, and then she went to bed. Aereon, pinned to a wall, found sleep more easily than she might have expected, but it was good that he was going to be fresh. She'd hate for him to miss anything.

'Good morning. Are you comfortable,' Arburella purred, as she circled the room.

Aereon might have shrugged if he could have. 'I've felt better,' he conceded.

Arburella smiled, making her way to her treasure chest. 'Yes, I image you have.' She lifted the lid effortlessly. 'What shall we start with today...?' She began selecting items seemingly at random, she hummed and hawed with each, but none seemed to quite fit the bill.

'That one looks pretty sharp,' said Aereon, helpful.

Arburella looked at the blade in her hand. It *was* pretty sharp; one of her favourites. 'An excellent choice,' she said, with her best maniacal grin that was sharper than the knife.

'Glad to hear I was able to help with something,' Aereon moped.

Arburella was too busy gleaming to notice. She walked to him and traced the knife from his wrist, down his arm, across his shoulder and onto his chest... it was here that she often made her first cut. Her victims were usually hyperventilating at this point and it was easy. All she did was keep her hand steady the subject would do the rest.

Aereon's mousy chest was operating in its usual dull wheeze. She frowned slightly and continued to his other shoulder and up his arm to his wrist.

She stepped back. Aereon didn't even have the good grace to look pleased with himself, he just stared at her. Or through her it seemed.

She looked from his gaze and studied his body instead. 'Did I do that?' she asked.

'Yes,' said Aereon, without looking.

'It looks painful,' she said.

'It was,' Aereon agreed.

It was inflicted onto his stomach during one of his final nights before he left Krank. When Arburella had stuck him with a white-hot poker.

'It was by accident, as I recall,' said Arburella.

'If you say so,' said Aereon.

'It was,' said the Queen, sharply. 'Imagine what I could do if I was really trying.' She tilted the knife so light pierced into his eyes.

'I'm sure I will be given front row seats,' said Aereon. 'Actually, audience participation would probably be a better analogy,' he added after giving it further thought.

Arburella's arms dropped to her sides. 'You're really taking the fun out of this, you know?'

'My apologies, I don't seem to be able to do anything right lately.'

Arburella sat down on her box and, with great threat to her personal wellbeing, contorted her face into a pleasant smile and asked, 'What's the matter?'

Aereon was so shocked that he stopped staring at nothing, 'What?'

Arburella crossed her legs, 'Look, this is how it works: you come down here stricken with fear. After all, you're not supposed to want to be tortured. Being tortured is *bad*. And then I, over the course of a few days, break your resolve. How am I supposed to do that if you are already broken?'

'Sorry.'

'Shut up! This is what's going to happen. I am going to get you to a point where the world is not so doom and gloom, ok? Then when your senses have returned, we shall begin. Now, I can't fix things until I know what is wrong. So, tell me, is it your parents, the boy or the girl?'

'All four,' said Aereon.

'Well, let's start with someone who might actually want to speak to you, shall we?'

'Does such a person exist?' moaned Aereon.

'Stop that! Lirna might be if you get your act together.' Aereon scoffed, but Arburella continued, 'She doesn't know that you know yet. So to save face she will be keen to play the role of loving girlfriend.'

'That's not exactly what I had in mind when I imagined Lirna and roleplaying.'

'Well it's all you're getting,' snapped Arburella, heartlessly. 'Honestly, you're lucky you are not covered in your own insides by now. I feel I am being more than accommodating. But, and I want you to listen very carefully, I am not doing this so that you can get your jollies!'

Finding the dwarves was simply a matter of following the streaming, possibly screaming, crowd, which was still opting to stay at a clear distance and dived behind buildings whenever Volris or Silvor turned around.

The dwarves, for their part, were curious why the people always seemed to be behind them. They tried changing direction several times but the crowd always dispersed like tetras before shoaling behind them again.

After a whole morning spent like this, they gave up and walked around the island until they found a congregation that wasn't particularly interested in them. Everyone was looking out across the water. Coming towards them was a redheaded boy and people were cheering him on.

Volris and Silvor shared a look. 'Floyancy,' they said together.

'What do you think of it?'

The dwarves turned to see the Creators striding towards them.

'Most ingenious,' said Volris, turning back to the device.

'It's nothing on the original, of course,' said Edin. 'But, he did alright.'

'I thought the original fell to bits on its first voyage?' asked Silvor.

'That's because of your bloody mountains!' said Edin. 'No fault of ours or the floyancy. A silly place to leave a mountain lying around.'

Silvor looked like he was ready for an argument, but Volris butted in. 'He seems very popular.'

'Yes,' agreed Koel. 'Riding on our coat tails.'

Volris looked around, not one person in the crowd was paying the Creators any attention. 'Looks to me like he's stolen the coat.'

'Hah!' exclaimed Edin. 'You're right there. Theft, that's

what this is.' He waved an accusing hand to the scene at large. 'Time for some comeuppance. Come on you two.'

The Creators parted the crowd as they made their way to the now beached floyancy. A few members of the population were eagerly aiding Juta in unloading.

'A fine haul,' said Koel.

Juta looked up. 'I heard you two were back,' he said, oblivious to any ill feeling. 'And… uh, Aereon too…' he looked past them for a sign of his friend, and was momentarily relieved, until he spotted Silvor and Volris. He had, of course, been told about them, but words can never equal the gravity of meeting dwarves in the flesh.

'Yes, he is around somewhere,' said Edin, impatiently. 'I see you've become quite the celebrity in our absence. Pray tell, how did that come about? Come on, talk us through the motions. We're anxious to hear.'

'I don't know about celebrity,' said Juta, in a tone which he thought would pass for modesty. 'It just sort of happened, I built the floyancy and everyone was so relieved that…'

'Whoa, now. Don't skip over that part. I bet that's an interesting story,' said Edin, hand on his chin.

'I suppose it is. There were a few complications along the way. I um… oh… now there was a little mishap in your Shack…'

'Really?' said Koel.

'Yes, I'm sorry about that… I um…'

'Blew the place up?' offered Edin helpfully.

'…Yes… but…'

'Silvor, how would you describe that action in a word?'

Silvor took a moment, 'Arson,' he concluded.

'Oh… now. Accidents happen… and I'm bringing in

materials that can replace the damage caused…'

'And Volris, what do you make of that tissue damage on his face?'

'Places him at the scene of the crime,' declared the dwarf.

'Well, yes… I'm not trying to hide anything.'

'We're just trying to make sure we have the facts straight,' said Koel. 'Would you say there is sufficient evidence here for a trial?'

'I'd say so,' said Volris.

'Silvor, take this man into custody.'

'Right you are,' said the dwarf, stepping forward.

'Oh, come on now,' said Juta. 'The King will explain everything.'

'Am I to understand that you will be resisting arrest?' asked Silvor, gleefully.

Juta looked at the manic dwarf. '… No,' he concluded.

'Oh, go on. Please,' said Silvor.

There was silence. In general, Arburella quite liked the sound of silence, but for progress to be made she needed these two kids to communicate.

'Aereon, don't you think Lirna looks pretty today?' She never said she wouldn't try have some fun with it.

'Yes, very pretty,' said Aereon. Credit to him, it wasn't a mumble. He raised his head to her and seemed to come to the honest conclusion.

Lirna smiled weakly, 'That's sweet of you to say.'

'How have you been?' Aereon asked.

Lirna approached the chest to sit on it, but she noticed the knife still lying on the lid.

'Oh, silly me,' said Arburella getting to her feet. She lifted the knife and lid and dropped the blade inside. 'I'll just lock this. I know how provocative Aereon can be and I would hate there to be an accident as the result of something said in the heat of the moment.'

Lirna sat down carefully. 'I've been good,' she said, with equal care.

'Oh, yes? What have you been doing that's good?'

'This and that,' she said at last. 'Just trying to keep myself busy. I'm sure your stories are far more exciting than mine,' she said, quickly. 'What adventures have you been on?'

Aereon gave her the brief notes. Choosing to skip over many of the details and keeping things as simple as possible. 'You don't seem particularly surprised to see me like this?'

Lirna looked at him hanging off the wall. 'You did defy the Queen,' she ventured.

'Ah yes,' said Aereon recalling. 'The first on my list of royalty spurned. Who died and made her Queen. Don't answer that,' he snapped. Arburella's closed her mouth. 'The point I am trying to make, is they are just people. That's what I've learned most. People who were born with the luck of the draw, there is nothing special about them.'

There was a cough.

'Alright, you have an exceptional amount of guile and malice. Happy?'

'It's nice to be appreciated,' said Arburella.

'But, I do not believe that makes you fit to rule over people. Not over me. No one deserves that power. No one is special.'

'Don't you think I'm special?' Lirna asked in a mousy voice, tucking her hair behind her ear.

Aereon stuck out his bottom lip. 'No, not anymore.'

Lirna's expression changed. 'Well that's good, because

I'm over you anyway.' Aereon's expression did not change from its vacant stare. No pain registered across his cheeks. 'Your friend Juta kissed me and I kissed him. What do you make of that?'

'I hope it blossoms into more,' said Aereon.

'Well it has!' said Lirna, furiously. 'I love him and he loves me.'

'I wish you nothing but happiness,' said Aereon.

Lirna produced an exaggerated exhale and folded her arms.

'Good call on the lock, right?' said Arburella.

There was a knock on the door.

It was Arburella's turn to wrinkle her brow. 'Who could that be? You,' she said pointing to Lirna, 'don't throttle him while I'm away. I'll be right back.'

She disappeared upstairs and they heard the rumbling of Hule above.

'Yes, alright. I'll take him, I have space. Bring him down.' Arburella returned, 'Buckle up folks – good job Aereon, you're ahead of the game – things are about to get interesting.'

She turned just as Juta was shown into the room. Aereon raised his eyebrows and Lirna gasped.

'Stick him up over their Hule.'

Hule secured Juta to the wall next to Aereon and then returned to his post.

Juta did not look at Aereon and Aereon did not look at Juta.

'Isn't this exciting?' said Arburella, with feeling.

'What's going on?' Lirna asked Juta.

'The Creators have charged me with arson. They want a trial. It's all Aereon's fault. This is his doing! He planned this!'

Aereon took a laboured look at his restraints. 'You caught

414

me. This is all part of my master plan.'

Arburella smiled, 'Delightful. Come along Lirna. I know guy talk when I hear it.'

'I am not leaving,' stamped Lirna.

'Excuse me?' said Arburella. 'You'll come with me or I will find a place for you on my wall and I'm all out of fastenings so I will have to get *creative*.'

Lirna shrunk away. 'I'll help secure your release,' she told Juta. 'The people won't stand for this.'

Arburella pushed her towards the stairs. 'I'll be back to see you tomorrow,' she smiled at the boys. 'I'm sure you two have lots to catch up on.'

When Arburella returned the next day, it was still silent in the cave. 'Now, there is no use letting a girl come between you, is there? Wouldn't want to spoil a friendship, would we? Let's get the lines of communication going. Aereon, would you like to start?'

'Don't see why I should. I'm the one who got stabbed in the back.'

'Because I can make that term more literal if you don't,' snapped Arburella. Her patience was wearing thin having to deal with all these moody teens.

'Fine! What's it like kissing a girl, knowing that I kissed her first?'

'It's really good,' Juta retorted. 'Do you miss it?'

'Can't say I've ever kissed someone after you have,' said Aereon.

'I meant Lirna in general!' said Juta.

'And you referred to her as an *it*? Not very flattering.' Arburella's eyes gleamed.

415

'You're twisting my words,' protested Juta.

'Aereon, is life worth living yet?' Arburella asked.

'Getting there,' said Aereon. 'If only for the purpose of winding up this twit.'

'Excellent,' said Arburella. 'I shall go and fetch my poker. It should be ready by now.'

'What? Oh, damn!'

Arburella rushed back upstairs. When she returned, she was holding her faithful implement, which glowed with anticipation.

She stopped in the middle of the room. 'Now, a thought occurs to me... there are two of you.'

Juta widened his eyes. 'You can't torture me! I'm awaiting trial. The people love me. I'm a hero. They wouldn't stand for that.'

'Really? Even if I had an excuse? Even if it was self-defence? After you were able to get your hand out of your restraints?'

'No one would ever believe that!' said Juta, though he was beginning to sweat.

'And why not? After all, I have a witness.'

'That's right,' said Aereon. 'He took a swing for you. I saw it with my own eyes.'

'What? No. No!' Juta tried to wriggle himself free.

Arburella smiled and started to advance on him.

'No! Please! I'll do anything you want. Please!' Arburella didn't even wince at the word, she was having too much fun. Juta started to weep. 'I'll pay for the damage! Aereon, stop her. Please! I'll stop seeing Lirna. I swear!'

Arburella pulled the poker back and prepared for the jab.

'Alright, that's enough.' Both Queen and victim turned to

Aereon. 'Leave him be, Arburella. Juta, thank you.'

'I mean it,' he said. 'I'll leave her alone. She'll be all yours.'

'Don't bother,' said Aereon dismissively. 'You two deserve each other. No, thank you for being a coward. Thank you for showing me that. It doesn't matter if no one else on this spit sees it, because I know. I will always know and so will you. Ok, Arburella, I'm ready.'

'Life worth living again?'

'Yes.'

'And you're not going to enjoy this pain in anyway? Feel like you deserve it or something stupid like that?' she asked.

'No, the way I see it, I'm actually alright compared to the rest of you. And this is really going to suck. I do have one request. Could you make it so it matches the other side? A bit of symmetry, you know?'

'I shall try my best.'

She skewered him. Not hard, it didn't need to be hard. Aereon screamed. Juta looked away as skin began to boil. Arburella was quite satisfied.

She pulled the poker back and inspected the steaming, stinking flesh stuck to it. Then she looked at Aereon's oozing wound. 'There, that should heal, nicely. Now, where would you like the next one?'

Aereon was panting. His skin was pale and glistening with sweat. His tongue seemed like a foreign object in his mouth and refused to work.

'Alright, I'll choose, shall I?'

But they never found out what Arburella's choice would have been.

The walls shook with the crash. Arburella's poker fizzed

when she dropped it as she tried to steady herself.
'What was that?' asked Juta.

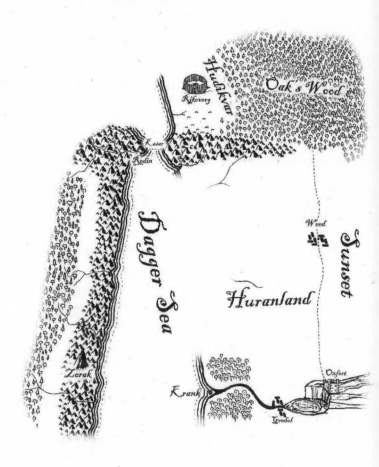

Moonrise

Sunrise

Sunset

Moonset

Hudkvat

Oak's Wood

Rikoverg

Kazar

Dodin

Dagger Sea

Weed

Huranland

Zorak

Krank

Gredel

Oxfort

The Subtle Knock

With a bang, the Juta exploded and water shot into the sky. People shielded their eyes and bodies from the blast. A rock fell from the sky and splashed into the river. So close, the beach dwellers got wet.

Flags billowed on the distant shore in the coastal breeze above ranks of soldiers. Something rose high above the land scape. Something structural. Something wooden. Something war like, with a certain mechanical quality. An arm swung up, releasing a boulder into the air. It landed in the shallows, mere metres from the beach. Sand and salt sprayed over the retreating Krankians.

The river settled around the boulder. Its upper half a new topological feature of the island.

A few seconds later, another rock thudded into the sands of Krank and was still. They waited, but no more shots came.

'Maybe they've run out of boulders?' suggested an optimistic citizen.

'Hey, there's something written here.'

A side of the stone had been smoothed out and polished. Upon it someone had chiselled in a message.

WE CAN FIRE FURTHER.
WE WOULD PREFER IF WE DID NOT HAVE TO.
WE WOULD LIKE TO SPEAK TO AEREON.
YOU HAVE UNTIL SUNDOWN TO GIVE HIM TO US.

Hardly anybody had seen Aereon since he'd arrived and, all of a sudden, his name was a curse. He was branded a meddler and accused of bringing unnecessary danger to their door.

'Hey!' Codrich shouted out across the river. 'Get Your Bleeding Rocks Off My Island!'

Arburella had arrived and was studying the message. Aereon and trouble did seem to go hand in hand.

She had to hand him over to the people now. It would not do if word got out that she had harboured him when she could have turned him over to these visitors. The people may not be in a mood to be particularly nice to him, but they would be a picnic compared to her.

She scowled and made her way back to the outhouse. Hule stood aside for her and she descended the steps.

'Well?' asked Aereon.

'Friends of yours,' said Arburella.

'Friends of mine?'

'Yes. They've been firing boulders at us from the bank. The last struck the island and had a message asking to speak with you.'

'Ah,' said Aereon.

Juta was hanging around, looking confused.

'Something you want to tell me?'

'Not particularly,' said Aereon, honestly.

'How do they know we can even get you to them?'

demanded the Queen.

'They saw me off the island once. It's not a huge leap for them to assume I could do it again,' said Aereon simply.

'They know you are from here. What have you been telling them?'

'Oh, bits and bobs. Nothing really, I gave them a few books to read, that's all.'

'Books?'

'Yes, old stuff, you wouldn't be interested.'

'Why do I get the impression you are hiding something large and important from me?'

'I couldn't possibly know,' said Aereon.

Reluctantly, Arburella unlocked his wrist restraints. His arms were dead and he tipped off the wall onto his face. She moved to his ankle locks.

Arburella crouched in front of him. Her face inches from his.

'Are these people your friends?'

'No, I wouldn't say friends.'

'Is it likely the rest of us could make a mutual enemy out of you?' she enquired.

'Could be,' Aereon nodded.

Arburella dragged him to his feet. 'Do not get us all killed,' she said shoving him towards the door.

'You're letting him go!' protested Juta.

'There are people firing great big stones at us, Juta,' said the Queen levelly, 'and right now, for whatever reason, it seems Aereon is the only one who can get them to stop.'

'How is he going to get to them? He's not using my floyancy,' declared Juta.

Arburella left Aereon to struggle with the stairs and

rounded on Juta. 'Do you remember how pliable you were when I had that poker in my hand? I can have another fire started at a moment's notice.'

Aereon struggled through the door and collapsed into Hule.

Hule held him easily in his arms, 'You allowed be out here?' he asked.

'If I wasn't, what would you do differently?' asked Aereon, philosophically.

'It's all right, Hule. You can let him go,' said Arburella, emerging from the stairs.

'Aw, does he have to?' asked Aereon.

'Yes,' said Arburella. 'I'm not having my men associated with you. Let go of him Hule, you don't know where he's been or who he's been talking to.'

Hule dropped Aereon.

Aereon winced as the sand stuck into his wound. 'Can I at least get some clothes before you kick me off Krank?'

'That is up to you,' said Arburella, stubbornly.

'I am going to be representing the country, you realise? It would be beneficial if I did not make us look like naked buffoons.'

'Fine. I will have someone pick something up for you, but you're not changing anywhere near us. Your clothes will be dropped off on the Sunrise point. It should be quiet there, what with everything that is going on.'

'Thank you. Plain pastels, please, and some bandages for this thing if you'd be so good. Don't want to get blood all over my new clothes now do I?' said Aereon, before staggering off as quickly as his legs would allow, hoping not to be noticed.

He made it to the Sunrise beach and hid behind a building

there. He would have to confront the people at some point. A speech of some sort was probably in order, but he would be damned if he was going to give it in his underpants.

He spotted one of Arburella's cronies looking around dully. Aereon paced over and snatched up the garments he was holding and quickly returned to the shadows. He patched himself up as best he could, put on the new trousers, fresh shirt, crisp socks, sturdy shoes and a replacement pair of pants and most importantly: not in that order.

He stepped out and walked to the water to wash his face.

A layer of grime removed, he turned and boldly made his way back into Krank. People started to point and whisper. He marched to the incriminating boulder, the crowd parted for him. He read the words and smiled before climbing atop them.

'Good afternoon.' Nobody seemed prepared to return the sentiment. 'I suspect you are all feeling apprehensive about what the future holds, but I assure you, there is nothing to fear. A little misunderstanding with the boulders, is all. You understand, it's the only way they could get a message to us. Please, do not take it as a threat.'

'It says they could fire further if they wish!' a heckler shouted.

Aereon pointed him out, and the crowd parted, leaving the man exposed. 'What's your name?'

'Yiron.'

'Well, Yiron, how well can you see the bank from here?'

'I can tell that there is an army there!' he stamped, which was met by a general murmur of agreement.

'Yes,' agreed Aereon. 'I, will get to that in a moment, but if we fired a boulder at them, would you be able to see exactly where it landed? How would you know it landed the right way up?' Yiron did not have an answer. 'That is all this message means. They are simply saying that if I am not there by sundown they will assume that we were unable to read this one and will send another message. Their machine obviously struggles at distances beyond here so they are not keen on firing further. That is all there is to read into this.

'As for the army, well, across that water sits a Prince. The individual who composed this message. A man eager to speak with me on an urgent matter, which I will not be going into the details of at this time. There is nothing to be worried about. We have a place in the world now. Change is good. I should not keep our new friends waiting.'

He jumped down and his face did not show any of the sharp excruciating pain his stomach was telling him there was. The people divided before him. They did not give him much room though, once he'd passed, they followed and hounded. In his silence, the spell had worn off and the heckling resumed.

Aereon crossed the island in quick time and made his way down to the floyancy.

'We can't let him do this!' someone shouted.

'Who knows what he's plotting,' said another.

'I for one do not have total faith in his interpretation of that message.'

'He could be in cahoots with them!'

'How do we know he isn't just going to do a runner as soon as he gets into the water?'

'That's what he did last time.'

Aereon tensed. 'If there is any chance you think that is a possibility, then you should not let me leave.'

'I think it is a damn great big possibility!'

Aereon walked up to the speaker and slammed the paddle

into his chest.

'What are you doing?'

'Delegating responsibility,' said Aereon. 'You want some? Off you go.'

'That's not exactly what I meant.'

'Oh? Then perhaps you're suggesting no one should go? And we just sit here and wait to be smashed to pieces?'

Someone else raised a hand.

'Yes, what?'

'I thought you said the message wasn't a threat?'

'Well, I lied, ok?' said Aereon, testily. 'They are a few hours away from turning Krank into a nice boulder field. Admittedly, I am partly to blame – marginally. It's really just a little misunderstanding. Are you going to let me go fix it or are we going to sit around here arguing and see who gets turned into veneer first?'

'Alright old chap, no need to be like that... just, uh, making sure.'

Aereon snatched the paddle back. 'I'll be back as soon as I can.' He pushed the floyancy into the Juta and jumped in.

At the mouth of the river he continued straight into the sea. Aereon hoped it might cause some steam blowing from the people of Krank, but that was not the main reason; the floyancy was the greatest thing to ever come out of Krank and he was not going to spill its secrets if he didn't have to. He took a wide arc away from the banks of the Juta and away from the eyes of Elijah's army. He brought it back in behind the ranks of the enemy as dusk was setting in and headed for the camp fires.

He found a few soldiers having their dinner and approached them, arms raised. 'Take me to your leader.'

One of the men dribbled his soup while the rest struggled to their feet.

He was taken deeper into the camp and more and more spears were pointed at him. They moved away from him as he approached and closed in behind him again. Their silver tips glimmered like fish, and Aereon was a shark gliding though their shoal.

He was presented to a tent and after a few moments Lord Visma emerged from the deep blue canvas. 'Ah, you received my message. It's alright, he's unarmed,' he called over his shoulder.

'Shouldn't you search me before making claims like that?'

Visma gave him another look, 'No.'

The curtains of the tent parted and Prince Elijah stepped out. 'If it's all the same to you, *I* would prefer to be more thorough than relying solely on your unfathomable self-assurance.'

Visma rolled his eyes and nodded to a couple of guards.

After a few uncomfortable moments of Aereon having his bits padded it was concluded that he was clean.

'Satisfied?' Visma asked.

'For now,' replied the Prince. 'Bring him in.'

Aereon was taken by the elbows into the tent. The Prince was travelling in some comfort. Carpets lined the floor and fur much of everything else. Elijah sat in the most comfortable looking of the chairs. He offered one of the others to Aereon.

'Prefer to stand, thank you,' said Aereon, who did not wish for any bending motions at this time.

'Very well, something to eat?' asked the Prince.

Aereon glanced at the offered food. 'No, thank you, vegetarian.'

'Really? Fascinating.'

'Leave us,' Visma said to the guards, somewhere behind Aereon. The Prince raised eyebrows to his Lord. 'A delicate subject, sire. Best to keep things private.'

'Oh, fine. Wait outside.'

The soldiers bowed out.

'It is good to meet you in person, Aereon,' said the Prince. 'As you can see, your short visit to Oxfort has caused quite a stir.'

'Yes,' said Aereon, still studying the tent. 'Out of curiosity, what justification did you give them for going to war?'

'Are we at war?' asked Elijah.

'At the drop of a hat,' said Aereon.

'Or at the consequences of your actions,' said Elijah. 'But at this moment, we are not at war. What happens next is entirely up to you, Aereon Cusith of Krank.'

'I am pleased to hear it,' said Aereon.

The Prince removed a throw covering a stack of books. 'Who else have you told about this?'

'I hope your library permits you to take those out for an extended period and on such a long journey,' said Aereon.

'Answer the question,' said Lord Visma.

'Everyone,' said Aereon.

Prince and Lord shared a look. 'That was a foolish thing to do.'

'If I hadn't then you would just kill me and the problem would go away.'

'Tell us,' began Visma, 'if everyone knows, what is the point in keeping you alive?'

'Oh, not a great deal, I'll grant you,' conceded Aereon, 'but there isn't a great deal of incentive to kill me either.'

'Don't be so sure,' sneered Visma.

'I am an ambassador,' said Aereon. 'Killing me *will* start a war.'

'A war which we will win,' said the Prince.

'Without question,' said Aereon. 'But if that was what you wanted you would have started already. I've seen your people though, a diverse lot. You prefer to conquer – although I'm sure you prefer to use a word like *assimilate* – rather than abolish. Well, if you can conquer us without spilling any blood, wouldn't that be something?'

'And how do you propose we do that?' asked Elijah.

'You know the answer to that,' said Aereon. He looked over his shoulder.

'I've made the suggestion,' said Visma. 'He is somewhat reluctant.'

'What do we get out of this *assimilation*?' demanded the Prince. 'You will gain our info-structure, our knowledge, our defence, access to our trading routes. What do we get from you?'

'Something of merit. I can't tell you what it is without your word that we have a deal.'

'You have our word,' said Visma.

'Ha, nice try,' said Aereon. 'I want to hear it from him.' Elijah said nothing. 'Aren't you curious how I got here tonight?'

'That would be via floyancy, I would imagine.'

Both tilted their heads to Visma.

'How do you know about that?' demanded Aereon.

'About what?' asked Elijah.

'I had a lengthy conversation with Edin. He was all too

eager to reveal it to me,' said Visma, coolly.

Aereon cursed the loud-mouthed Creator.

'Am I to understand that your bargaining chip has now disintegrated?'

'But you haven't seen it,' said Aereon. 'You do not fully understand it. The deal is still the preferable option. Should a war be started, should all those people die just so the Prince doesn't have to do something he doesn't want to?'

Prince Elijah gave it a lot of thought. 'If I agree, to not go to war and to include you in our empire that should be sufficient. I do not have to do the other thing.'

'No deal. You owe us more than that. We are all of stronger blood than you after all, purer blood. Like a single crimson drop splashing into a glass of water, yours has mixed and blended. Contaminated. Faded. Ours remains resolute.'

'Is that why you do not call me *sire*? Out of some sense that you are nobler than I?'

'No,' said Aereon, truthfully. 'I just don't do that sort of thing anymore.'

'You don't respect blood?' asked the Prince.

'No,' said Aereon. 'But, other people do, which is what makes it such a key part of my argument.'

Visma was smiling underneath. 'Have you ever thought about a life in politics?'

'Can't say that I have.'

'Wasted talent,' said Visma.

'What do you respect?' asked Elijah. 'God?'

'No. Krank has been without religion for most of my life and has been getting on quite well,' said Aereon. 'Do we have a deal?'

'You have a deal.'

'Excellent,' said Aereon. 'Shall we seal it in blood?'
'That was in poor taste, Aereon.'

Dethroned

T he people of Krank held their collective breath as the floyancy approached. It was low in the water with the weight of three people. When it hit the sand, two woozy soldiers stepped out, still a little shaken from the experience. Aereon climbed the beach and addressed Krank.

'Hello all. Behind me are two stand out individuals from the Huran Empire. They are our guests. Introduce yourselves, be nice to them. Do not harm them. In fact, where are the dwarves? Silvor! Volris!'

The dwarves waddled out of the crowd.

'I am putting you two personally in charge of making sure nothing happens to these fine gentlemen. Understand?'

'We're on it,' said Silvor, as he and his brother took up positions in front of the soldiers.

'Did you hear that?' Aereon asked the Krankians. 'Anything happens to these two and you'll have the dwarves to answer to. Now, I'm off to bring over another two of our new friends. While I am away, could I ask any eligible women to start forming a line. I suggest you spruce up your hair and put on your best outfit. Oh, and let's get some food going, shall we? Come on folks, don't look so petrified, this is a night for celebration.'

Aereon repeated the journey another fifty times. To begin with he gave the spare paddle to one of the soldiers travelling, but after a few trips he handed both over and guided them through the technique.

Then it was time for the Prince and the Lord. Neither elected to paddle, even after a bit of prompting. They arrived to "oooh"s and "ahhh"s. No one on Krank had ever seen such garments.

'May I introduce Prince Elijah and Lord Visma. In case you needed help, the Prince is the young, handsome one, with hair and he is here for a very special reason. Over to you. Your big moment.'

Prince Elijah stepped forward, now protected by two dwarves and a hundred men. He cleared his throat. 'Yes, as Aereon said, I am here for a very special reason. For years, I have been searching, to no avail, for a woman to marry. A woman to help me rule. Thanks to Aereon's research it has come to my attention that everyone on this island is of royal descent.

'I see you have assembled yourselves accordingly. Tonight, one of you will become my betrothed. Symbolising the uniting of our nations and Krank's allegiance to the crown of Oxfort.'

There was rumbling in the crowd which Visma noticed, he also noticed the gasps from the single women at the indication of one of them becoming Queen. He gave Aereon a sly look.

Much of the crowd did not like the sound of being ruled, but the more they thought about it, the smaller their number became. First the parents of allegeable daughters saw the upside. Then others started to entertain the idea of Arburella having someone to answer to. Finally, people buckled under the anticipation. Things were just too exciting to cause a fuss.

The Prince approached the aspirants and, with Visma in his ear, reduced their number significantly.

The crowd looked at those who remained and generally murmured in agreement.

'Would it be possible to sit down for the next part?' enquired the Prince. 'That way I can get to know each more intimately.'

Chairs were set around a fire and food provided for the spectators. Even the Prince's men were getting right into the event.

However, as everyone sat intently for the next round. Codrich burst onto the scene.

'Alright, what's all this then?'

'Haven't you been paying attention?' asked Aereon.

'No, I've been eating. Who's this chap? Why does he look so fancy?'

'Do we have another chair?' asked Aereon. 'This could take some explaining.'

The crowd weren't upset by the interruption, some of them could do with a few points being gone over again.

'You never told us you had a King and Queen,' Visma complained to Aereon.

'They are not what you would call conventional. On Krank royalty are selected on strength.'

'That's right,' said Codrich. 'You wanna go, sunny boy?'

Prince Elijah gave him a funny look, 'What?' he asked, baffled. 'I have an army.'

'Individual strength,' said Aereon, helpfully.

'Ah, well I am not going to play by your customs. And you can no longer declare yourself King of this land,' said the Prince. 'However, I have the power to make you Lord of it.'

'Lord eh?' Codrich was intrigued. 'What's that then?'

'Well, you would be in charge of this land. The people would be under your rule and protection.'

'Lording sounds awfully similar to Kinging,' Codrich concluded.

'It is in many ways,' agreed Elijah. 'But, with a few differences. The first one's an easy one,' the Prince began, and had really assessed the challenge in front of him quite well, 'people call you Lord instead of King. Two: you will have to stop wearing that crown. And Three: a Lord answers to his King, which will be me.'

'Ah huh, and what sort of things are you likely to ask me to do?' asked Codrich, eyebrow cocked.

'Whatever I see fit,' said the Prince, losing patience.

'And what if I just say "arm wrestle right now, winner takes all"?'

'I would decline.'

'What if I didn't take no for an answer?' asked Codrich.

'Regrettably, I would have this man here,' Prince Elijah gestured to a soldier, 'stick you with his sword.'

Codrich eyed the soldier, 'Reckon I could take him.'

'Him as well then,' said the Prince.

'Would still be close.'

'Alright, those five too!'

'Oh, you're a shrewd man,' said Codrich oblivious to any tension. 'I can see we're going to get along well. Lord it is then.' Codrich tossed his crown onto the sand, grabbed a chair and with his behind still on the seat, shuffled around so he was next to the Prince. 'Right, bring forward the contestants.'

Prince Elijah was perplexed. Lord Visma was giving Codrich a look like he might explode at any moment.

'Probably best to move on,' said Aereon. 'He's usually quite cooperative when he's in this sort of mood.'

'That's right. Never let it be said that Lord Codrich is a burden to his King. How was that?'

Elijah looked at the grinning idiot next to him. 'Technically I'm your Prince, at the moment.'

'Ah right, and I have to obey him too, do I?'

'Yes!'

Codrich clicked his fingers, 'Damn. Thought I'd found a loop hole then.'

Somewhat apprehensively Prince Elijah asked, 'Who is first?'

Visma produced a notebook and flicked it open. 'We have Frilla... no last name, just Frilla,' said Visma. 'Don't be shy, step forward into the light.'

The young woman came forward and the light of the fire found her soft features.

'Hello,' said the Prince.

'Hello,' replied Frilla in a husky voice.

'Excellent,' said Visma. 'Niceties established,' he made a little *tick* in his notebook. 'First question: Why would you like to be Queen?'

All eyes were on Frilla as she twiddled her thumbs. She knew why she wanted to be Queen, so did everyone else, but she couldn't say that. She had to think of something less malevolent.

'I would like to live with you, and keep your bed warm for you at night?' she ventured.

The Prince said nothing. Visma made a note. 'And why do you think that you would make a good Queen?' he asked.

Again, Frilla did not have an answer prepared and she stumbled. 'I feel that going first is a disadvantage,' she complained. 'Everyone else is going to have a chance to memorise answers. You should have given all of us the questions before, so we could prepare.'

'The purpose of this exercise is not for you to prepare false answers. We would like to hear your genuine thoughts,' replied Visma, levelly.

'The others won't give you theirs. They'll cheat!'

'Perhaps they will,' said Visma, 'but that is no longer any of your concern. Thank you.'

Frilla was ushered away and Lord Visma called for the next contestant.

'Hello, Maggie, why would you like to be Queen?'

'Well, I think that Prince Elijah looks like an interesting man. I would like to get to know him and experience your culture.'

Lord Visma look pleased as he jotted down some notes. 'And why do you think that you would be a good Queen?'

'As well as being interested in embracing the cultures of Oxfort, I would be helpful in bringing the flavour of Krank to the Kingdom to ensure a smooth immigration of the country into your empire.'

'Very good,' said Visma. 'Lastly, if you were to become Queen, what would your main goal be?'

'To achieve world peace,' said Maggie.

'Excellent,' said Visma. 'Very good answers. We shall send for you shortly. Don't go far.'

Maggie disappeared with a smile and a curtsy back into the

shadows.

'She was good, wasn't she?' said Codrich. 'I liked her.'

The Prince offered a weak smile.

'Let's see,' said Visma. 'Next we have… oh yes Timadila. Timadila?' he called a little louder.

A woman stepped forward and was met with inhales.

Lord Visma seemed not to notice. 'Now, why do you want to be Queen, Timadila?'

'I'm not Timadila.'

'No?'

'No, she said she couldn't make it,' said the woman.

Visma consulted the next name. 'You must be Odele then?'

'She couldn't make it either.'

Visma took another look at her, 'Were you in the first round?'

'No, I wasn't, you can add me now. My name is Arburella. Two Ls.'

Visma consulted the Prince, who nodded. 'Very well, Arburella with two Ls, why do you want to be Queen?'

'Because I've been doing it most of my life,' Arburella answered.

'Hang on a minute,' said Codrich. 'That's my wife!'

'What?' exclaimed the Prince.

'That's my wife,' Codrich reiterated and pointed an accusing finger.

'Hello, dear,' said Arburella.

'Visma! What are you writing down?' Prince Elijah demanded.

'Previous experience,' replied Visma, without looking up. 'Could be very useful.'

'You can't be serious?' asked the Prince. 'She's married!'

Visma lowered his quill. 'Is she? Who married them? Aereon told us that there is no religion here. That means no priests. Lord Codrich, how were you two married?'

'Well I had just won my claim and become King and then I just sort of said "that one" and that was it really.'

'You see sire, they are not truly wed,' said Visma.

'But she will have been *with him*.'

'I hate to break this to you,' began Arburella, 'but there is not a single candidate on your list who has not done the deed with a man on this island.'

Somewhere in the crowd Edin shouted, 'Guilty, as charged.'

'Well what about him?' the Prince pointed at Codrich. 'I don't want to spoil this friendship with a new Lord by stealing his wife.'

'Again, sire, not married,' said Visma.

'You know what I mean! She might not be married, but she has consummated, whatever it is she is.'

'No fear there,' said Codrich, who was about caught up on what was happening. 'No hard feelings. Way I see it; you're being very charitable not having your men stab me as it is. That's what I'd do if things were the other way around. No offence, of course.'

The Prince gawped at him.

'The honesty of a saint,' said Visma. 'I'm not saying we should decide this second, sire, but she deserves to be in the running.'

'Fine, fine,' conceded the Prince. 'Continue with your questioning.'

'Well, I suspect that *why you would be a good Queen?*

Would also be answered with *because I've been doing it most of my life.*' Arburella nodded. 'So, we'll move right along to: what would you like to achieve as Queen?'

'I would like to continue to keep my people happy, by establishing strong laws to ensure their protection and freedom. I want to help the Prince become a King who will be remembered through the ages as well as keep him happy while he is alive.'

'Another strong contender,' said Visma as he took down further notes.

'You say that you want to continue to keep the people happy. Your people are happy now, are they?'

'Ask them,' said Arburella.

'Very well,' said Elijah. 'Does anyone here know of any reason why this woman, Arburella, would be unfit to be my Queen?'

Arburella didn't even have to look around the crowd. She just looked forward with a trace of smugness as nobody said anything. This so-called Prince had been here for only a few hours. Could he really contain Arburella? Was he really their saviour? You couldn't blame the people for playing it safe and keeping their heads down. Better to suck up the villain you know, then put faith in the saviour you don't.

'Incredible, said Visma. 'One-hundred percent approval. We could be on to a winner here. We will call for you once we have finished with the other candidates.'

Arburella gave a short bow and moved out of sight. Visma called for Odele. 'Oh, that's right she's gone isn't she. Carylron? Are you here?'

She wasn't.

Visma moved on to the next name on the list, but as he was

soon to discover, every other candidate had mysteriously disappeared.

Codrich was smiling, but said nothing. This was bringing back memories of his wedding night.

Aereon was not surprised, but also said nothing. It was quite impressive to see Arburella's work unfold. Particularly when you knew that you weren't in the running for any mishaps. She was getting to flex her muscles again, which were toned to a devious taut.

Some fuss was made and eventually a few of the women were found or prompted to come forward. They all thanked the Prince for the opportunity, but they had had second thoughts and decided that it wasn't for them or they weren't suited for the task. Oddly enough they were all very quick to show their support for Arburella. Their endorsements were acknowledged and they were sent away.

Arburella and Maggie were asked to return.

Both did so, and every Krankian knew what was going to happen next.

Maggie opened her mouth. 'I would like to withdraw from the running.'

Visma raised a hairless eyebrow. 'Are you sure?'

'Yes, it is a position which I would thoroughly enjoy. However, I could not rightly take it knowing that there is someone more suited for it than I. Arburella would make a fine Queen of Huranland,' she said, solemnly.

'That's very flattering of you,' said Arburella. 'Personally, I think you would have made a fine Queen also.' Maggie almost opened her mouth again. 'But, I respect your decision to withdraw,' finished Arburella.

'Very well,' said Lord Visma, waving Maggie away. 'It

would appear we have your proposed Queen of all Huran. Does she please you, sire?'

The Prince scrunched his face a little. 'Are you sure that there are not any woman who have not previously been unlawfully married?'

'Trust me,' Codrich began. 'Experience, that's what you want in a woman. Am I right?' he nudged the Prince in the ribs, who remained unconvinced.

Visma sided with Codrich. 'I agree with Lord Codrich. Some experience could be exactly what you need.'

Prince Elijah glared at him.

'She is very beautiful, your grace, and proven in the manner of rule. I find it hard to believe we will discover anyone better suited.'

'Yes, yes. Alright.' The Prince rose to his feet and sorted his clothing. He took Arburella's hands. 'My dear lady, do you accept this proposal to be my Queen?'

Arburella smiled, 'I do.'

Empty Pockets

Hule was still stationed outside Arburella's pit. Aereon was hardly surprised, but a sigh found its way across his mouth.

'Hule, what are you doing here?'

'Someone need stay and guard Juta,' he replied.

'No, they don't. No one is thinking about him,' said Aereon.

'Lirna,' said Hule, thoughtfully.

'She wouldn't have the backbone to do a thing.'

'While you away she and Juta had backbone to –'

'Yes. Yes. Thank you,' snapped Aereon. 'It doesn't matter anyway, because I'm letting him go.'

'Does Queen know?'

'Hule, just for tonight, sod the Queen!' Aereon ignored the sharp inhale and Hule's hand, which covered his mouth in shock. 'We won today. Her above all,' he added. 'She is not going to care about what happens with Juta. She has bigger fish to fry. Go let your hair down. Have a drink.'

'I don't know bout dis Mister Aereon.'

'Hule. I am ordering you to relax. Now go.'

Begrudgingly, the hulking figure left and did not see

Aereon pick up a rock.

Aereon took the stairs slowly. He was sure he could hear a wince every time his foot echoed off the stone.

He reached the bottom and did not look at the prisoner, but Juta's eyes were on him as he walked to Arburella's chest and smashed the lock open with the rock.

Aereon lifted the lid and inspected the contents.

Juta listened in horror to the sounds of rummaging.

Aereon tossed a few unsatisfactory implements over his shoulder before eventually settling on an axe. He tested the edge with his finger.

'Aereon, old buddy, this is a bit dramatic, isn't it?'

'Desperate times call for desperate measures,' Aereon replied, as he advanced.

'Please, you must have mercy. You must forgive me!'

'I will never forgive you. You stabbed me in the back, Ju Daas.'

Aereon cut him down.

Juta pulled off the remaining ropes and chains and hastily got to his feet. He really was quite tall, but Aereon had grown on his travels and was not the same boy who had left.

'Why did you do that?' Juta asked.

'Because I had nothing to gain from not doing it,' said Aereon.

'What did you gain from doing it?'

'Free labour. There is a party going on. I'm afraid you've missed most of the exciting stuff, but I daresay someone will be able to fill you in. However, chit-chat will have to wait. Krank is in celebration and at the moment the people on the bank have no idea. Arburella would like you to begin ferrying them across. And you are not to stop ferrying them until they have all been ferried. Is that understood?'

'How long will it take?' Juta asked.

'I would imagine it will take you all night.'

'I'll miss the party!'

'Oh, bother,' said Aereon.

'I'm not doing it!'

'Arburella. Poker. You. Yes, wrinkle that brow. Now go, before I start getting clumsy with this axe.'

Once Juta was gone, Aereon packed everything back into Arburella's chest, climbed the stairs and closed the door behind him.

'It's a lovely night you have here.'

Lord Visma emerged from around the wall.

Aereon looked up at the stars and the moons. 'I suppose it is.'

'They'll align in a few hours and Endos will slip behind Cicar. In Oxfort, we call that the lying moon. Have you heard the term?'

'Can't say I have,' said Aereon.

They started to walk.

'Really? I would have thought you and the lying moon would be well acquainted,' said Visma. 'You didn't tell anyone what you discovered in our library did you?'

'I did not,' said Aereon.

'Why?' asked Visma, coolly. 'If we had killed you then these people never would have known. They would all have been oblivious why they were being killed.'

'I don't owe these people anything.'

'And yet you fight for them,' said Visma. 'You could have taken that device of yours and left. We never would have known.'

'While I'm still alive I can change their opinion of me. If you had killed me, I'd be dead and then what'd be the point?'

'I have to say Aereon, you are a curious individual. You show little to no regard for the preservation of others, in fact by all accounts the evidence shows you actively dislike most people, yet you will fight tooth and nail to be one of them. Tell me, do you really believe you are descended from royalty?'

'Oh, who knows?' said Aereon. 'I knew there was enough of a chance to scare you, that's all.'

'Very well played.'

'Although I had no idea it would scare you this much. My only goal was to free Edin and Koel. That information was simply to be used as leverage.'

'Never!'

'Honestly,' said Aereon.

Visma chuckled. 'Well, too late to do anything about it now. There is to be a wedding.'

'Indeed.'

'And what of this Arburella? What do you make of her?'

'Oh, she's a peach,' replied Aereon. Well, he didn't owe Visma anything either.

Edin stood waiting for the mists to part. On his back was a large pack, a stack of logs was tucked under his right arm and he held a watering can in his left hand.

The mists billowed and the floyancy approached.

Juta guided the device onto the beach and two soldiers stepped out. They were given directions to the party and went on their way, towards the noise and the light. Juta was getting himself ready to leave when Edin climbed in. 'Take me across.'

Juta did not argue. It was not a tone of voice to argue with.

Edin sat in silence as Juta paddled him across the foggy water and made no comment when they reached the other side. Edin strolled past the soldiers and up the beach. He walked through the remains of their dwindling camp and through the other side. He continued until the flickering flames were out of sight and the twinkling stars sang above.

Aereon had shaken Prince Elijah's advisor and was beginning to think about enjoying himself. It had been a long time since he'd had an evening to himself. An evening with nothing to do. Yes, there was the night he'd spent chained to Arburella's wall, but somehow, he didn't feel like that should count.

Long before he'd left Krank, he was often forced to work into the night, to carry out the King's wishes. Well, Codrich wasn't a king anymore and Aereon saw that as a good a time as anything to terminate his statute of employment.

He didn't know what he'd do next and he didn't know if he liked the blank void ahead of him, but it was something new. Something different from what his life had been to this point and he had the rest of the night to figure out how other people relaxed. For the first time in years he had himself all to himself.

'Aereon!'

He turned to find Lirna striding towards him, holding a rabbit. He couldn't quite put his finger on why, but Aereon desperately wanted to laugh.

In the dim, he stifled his bemused amusement as she approached him.

'Hello, Lirna,' he managed.

'Hello,' she replied.

'I guess this must be Tingo,' he said.

'Tingina, actually. We made a little discovery.'

'Ah,' said Aereon. 'I suppose you are here to shout at me.'

'Why? What have you done?'

'Nothing. That just seems to be the running theme on Krank nowadays. Oh,' he said remembering, 'I did send Juta away to bring the rest of the soldiers from the bank.'

'The Queen let him out, did she?'

'No,' said Aereon. 'I did.'

'After orders from the Queen?'

'No,' said Aereon.

Lirna gave him an odd look. 'I'm sure he can cope with that. It will give us a chance to talk.'

'You would like to talk?'

'Is that alright?' asked Lirna.

'Why not?' said Aereon.

'Can we walk?' she asked.

'Walk and talk? Sure.'

Volris was in heaven.

He'd read the books. He'd seen the cities. But this... this was something else. This was an *event*.

Codrich's fondness of the dwarves had granted them prime seats next to the action.

The flavourful food they'd sampled was gone and Volris sat with his legs crossed digesting what was going on.

Marriage was a term he understood in theory, but the mechanics of the practical side of it still confused him. He'd read about it and deduced that at face value it was a contract. Two individuals came together in holy matrimony in front of witnesses and some sort of judge, who carried out the proceedings to make sure the right things were said at the right times. Volris had been surprised when he discovered that there was even a special section for people who had a problem with the marriage to have their say. There had even been examples. If one or both of the individuals was already married for instance. Volris understood that, just standard breach of contract. However, there were other wordings that he had more trouble with. Adultery for example. Now, Volris understood that this was part of the married agreement, to be faithful, but if an incident occurred prior to the signing of papers and shaking of hands he didn't see what relevance it was. But he had read several accounts from angry spouses who found out hanky-panky had occurred prior to contracts signed and they thought it was really quite relevant indeed.

It was at about this point that the sticky word *love* popped into Volris's head. A further notion he could not get to grips with. Neither could humans, in his opinion. It seemed to be at the root of most of their problems. Wars had started over it. Volris tried having Aereon explain it to him, but the best comparison Aereon had made was between dwarves and gold. Volris hadn't understood that, because there was lots of gold in the world. So Aereon had tried a steak analogy. Still Volris was unconvinced so Aereon suggested to Volris, "What if someone said you could never eat a steak again?" "I'd chop his head off" Volris had said. Aereon said "That's love".

He appreciated Aereon had tried, but it still didn't make a lot of sense to him. You had to love steak, because it was fleeting. It only lasted for a moment. What was the point in loving a person? There were millions of them about, and they lasted for ages.

Volris lifted his eyes to the happy couple.

The Prince looked a bit nervous. Although, as Volris understood it, that was not uncommon. Personally, Volris never got nervous about eating steak. The man had an odd grin on his face and seemed to be nodding a lot. Volris thought he looked uncomfortable and his assessment was that this man was not in love.

He turned to Arburella.

Ah, now this was more like it. Her eyes were wide. She leaned towards her bethrothed in her chair and her hand was placed delicately on his thigh. A fact that the Prince seemed to be very aware of. She looked intense. Interested. She hung on his every word. But, and it was a big *but*, there was no gleam in her eyes. They were wide and they were focused and they looked hungry, but Volris had a gleam in his eye whenever he found a rare steak before him.

That would be the end of it, he mused. The wedding would probably be called off by sun up.

Aereon and Lirna meandered away from the crowds. That part they could do. Walking was fine. Conversation was proving an issue.

Aereon was still hopeful he might get that quiet night after all.

She walked him to the coast where she sat down.

Aereon took a seat next to her. Out of the corner of his eye he watched her put Tingina down and ye gods it has a collar and a lead! He couldn't help it.

'What was that?' asked Lirna.

Aereon cleared his throat. 'Nothing. Just clearing my throat.'

450

Lirna seemed to accept that was what had happened. 'I *am* sorry you know.'

Ah, so that's what this was about. 'I know,' said Aereon.

'I hope you mean that, because I do.'

Aereon sighed. 'How did it happen?'

'It just sort of did. It wasn't like we planned it,' she said, hastily. 'After the accident, I felt so guilty. I wanted to spend more time with him, to show my support. Then one day, we were kissing. And that was that.' Aereon did not offer comment. 'You know,' Lirna continued, 'if you had told me what was on that piece of paper none of this would have happened.'

Aereon smirked.

'What's funny?'

'Oh, just if you'd told me that a day ago I probably would have screamed.'

'What happened in Arburella's dungeon?'

Aereon's fingers tickled his bandages. 'I got some perspective,' he said.

Lirna had no idea what that meant, but it gave her an ugly thought. 'Do you like the Queen?'

'Queen to be,' corrected Aereon. 'Like is a strong word. I am beginning to understand why she does what she does.'

Lirna made a noise at the back of her throat, 'I don't understand how anyone could make sense of that woman.'

Aereon studied her, yes, I believe that's true.

'Do you forgive us?' she asked. 'Do you forgive me?'

'Yes,' said Aereon.

'So, we can still be friends?'

'Oh, I don't know about that,' said Aereon.

'What?' squawked Lirna. 'But why? You said you forgive

451

us.'

What I mean is I will not retaliate.' His eyes found hers. 'Trust me, Lirna, you don't want me as a friend. And you certainly don't want me as an enemy. You're getting the best deal possible.'

Lirna's cracked face organised itself into a smile. 'You're just saying that. We'll still see each other, on a daily basis, I'll bet. You'll have no choice but to be my friend.'

'I'm not staying, Lirna,' said Aereon.

'Now I know you're talking nonsense. You're not staying?' she scoffed at him. 'Where are you going to go?'

'There is more to the world than Krank.'

'Yes, and I'm sure it's lovely to visit, but it's not home, is it?' she said, triumphantly.

'I don't have a home,' said Aereon. He did not sound morbid; it was said in a *matter of fact* fashion.

'What will you do?' said Lirna. 'If you're not here, where will you go?'

'I don't know yet. I've got a bit of time to figure that out. I'll be tied to Krank until I can build another floyancy, so you'll see me around for a couple of weeks at least,' said Aereon. 'Maybe I'll go see the dwarves and speak with a golem once more. Or return to the elves and see if *Quercus* has anymore words of wisdom. While I'm there, I could check in on Hudikvar and see if Victarian is dead yet.'

Lirna didn't understand any of this. It was like Aereon had left and the world had given back something else. She said this to him and he agreed that she was probably right.

'Who I was yesterday isn't who I am today. What I've lost in dignity, I've gained in wisdom.'

They talked a little more, but the conversation slowly

faded.

Lirna declared she was going to the party, she asked if Aereon would come with her. He told her he wasn't interested.

They said their goodbyes and he watched her walk up the beach with Tingina hopping after her on a little brown lead.

Aereon waited until they were out of sight. Then he laughed. He laughed so hard his wound screamed and he rolled onto his back and laughed some more. His amusement carried far across the Juta, but nobody heard him. At last, Aereon had himself to himself.

The noise and light of Krank was behind Edin. Beyond a small ridge; he felt peaceful in the quiet.

He'd constructed the logs into an airy structure and lit the kindling beneath. He undid his pack and began assembling the contents. It was a steam collector. At the base, on a stand over the fire, he placed a container filled with water. A tube was secured on top, taking the steam up, where it would collect in the chamber which was fastened above, before the droplets trickled down the other tubes, away from the fire and eventually end up in his watering can totally salt free.

He reached into his left pocket and took out a string, a small drill and a curiously long and sharp cone. He held the last item up to the light of the fire. He could almost see through it. He could certainly see into the opaque ivory. A tooth from a goblin. There was a channel right down the middle where venom had once flowed. Where venom had once flowed into him. Kicking that vile gremlin in the chin seemed like a long time ago.

He wiggled his toes, a very long time ago.

He shook the thought away and delicately pressed the drill at the top of the tooth and started to twist.

Every now and then, he would remove the drill and blow away any excavated material. He'd peer at the hole and inspect his progress, then he would begin again.

Once through the other side, he took the string and wetted the end with his lips. Carefully, he fed it through the hole and pulled it out the other side. Edin reached behind his neck and tied the tooth to him. It rested against his chest, almost three inches long.

He sat for a while, letting the fire die next to him, watching the silver capped waves roll into the coast.

When the logs were nothing but embers, he picked up the watering can and walked into the black.

His eyes adjusted without the fire and he strolled further from Krank, looking down at his feet as he went.

At a slight dip in the landscape, Edin stopped. It wasn't much cover, but the surrounding ground did rise and provide a bit of protection.

Edin got down onto his knees and dug a small hole with his hands. Under the sky's watchful eyes, he reached into his pocket and took out an apple seed and placed it into the hole. He covered it and smoothed the soil on top with his palm. Edin picked up his watering can and gave Kalei's seed a drink.

Epilogue

The streets where nice this time of morning. Empty, if you didn't count the cats and the rats. The rats kept to themselves for the most part. The cats on the other hand, wouldn't leave him be. Regardless of gender. The females were always brushing against him and wafting their tails in his general direction. Their actions brought the attention of the males in the area. Roland tried to explain that he really wasn't interested. He was attracted to strong, independent felines, but there is only so much that one can convey with *meow*.

It wasn't that Roland didn't have urges. It was just that alley cats did nothing for him. Roland had high standards and was convinced there was kitty out there for him.

So every night, he escaped from his new owners' kitchen window, after a peruse over whatever had been left on the counter, and wandered into the night.

Tonight was Roland's lucky night. Not to actually *get lucky*, but the way he saw it, finding the cat was the main issue. Wooing such a specimen would be trifling in comparison. Roland could purr the quilts off a granny's lap.

Recently, he'd been heading towards the outskirts of town. The houses were generally bigger, with fewer cats around, but he hoped those that were there may be of fine heritage. Roland's tail formed into a hopeful question mark over his back.

Half the sun was over the horizon and Roland's ears were beginning to pick up the sounds of day, mostly bird orientated. But, his nose was telling him that there was something strange around. Something new. It wasn't particularly unpleasant. In fact, it wasn't unpleasant at all, but it carried a certain threat.

The scent strengthened and Roland slinked into a shadow.

A woman stepped over the horizon, dressed all in black. She had hair to match and milky skin, none of which was of any interest to Roland.

Every sense in his body tingled as a second figure stopped little more than two feet from him.

The magnificent feline in front of him did not sit but stood with its tail slowly swooshing from side to side. Her fur was that of the shimmering sands from a far away land, her face in a pale black mask and her eyes glowed green in the faint light.

Roland looked up at the golden mountain lion and knew his heart would never want anything else ever again.

'Well, Salique,' said Jillian, 'We're here. The great Oxfort, Capital of Huranland. Time to have some fun.'

Jillian and, more importantly Salique continued on to the city, with Roland darting from alley to alley behind them, keeping himself out of sight and sound as best he could.

The gates of Oxfort had not really been designed to withstand a siege. A few well-placed battering ram blows and the hinges would buckle. But it looked pretty, and was still a barrier for people with no siege equipment.

Jillian walked to the metal bars and touched one. She rubbed her fingers together, as if removing a fine powder.

She spoke a few words and touched the lioness. Shalique walked through the bars as if they weren't there. Jillian followed. Roland sprang from the bucket he was hiding in and jumped in between the bars and into Oxfort.

Oxfort was just as desolate in the night as the town outside. No guards patrolled the walls or armed the turrets. Huran was an empire at peace, something which Jillian felt was a mistake. She firmly believed humanity was at its best when forced to fight for something. Comfort breeds complacency.

'You're looking well.'

Jillian rolled her eyes. 'I was wondering if you three would turn up.'

'No, you weren't,' said the Teller. 'You were wondering *when* we would.'

Jillian ignored the comment and walked on.

'Can't we interest you in our services?' the Trickster called after her.

'Your fortune, perhaps,' said the Teller.

Jillian stopped and walked back to the dark alley. She glanced at the sign. 'The Three Hags?'

'You got a problem with that?' asked the Dealer.

'No problem. I just thought it was more traditional for a coven to only have one,' said Jillian.

'We are not traditionalists,' said the Trickster.

'Clearly. I wouldn't dream to embarrass any of you by asking why none of you thought to be the maiden, but why no mother?'

'You're one to talk,' mumbled the Teller.

'We've all done the mothering. It's behind us. Croning offers a more enjoyable career,' said the Dealer.

'It's the one liners,' commented the Trickster.

'Right,' said Jillian. 'So, if no one fancied the mother position and maiden is out, who's the sane one?'

'None of us fancied that much either,' said the Dealer.

Jillian nodded, she could tell they meant it. 'There is one thing you could help me with.'

'Excellent,' said the Teller, beginning the shuffle.

'Put those away,' snapped Jillian. She sat down and Shalique padded down the alley.

'How may we help you, Jillian?' asked the Dealer.

'Don't call me that!'

The Dealer's hands appeared from the darkness raised apologetically. 'Sorry. How may we help you, oh thee Great Temptress?'

Jillian scowled. Her hand reached down and plucked Roland from the darkness and dropped him on the table. 'You can tell me why this is following me.'

The three chairs opposite creaked as the Hags leaned in for a closer look.

'I think he's a shifter,' said Jillian. 'A good one too. Not even a shimmer of his true self. Even when threatened like this. What do you reckon? A warlock?'

The Dealer's hand came out of the dark and picked up Roland by the scruff of his neck.

'I'm not sure he's been following you,' she said.

'Of course, he has. He's been at my heel since I reached the falls.'

Roland's eyes had not yet moved from Salique, who

458

continued to treat him with indifference. The three Hags cackled away.

'I really wish you wouldn't do that,' said Jillian. 'Here I am trying to modernise witchcraft and you three crones are sitting here, in the capital, undoing it all.'

'Excuse me,' began the Teller, 'did we not just establish that three crones is pretty untraditional?'

'Oh yes,' groaned Jillian. 'Forward into the pages of history we go.'

'We are taking witching forward, just the same as you,' said the Dealer.'

'Well, not just the same,' said the Trickster.

'No that's true.' The Dealer gave a shudder. 'How do you manage it? Sounds very icky.'

'Sounds alright to me,' said the Trickster.

'Shht!' hissed the Dealer.

'I manage just fine, thank you,' said Jillian. 'How do you find lugging around that wrinkly old skin all the time?'

'It is a minor burden compared to what you have to take with you wherever you go,' said the Dealer.

'Suffering builds character,' said Jillian.

'That it does,' mused the Hags.

'Can we get back to the cat? Don't the three of you have enough collective wit to coax it out of there?'

'How do you expect us to go about coaxing a cat out of a cat?'

'What?' said Jillian.

'Yes,' said the Dealer. 'What we are looking at here is simply a lowly alley cat. Although a very handsome one at that,' she added tickling under Roland's chin. 'A-cutchy-cutchy-coo. It appears you did not have the wit to see it.'

'You can't be serious? Why would an alley cat follow me? And don't give me that cats are drawn to witches talk.'

'I already told you,' said the Dealer, 'he wasn't following you. This cat is drawn to something else.'

On cue, Roland hopped down off the table and proceeded purring vigorously in Salique's general direction. Her mood remained indifferent.

Jillian's eyebrow shot up. 'He can't be serious?'

'He's a plucky little devil, I'll give him that,' said the Dealer.

'She could crush him with one paw!'

'Hence the plucky.'

'She's a lion!' stamped Jillian.

'So he's ambitious? Is there anything wrong with that?'

'In a household cat? Yes, a little,' said Jillian.

'I get that,' agreed the Trickster. 'It's a little jarring. Somewhat disconcerting. Now he wants to conquer a lioness. What's next? The world?'

'Well, I think it's sweet,' said the Dealer.

'What are you here to conquer?' asked the Teller.

'The world?' asked the Dealer.

'Afraid of a little competition?' asked the Trickster. She nodded to Roland, who was rubbing his head up and down Salique's leg.

'I'm not sure what I'm here for yet,' said Jillian. 'I just got this body again. For now, I'm just going to have some fun.'

'Yes, we heard about your lust. Or should that be his lust?' said the Dealer.

Jillian smiled. 'My, you three are well informed. Do I deserve the honour of your secrets?'

'We had a little run in with Aereon,' said the Dealer.

'Aereon, eh?' said Jillian. 'Interesting character, isn't he?'

'Very,' said the Hags.

'We were surprised that you didn't go for him.'

'I was tempted,' admitted Jillian, 'but I love a story to come full circle.'

'Not your blasted apple tree?' said the Dealer.

'The very same.'

'Still, to miss out on Aereon's determination was a big call to make,' said the Dealer.

'Perhaps my narrative instinct got the better of me. Maybe I will look back and think I should have taken it, but there is always time for seconds.'